SACRED ARMOR TRILOGY—BOOK TWO

SACRED ARMOR TRILOGY—BOOK TWO

Ralene Burke

PUBLISHING THE POSITIVE

ELK LAKE PUBLISHING INC
Plymouth, Massachusetts

Cover and Interior Design: Derinda Babcock

Editor(s): Linda Rondeau, Deb Haggerty

Author Represented By: the Seymour Agency

PUBLISHED BY: Elk Lake Publishing, Inc., 35 Dogwood Drive, Plymouth, MA 02360, 2019

Library Cataloging Data

Names: Burke, Ralene (Ralene Burke)

Sword of Soter—Book 2, The Sacred Armor Trilogy / Ralene Burke

306 p. 23cm × 15cm (9in × 6 in.)

Description:

Identifiers: ISBN-13: 978-1-951080-24-2 (trade) | 978-1-951080-25-9 (POD) | 978-1-951080-26-6 (e-book)

Key Words: Speculative fiction, fantasy, good vs. evil, quest, young adult, courage, self-confidence

LCCN: 2019948012 Fiction

DEDICATION

For my husband,
MY love, MY forever,
My perfect match.
Thank you for believing in me!

CHAPTER ONE

Karina thrust the sword toward Tristan's gut, but he sidestepped her advance. She stumbled forward a couple of steps, then growled, spun around, and lunged again.

"No." Tristan batted her blade away with his and swatted her behind. "You're too impatient. You have to wait for the right opening."

Karina sucked in a breath. The more she trained with Tristan, the more she wanted to take the dull blade in her hand and run him through. Releasing a long breath, she squared her shoulders, turned around slowly, and smiled as sweetly as she could manage. "I am sorry. I have no idea what has come over me." She fluttered her eyelashes.

Tristan smirked and crossed his arms, the sword still dangling from his right hand. "Don't think you're going to pull one over on me, Your Majesty. I've met too many women to be swayed by a little eye-batting."

Such arrogance. She pushed a strand of dark hair away from her face and chewed on her lip. Tristan had been favoring his left leg ever since the battle at the Aletheian temple. He had refused to let Rashka heal him, saying the limp was nothing … he would manage just fine. Men! However, the limp did mean his left side was weaker. If she forced his weight onto that foot, she could throw him off balance …

"Your eyes betray you, m'lady." He chuckled. "You're staring so hard at my left arm, there's no way—"

She lunged so quickly he had to take two steps back. Without slowing, she swung her sword in from her right side. He tried to parry but lost his balance. He deflected her attack at the last second but still winced and fell back.

She ambled over and put a foot on his chest, her sword hovering over his heart. "Maybe so, good sir, but you seem to have landed on your backside." With a smirk of her own, she pivoted on her heel and walked as calmly as possible to the fire pit.

Sitting at the edge of the small fire, Sam leaned over, his light brown hair flopping around as he stirred a stew of potatoes, carrots, and spices. Unlike Tristan, Sam had allowed Rashka to heal his wounds once they had reached River Branch, before crossing into the kingdom of Soter. No one would know he had barely been able to walk a week ago. He appeared as fit as ever.

With a wry grin, he handed Karina a piece of dry meat. "I knew you had some fight in you. It's about time you showed him a thing or two."

She tossed her hair out of the way, casting a casual glance over her shoulder as Tristan sauntered over to them. She shrugged. "I guess I learn quicker than he anticipated."

Tristan muttered something as he pushed by her to grab the bag of dry meat. Karina giggled. When he glared at her, she shoved her piece in her mouth.

They were silent for a long time, and Karina was content to enjoy the quiet—however long it lasted. The sun sank behind the trees, painting the clearing in long shadows, while the first stars appeared in the sky. Karina breathed in deep and let the cool spring air relax her muscles.

"So, how much further to Gundow?" Sam pulled out four small bowls and scooped in generous amounts of potatoes and carrots.

Tristan leaned forward, elbows on his knees. A lock of brown hair fell over his eyes. Karina wished she were a little closer so she could tuck it back into place. She looked away, focusing instead on the flames before her. Now was not the time for romance. They had a mission—an important calling from the Creator.

Tristan cleared his throat. "Not sure. We stopped for those three days to rest, and we're only three days into our journey. I'd say we have—"

"About another week."

They all spun toward Rashka's voice. She appeared from the depths of the forest, her black hair tied back in a braid and a long bow strung across her back.

Sam raised an eyebrow but did not say anything, instead, handing bowls to everyone.

"Normally, the trip from River Branch to Soter's capital would only take six or seven days, but we must go around the wetlands."

"Go around?" Tristan scowled. "Why?"

"Even under the best circumstances, the swamps are dangerous this time of year. But I have heard rumor of ogres venturing inland as of late."

Karina cringed and glanced at the already-darkening shadows beyond the tree line. Were there some kind of giant monsters out there ready to kill them in their sleep? She sighed. *There goes another night of good rest.* Not that she had slept well since this quest had begun.

Tristan swallowed a bite of the stew. "Ogres? I thought they kept to the mountains on the east coast?"

Rashka nodded as she sat on the ground by the fire. "That is where they usually stay. I do not know why they have come so far inland. But having them in the Heart of Soter makes the trek all the more dangerous, and we should avoid them if we can."

Tristan nodded and stuffed another bite in his mouth.

Karina stared at the contents of her bowl, suddenly losing her appetite. While she would prefer crawling over to her makeshift bed, keeping her strength up was important. She used the wooden spoon to mash the potatoes and carrots together, wished for some creamy butter to stir in, and bit into the slightly sweet concoction.

Rashka and Tristan continued to discuss the best way to get to Gundow while avoiding the most dangers. Karina ignored them. Instead, flashes of her time in the tunnels at the Temple of Aletheia, before she retrieved the Belt of Truth, crossed her mind. She was supposed to lead this group to the other two temples to retrieve the rest of the Armor of the Creator, four more pieces all together. Although she had accepted her quest and understood the Creator's trust in her, she still did not know how to accomplish the rest of this monumental task. Nor did she entirely believe they would come out of this unscathed, much less successful.

She glanced at Tristan as he argued with Rashka. Tristan was worldlier than she was. He understood the various cultures of the Three Kingdoms. Raised in a royal house like she was, he could fraternize with nobles or—given his years as a bounty hunter—could converse with commoners. She had been but a girl the last time she had ventured from Aletheia.

Rashka let out a condescending laugh, shaking her head as Tristan continued to drone on about something. The elf was a guardian for goodness sake! She talked to the animals and the trees. The knowledge she had of the Three Kingdoms probably surpassed even Tristan's.

Her gaze fell on Sam. While he might not be as worldly as Tristan or as knowledgeable as Rashka, he was still a skilled swordsman with a strong heart and the ability to lead. Her uncle had always said Sam had more potential than he realized and had offered to let Sam train as a soldier despite being an orphan.

And what was she? A healer? What part of medicinal training proved she could be a queen or a prophetess? Stooped with doubt, she shook her head.

She and Tristan already had the first two pieces of the armor—the Belt of Truth and the Shield of Faith. What two pieces would be next? Obviously, Sam and Rashka would complete the next challenges.

A hand landed on her shoulder, and Karina jumped. Tristan flashed her his trademark grin. "Why, hello, Your Majesty."

She shrugged off his hand and glared into the fire. "Stop calling me that."

"Better get used to it. It's your official title now."

"Not if I have anything to say about it," she muttered. If she really held such power, she would have done away with titles all together—tradition forgotten.

Rashka stood and brushed off her leather pants. "We will make our way to the western border of Soter, to the Cliffs of Morin, then south. From there, we will cut across the forest and head east."

Karina quirked an eyebrow. "Do we need to go so far west?"

"You weren't listening, were you?" Tristan smirked again.

She bit back a sarcastic retort, instead turning toward Rashka.

The elf laid her bow beside her and stretched. "We are not sure how far into the swamp the ogres have come. And the Heart of Soter is the most dangerous part of the wetlands on a good day. It is best to go all the way around."

"Very well."

"And with that decision"—Sam pulled the pot off the fire—"we should all get some sleep. I'll take first watch."

Karina grabbed her satchel, pulled out a blanket, and laid down. She was not sure she was ready for the next leg of the journey, but the Creator's call said she had little choice.

The next day dragged on. They plodded their way through the forest on horseback, following some sort of invisible trail. In fact, Karina was almost sure there was no trail. Rashka had shifted into her hawk form and flown on ahead to scope out the terrain.

Karina busied herself with thoughts of the past month. Her uncle dying. The former queen charging her with murder. Fleeing and then being kidnapped. She squinted ahead at Tristan. His back was straight, but his head moved side to side as he kept watch for any enemies hiding in the trees. A gentle breeze rumpled his dark hair. Did he ever think about the night he had kidnapped her or the days that had followed?

He turned around, and she quickly looked away. She blushed. Had he seen her staring? While pretending to study the trees, she peeked at him out of the corner of her eye. He had gone back to the trail—or non-trail—before them. Her heart thudded, but she rolled her eyes as she settled back in to the long ride. When had she become a silly romantic?

A hoarse screech resounded overhead. With a quick glimpse at the sky, Tristan signaled for them to halt while Rashka circled down and eased onto the ground. A flash of light, and she morphed back in her elven form.

Tristan dismounted and stroked his horse's flank before acknowledging the guardian. "What news do you have?"

Sam appeared at Karina's side, his sandy brown hair highlighted by the light filtering through the trees, and offered his hand. With a small smile, she allowed him to help her off Dom. She patted the flank of the humongous black stallion, resting her head against his mane. Although he was Tristan's horse, she and Dom had already become fast friends.

"You better see what Rashka has to say." Dom nickered and nudged her forward with his nose.

"I am going." She offered Dom the last carrot from her bag before she followed Sam to where Tristan and Rashka waited for them.

"How much further?" Sam asked.

"Oh, we will be heading west for at least another day." Rashka patted her own horse, which had been following behind Tristan. "There is a small village up ahead with an inn—Greenhorn. We should reach the inn by nightfall, and I have already arranged rooms for us."

Karina let out a relieved sigh. Her muscles fairly sang at the thought of a hot bath. She must be a sight after several days on the road. She raked her fingers through her ratted hair, but they became caught in the tangles.

Groaning inwardly, she pulled out a strap of leather from her satchel and harnessed her hair at the nape of her neck.

Tristan watched her with an odd smile. Why did he look at her like that? And why did she always blush when he did?

"There is one thing." Rashka gestured in the direction from which she had come. "I sensed evil as I entered the village. I could not tell what it was, but I have only felt that kind of evil when we were in the tunnels in Tzedek and at the royal house in Aletheia."

Karina furrowed her brow. "Should we be staying there then?"

"I did not sense the evil as strongly at the inn, which sets on the north side of Greenhorn. I believe if we circle around and come in from the north, we can avoid most of the village."

Karina's stomach twisted, making her nauseated. "I am not sure about this, Rashka." She looked over at Tristan, hoping for some support. As much as she wanted a hot bath, she would rather live through the night.

He glanced to the west, then back at her. "I think we'll be fine if we do as Rashka suggested. We'll continue to stand guard, just like we do when we're out here. If something is amiss, one of us will be awake to warn the others."

"Well …"

Sam swung his arm around her shoulders. "Hey, we aren't going to let anything happen to you." He wriggled his eyebrows.

She shoved him away. "I do not need protecting."

He grinned. "Just because you bested Tristan one time does not mean you are an expert swordsman. Like me."

Tristan growled. "She didn't best me."

"Uh-huh."

Tristan took a swing at Sam, who ducked out of the way and danced back to his horse. Karina rolled her eyes at the both of them. Silly boys.

With the trees swaying overhead and the birds singing in the branches as the sun shone down, she could almost imagine this was a nice outing with friends. With no impending doom awaiting them in the not-so-distant future. No crazy warlock bent on destruction. Karina trudged back to her horse. If only …

CHAPTER TWO

Day had nearly descended into night when Tristan brought the group around the outskirts of the mid-sized town of Greenhorn. He had been through here many times, especially when visiting Gundow, both as a child and as an adult. As they crested the hill, hearth fires and candles lit up the small homes. Yet a larger bonfire in the middle of the town glowed brighter than any of the others.

The hint of a memory poked at the edge of his mind: Father, all smiles and crimson robes, lifting him to sit on his shoulders before a massive bonfire in Andor's town square as the townspeople danced and sang.

Sam rode up beside him. "I wonder if they're having a celebration tonight."

Tristan shook his head without taking his eyes off the growing fire. "Must be a local thing. I don't remember any ritual celebrations this time of year." He finally glanced back. "Either way, we stay inside the inn."

Sam nodded.

The quartet guided their horses down the hill and up to the front of the inn where Rashka slid from her horse with all the grace the elves were known for. She held up her hand. "Stay here. I will send servants to take the horses to the stables out back."

Tristan dismounted and held the reins of both of their horses. He'd much rather be riding Dom, but he had promised Karina she could ride him. One would think Dom belonged to her the way those two behaved most days. Like he and Dom hadn't been through scores of tight scrapes together. Where was the loyalty? He snorted. Did horses know what loyalty was?

Dom trotted up to Tristan, and Karina smiled down from atop his back. "Dom says you have a jealous look about you, and I am inclined to agree. Whatever is the matter with you?"

"Nothing." He turned away.

A moment later, he heard her dismount. "Hey." Her soft whisper tickled his ear, sending a delicious shudder down his spine. "Please. Tell me what ails you."

He groaned, dropping his arms to his side. This woman would be the death of him. He could not stay cross with her, even if he wanted to. "Nothing, I promise." He forced a smile. "Just me learning how to be around other people, I suppose."

The corner of her mouth curved up. She dipped her head, looking up at him from beneath her pretty long lashes. He couldn't take his eyes off her. With another groan, he ran his hand over his face. "Remember, I'm a bounty hunter who's used to going at it alone."

Her eyes softened. She was about to reply when a door slammed rather loudly.

Two freckled boys, no older than twelve summers, ran up to them. "We'll be minding your horses, sir." They bowed their heads to Karina. "M'lady."

She bowed her head in return, flustered by the formality, which made Tristan's lips twitch. When the boys led their horses away, she leaned toward him. "Do they know who I am?"

He shook his head. "They probably assume you are a lady of station, given your clothes and the fact that you were riding Dom."

She mouthed an "Oh."

He took her arm and led her into the small inn. Small was indeed a good description. The main room held only three tables with four chairs each. A bar—if it could be called such—sat in the corner with a fireplace blazing in the opposite corner. The tantalizing scent of fresh bread and roasting meat gave the room a homey feel. If memory served, he had stayed here before once or twice on his travels.

Rashka stood by the kitchen door, talking with a woman who seemed no wider than a broomstick. When Rashka noticed their presence, she escorted the woman over. "This is Mable. She and her husband own the inn."

Tristan took her hand and bowed his head. "A pleasure, madam. Thank you for your hospitality."

The woman blushed, putting her other hand to her thin lips, but quickly recovered. "The pleasure is ours. There are four rooms upstairs. None of them are taken, so you may have rooms to yourselves. Unfortunately, we only have two bathing tubs, one in each of the first two rooms, already filled with hot water. By the time you have all bathed and dressed, my husband and I will have a hearty dinner waiting for you at one of the tables."

Tristan wasn't sure about the safety of this inn. But then his stomach gurgled, and he did not want to think about how he must smell. He nodded to the innkeeper, who led the way upstairs.

"Women on the right, men on the left." He shoved the door open and dropped his bag on the floor. The room contained the essentials—a bed, a chair, and a small table with a basin and water pitcher on it. In the middle, steam swirled from the surface of still water inside a wide wooden tub.

Sam poked his head in. "I'll settle in my room. Let me know when the tub is available."

Chagrined for not offering Sam the first bath, Tristan shot him a sheepish grin. But Sam had already shut the door, his boots echoing down the hall. Tristan shrugged. That was all well and good. He wanted nothing more than the steaming hot bath of fresh water.

He peeled off his traveling clothes and dropped them on the chair. Easing into the tub, he sucked in a hiss of air. Was the madam trying to boil them alive? When his muscles began to relax, he leaned back and closed his eyes.

His mind would not shut down, his thoughts everywhere. Was Karina well? Were they in danger? Was there a road leading south? How had he gotten himself into this mess? That last question brought him around to thoughts of his brother. He frowned. Anger and resentment heated his blood hotter than his bathwater. If only he'd had the courage to kill Faramos himself, they wouldn't be on this journey now.

He growled. No use dwelling on the past. Karina and her quest were the best way to get back at Faramos for all the pain and heartache his brother had caused him.

He opened his eyes. A bar of soap and a towel lay on a small stool beside the tub. He scrubbed his body down quickly, letting all the frustration melt off him along with the suds. He was about to step out of the water when a knock sounded at the door.

"Yes?" he called.

The door opened. "I was wondering if you were—" Karina stepped through the opening. "Oh!" Her cheeks flushed a bright crimson before she averted her eyes and spun away from him. "Forgive me. I thought you would be dressed by now."

He chuckled. "Well, as you can see …"

Karina let out a sound like something between a cough and a giggle.

"If you would kindly close the door, I will join you in the hall in a couple of minutes." She turned to leave but didn't move all that quickly, so he couldn't resist adding, "Unless you'd like to watch?"

She spun around, glaring, ready to unleash her rage on him. Then she froze. As if in sudden realization of what she'd done, she yanked the door open, stepped out, and slammed it shut.

Tristan smirked. Making her squirm was kind of fun.

When dressed, he adjusted his belt over his dark-blue tunic and brown pants. His damp hair clung to his forehead. No time to fuss further with his grooming—Karina was waiting.

He opened the door and found her standing alone in the hall. When she saw him, her cheeks pinked again. Without a word, she hurried toward the stairs. Tristan bit his lip to keep from smiling. This was going to be an interesting evening.

Down in the main room of the inn, they found plates with bread, meat, and vegetables on the table closest to the fireplace. The delectable smells made his stomach growl again. He escorted Karina over to the table and offered her a chair.

When they had been seated, the matron came over with a pitcher of watered ale. Tristan gladly accepted a glass. Karina smiled and thanked the woman as she poured the drink. The fire crackled loudly in the face of the silence that followed. Karina kept her eyes on her plate, pushing her food around, not taking a single bite.

He should say something. Yet, every thought that came to him was lousy. Instead, he hunched over his own food and scarfed down a piece of the bread, the warm, buttery deliciousness melting in his mouth. He wanted nothing more than to groan with pleasure but decided against such obvious delight … not very polite. This food was heaven compared to the fare available on the road.

He must have sighed or something because Karina peeked up at him between her long lashes again, a smile pulling at the corners of her mouth. When he tried to catch her eye, she quickly glanced at the fire and then back to her food.

"It's nice to have a home-cooked meal, isn't it?" he finally asked.

She nodded.

"I wonder if the matron has something planned for dessert. What kind of delicacies do you fancy?"

She stared at him. Did his question take her by surprise for some reason? Then she shrugged. "Citrus puffs are my favorite. I suppose I enjoy small cakes too. The cook at the royal house used to make small lemon cakes for me on my birthday."

He grinned. "Sounds delicious."

"What kind of desserts do you—"

"I am starving." Sam plopped down in the chair on Tristan's right.

Rashka sat down much more elegantly on his left. "The food smells wonderful."

"It tastes as good as it smells." Karina's eyes twinkled as she glanced his way.

He cleared his throat—and decided to change the subject. "I wish we could tarry here for another day or so, but we must leave first thing in the morning."

Rashka nodded. "I agree. No time to waste."

"As soon as we're done eating, I suggest everyone seek their dreams, so we will all be well-rested for the trip. I do not believe we will have another inn to stay at tomorrow night."

"We will pass through a few smaller villages over the next couple days. At least we will be able to keep our supplies full." Rashka pulled a small piece from a bread roll and popped it in her mouth.

The matron came out and filled everyone's cups again. She put a hand on her hip. "I do hope you all are able to rest tonight with all the noise out there."

"Yes," Sam said, chewing a bite of vegetables. "We noticed the village is preparing for a celebration."

The matron harrumphed. "Not the kind we should be having, if you ask me."

Interesting. Tristan shifted in his seat.

"What do you mean?" Karina asked.

"They be celebrating a union with that rotten king of Tzedek."

Tristan dropped his fork. "What?"

"Oh yes. Tzedekian soldiers have been haunting the towns on this side of the river for a while now. Threatening to burn down homes in villages refusing to bow to their king. Our town didn't even need that kind of convincing. Just rolled over on our loyalties. Right odd if you ask me."

Karina's wide eyes mirrored Tristan's sense of urgency. They were running out of time.

"I'm sure we will be able to sleep just fine, matron." Sam smiled and stuffed another bite of meat in his mouth. "Especially after such a delightful meal as this."

The woman fairly beamed as she bowed her head and then hurried back into the kitchen.

Tristan picked up his fork once again. "I'll take first watch tonight."

CHAPTER THREE

Karina sat up in her bed. Something had woken her, but she could not place what it was. The quiet room was cloaked in darkness as only a bit of light slanted in from the window. A small table was set against the opposite wall from the bed she lay in, a chair pushed up underneath. The tub had been removed during their dinner.

An echo of laughter, followed by several shouts, interrupted the quiet stillness. The noise came from outside—probably from the big fire pit in the middle of the village. Why were they all not in bed by now? It had to be after midnight.

She sighed and lay back against the feather pillow—a special gift, the matron had said when she had made her way upstairs after dinner. Staring at the ceiling, she listened to the din outside, waiting for sleep to claim her again. Perhaps a lost cause since comfort eluded her.

The air shifted. Outside her room, the tone changed. No more laughter. No more friendly shouts.

Instead, a steady murmur of voices rose in the night. The same cadence, the same pitch. They were not singing—chanting, maybe? Whatever the sound, she trembled despite the warm blanket.

Karina threw off the bedcover. Sweat dampened her skin and chilled her bones. Something felt very, very wrong. She stepped toward the door.

A flash of light blinded her. With a squeak, she stumbled back and fell onto the bed.

The brightness faded, and a glowing figure became clearer in the shadows. Karina's heart raced as she scrambled up against the wall.

"Fear not, Prophetess."

A familiar voice. She gasped. "Garon. What are you doing here?"

He stepped into a patch of light shining through the window, no trace of humor on his stone-like face. The pale moonlight added to his pallor. She imagined this is how ghosts of old stories would appear.

"Prophetess, you are in danger."

She sat up straight.

"There is evil in this village determined to destroy you if your presence is made known."

Karina hesitated to even breathe. So, the unsteady feeling in the pit of her stomach had been the evil outside. She pushed off the wall and climbed out of bed again. "I will tell my friends. We will leave at once."

"No. You cannot leave yet."

"Why not?"

"Outside, the evil would sense you. You should stay hidden until the village sleeps. Rise and leave before dawn."

She nodded, gazing out the window. "Garon, what kind of evil are you referring to?"

When he did not reply, she turned, only to realize he had already disappeared again. She shivered, whether from the cold or from fear, she was not sure. Would all her nights be fraught with danger from here on out? Would she always be looking over her shoulder? Always afraid to sleep?

She pulled her cloak from the hook by the door and wrapped it around her shoulders, then slipped out the door. With a deep breath, she took a step toward Tristan's room, where voices came from inside. Was she not the only one awake?

Without knocking, she opened the door and peeked in. Tristan, Sam, and Rashka huddled around the small window. Firelight danced like halos around their heads, which added to the supernatural feel of this night all the more. When the door creaked, all three went for their weapons.

"I did not mean to startle you," Karina whispered. "Is there something wrong?"

"I don't like it. Don't like it at all. We should leave." Sam stepped away from the window, his muscles taunt in the firelight.

"We cannot." Rashka moved closer to the door, her features hard. "The night is rife with danger."

"How is it dangerous if we leave the way we came? We'll be going away from the fire and the—the odd chanting."

"He has a point. Everyone is still distracted." Tristan continued to stand guard at the window.

Karina sidled up next to him, goosebumps rising on her skin. What had appeared to be a celebration earlier in the evening now made her tremble inwardly. The fire, a peculiar whitish-green color, stretched high into the sky, towering over the people. Instead of the usual frivolity associated with a festival, everyone crowded in a circle around the fire pit, solemn and unmoving.

"What are they doing?" she asked, barely daring to breathe.

"Chanting." Tristan's mouth was close to her ear, his warm breath teasing her skin. While his nearness should have made her stiffen, she relaxed into the safety she found when he was this close.

She inhaled deeply and returned her attention to the terror outside the window. "Chanting? What are they saying?"

He shook his head and stepped away. "I'm not sure."

Almost immediately, her body chilled. She frowned. Leaning her hands against the side of the window frame, she continued to observe the spectacle. Her stomach was unsettled, and her heart beat irregularly—or so it seemed. The sense of evil emanating from outside strengthened with the fevered chanting.

Behind her, the other three continued to argue about whether they should leave now or wait until morning, their whispers rising to shouts as the arguments intensified.

Karina sighed and retreated from the sinister scene outside. "We cannot leave now."

"Why not?" Sam sat in the only chair in the room, stretching his legs out in front of him.

"A Servant of the Creator appeared to me. In my room."

Tristan took hold of her elbow. "What? When? Why are you just now saying something?"

She swallowed the growing lump in her throat. "He was Garon, the same servant who gave me this quest. He warned me leaving tonight would be too dangerous—the evil out there would sense me." At the confused expressions on everyone's faces, she took a deep breath and related the whole tale. "Garon said to leave after the townspeople are asleep, before dawn."

Rashka nodded. "That is good advice."

Tristan let out a long sigh. "You all should return to your rooms. Get some sleep. It'll be a long day tomorrow."

Nobody moved.

CHAPTER FOUR

Karina yawned as she grabbed the bag Tristan handed her. "What is this?"

"Supplies. The matron was kind enough to give us food and blankets for the road."

She smiled. The woman had been kind indeed—maybe she sensed their intentions or their mission somehow. "Should we—"

"Don't worry. I left several coins on the table in my room."

She nodded. He knew her so well after so little time—though being around another person all day for several days did force people to get to know each other quickly. He had left the coins because she would want to return the kindness.

"We need to hurry, Karina." Tristan stroked her arm, causing her muscles to ripple involuntarily. His lips twitched. He cleared his throat and said, "Sam and Rashka have already saddled the horses and are holding them out back."

"By the stable?"

"We needed to avoid being spotted." He handed her another sack and inclined his head toward the kitchen door.

They made their way outside. The moon had dipped low on the horizon, no longer affording enough light. A little darkness was surely not as bad as whatever lurked in this town. Karina shivered.

The matron stood in the doorway, hands on her hip and a worried pinch to her face.

"Wait!" Karina tossed the sacks to Sam and ran to the older woman. "You should leave," she said between gasps of air.

"Pardon me, m'lady?" The woman placed a hand over her heart.

"You need to leave. It is too dangerous here. You do not know what is coming. Take your family and anyone else you hold dear, make your way north to Aletheia."

"To Aletheia?"

Karina bit her lip. How much should she say? "Make your way to River Branch, a town just over the river. At the inn, tell the owner Tristan sent you. He will help you from there."

The woman looked like she wanted to argue.

"Please, madam. I am only trying to help you."

The woman nodded and then, without a word, shut the door. As Karina hurried over to Dom, she prayed the woman would heed the warning.

Tristan handed the reins to Karina but did not let go immediately. Instead, he placed his other hand over hers. His eyes were hooded by shadows. Why did he stare at her so intently? The faintest breath escaped over her lips. "You are a good woman, Karina," he said. "You will be an amazing queen when the time comes."

She ducked her head. He did not need to say such things, especially since he added a humorless, "If we live through this." Did he really expect they might not survive?

"Indeed."

They mounted the horses, and Tristan led them up the hill behind the inn. When they reached the top, a screech pierced the darkness, echoing throughout the town. Dom's muscles tensed beneath Karina. The other horses whinnied and pranced.

"By all that is created, what was that?" Sam's whisper was harsh against the silence following the earsplitting interruption.

"I am not sure." Rashka nudged her horse forward. "We should get out of here."

Karina glanced back as the horses broke into a gallop. Something between a dark cloud and black smoke hovered over where the now-doused bonfire had been. "Tristan …"

"I see it. Keep up."

She said a quick prayer and urged Dom onward. Her breath kept time with the stallion's hoofbeats.

The group was silent as they circled wide around the town and headed south. The road stretched before them for some time before the hint of dawn lightened the horizon.

Most of the day, they traveled in silence, with only short commands uttered when necessary. Everyone was spooked. Karina's stomach still had not settled. She let out a sigh. Her muscles were sore, her brain was tired, and all she wanted to do was sleep.

"Careful there."

Karina startled, gripping Dom's reins. She regarded the stark land, the sky, the birds before realizing Dom had spoken. "What is wrong, you beast?"

"Nothing is wrong with me. You were the one about to fall off my back. Do you not know better than to fall asleep while riding a horse?"

Her cheeks heated. "I—I was not—"

"You were. I could tell."

She bit back a sharp retort. Yes, she was tired. "Thank you for keeping me awake."

The hours had passed into late evening before they stopped to make camp. Tristan had wanted to put as much distance between them and Greenhorn before they rested. They had already skirted two other villages and were on a stretch of flat land with few trees.

The sound of rushing water caught her attention as she dismounted. Just ahead, the land appeared to fall away. Casting a quick glance at the others, who appeared not to notice her or the rumbling sound, she padded over to the edge.

A river tumbled through the chasm between two cliffs. While not quite as high as the cliffs they had crossed in the Barrens or the natural barrier of the Aletheian temple, the Cliffs of Morin were still staggering. Below, naturally hewn stone amplified the roar of the rapids. The height, along with memories of the screaming horse, made her dizzy as she breathed in the damp air.

Behind her, raised voices interrupted her reverie. She turned and inclined her head.

"No fire tonight." Tristan yanked his pack off the brown mare, muttering under his breath.

"What? Why not?" Sam held up two handfuls of vegetables. "I've got the makings of a decent stew from the innkeeper."

Tristan towered over Sam. "With no protection, anyone can spot our fire and know exactly where we are. No. Fire." He stomped away.

Sam wrinkled his nose and made a mocking gesture.

"Sam!" Karina hissed as she made her way over to him.

He grinned and picked up another bag. "Well, if we can't have stew, I suppose we can eat bread and dried meat." Humming softly, he unwrapped a small loaf of bread and broke it into four pieces. Then he opened a brown leather bag to pull out a handful of dried meat. He held some out to her, which she accepted with a smile and a nod.

She eased down beside him as Tristan and Rashka circled around and took their portions. Everyone sat in a line and chewed quietly. At the same time, both Tristan and Sam leaned back on their elbows.

Karina raised her eyes to the velvety night sky, alive with the twinkling and dancing of stars. She smiled as a warmth enveloped her heart. So many stars, and the Creator still called her by name. "I do not remember seeing so many stars."

"One of the perks of not having a fire." Tristan stuck another piece of dried meat in his mouth.

Rashka crossed her legs and arched her neck. "My people used to believe the stars were made up of the host of Guardians and Servants."

"Used to?" Sam turned toward Rashka and so did Karina. "Not anymore?"

Rashka grunted. "Of course not. The stars were made by the Creator to light the night sky, along with the moon."

Sam snickered as he drew his gaze back to the diamond-studded sky.

They sat like that for a long time. When the chill in the air became too much, they gathered their packs and made a circle of make-shift beds. Sam plopped down. "I am exhausted."

"Well, after a night of no sleep …" Karina yawned.

A long, low howl ripped through the quiet of their night.

"Lupens?" Karina shivered. "This far south?"

"You don't think it's Brusho again, do you?" Sam stood, pulling out his sword.

"No." Rashka pushed aside his hand holding the hilt. "The last time was the end of him."

Tristan stared off in the direction of the sound. "That definitely lends to the mystery of what lupens are doing this far south."

Another howl echoed through the chasm and across the plains. Karina took a step toward Tristan. An answering bay came from the east, from the distant woods. More than one? Her heartbeat skittered.

A chorus of howls brought frightened whinnies from the horses. Dom stomped his feet. "We need to go, Prophetess."

Karina glanced at the black stallion, then back toward the trees in the distance, and then at the chasm. There was not much they could do if lupens decided to attack. Not from out here. Not right now.

Tristan drew his sword before he stepped in front of her, sliding his free hand back to grab hers. When she saw the ring on his finger, she breathed a sigh of relief. The Shield of Faith. She closed her fingers around his.

Rashka readied her bow. Her magical arrows would appear when she drew the string. They all stood, poised, ready to fight. Whatever came at them. At least from out here, they could see whatever attacked.

Karina surveyed the blue-gray landscape around them. Nothing. No lupens. No rogue elves. She lifted her gaze to the sky—nothing but stars … no dragons.

More howls echoed in the night. Where were the beasts? What were they waiting for?

Rashka lowered her bow. "If I did not know any better, I would think they were trying to bait us."

"What do you mean?" Tristan asked without moving.

"I mean, they want us to know they are here. But they are not attacking. Why? For what other reason?"

Sam eased his sword to his side. "So, what are we supposed to do?"

Rashka shrugged. "I say two of us should sleep while the other two stand watch."

Karina grunted. "I do not think any of us will sleep with the lupens howling like that. I know I will not."

Instead, they all watched in silence awhile longer. Karina leaned into Tristan's back, the warmth of his body soaking through his tunic as his adrenaline spiked. She told herself to breathe normally until there was something to worry about.

And then a piercing yowl broke the silence—so close. The horses fought their ropes, rearing back.

Tristan and Sam raced over to the animals. "Whoa there." The ropes snapped, and they all raced off, including Dom. The men tried to run after them but were unsuccessful.

Karina turned away, back toward the eerie sounds. Yet, nothing moved. Lupens were massive beasts with eyes that glowed red in the dark. She should be able to see them coming. She sucked in a breath, and her hands shook as she grasped the cloak draping her body.

"We should go." Rashka appeared beside her as Tristan and Sam approached.

"In the dark? On foot?" Tristan raised an eyebrow. "I don't think that's a good idea."

Rashka crossed her arms over her chest. "What do you suggest?"

"I don't know."

The guardian shook her head, dropping her arms to her side. "I can change into my griffin form and carry Karina away from here. You two can make your way on foot. I will come back in the daylight."

"Would splitting up not encourage the lupens to attack?" Karina steadied her trembling hands, her quavering voice. She did not want to leave Tristan and Sam, her protectors, her friends. She inhaled deeply, the edge of panic easing up on her.

"It would be a possibility. If there are only one or two lupens, they may sense they are outnumbered. Might be why they do not attack."

Tristan raked his hair, his eyes wild. "I think Rashka is right."

"No, I will not—"

Tristan grabbed Karina's shoulders, his green eyes boring into hers with such intensity. "Keeping you safe is the most important thing. More important than my life or Sam's."

"But—but you h-have the r-ring." Tears welled in her eyes though she refused to let them fall. She could care less about the stupid ring at the moment. If she were honest with herself, she felt safer when Tristan was around—not that she would tell him that.

Tristan's gaze fell to the ornate ring with the sunstone on his right hand. "Then you should know Sam and I will be fine. I have the ultimate defense."

She shook her head. He was right. She knew he was right. But there had to be a way to get them all out of here … together.

A burst of light interrupted their argument. Karina startled. Rashka morphed into her griffin form moments before her thoughts entered Karina's mind. *We must go now.*

"But …" She glanced at Tristan. Then at Sam.

Sam's slumped shoulders belied his cheeky grin. "C'mon now. You know we'll be fine. We'll be able to focus better knowing you are safe."

At that moment, she loathed them. All of them. She huffed, spun on her heels, and marched over to Rashka. "If either of you manages to get

RALENE BURKE

yourselves killed, I will find a way to bring you back just so I can kill you myself."

All Karina heard were chuckles as she mounted Rashka's back. Then came another eerie howl. Karina glanced behind them. Nothing.

Here we go. The griffin took off and circled into the sky.

Karina searched the ground for lupens, for glowing eyes in the forest. Nothing.

23

CHAPTER FIVE

Tristan watched Karina and Rashka until they disappeared over the distant trees, heading south and east. Hopefully, they would find a place to rest for what remained of the night.

"What now?" Sam stretched his arms above his head.

Tristan sighed and gathered up his pack. "We make our way in the same direction. Keep your sword at the ready."

Sam nodded, picked up his bag, and slung it across his back. He kept his blade up even as his gaze swept back and forth. Obviously, the lupens had him on edge too.

Tristan had never known lupens to act like this. They hunted, sure. But they didn't play with their food. They didn't betray their position with howls when they were on the hunt.

"Is it possible they're not after us?" Sam asked as they quickly made their way across the open field.

"I suppose anything is possible. But I do not believe it is a coincidence they are here, not far from Karina." Tristan growled. How he detested being separated from her, unable to keep her safe. If anything happened to her …

He growled again.

Sam watched him from the corner of his eye. "She'll be fine, you know. Rashka can keep her safe."

"I know that."

"Of course."

They walked on in silence, though it was not long before Tristan picked up the pace. They would be better off under the protection of the trees. Even if it put them too close to the ogres—they could deal with them later. One danger at a time.

The baying continued. While their howls did not seem to get any closer, they also did not fade away.

"The lupens are following us," he whispered, loud enough for Sam to hear.

Sam glanced over his shoulder as he followed. "I figured."

"We need to run."

"We won't be able to outrun them."

Tristan nodded. "We only need to get to the trees. Move a little faster."

They quickened their steps, but Tristan continued to watch behind them. No sign of the beasts except for the occasional howl. He hardly dared to breathe as he listened for hurried paws or labored breathing. Some sign they were being tracked. Yet he saw nothing nor sensed anything unusual. The whole situation baffled him.

Still, he pressed on. Though he might have the power to incinerate anything attacking him on contact, he may not have the power to protect Sam. Tristan sighed. Karina would kill him if he let anything happen to her best friend.

Another howl stopped him in his tracks. The eerie sound had come from in front of them.

Sam slowed and turned in a circle.

A chorus of howls echoed through the night. They were surrounded.

"What do we do?" Sam whispered.

"Keep moving forward. Be ready to fight." Tristan narrowed his eyes. The sounds were coming from all around—why couldn't he see anything? "None of this makes any sense."

Tristan stooped from the bag's weight. He chanced a quick glimpse toward Sam, his hair and tunic drenched with sweat. Was it from fear or running? Both? If they dropped their packs, they might distract whatever lupens followed them, perhaps move more quickly. Then again, they would also lose their supplies. While Tristan knew he could survive in the woods with only his sword—and ring—he didn't want to.

He ground his teeth. He hated not knowing what was going on and this feeling of helplessness. This was Faramos's doing—whatever this was made his blood boil.

"Hurry. We're almost to the tree line." Sam went from a fast-paced walk to a full-out run.

"Wait." Tristan rushed after him. If lupens were indeed following them, then running like this would only fuel their aggression. "Sam!"

Out of nowhere, Sam stopped. He didn't move, didn't say anything.

Tristan slowed, blew out a deep breath, and clapped a hand on his shoulder. "What are you doing?"

A low growl emanated from the trees not five human lengths away. Red eyes appeared in the darkness.

Tristan's breath froze in his lungs. Now would be the moment of the attack. He flung his bag away from him. Sam did the same. Luckily, there were still no lupens out on the plains. Dragging in a slow breath, he processed their predicament.

A gigantic lupen stepped from the woods—the largest he had ever seen. Its massive paws were the size of his chest. His heart pounded, and his throat went dry. This couldn't be a lone lupen, more had to be hiding in the trees, given the multiple howls they had been hearing all night.

"Why is it not attacking?" Sam whispered, his voice shaky.

Had Sam ever faced a lupen? Then, Tristan remembered the time he had sent Sam and Karina off into Shadowed Woods when they'd faced Brusho. While Tristan had taken on two lupens accompanying Brusho, Rashka had fought the evil elf in his lupen form. Meanwhile, Sam and Karina had been chased by yet another lupen, fought off by a temple priestess—not Sam.

"Are you up for this?" Tristan asked.

Sam stopped shaking and his face hardened. "I am."

Tristan's eyes narrowed in on the lupen, his muscles tensed to react at the slightest movement. Why was the beast not attacking? It stood as if frozen, staring at them. Was it waiting for something—or someone?

Tristan let out a yell and stepped forward, swinging his sword down across his body, then back the other way.

The lupen did not move. Didn't even flinch.

Tristan dared to take another step, shouting louder. "Get out of here! Get!"

The lupen licked its lips, drool leaking out the sides of its mouth.

"Don't get any closer," Sam said in a harsh whisper.

Indeed. Closer would not be a good idea until the lupen decided to attack. What he wouldn't give for Rashka's bow right now. Instead, he brought his sword up.

A howl sounded from somewhere behind them—far off.

The lupen growled, its eyes fixed on them, then took a step forward.

Karina let out a discouraged sigh. The air up here was freezing, and she was exhausted. She needed a good night's sleep. If she were not afraid of tumbling to her death, she would have fallen asleep long before now, her head buried in Rashka's soft feathers.

It will not be long, Your Majesty. Rashka's soft voice soothed Karina's haggard mind.

"I thought we would have found a place to rest by now."

I am trying to get as far south and east as I can.

"Why? That will put too much distance between us and Tristan and Sam."

Perhaps. But it is more important for us to put enough distance between you and Faramos's lupens, so they cannot track you.

Karina was not sure she agreed and let out another sigh. "The sun will be rising soon," she muttered.

You will have plenty of time to rest when I go back to search for Tristan and Sam.

"What? No! I will not let you leave without me."

You will be safe where we are going.

"My safety is not my primary concern. What if Tristan and Sam need help?"

Rashka did not reply. Karina squeezed her eyes shut, praying hard. Logically, Rashka could fly faster and longer without carrying her. Worst of all, if there were trouble, Karina would only be in the way—a distraction that must be kept safe. She pressed her lips together, frustration knotting the muscles in her shoulders.

After a few minutes of silence, Karina asked, "Where are we going?"

To the home of a sister guardian.

"You have a sister?" After their discussions about Rashka's brother, Asharan, Karina was surprised she had never mentioned a sister. Did she have more family out there in the Three Kingdoms?

Karina could almost sense the smile on Rashka's face—if griffins could smile—as her thoughts came to Karina's mind. *She is not a biological sister, just another guardian. Her name is Danna. She has a cabin across the pond ahead.*

Karina could not see much below them. The spread of trees looked like a gray-blue blob rising and falling with the variations of the land, like a dark sea. On occasion, a large clearing would open, an odd hole in the sea of a forest.

Above her, though, she could get lost in the stars. As high up as they were, the jewels in the night still seemed so far away. Jace, the royal healer in Aletheia, had once told her the stars were so far away one would never be able to fly high enough to reach them. Maybe he was right. Still, up here, so many millions of stars appeared, and the sky swarmed with glittering light.

Hang on, Karina, we will be landing in a moment.

She gripped the griffin's feathers tightly. Before now, she had been nervous about hurting Rashka. But the guardian elf insisted she hardly felt Karina's grasp … most of the time.

They soared in a large circle as they descended through the air. Karina finally caught sight of the pond Rashka had referred to. In the east, the horizon began to lighten, a glorious dawn of light pink hues. She held her breath in awe.

Somber reality melted her momentary joy as they came to rest on solid ground. With a groan, Karina dismounted, her legs like jelly. She had not ridden so far on Rashka since their trek from the Temple of Aletheia to Calliope. Her whole body ached, and she longed to sink to the ground in an exhausted pile.

A burst of light signaled Rashka's return to elf form. She tucked her raven black hair behind her pointed ears. "Well," she started with an unusually bright smile, "let's see if Danna is home."

The cabin was built into the side of a hill, with a small porch sticking out beyond the rise of ground and a window on both sides of the door. The idea of an underground house such as this fascinated Karina. Who could live in a house surrounded by dirt? What would keep burrowing creatures out? Karina had lived in a cave for a bit after the orphan caravan had been destroyed, but at least the cave had been surrounded by stone.

A line of plants had begun to bloom around the porch. Leading away from the house, a dirt path split right, toward the pond, and left toward the trees.

"Are you sure about this, Rashka? She might still be asleep."

Rashka shrugged. "Danna is an early riser. If she is not yet awake, she will be in a few minutes."

Karina nodded as they approached the quaint cabin. On closer inspection, or maybe as the dawn provided more light, Karina noticed the door hung slightly askew. Why would someone leave the door open?

Beside her, Rashka stopped and gestured for Karina to hold back. Rashka raised her chin, her eyes darting back and forth. "Something is wrong," she whispered. "Stay here."

All too happy to oblige, Karina swallowed past the lump in her throat, willing herself to breathe normally. Her palms had already begun to sweat, and her body shook ever so slightly. The silence she had mistaken for early-morning quiet took on a menacing edge. Something was definitely wrong.

Rashka crept forward. Without a sound, she pulled a dagger from the sheath at her belt. One of these days, Karina would ask her elven friend what happened to her weapons and clothes when she was in griffin form.

Rashka crouched in front of the porch, cocking her head. A finger to her lips, she stepped onto the rickety boards. A loud creak echoed around them. Rashka froze.

Karina's heart beat wildly, threatening to leap out of her chest. Glancing around, she did not notice any disturbances outside. She squatted for a moment and then stood again as she sent up a quick prayer to Creator.

Rashka pushed the door aside and disappeared from Karina's view.

The deafening silence still haunted the woods and the pond. No insects, no morning birds—not even the wind. Was something coming? Karina shivered, wishing Tristan and Sam were here.

"Danna!" Rashka's frightened voice—Karina was not sure she had ever heard her scared before—sounded from within.

She rushed to the porch and peeked into the cabin. Her friend crouched over a figure lying on the floor in the middle of the room. "Is everything well, Rashka?"

She shook her head.

"Is she … is she …"

"Yes, Karina, she is dead." Rashka spoke with breathy, tear-filled whispers.

She entered the cabin and placed a hand on the elf's back. "I am so sorry, Rashka."

Rashka straightened, sitting back on her haunches. "We trained as guardians together. She was strong but sweet-natured. We would meet for fellowship at the river between Aletheia and Soter many times throughout the year."

Karina did not know what to say. Two of the three Guardians—were there only three?—were dead. Would someone—or something—be coming after Rashka now too? The thought sent a shiver down Karina's spine. She gritted her teeth. They would deal with whatever was to come. Right now, she must concentrate on helping Rashka through her loss.

"Is there anything I can do?" Karina gently tugged Rashka to her feet.

"No. Please wait outside so I may send her off in peace."

Karina was not sure what she meant, but she bowed her head and stepped into the awakening forest.

CHAPTER SIX

Moonlight lit the world in hues of gray and blue, a sharp contrast to the glowing red eyes staring back at Tristan. He volleyed his weight from one foot to the other as he faced the advancing lupen. A miracle if both he and Sam survived this fight.

A low growl emanated from the beast, but Tristan stood his ground. The Lighted Realm would pass before he'd let a lupen make him quake in fear. With a mighty shout, he lunged forward, slashing his sword across its nose.

The lupen ducked out of the way and snapped its jaw at Tristan's outstretched arm, missing by a mere hand's span. Sweat trickled down the side of Tristan's face as he swung back around.

Sam rushed in behind the beast and plunged his sword into the lupen's shoulder. It whimpered and wrenched around, its mouth open wide, then roared. Sam fell back, rolling away, his weapon still stuck in the lupen.

Tristan gritted his teeth as the beast stalked toward Sam. He had to act swiftly or his friend would be the lupen's dinner. "Hey!" Tristan shouted.

The lupen remained fixated on Sam.

"Hey," Tristan yelled as loudly as he could and ran toward them.

Sam scrambled back on his hands and feet. The next moment, his face hardened, his fear seemingly giving way to determination. He glared at the lupen.

The beast attacked.

Sam rolled to the left and leaped to his feet. Using both hands, he grabbed the hilt of his sword, yanking it from the lupen's shoulder. With a yelp, the beast flinched. Before Sam had a chance to move, the lupen bit into his arm. Sam let out a sharp cry, pain lacing his features. Still, he managed to smack the lupen's nose with the hilt.

Tristan sent up a quick prayer, gave another shout, and then drove his sword into the lupen's spine. He may not have had a kill shot from behind, but that should do some damage. He gave the sword a twist.

The lupen whimpered, then shifted to the right, growling as it swung its head around. Large white teeth flashed in the moonlight. Its front paw swung out.

Tristan tensed. Squeezing his eyes shut, he prepared for the impact, ready to roll with the force. Nothing happened. Sam gasped, and Tristan dared to look.

The lupen was gone. All that remained was a pile of ash.

Of course. He held up the ring on his finger as the light from the shimmering sunstone faded. How could he have ever doubted? Why had he not asked for help to begin with? *Forgive me, Creator, for being a stubborn mule of a man.*

Sam, holding his wounded arm to his chest, retrieved his sword. He clumsily wiped the blade across his pant leg.

"Here, let me. We need to look at your wound too." Tristan held out his hand for the sword.

At first, Sam's face hardened, but then he let out a frustrated growl. Wincing, he turned over the blade before holding onto his wounded arm again.

"Sit." Tristan retrieved their packs, pulled out a cloth, and wiped down both of their blades. He was pulling out another piece of cloth to rip into strips for bandages when an unnerving howl echoed across the stillness of the night.

Sam's eyes widened. "You don't think …"

Another howl joined the first. They weren't too far away.

Tristan sucked in a deep breath. "We need to get going. Now. First, let me wrap your arm. I'll have to clean your wound later when we find a safe place to rest." He ripped the cloth into three strips. "Let me see."

Sam held out his arm. Large teeth had gouged chunks of flesh that now oozed with blood. His arm resembled ground meat ready for the frying pan.

Tristan shook his head. "I'm not sure I can patch that up. You need a real healer."

"Trust me, it hurts worse than it looks," Sam managed to say between painful breaths.

"Still able to joke? Can't be too bad."

Sam let out something between a sigh and a laugh. "Got anything for the pain?"

"I don't think so." He rummaged around in both the packs. If only they'd thought to bring Scorch flower ointment—Karina probably had some in her bag. No help to them now. He faked a smile. "Let's get the wound wrapped so we get out of here."

Tristan quickly wrapped all three bandages around the oozing teeth marks. Sam hissed at every movement, flinching and jerking his arm around. Not that Tristan could blame him. He was kind of surprised the lupen hadn't ripped the lower part of Sam's arm off completely.

The howls started again.

Tristan looked back toward the east, though he couldn't see much above the forest towering over them. Light? Dawn had arrived. Whether that was a good thing or not remained to be seen.

He turned to the plains again where multiple moving shadows, though still a good distance away, closed in.

"We need to go." He stuffed everything in the packs.

Sam struggled to push himself off the ground. "Where did they come from? They weren't there a minute ago."

Tristan grabbed Sam's good arm and yanked him to his feet. He snatched the bit of thin rope he'd left out, then circled it around Sam's neck and his wounded arm, forming an awkward sling. Not the greatest result, but good enough for now.

When Sam reached for his sword with his good arm, Tristan realized the beast had attacked his companion's dominant hand. Sam would not be able to wield a blade now.

"Put your sword away. Focus on running." Tristan swooped up both bags and slung them over his shoulder, his sword in his hand. He paused and blew out a breath. This was bad. Really bad. *Creator, we desperately need your help. I am not sure I can save us without it.*

The lupens trotted confidently toward them, their heads hanging low. Forcing down the knot in his throat, Tristan hoisted the bags higher on his shoulder. "Let's go!" He pushed Sam ahead of him, and they took off into the woods.

When Tristan cast a glance backward, one of the lupens let out a growl as it charged.

"Faster!" he shouted at Sam.

Red-faced and slicked with sweat, Sam fell behind. Tristan had to slow to match his pace. As his breathing became more labored, Sam stumbled along the forest floor, unable to swipe limbs, bushes, and other forest hazards out of his way.

Behind them, the sounds of breaking branches and crunching leaves hailed the lupens as they tore through the trees.

What now? Tristan was not familiar with these woods. The danger of wet ground that sucked people into the earth lurked in the Heart of Soter. He was not sure they were far enough south to avoid the natural traps.

Ahead, Sam tripped. With a cry, he threw his arm out to catch himself but didn't have the strength and rolled across the ground. A fresh cut appeared on his cheek.

Tristan paused, offering his hand to help Sam up.

On his feet again, he blew out a breath. "This isn't working."

"No, it isn't." Tristan surveyed the forest around them, assessing the situation. The sounds of twigs snapping and leaves crunching drew nearer every moment they delayed. This wasn't safe. His temples ached as his pulse raced.

In Sam's condition, they would not get very far. Should he leave Sam behind? His old self would have deserted him earlier. Survival of the fittest. He shrugged off the thought. Not only would Karina never forgive him if he lost her best friend, but Tristan was no longer that kind of man.

A thought struck him. He pointed upward. "Well, if we can't run away, perhaps we could—"

"Climb the trees?"

Tristan nodded. "As far as I know, lupens can't climb."

"I'm not sure I can either." Sam held up his wounded arm, then winced.

"Yes, you can. I can give you a boost. You can use your legs and your good arm. If you get high enough, a lupen can't jump and snap your leg. Come on." Tristan scanned the trees around them. Most didn't have low-hanging branches. He jogged a ways and searched again. He spotted a solitary tree standing in the middle of a small clearing. Its trunk was thick, and its branches appeared strong. "Over here, Sam!"

Breathing hard, Sam followed Tristan into the clearing.

Tristan circled the tree while staring up into its canopy. When he'd found the easiest path up the tree, he knelt and knotted his fingers together, ignoring the crashing sounds of the approaching lupens. "Hurry."

With a boost from Tristan, Sam reached up with his good hand to grab a higher branch. He pulled while Tristan pushed him higher. Sam hopped onto the lowest limb, then moved up into the branches.

A howl echoed through the clearing as a lupen stepped from behind nearby bushes.

Tristan froze. Glancing at the packs on the ground, he reached up to find the lowest branch. Another lupen appeared to his left. And then another between the two. There had to be at least two more out there. He sucked in a breath.

"C'mon, Tristan," Sam hissed.

Having not found the branch by touch, Tristan looked up. In the next second, he heard the charge, the pounding of paws. No time to climb. He pulled out his sword. "Sorry, Sam!" He spun on the lupen to his left and swung at his snout.

The lupen ducked out of the way, barring its teeth as Tristan danced to the side and around the tree trunk.

Snatching up his pack, he turned toward the trees on the other side. "I'll lead them away. Don't get down until you are sure they're all gone."

"Tristan, why don't you …"

Tristan ignored Sam and headed into the forest. His pulse thundered, and his breath came in short gasps. This would never work. He was going to die.

CHAPTER SEVEN

Karina skipped stones across the pond. The early morning sun brightened one side of the pond yet cast shadows on the side where she stood. The world seemed peaceful. Calm. Birds twittered in the trees as they went about their morning chores. A light breeze rustled the grass and skimmed the water. She breathed deeply and thanked the Creator for the respite.

She had not had a moment's peace since her journey began. Every breath spent training, praying, worrying, fighting. On the rare nights when she slept, she dreamed … well, she was not sure what she dreamed. The future? The present? Or were her worries leaking into her slumber? She sighed and sank down on a flat boulder at the edge of the pond.

Life was too hard. Being a prophetess was too hard. Being a queen was too hard—even if she'd only served in name alone. Thoughts of home reminded her of Mauri and Jace and just how much she missed them. Of her uncle … a tear trickled down her cheek, and she hastily swiped it away. No time for pesky emotions right now.

"I am sorry for what you had to see back there, Your Majesty."

Karina startled, then turned her head to Rashka, who walked lightly down the path to the pond. Karina straightened her tunic and cleared her throat. "And I am sorry about your friend."

Rashka nodded as she put her hands on her hip.

What should she say? Were there any words to lessen the sting of death? No one had been able to speak to Karina after her uncle died. As her eyes filled with unshed tears, she knew the answer. Her heart still ached for her parents, her uncle, even for Anaya. She rose, moved to Rashka's side, and gently touched her shaking shoulders. Instead of saying anything, Karina prayed the Creator would help Rashka find the strength she needed to get through this. She too had lost so many in the short time Karina had known her.

After a few minutes, Rashka wiped at her eyes. "I wrapped Danna's body in a blanket and buried her in a shallow grave behind the hill." When Karina remained quiet, she continued. "Now I must go find Tristan and Sam and bring them here. Danna's death means Faramos's evil is spreading."

"Are you sure?"

She nodded. "I found evidence of lupen tracks around Danna's home and Faramos's symbol carved into the table."

"Symbol?"

Rashka quirked an eyebrow. "From the crest of Tzedek's royal family."

Karina shook her head. She tried to picture the family crest but had no recollection of ever seeing it. Though she must have when Faramos held her captive.

"A dragon. The crest is usually a black flag with a silver dragon."

"Not much of a crest."

Rashka smirked.

"So, Faramos's minions are reaching farther than we thought."

She nodded.

As an uneasiness settled over her, Karina wrapped her arms around her stomach. Had the king of Tzedek's evil spread to the capital city yet? Surely not so far. If so, they might be in for a bigger struggle than they had anticipated. She cleared her throat. "I do not want to be insensitive, Rashka. But how long had Danna been dead?"

She sighed. "Two days. Her death was likely a direct attack on the Guardians and not in anticipation of her helping you."

Karina stared at Rashka. "You thought this might have been because of me?"

"No." She took Karina's hands. "We are on the brink of a great war, Karina. One in which you are a leader. Our people will fight *for* you and *with* you. Faramos's best strategy is to destroy as many as he can before the war begins."

Tears filled Karina's eyes, and she eased back down on the flat stone. She did not wish for anyone to die for her sake … for just the chance they might help her. Rationally, being queen and a prophetess meant people would sacrifice themselves for her cause, but her heart still ached at the thought that anyone would do such a thing for her. Her life was not worth more than theirs.

Rashka knelt before her. "Karina, you must not dwell on these things or you will go mad. You are a representative of the Creator. It is his war we are fighting—and we do so gladly because he is the Creator."

Karina nodded and squeezed her eyes shut, pushing back the tears.

"I must go now."

She snapped open her eyes. Go? "Are you sure it's safe?"

Rashka nodded. "Whoever was here has moved on. I do not think there is need to worry. They accomplished their goal." Grief passed over her face briefly before her features hardened again. "I will return before nightfall, regardless of whether I find them or not. If I do not, then I will go out again tomorrow." She locked her gaze with Karina's. "If I do not find them after tomorrow, we may have to make other plans."

Panic constricted Karina's lungs. No, leaving them behind would not be an option. Never. Karina opened her mouth to protest, but Rashka continued as she moved away from the cottage.

"I noticed some bread and dried meat in the house. You should eat and then rest." She raised her hands over her head and, with a flash of light, became a hawk.

"Be safe," Karina urged, pushing off the small boulder. "And please find Tristan and Sam."

Indeed, Your Majesty. You be safe as well. Do not wander off. Rashka flapped her great wings, rose into the sky, and then disappeared over the far treetops in the west. With a sigh, Karina let her arms fall to her side and soaked in the stillness of the pond. Unlike earlier, this peace had an eerie edge.

She was alone. Flashbacks flitted through her mind. She had been alone in the woods before, after her parents died. And again after the orphan caravan had burned. Scavenging for food, constantly fearing for her safety, sleeping with one eye open. Sweat dampened the back of Karina's tunic. Her hands shook. She breathed in deep and willed herself to calm down. This situation was not the same. Rashka would be back, and she would bring Tristan and Sam.

And you always have me, a small but powerful voice echoed in her mind.

Karina startled, but then her muscles relaxed. Of course, she had the Creator with her always. Still, the thought of her past stole away her thin smile. She turned away from the pond, with all its quiet serenity, and headed up the dirt path to the house in the hill.

The wind waved the tall grasses and riled up the trees. Clouds darkened the sky to the west. Why had she not noticed this before? Hopefully, the sky welcomed a gentle rain—unlike the brutal storm in the Barrens. Back in Calliope, she loved to curl up by the fireplace on a rainy day to read or nap. Her uncle always teased her about being a slugabed, but she never minded.

The wind pushed harder, swirling her hair around her face. She wrapped her arms around herself, quickening her pace.

The house came into view ahead. At least, being beneath a hill meant she only had to worry about an attack coming from one direction. Of course, it also meant there was no escape. She shook her head. No use worrying about something that was not likely to happen, like Rashka said.

A boom of thunder rattled the broken door. Maybe this was not going to be a nice little rain shower after all.

Sam waited until well past dawn before he dared to move from the tree. The overcast sky hid the world in shadows, and he dreaded the coming rain since he had no place to take shelter. He didn't even know which way to go. He had hardly ever been outside of Calliope, let alone Aletheia. And when he had, his travels had been north, through the passways to the sea with his father.

As he dropped to the ground, he hissed at the pain vibrating through his injured arm. The wound stung like crazy—and, in addition to his shredded flesh, the bone was broken. The mad dash through the trees had left no time to splint his arm properly until he'd been stuck in the tree. But splinting a broken arm on his own had been a tedious process. Not that he'd known what he was doing anyway—he'd almost passed out from the agony a couple of times.

He ground his teeth against the pain. Sweat trickled down the sides of his face, and he tried to wipe it away with his good arm. He closed his eyes, sucked in a deep breath, and shook his head. He had to think straight.

Their plan had been to head south and then east. When the lupens began stalking them, Tristan had headed straight east while Rashka had taken Karina directly south and east. Should he go after Tristan or Karina?

He looked at his arm. He'd be of no use to Tristan, especially if the lupens were still after him—or if they'd killed him already. Best to find Karina and tell her what happened.

His heart thudded a bit faster at the thought of her. Her smile. Her laughter. When was the last time he'd heard her laugh? What he wouldn't give … He hoisted his trampled bag over his shoulder, determined the best direction, and trudged off through the woods.

CHAPTER EIGHT

Tristan's side ached like never before. He could barely draw in a full breath. If he didn't think of something fast, he'd be dead in a matter of minutes. Maybe less than a minute.

Above the trees towering over him, thunder cracked so loud he cringed and ducked to avoid an invisible blow. With a quick glance over his shoulder, he confirmed the lupens were still following him … three now. Where had the other two gone? Had they gone back for Sam? He cursed under his breath. Karina was going to kill him. Granted, he might not survive to face her. Death by lupens would be preferable to delivering such news to Karina.

Creator, please take care of her as I was unable to.

A drop of water landed on his nose—another on his arm. He looked up as lightning split the belly of the clouds and opened them wide. Rain poured down. Was this a blessing or a curse? The rain would hide his scent and his footprints. On the other hand, the ground would become muddy and slow him down.

His legs were numb. He had no idea how long he'd been running. Normally, he was much better at finding a way to disappear. These woods did not hide the secrets the other forests did—caves and the like. Even the limbs on these trees were too high. He could not climb up into the safety of a canopy like Sam had done.

His foot smashed into a rock, and he fell forward. He hit the ground in a roll, letting momentum throw his body back to the upright position. His arm flailed as he stumbled a couple of steps, but then he was running again.

Creator … A warmth spread through him, rejuvenating his body. His Creator was watching out for him.

A great white light flashed, followed closely by a massive boom. Behind him, the lupens yelped.

He paused long enough to realize lightning had set the tree in front of him on fire, and the flames spread quickly from one tree to the next.

A grin pulled at Tristan's lips. Praise the Creator!

He skirted around the tree, ducking below the fiery branches, which continued to spread despite the downpour. A holy fire, indeed. He peered through the trees, trying to see through smoke and rain.

The lupens had stopped on the other side. They paced back and forth, sliding off each other, waiting, searching.

Tristan watched a moment longer, then curved back to the woods. They would not need much longer to figure out how to go around the fire. If he hurried, they would also not be able to track him.

He ran until he couldn't run anymore, keeping a brisk pace through much of the morning. Eventually, he came to a small river. On the other side was a village. Did he dare attempt to find rest and food there? Would the lupens be able to find him and tear through the village? No, he couldn't risk the possibility. He turned south with the river and followed its swollen banks.

A way down he found a massive tree with wide branches. He needed to rest. He could hardly collect his thoughts, much less continue to pick his way through the forest. He climbed up in the tree and settled in the crook of a branch. His stomach growled, and he groaned. Sleep would elude him until he filled his stomach. He pulled some dried meat from his pack. Not that this was the meal of kings.

He needed to find Sam. And he needed rest. Perhaps after a few hours of sleep, he'd venture back into the forest. Part of him hoped Sam had stayed in the tree. Much easier to find him if he had. The smarter part hoped Sam had headed south, making it harder for the lupens to find him.

Tristan's eyelids refused to stay open. His muscles relaxed … just a little bit of sleep.

Sam trudged through the rain. Was he going south? He couldn't be certain without looking at the sun. An old wives tale told of moss growing on a certain side of the tree. Could be true. Then again, he could not see the moss in dim light. He was sure the noon hour had come and gone because his stomach rumbled like a thunder's echo. The earlier storm had now quieted to a constant torrent of rain. If he could find a dry place to rest, he could eat some of the bread in his pack, assuming it wasn't a sopping mess by now.

Why had he let Tristan convince everyone to split up? Why had Tristan left him? Tristan had the Ring of Faith, or whatever it was called. He could have done away with the whole pack of lupens.

Sam stopped and cocked his head to the side as the rain slid down his face and over his already-soaked body. Maybe Tristan's plan had been to separate them all. How else could he get rid of Sam without Karina fighting him? Maybe Tristan wanted Karina all to himself. Like Sam hadn't been her friend for years, waiting patiently, enduring without complaint.

Karina's beautiful smile invaded his mind, her light peal of laughter rang in his ears. The way she touched his arm when they sat on the edge of Mount Jyal and talked for hours and how he inhaled her enticing lavender scent whenever he was near her.

He growled, clutched his arm to his chest once again, and stalked through the trees. No way was he going to let some two-bit bounty hunter keep him from Karina. If he wanted to get rid of a rival, that lowlife would have to do worse than leaving him alone in the forest. Sam snickered at the thought. He might not be an experienced outdoorsman, but he had determination … a purpose.

Sam didn't know how long he'd been walking when the rain finally gave way and the clouds began to break up. Warm rays of sunshine protruded through the heavy clouds.

When he wanted to drop from exhaustion, he came to a swollen river. Water had never looked so enticing! He raced over and laid flat on the bank, drinking greedily from the rushing streams. When he had his fill, he pulled out his water skin and filled that as well.

At last, he leaned back with his good elbow against the mushy bank for a well-deserved rest. Breathing in the warm air, he tried to relax … until his stomach broke the quiet of the moment with an angry growl.

Fine. Sam grabbed his pack and pulled out a loaf of bread wrapped in cloth. Thankfully, only the outer layer of cloth was wet. The bread was dry. He stuffed a piece in his mouth. The sweet, doughy goodness was gone before he could chew it properly. He let out a groan of pleasure, then devoured the rest.

He sat at the river longer than he'd intended, glad he was able to rest despite the constant throbbing in his arm. He needed a healer. Yet another reason to find Karina. Then the descending sun caught his attention, and he curled his lip. No, first, he needed to find shelter for the night.

"Well, well, well, Bogey. What do we have here?"

CHAPTER NINE

"What is it that I spy up in the tree?"

Tristan startled, and his feet slipped off the sturdy branch. He grabbed the limb above him to keep from toppling to the ground. What in the world? He noticed the shadows cast by the waning sun. Was it so late? He was only supposed to sleep a couple of hours. His stomach tightened. He'd never find Sam before dark now.

"Tristan, what are you doing?" the familiar voice shouted up at him. Rashka.

"What am I doing?" Pulling his pack over his shoulder, he hopped out of the tree, bending his knees as he landed. He wiped his hands on his trousers. "What are *you* doing? Where's Karina?" His heart stuttered at the question, his mind almost immediately shutting down, refusing to believe anything ill had happened. "Is she well?"

Rashka nodded. "She is safe. I have come to ensure you and Sam are well and bring you to her." She looked up at the sky, shielding her eyes with her hand. "I fear I may not be able to get both of you back to her tonight, though. The hour is already late." She placed her hands on her hips with a scoff. "Of course, if you were not hiding in trees where I could not spot you, finding you would not have taken me all day either. How did you end up here?"

Tristan let out a wearied sigh. "Lupens. We were chased."

Rashka quirked an eyebrow and tossed her black hair over her shoulder. "Where is Sam?"

"About that …" Tristan looked out over the rushing river. "I had to leave him behind. He was injured."

Her eyes flashed and then narrowed in on him.

"No, I didn't leave him to die. I helped him up into a tree and then led the lupens away from him."

She crossed her arms. "Why did you not allow the lupens to attack and let the shield protect you both?"

"Because there were too many of them. Because I didn't want any more to be able to track us. Because …" He let his shoulders fall forward as he kicked an imaginary rock in the grass. "My first instinct is still to fight."

Rashka dropped her arms to her side and nodded. "Well, what is done is done. Let us go find him. I need to return to Karina tonight. At least I can reunite you and Sam before I go." She raised her arms over her head, and with a burst of light, she morphed into her griffin form.

Tristan groaned. He didn't want to be atop a bird now or ever.

Come on, bounty hunter. We need to leave.

"Don't call me that," Tristan growled. He was pretty sure griffins couldn't smile, but he could have sworn Rashka did. Muttering under his breath, he climbed onto her back and sat where she instructed. How Karina did this so often with Rashka, he had no idea.

With a couple running steps, Rashka flapped her wings and lifted off the ground. Tristan clutched tight to the feathers around her neck. An odd mix of exhilaration and horror rushed through his body, tingling his spine and tensing his muscles at the same time.

Which way?

"To the west. I tried to head straight east when I led the lupens away."

Rashka soared low above the trees and angled her body to the west. *Do you think Sam would stay in the tree until you returned?*

Tristan shook his head—then paused. Rashka couldn't see him. "If he were smart, after a while, he would have headed in another direction."

Well, let us find the tree and then go from there.

They flew over the treetops, searching the ground. Tristan wasn't sure he could pinpoint the tree from up here. Everything looked different from a bird's-eye view. The forest blurred as they flew by so quickly—much faster than riding a horse.

"How am I supposed to see anything," he shouted.

Do not worry. My eyes are better than yours.

"But you don't know where I left Sam."

No, but if we reach the edge of the forest and have not found him, we will know he is not there.

"I was in a tree, and you hardly found me."

But I did.

Tristan glared at the back of the griffin's head. She acted like she knew everything. Guardian of Shadowed Wood she may be, but that did not mean she was perfect.

Eventually, they reached the western edge of the forest with no sign of Sam. Rashka eased down to the ground, and Tristan dismounted. His legs were shaky, as wobbly as a newborn foal. He plopped down on the ground and lay back.

We do not have time to search the woods. Rashka's talons scraped the ground.

"What do you want to do?"

I need to return to Karina so she does not worry. You will come with me.

He didn't fancy another ride on her back, though he didn't have much choice. Staying here would not be safe. "Fine."

Tomorrow, we will resume our search for Sam. We do not want to leave him behind.

Karina wouldn't let them anyway. Not that Tristan had any desire to lose Sam—he was a decent swordsman and someone who could one day be a true friend. Tristan closed his eyes and groaned. Karina was still going to have his head for leaving Sam in the first place.

Come on. Let us go now.

Tristan groaned again as he rolled to his side and stood.

She will not be as angry as you think.

He snorted. Obviously, she did not know Karina very well.

The sun had slipped below the horizon by the time Rashka landed by a small pond and turned back into her elven self. Stars were just beginning to twinkle, and the moon, at its half phase, made its way up into the night sky. Tristan did not see a house of any kind, let alone a village.

He spun to face Rashka, his jaw grinding. "Where exactly did you leave Karina? Did you leave her by herself?"

She thrust her hands on her hips and glared back at him. "I told you she was safe. Though she is alone, there is no reason to worry."

Tristan growled and took a step forward.

"Rashka!" a delighted voice shouted.

Karina ran out of the tall grasses lining the pond. Her bright blue eyes danced, and her dark hair bounced around her shoulders. He sighed. Karina was well.

"Your Majesty. It is good to see you. I trust your day was restful." She arched an eyebrow as she glared at Tristan, and he resisted the urge to roll his eyes like a young girl.

"Oh yes, I …" Rashka's tip must have registered because she stopped and then turned toward him.

"Tristan!" A smile of apparent joy brightened her face.

"Hello, beautiful."

She rushed over and threw her arms around him. He hesitated for a moment, then wrapped his arms around her, pulling her close, cherishing the warmth of her embrace. She would be hurling insults at him as soon as she heard his news.

"I'm so glad you're safe," she said, her voice muffled by his tunic.

A stab of remorse shook him as she pulled away.

Karina looked around. "Where's Sam?"

Tristan ran his hand through his hair. Boy, he did not want to have this conversation. He'd rather be up on Rashka's back again. He let out a long sigh. "We got separated."

"What?" Her hand flew to her mouth, and she took a step back. "What do you mean?"

"There were lupens on the plains. Lots of them. He got injured and couldn't fight or run. I helped him into a tree, then led the lupens away."

She bit her lip as tears shimmered in her pretty blue eyes.

He sucked in a deep breath. "When Rashka and I went back to look for him, he was gone."

She stared wordlessly at him.

Rashka stepped forward. "Do not worry, Your Majesty. We will return to the Heart tomorrow to search for him. For now, we should eat and then seek our dreams."

Karina would do nothing but worry until Sam stood before her. The fact made Tristan's heart ache, knowing he was to blame for her pain. He clenched his hands into tight fists.

Karina nodded, turned on her heel, and trudged back through the high grasses.

He let out a groan.

Rashka clapped her hand on his shoulder. "You do not worry either, Tristan. She will be fine. Come, let us eat."

Food? His stomach growled. The dried meat he'd consumed hours ago had not filled him for long. Indeed, dinner would be nice.

He followed Rashka through the grasses to a house built into the side of a hill. He'd heard of such dwellings but, as the son of a king, had never seen one. The dilapidated boards creaked as they stepped onto the porch. Everything was worn, but strong—except for the door, which hung at an odd angle.

The scent of vegetables and meat wafted out of the open door. Savory spices mixed in with the smells. His mouth watered as he stepped inside.

Karina stood by the fireplace, stirring a pot that rested over the flames. She did not look up when he entered. Though small, the one-room home was neatly arranged. The table in the middle of the room held a loaf of bread and four plates. Another kick in the face. She had expected Sam to be with them.

Rashka grabbed a wood pail by the door. "I will retrieve fresh water from the well." She shot Tristan a meaningful glare and whisked out of the house.

He let out a long sigh and sunk into one of the chairs around the table. The only sounds were Tristan's breathing and a soft click as the spoon hit the side of the pot over the fire.

Karina laid the ladle on the fireplace mantle. She turned but didn't bring her eyes to his face. Instead, she busied herself with domestic work, returning the extra dishes to the shelf, gathering dirty dishes in a small tub.

Tristan cleared his throat. "The stew smells delicious."

Her gaze flicked to him and then away. Silence.

Tristan rubbed his face and leaned forward. She couldn't stay angry with him forever. "Karina, I am sorry. I don't know what else to say."

Fury washed over her delicate features and then melted into sorrow. "I know," she whispered. "And I know this is not your fault. You were doing the best you could."

The best he could? He had never felt so inadequate in his entire life. He used to be a bounty hunter—a trained assassin. Kings had hired him to do their dirty work. Well, one king—his brother. Other nobility throughout the Three Kingdoms as well. He had escaped more snares than he could count. His name had been feared and revered.

Now he couldn't even keep track of one lame man—one who meant so much to the woman he cared about more than he had cared for anyone since his parents had died. How could he fail so miserably?

"I will find him."

At last, Karina looked up at him, her eyes still shining with tears. "I know you will, Tristan. Of that I am sure."

CHAPTER TEN

Sam froze. The voice behind him sent shivers up his spine.

"I don't know, Madge. Looks like a puny human to me."

Sam swallowed and spun around.

Two humanoid men stood in front of the trees. They were abnormally large, taller and wider than any man he'd ever seen. From this vantage point, he guessed they would stand head and shoulders above the tallest man he knew. One black eye was stuck in the middle of their slightly disfigured bald heads. Animal skins covered their bodies.

Ogres.

Sam stumbled back a couple of steps, aware of the still-rushing river behind him. Rashka's warnings echoed in his ears—too late to make a difference.

"Puny or not. I'm hungry." The ogre on the left grinned. His voice was the same as the first speaker, so he must be Madge—which made the one on the right, with the scar on his left cheek, Bogey. Other than the scar, they looked exactly alike.

Sam clenched his jaw, determined not to show fear to these stooges. Though twice his size, they clearly did not have the brains to match. If not for his broken arm, he could easily escape.

"Should we roast him over a fire or eat him now?" Madge took a step toward him, and Sam shuffled back toward the river. He could jump. Maybe he would have a better chance in the river.

"Wood's too wet from the storm. We'd have to take him back to camp to cook him over a fire." Bogey stroked his large axe.

"Raw it is. I like raw human for a snack anyway. Chewy." Madge grinned, revealing a row of rotting teeth that made Sam cringe.

He surveyed the land, the trees, the river, trying to determine the best escape plan. Who knew how fast the ogres were on their feet—he might not be able to outrun them. If he jumped into the river, he could swim away. Then again, he only had one arm with which to swim, and the current might be too strong. He could drown if he were pulled under. Could he talk them out of killing him?

"My dear friends," he started, then coughed. The ogres turned their attention to him, their snarls not at all friendly. "You don't want to eat me."

"Yes, we do." Madge said with a grin.

"No, no, no." Sam raised his good hand, shaking it. "Bogey was right, I am much too puny. I am much more valuable as a—a—" He searched his mind for something, anything, he could say to distract them. "A prisoner for ransom."

"As a what?" Bogey peered down at Sam with his one big eye.

"A prisoner. For ransom." Sam shrugged his shoulders. "You know, like someone you trade for money."

Bogey smirked. "We don't need no money. We take what we want."

"Well, you could trade me for other stuff as well. Food, supplies … maybe even a peace treaty. I am a special adviser to the queen of Aletheia." While that was not even remotely true, Sam was pretty sure Karina would forgive him this little white lie.

"A what?" Madge's continued confusion shown in the creases on his face.

"Adviser. The queen shares her issues with me, and I help her decide what to do."

Bogey took a step toward him, backing him up against the edge of the rushing river. Nowhere else to go.

"Is that a fact?" the giant ogre asked.

"Uh—yes. We have been friends since childhood. Best friends. Now that she's queen—well, uh, she would give you whatever you want in exchange for my safety."

"Too bad she's not here, then."

Madge chuckled and rubbed his hands together.

Sam swallowed his rising panic. The river was his best shot. Now or never. He had to jump. Balling his good hand into a fist, he took a half-step back. His heel found the lack of sturdy ground. One more step …

"Stop!"

Madge and Bogey halted, then spun around. They searched the ground and the trees, but Sam did not see anything either. The voice came from all directions.

"Over here, you big lugs." A woman approached from the left. Her green dress blended in well with the surrounding flora. She used a walking stick to help her maneuver around the river rocks and bushes. Her bright red hair had flowers and vines interwoven with her braids.

"What do you want?" Bogey asked.

"Yeah, you're ruining our snack time," Madge retorted.

"And what has you two stooping to eat humans again?" The woman paused before the two ogres and raised her head to meet their glares with one of her own.

Bogey jerked his thumb in the other ogre's direction. "Madge's stomach."

"What have I told you two about engaging with innocent folk?" The mysterious woman crossed her arms. From here, Sam could tell her eyes were a beautiful emerald green, the same color as her dress. No wonder she hid so well on her approach. Whoever she was, at least she seemed to be on his side. Or at least on the side of not letting the ogres eat him.

"We're sorry, Sabreen."

"An apology does not answer my question."

Madge dropped his gaze. "We're not supposed to get in the way of humans, and we're not supposed to eat them."

"Now, our agreement says I let you come down from the mountains to find more suitable food as long as you leave the humans alone. Is that clear?"

"Yes, Sabreen," they said in unison.

"Very well. Off with you. Alert the camp, for I am on my way." With a sly smirk, she winked at Sam. "And I shall be entertaining a guest. Ensure the tents are prepared."

"Yes, Sabreen." The ogres ambled off without another word and headed down the river where Sabreen had appeared. Madge shot a forlorn look his way until Bogey elbowed him.

Sam gawked. How was this woman able to control the ogres? Rashka had made them sound so much more dangerous, more like wild animals.

"Please excuse my friends, they tend to think with their stomachs." When Sam turned back to the pretty red-head, she extended her hand. "I am Sabreen."

He shook her hand gently. "Sam. Who—how …?"

She giggled. "I grew up in these wetlands and forests. I tend to take care of all living things here—the ogres quickly realized my authority when they ventured down from the mountains."

"So, are you … like … a guardian?"

An unreadable expression crossed her face, then she broke into a small smile. "Not exactly. I suppose what I do could be compared to the responsibilities of a guardian. Especially since, from what I understand, the Guardian of the Wetlands has died recently. A tragic loss." She glanced away and down at the ground, then, with a bright smile, gazed back at him. "But I do take care of the wetlands and all the creatures within."

Sam nodded, unsure of how to respond. Did Karina and Rashka yet know about the guardian's death? Were they even safe now?

"Come, my new friend." Sabreen looped her arm around his good one and pulled him along. "Let us make our way back to the ogres' camp. I am sure we can find you dry clothes and a hot meal, and I can also assess your wound. Not to mention you must be exhausted to have reached this far into the Heart of Soter with no steed or companions."

A lot of bubbly words from this exuberant beauty. "Well, I was separated from my friends. We had horses, but they were spooked off by lupens."

Sabreen's perfectly shaped eyebrows rose. "Lupens? In the wetlands?"

"Indeed. They followed us from Aletheia."

"Why in the world would they follow you so far?"

Sam regarded Sabreen. She seemed innocent enough—kind and generous for sure—but should he reveal their true quest here in Soter? Maybe not yet. For her safety as much as his. "We killed a few that attacked us in Aletheia. Maybe they want revenge?"

Sabreen smiled—apparently accepting his explanation—then led him along the riverbank. Despite the rushing water, the walk was rather enjoyable. The temperature had warmed in the heat of the mid-day sun, and everything around him was the new green only found at the beginning of spring.

Next to him, Sabreen continued to ask questions, genuinely interested in who he was, what he did, and where he came from. She didn't venture any further into what had brought him here.

They came to the edge of a small waterfall that plunged into a pool below. A small village of tents circled the pool. Despite the distance, he could make out people—ogres—moving around the tents.

"Welcome to Dunria," Sabreen said with a sweep of her hands and a cute giggle.

Sam followed her down a winding path from the top of the waterfall to the tent village below. He tried not to gawk at the gathering of ogres, and they seemed to regard him with some confusion as well.

Made from tanned animal skins, the tents were large, each meant to hold a couple of the ogres. They were spaced apart much like an army traveling together in the heart of winter. Oddly, there was a single, massive tent in the center—a sprawling beauty with skins dyed red.

Sabreen offered him a small smile as she led him into the center tent and away from prying eyes. The floor was covered with soft rugs of animal fur. A large bed lay to one side, while a roughly hewn table and chairs sat on the other. He marveled at the series of shelves adorned with various trinkets and bottles in the back.

"Welcome to my home. Or rather, my temporary abode." Sabreen eased down on the edge of the bed.

"Thank you. Temporary? Well, obviously, since this is a tent. Where do you hail from, then?" Sam stood awkwardly in the middle of the room as he scanned Sabreen's abode.

"I have a permanent home northeast of here, near the edge of the mountains. I traveled here with the ogres." She regarded him as if deciding if he were trustworthy or not. "Partially to ensure they did no harm while they were down here, and partially to collect special herbs found only in the Heart of Soter."

"Are you a healer, then?"

She did not respond right away, her eyes critical. At last, she nodded. "And more." She rose from the bed and ventured over to the table, which held a pail of water and a cup. She continued as she poured the water. "I am a caretaker of this land, and I am familiar with all the plant life and their variety of uses. But I do not care to venture this far into the Heart without accompaniment. Since my mother passed away over the winter, the ogres' sojourn was quite fortunate."

When she handed him the cup of water, he nodded his thanks. "How long will you be here?"

"I am not sure. I have mostly accomplished my task, but I do not want to leave the ogres unattended. They may cause more trouble than we care for." She gave him a knowing look.

Sam wondered if the herbs had been worth the risk, although Sabreen had some control over the giant ogres. Maybe they were just dumb animals. Still, the thought of all the monstrous men mere steps outside this tent …

"Do not worry, Sam. I would not let them harm you."

He grinned. "I was not worried about myself. Only for your safety."

She laid her hand on his arm. "That is sweet of you. I assure you neither of us is in any danger tonight."

As Sam relaxed against his chair, his energy waned as if being siphoned off by a leech. He must have lost more blood than he thought, or the walking had wearied him. He tried to take in a deep breath, but his lungs resisted.

"Here, let me look at your arm."

Barely able to raise his head, he managed to meet her gaze. Sabreen looked equally concerned and curious with her furrowed brow and bright green eyes. The way her lips twisted to the side—not quite a smirk—made his mind fuzzy.

"What—what …" His mouth didn't want to work correctly either. Something was wrong.

"Do not worry, Sam. I will take care of you." Sabreen offered him a genuine smile as darkness slipped over the edge of his vision and devoured him whole.

CHAPTER ELEVEN

Rashka landed in front of the dilapidated underground cottage. Her muscles were sore, her head ached, and she longed for rest—more rest than she had been granted of late. With an exertion of energy, a warm light overtook her body as she shifted from her hawk form into her elven form. She stood there for a moment, willing the weariness not to send her into sleep before her time.

She had returned to the woods where she had found Tristan the day before to search for Sam—to no avail. Not a trace, which she thought was odd. There should have been some clue as to what happened to him. Torn clothes, trail of blood, footprints … something.

Of course, Tristan had no memory of where he had left poor Sam. They had no starting point, save the place they had entered the woods. She had tracked that trail for a while until it disappeared. Both trails.

The tracker in her itched to be released again. People did not just disappear. Ah, this failure frustrated her beyond the telling. She needed to find Sam. They were falling behind on the bigger quest, and she was not sure Karina would allow them to continue without him.

"Any luck?" Tristan stepped out of the cottage.

She shook her head, not having the heart to answer with words.

His head fell forward as he let out a long sigh. She could not blame him. Sam's disappearance weighed heavily on all of them—none more than Tristan. Of course, he probably thought there was more at stake with his budding relationship with the prophetess. He assumed Karina would not forgive him his lapse of judgment. While he could be right, she did not think Karina quite so unforgiving.

"Do not lose heart, Tristan. I am sure he is well. Perhaps he found someone in the woods to take him in for a while."

She knew his forced smile belied his actual thoughts. He no more believed her words than she did. If Sam had been injured and there was no trace of him, he was likely no longer alive. A sad fact, indeed.

"I will try again tomorrow. How is the prophetess?"

Tristan's shoulders slumped all the more. "She sits in front of the fire, staring into it like an invalid." He kicked at a stone, sending it skittering across the damp ground.

"She will be fine as well, Tristan. No matter the outcome." Still, her heart squeezed within her chest. Aching for the situation they were in, worrying for the timing of this mishap, and grieving for the most likely outcome.

He refused to meet her eyes as he gestured toward the cottage. "There's vegetable stew hanging in the fireplace. Lucky your friend had a garden out back."

"I am famished. And I will need to rest so I can continue the search tomorrow." She strode past him and into the cottage. The room had darkened quite a bit, highlighted by the flames dancing in the fireplace.

Karina barely tore her gaze from the flames when they entered. She sat in a chair by the stone fireplace, exactly as Tristan had said. "Still no sign of him?" she mumbled.

"I am sorry, Your Majesty."

Tears welled in the girl's eyes, though she managed to hold them at bay. "I do not suppose there is any hope in finding him now."

Rashka knelt in front of Karina, taking her hands in her own. "Do not give up hope. Sometimes it is all we have. I will go out again tomorrow."

Karina nodded.

"Look at me, Karina."

She turned her gaze as if moving away from the flames was too painful to endure.

Rashka stayed her own heart at what she was about to say. "If I do not find him tomorrow, we must move on toward Gundow. We will have to trust the Creator to care for Sam as we continue the quest—trust that we will see him again."

Karina shook her head in a slow, repetitive motion. Rashka would let the truth of their situation settle in Karina's spirit a bit before pressing the importance of moving forward with their mission. The Creator would heal Karina's heart in time. He had done so for her so many times over the years. Not that the grief of loss ever went away completely, but the pain did lessen with time. Joy could be found again.

Tristan, who had not said a word since they had come inside, handed Rashka a piping hot bowl of stew. The sweet scent of carrots and other veggies blended together in an enticing aroma. She took her bowl over to the table and thanked the Creator for the provision.

Tristan sat next to her and dug into the stew. "Did you see any signs of lupens while you were out?"

"Other than the ashes of the ones you killed … no."

"That's one good thing. At least we do not need to worry about those crazy beasts for the time being."

Rashka shook her head. "Soter is a large kingdom, and I only scouted a small portion of the area. We know only there are no lupens in the Heart of Soter, the wetlands."

Sam struggled to open his eyes. Blood pounded through his brain like a smithy's hammer. Despite his lack of vision, his other senses reached out beyond him. He could hear cloth flapping in the wind nearby and the sounds of water, like rain but harder, faster. Hoarse voices called out orders above the din. Since the air was cool, he nestled beneath soft blankets.

Where was he? The only thing missing from the throng around him was Karina's familiar presence. His eyes popped open. Karina? Was she well?

His vision blurred as he pushed himself into a sitting position. Several animal-pelt blankets fell from his chest. His bare chest. He peeked underneath, grateful to find he still wore pants—though not his pants. These leather pants were nothing like anything worn in Aletheia. Maybe they were better suited for the wetlands?

The perky red-head … Sabreen—had she poisoned him? Or not poisoned as he would be dead now. Drugged him? He surveyed his surroundings. He was still in her tent, lying in her bed. Suddenly feeling rather uncomfortable, he clamored from the comfort of the bed, his limbs numb, nearly falling to his knees.

"Ah, so you finally decided to join us in the land of the living again." Sabreen appeared at the entrance to the tent. She giggled as she threw him a light blue tunic before moving to the table.

"Land of the living?" he spat. "What did you do to me?"

Her normally vibrant smile vanished, replaced by a solemn expression as she held up her hands. "Easy there, Sam. I had to send you to unconsciousness."

"What?" He yanked the tunic over his head, then stormed over to where she stood by the table. He towered head above her, glaring. "Why? What did you do to me?"

She took in a deep breath before forcing an encouraging grin. "Why, to heal your arm, silly."

"To heal my what?" He looked at his arm, remembering the lupen attack—his shredded flesh, his broken bone. Sure enough, now the arm appeared relatively normal. A long red scar ran from his elbow to his wrist, with only a twinge of pain when he flexed his hand. Still, a marked improvement from his previous condition. He stared at Sabreen, mouth ajar. "How?"

"The wonders of the Heart of Soter." When he clenched his jaw, her features softened. "I assure you, Sam, I would never hurt you."

His cheeks heated … something in his stomach roiled as if he had eaten some rancid meat. Of course, his reaction could be the side effect of herbs or whatever she had used to subdue him. "You could have told me. I would have let you heal my arm."

She nodded. "Perhaps. However, healing is not always a painless process. Being unconscious saved you from unnecessary pain."

Supernatural healing that caused pain? When Rashka had healed his wounds after the battle at the Aletheian temple, there had been a brief sting of discomfort. Then a warmth had spread through his body. What made Sabreen's remedies different?

He must have been staring at Sabreen for too long for a dark shadow crossed her face. "A thank you is not necessary," she said gruffly as she set about throwing items in a bag. The hurt in her voice was evident.

He chastised himself for not being more grateful, for questioning her methods and motives. "Sabreen, really, thank you for healing my arm." When she didn't acknowledge him, he took her hand, stilling her harried motions. Then he waited until she looked at him. "Thank you."

"You are welcome." She offered him a small smile, then pulled her hand away and continued packing her bag.

"What are you doing?"

"We have a long trek ahead of us. We will need supplies."

"Trek? Where are we going?"

Amid her packing, she gave him an incredulous look. "To find your friends, of course."

Finding his friends was his top priority, indeed. Yet, he was also curious about Sabreen and her life here. Fascination over how she lived in harmony with the ogres brought up so many questions. He sat down on the edge of the bed. "But I just got here. You have not shown me around or anything."

"Why, Sam, are you curious about my life?" She shot him a teasing grin.

"Well … I …"

She furrowed her brow and shook her head. "It is not safe for you here."

His back went rigid. "What do you mean?"

"I mean"—she let out an exasperated sigh—"if I have you traipsing around the camp, there is no telling what these giant brutes would do."

"Then why did you bring me here? You said it was safe!"

She waved her hand. "As long as you are in this tent, they know you are mine. Plus, the whole out-of-sight thing. If you are out in the camp, it's like dangling meat in front of a lupen. They could only resist for so long."

"I thought they obeyed you."

"Obey?" She chuckled. "Hardly. They heed my warnings. And, sure, I could handle one or two of them if they gave me trouble. Any more, and I would be on the dinner table."

Sam stood, searching for ways to help. If it really was that dangerous here, then he needed to get out. Find Karina. Get on with the quest. "I should leave quickly."

"Indeed." She shoved a large pack at him and then grabbed another one. "I am going to the food tent. You stay here. Do not come out of the tent."

He nodded, and she disappeared beneath the flap of cloth covering the entrance. How did he get into this mess? His resentment toward Tristan flared again. If he hadn't left him in the tree, alone, Sam would be safely at the fireside with them tonight. With Karina. Keeping her safe.

No, she preferred Tristan. A bounty hunter. Why did women always prefer the bad ones? Not that Karina had really shown much interest in any man before Tristan came around. Sam had always hoped Karina would one day open her eyes and see what was right in front of her.

He had to push those thoughts aside. Karina's quest was more important than his feelings for her, or the lack of such for him on her part.

Impatience made him antsy, had him pacing around the tent. He ambled over to the door and stuck his head out from beneath the flap. One-eyed ogres roved around beyond the tent—life in a regular village, only on a larger scale. Some ogres worked together—with several arguing back and forth—to put up more tents, while others were skinning animals and preparing food. Still others sat around mending clothes or whittling wood. Where were the women? Did they look like the men? How did one tell them apart?

"Hey, Bogey, it's the human boy." Madge. Again.

Sam pulled his head back in and stumbled over to the bed. He could hear heavy footsteps nearing the tent.

"Leave him alone, Madge. We don't want to anger the witch again."

Witch? They thought Sabreen was a witch? Sam turned the word over in his mind. That would explain her knowledge of life in the Heart of Soter. What if she was? Witches were unheard of in Aletheia, outlawed by the Word of the Creator. Their powers, though based in nature, were outside the natural laws of life, the design the Creator intended. Perhaps that is why Sabreen's form of healing would have caused him more pain.

"Ah, she doesn't scare me. What does she need this puny human for anyway?"

"My plans are none of your concern," Sabreen's steely voice interjected with more power.

A thunder of footsteps. Some coughing. "Oh, he was joking around, Sabreen," Bogey replied.

"I think your particular strengths could be used by the watering hole."

"Y-yes, S-Sabreen," Madge stuttered.

Before Sam could move, the flap opened. Sabreen swept in with the food bag on her back. "Stupid overgrown ogres. And you!" Her nostrils flared. "I told you to stay in the tent."

Sam rubbed the back of his head. "I did. Mostly. Only peeked my head out for a minute."

With a grunt, she stormed about the tent. "Men! If only they would learn to listen, it would save my sanity." She grabbed a cloak from the bed before she turned to Sam. "Well, we best be on our way before those two ignite the interest of more ogres than I can handle."

"Don't they know you're leaving?"

"No."

"Are you going to tell them?"

"Didn't plan to." Without another word, she ducked out of the tent. "Are you coming?" she hollered back.

He grabbed the larger sack she'd given him earlier and rushed off after her. Keeping his head down, he avoided the curious glances of the ogres as they passed. Sabreen shouted greetings to a few. True to her word, she did not mention they were leaving.

When they neared the edge of the village, he sidled up next to her. "Will they wonder where you've gone?"

"No." She grinned. "They are used to me disappearing for days on end. Sometimes I am hunting for herbs or food or merely adventuring for a day or two. They know I will be back when I am ready."

"Are you their leader?"

"Not really. Although, they do look to me for advice. They view me as a seeker of justice."

"Why?"

She shrugged. "Not sure. When they ventured down from the mountains, they were pillaging everything in sight. I pointed out one day they were going to invite the eyes of the king, which would bring on the sting of the Soteran army. When I offered them a different solution, they showed their gratefulness by taking care of me."

"Taking care of you?"

"They made me the tent, brought me food, gave me a reason to use my arts."

By arts, she probably referred to her witchcraft. Sam resisted a shudder. He may have been taught witchcraft was evil, but Sabreen seemed anything but. She only wanted to help—first the ogres and now him.

They hit the tree line, and Sabreen proceeded into the woods without stopping. Sam scanned the branches that closed them in beneath their budding leaves. Spring had come in full force, awakening the sleeping foliage of the forest.

"Where are we headed?" he asked.

"First, out of the Heart of Soter and then to find your friends. Where were they headed?"

Right. He had not yet revealed the reason Karina had brought them to Soter. The truth was still not his to tell. Sabreen did need to know where they were going in order to get him there. "They were headed to Gundow."

"Ah, the golden city of Soter."

"Golden city?"

"Oh, you wait and see, Sam."

CHAPTER TWELVE

Karina stepped out into the early morning sunlight. She had not slept well yet again, despite the fact Tristan and Rashka had granted her use of the small bed in the cottage while they chose to sleep on the floor in front of the fireplace. They had alternated watch shifts the last couple of nights, refusing to allow her to do the same. Though they meant the gesture out of kindness or possibly loyalty, it still irked her not to be allowed to pitch in.

A nicker from her left startled her. A massive black stallion trotted down the path from the woods. "Dom!"

The friendly horse shook his mane and stamped at the ground. "Greetings, Prophetess. I am pleased to find you well."

When he stopped next to her, she nuzzled the side of his face. "What happened to you?"

"After I fled with the other horses, it took a long time for me to catch your trail. I think it was more the Creator's leading that brought me here."

"Well, whatever it was, I am glad you are here." She squeezed him a little tighter, relishing in the warmth of his hair.

Wood banged against wood. "What in the Creator's name is going on?" With a good bit more noise, Tristan clamored off the porch, sword in hand, with Rashka behind him, her bow poised with one of her magical arrows.

She laughed. "Look who found his way to us!"

Tristan let his blade droop, an equally bright smile on his face. "Dom! You know, I never tire of seeing you turn up, but you surprise me every time."

"Indeed. It is good to see you as well, old friend."

Karina patted his neck. "Dom says it is good to see you too."

Tristan ambled over and ran a hand down the stallion's neck and over his flank. "He appears to be uninjured."

"I am well."

"He says he is well."

Tristan nodded. "Good."

Karina basked in the joy of the moment before the current situation sunk back in. She let out a long sigh. "Dom, did you happen upon any sign of Sam on your way here?"

He whinnied and shook his head. "I was too busy avoiding ogres."

Her eyes widened. "Ogres? You actually saw them?"

Rashka, who had set her bow aside and had begun gathering supplies, froze. "Did you say ogres?"

Karina nodded. "Dom had to avoid some ogres on his way here." She turned back to him. "What happened?"

"It took me awhile to pick my way through the wetlands. Too much water and mud." Karina noted his mud-caked legs, but she let Dom continue. "I heard something crashing through the trees—large men with one eye and bad tempers. I was careful to go around."

"So, the rumors are true." Karina leaned against Dom's flank, closing her eyes. Only the Creator knew what had happened to Sam. Had he run into the same ogres?

Rashka laid her hand on Karina's shoulder. "Do not lose hope. Just because Dom saw the ogres, does not mean anything happened to Sam." She paused and waited until Karina looked at her. Though Rashka's expression was serious, a hint of sympathy lay behind her gaze. "However, it is time."

Karina's mind halted at those words. "Time? Time for what?"

Rashka pulled her away from Dom and helped her sit on the edge of the porch before she knelt next to her. "It is time to leave for Gundow."

"What?" She tried to stand, but Rashka held her still. "No! We have to keep looking."

"We have looked. We found no sign of him, no trail to follow."

"So, we try again!" Panic rose in her throat, and she struggled to breathe. Her arms and legs tingled with the desire to do something. Anything. They could not leave Sam behind.

"Karina." This time Tristan spoke, his voice firm. "Rashka, Sam, and I agreed back in River Branch …"

Karina put her hands over her ears, not caring if she was being childish. Instinct told her what would come out of Tristan's mouth next, and she did not wish to hear his counsel. She did not care what they had agreed to. She would not leave her friend behind. Any friend.

Tristan gestured for Rashka to move away. Then he knelt in front of Karina and moved her hands away from her ears. Tears welled in her eyes, but she refused to let them fall.

He lifted her chin and met her gaze. "We agreed the quest had to continue, no matter what. Even if it meant one of us would be left behind."

"I would never agree to leave anyone behind," she retorted through clenched teeth.

"You didn't need to. We are the ones who have to keep you safe, to keep you moving forward."

"But if Sam is supposed to complete one of the next challenges, who will take his place? There will be only three of us now."

Tristan shrugged. "I do not know how to answer that question, Karina. I only know the Creator is with you—with us. We have to trust him."

She pursed her lips. What Tristan said was true, but she did not have to agree. Before she could object, Tristan held up his hand.

"We are leaving." Without waiting for further argument, he stood and stalked into the cottage. He returned with two packs, which he strapped onto Dom's back without a word.

Rashka offered a sympathetic nod, then prepared her pack as well. They left her on the porch, not asking for Karina's help or input. Being left on her own angered her more. They were leaving Sam, and they were treating her like a child. A child! Granted, she was acting like a child … but that was not the point.

She inhaled slowly through her nose, willing her body to relax, to calm down. Her friends meant well. More often than not, they were more knowledgeable about—well, most things—than her. The Creator had provided these companions for the quest to complement her weaknesses.

She stood, resolving to remember her place in all this. She was a queen—but not just a queen, a prophetess—called by the Creator himself. Nothing was more important than the quest to retrieve the sacred armor. Nothing—and no one. Her heart broke at that last thought, crumbled into a million pieces. It took all her strength not to dissolve into a sobbing mess herself.

Instead, she brushed her hands over her leather pants, straightened her tunic and cloak, and marched over to Dom. "How far is it to Gundow?" Her voice cracked, but she managed to keep it from wavering too much.

Tristan raised his eyebrow. "I'm not sure, I don't even know where in Soter we are—other than south of the Heart."

Rashka ambled over and threw her pack on Dom's back. "It will be less than a two-day journey from here with Dom to help. We should arrive by tomorrow afternoon."

Karina eased down on the ground beside the roaring fire pit. Typical of early spring weather, the temperature had taken a nosedive. She huddled beneath her cloak. They had ridden most of the day, with Tristan riding Dom and Karina on the back of Rashka's griffin form.

Not long before sunset, Rashka had shown Karina from the sky where the capital of Soter, Gundow, fairly glowed before the sinking sun. Rashka had said the city was trimmed in gold mined from the southern cliffs. Though Karina had spent a few years in Gundow as a small child, seeing the city now from above—what a sight to behold!

Tristan rose from the other side of the fire, where he had been preparing a savory dinner of dried meat and crusty bread. She suppressed a smirk as he held out the delicacies to her, accepting them with a nod.

They were all too tired for much chatter. And Rashka and Tristan seemed to believe they should be quiet as Karina grieved for Sam, which was fine with her. She did not want to discuss the matter either. She let her chin drop. Oh, how empty she felt now. A Sam-size hole was left in her heart.

Tristan sat next to her without saying a word. After a short, companionable silence, Karina laid her head on his shoulder, accepting strength and warmth from him. After he finished eating, Tristan slipped an arm around her shoulders, pulling her close, and kissed the hair on top of her head. He held her for a while, and her eyes began to droop. His presence was comforting, and the silence allowed her to continue to process—to accept what had happened, to what the rest of them had all agreed.

Her eyes had just shut when the firelight brightened immensely, startling her. She opened her eyes to a shimmering green flame, reminiscent of the bonfire from their night in Greenhorn. She shrunk against Tristan's side. He nudged her farther behind him and stood, pulling his sword.

Masculine laughter rose from amid the unusual flames. Rashka, her face a stoic mask, rounded the fire with her bow poised as she made her way toward Karina.

"What is happening?" Karina asked.

"I do not know, Prophetess." Rashka fixed her gaze at the fire. "Stay back."

The eerie flames danced and grew, reaching higher than Karina was tall. From the fire, a green hazy smoke billowed, taking the shape of a man. In the next moment, Karina locked eyes with Faramos Lemur. His sinister smirk made her gasp, and she stumbled backward. His dark hair was slicked back, his traditional black clothes somehow see-through in the green smoke.

"By all that's created!" Tristan snarled.

"Greetings, brother." Faramos's gaze slipped from Karina to Tristan. "I see you all have made your way into Soter."

"What do you want?"

"To see how the journey is treating you."

"Why don't you come on out and ask me in person?"

The smoke figure cackled. "Do not tempt me, dear brother. It is not like you have given me any reason *not* to kill you."

"You're not here to make good on that threat." Tristan stood still, back rigid, though the ripple of his muscles proved he was ready to lunge. Karina had seen the stance often enough to know he expected danger. Was Faramos nearby?

"I see my former bride is still well." His gaze found Karina again. He took the time to look her over, a lustful heat burning behind his dark eyes. "My offer still stands to unite our kingdoms."

She shuddered. "Never. You have proven there is not a bit of good in your soul. You have been consumed by the evil you released."

Faramos's face contorted in apparent rage. "You would do well to remember your place, Your Majesty. In direct opposition of me is a dangerous place to be."

"I am not afraid of you, Faramos. I serve the Creator." She elbowed her way in front of Tristan, who grabbed her arm and held her back.

"Ah"—the smoke figure leaned forward—"but does he serve you?"

What did he mean by that? She shook her head. He was trying to confuse her, to throw her off. "He is with me always."

Faramos straightened and shrugged nonchalantly. "It seems to me this quest was doomed from the start. A queen who does not know how to lead, a bounty hunter who betrayed his own kin, and a guardian who has lost everyone she has ever cared about." He glanced around. "Say, are you missing a member of your ragtag bunch? Where is the boy who plays at being a knight?"

Karina's heart squeezed, and she pursed her lips at the reminder of their most recent loss.

He shot a mock sympathetic frown her way. "Did we lose our closest friend already?"

She raised her chin, refusing to dignify his question with a response.

"Well, well." Faramos rubbed his palms together. "Maybe this quest is not going as well as we thought it would."

"Either attack or leave us be," Tristan shouted.

"Now is that anyway to treat a guest at your fire pit?"

"You are no guest, Faramos. Guests are invited and welcomed—you are neither." Rashka lowered her bow. "We have no wish to converse with you anymore tonight."

"Very well. We shall be seeing each other soon enough." He turned to Karina. "Seek your dreams, Your Majesty. You have much to look forward to in the days and weeks to come. I cannot wait until we meet again in person."

Karina's skin crawled at the thought of being in his presence again. She prayed she could avoid the inevitable. Faramos would have to be defeated at some point. Hopefully, they had all the armor before the final battle came.

Faramos regarded them with a haunting smirk, then disappeared in a blinding burst of green light. When Karina blinked, the flames were a reddish-orange once again. Her legs went weak, and she sank to the ground. She focused on each individual breath as fear and doubt threatened to wiggle their way further into her soul.

Tristan knelt beside her and took her in his arms. "Hey, all is well," he murmured as he stroked her hair.

With her eyes closed, she breathed in Tristan's scent, let it wash over her and calm her mind. When her breath had steadied, she pulled away. "How did he appear like that? How did he know where we are? Is he near?"

Tristan looked back to the flames for a moment before meeting her gaze. "I do not believe he is close. He would not want to give away the element of surprise if he were. No, this appearance was a trick. He probably used something of mine to track us with his dark magic."

"Could he use this magic again if he sends an army after us?"

Tristan stood and dusted off his pants. "Maybe. I am not sure." His hands balled into fists, and his fingernails dug so deeply into his palms a trickle of blood dripped from his right hand. "Either way, he would still have to deal with me."

CHAPTER THIRTEEN

Sam pulled his foot from the murk. Each step felt as if he were stuck or as though the mire had devoured his foot. His shoes and half of his leg were covered in mud. And the stink of the swamps probably reached all the way to the Lighted Realm. He attempted to block the smell by covering his face with his cloak. No—not much help … only made his breath hotter and more irritating.

They had done nothing but traipse through swampy terrain for two days—on foot—and Sabreen said it would likely be another two days, if not more, before they reached Gundow. His muscles and feet ached, and his tunic was drenched in sweat.

"Will we be out of the Heart of Soter soon?" he finally asked as they skirted around a tight copse of trees. Sabreen had not been much for conversation while they were traveling, though, she had been more than happy to chat on breaks or in the evening after they had decided to rest for the night.

Sabreen stopped to survey the trees. "We have been out of the Heart for some time."

"Then when will we be through the wetlands?"

"Hopefully by tonight. If we keep moving."

He groaned. Lunchtime had come and gone a while ago, still several hours of daylight remained. What he wouldn't give for fresh-smelling air, some unfiltered sunshine, some—

The sound of rushing water brought him to attention. Fresh water. Perfect. He hurried past Sabreen, anxious for a drink of something that was not stale.

"Sam, wait!"

He heard her call after him, but he didn't care. His need for a change of scenery, a hope for something new, outweighed whatever warning Sabreen wanted to relay. He crashed through the trees, giving no thought to anything except fresh water. Through the trees ahead, he spied a sparkle or two. He was almost there.

And then the world crumbled beneath him.

He let out a shout as his arms flailed around for something to grab on to. Nothing. He fell several feet as dirt closed in around him. A trap.

He landed with a thud that shook the air from his lungs. A sharp pain shot from his ankle, up his leg, to where his hip ached from landing the wrong way. *Deep breaths, deep breaths.* Too much effort. All he wanted was for the intense pain to stop. This was worse than getting his leg sliced open during the battle at the Temple of Aletheia.

"Sam?"

Sabreen's voice sounded far off. He wanted to call back to her, but he couldn't catch his breath.

"Sam, are you hurt?"

He nodded, though he suspected she could not see his movement. He peeked through one eye. The same sunlight that highlighted Sabreen's crimson hair cast shadows across her face. Impossible to read her expression. He sucked in a deep breath, past the pain, past the fear. "I think I broke something."

"Something … like what?"

"My ankle? My leg? I'm not sure. My whole body hurts."

She put her hands on her hips. "Boy, you sure know how to get yourself into trouble." She continued to grumble incoherently, probably because she was no longer looking at him. After a minute, she turned back to him. "You have fallen into a trap meant for an ogre, which is why it is so large. I am not sure how to get you out of here."

"Well, I could really do with fresh water."

"Didn't water get you into this mess in the first place?"

"Possibly," he croaked, then smacked his lips. Dirt had gotten into his mouth. "However, water is no longer a want … more like a need." He didn't let on the agony was already wearing on him. Sweat moistened his brow and slid down his neck. Each movement sent waves of pain through his body—and not just from his leg. Something was seriously wrong.

"I am going over to the river to fill the water skin. I will be right back." Sabreen's voice sounded concerned. Maybe she could sense how serious his situation was. Maybe she knew something he didn't. That would not surprise him. He went to nod but was not sure he actually moved or if Sabreen was looking anymore.

He closed his eyes. For all his grace with a sword, why did he keep ending up in these situations? Was someone out to get him? Did the Creator hold a grudge over something he was not aware of?

Another wave of agony swept over him. He tried to steady his breathing, to use his will to conquer the pain. He could feel himself losing grip on consciousness.

A loud thump next to his right ear startled him. His muscles tensed, and he let out a shout. Pain vibrated through every part of his body. He could not even differentiate where the pain was coming from.

"Sorry." Sabreen's voice was soft now, full of concern. "Can you sit up?"

"W-what are you doing?" He tried to reposition himself. Unfortunately, the smallest amount of movement made him dizzy.

"Well, I do not believe we are going anywhere today. Not in the condition you are in. I have some of my herbs, but they will take some time to work. It may be best for us to stay down here tonight instead of trying to move you before you are ready." She held out the water skin. "Would you like a drink?"

"You'll have to pour it for me. I can barely move."

She nodded and leaned over him, letting the water dribble into his mouth a little at a time until he turned his head.

"Now let me assess your wounds." She set the water skin and her pack aside.

With lips pressed together, she poked and prodded all over his body. Each touch was like being punched by one of the guards during sparring matches behind the guardhouse. Only the guards were nicer and knew when to yield. Sabreen persisted, and Sam clenched his jaw to keep from screaming. When she twisted his ankle, an inhuman yell tore from his chest before darkness overtook him.

CHAPTER FOURTEEN

Gates plated with gold, etched with vines and leaves, were awe-inspiring, to say the least. Karina loosened her hold around Tristan's waist as they sat on Dom's back before the city's entrance. Rashka had said the gate was made of iron, the gold overlay for show. She had not remembered the awesome beauty and could only gape at the ornate structure.

As they had approached the royal city, the familiar gold-topped roofs glittered in the mid-afternoon sun. She had not been back to Gundow since her parents had been murdered. After that, she had been picked up by a family who immediately put her on an orphan caravan. As she gazed up from Dom's back, she could so much more appreciate the beauty now.

Karina could scarcely take her eyes off the gilded gates as they passed beneath the white-stone arch and made their way up the main road leading to the castle. Ahead, two more gates loomed over the surrounding buildings.

In this first section, all manner of people roamed about, attending to their daily activities. Although not many paid them any heed, those who got in the way of the massive black stallion ran for cover. Lining the roads were supply shops, merchant booths, and inns. Homes, barely passing for hovels, were hidden behind the store fronts.

The next gate was not as grand but still plated with gold. Simpler. Behind that gate, the next section boasted an array of middle-class homes and modest store fronts, even a few restaurants. As they approached the final gate, the homes were larger and more ornate, light reflecting off the many gold and crystal surfaces—the city homes for wealthy merchants and minor nobility if Karina remembered correctly.

The last gate was the most ornate of all, twice as large as the main gate, and the engravings were much more intricate, so life-like. Karina wanted to reach out and touch a leaf, until a memory surfaced.

"Momma, look. It's so pretty. Is it real?" Karina reached up to the golden leaf.

"Now, now, sweet child. Do not touch. We would not want to anger the guards." Karina looked up at her mother, whose eyes were tired. "We want them to like us, so they will take us to the king."

"But I just want to touch it." She eyed a guard a few feet away. "I can touch it, right?"

The guard barely tossed a glance her way before he shook his head.

Karina's brow furrowed and she crossed her arms. It wasn't fair.

It still did not seem fair, although Karina had more self-control now than she'd had as a child.

Presently, the gate was closed. Four guards in silvery steel armor with gold-trimmed helmets flanked the archway. The one on the left stepped forward as they approached. "Ho, there. What business have you at the royal house?"

Tristan dipped his head in acknowledgment. "We seek an audience with the king."

The guard shook his head. "The king is not seeing anyone today."

"It is urgent we speak to him immediately." Tristan's tone was relaxed, though his muscles tensed beneath his tunic.

"I apologize for the inconvenience. You will have to check in tomorrow." The guard regarded their attire. "Or you could leave your name and where you will be staying with the priests over at the public temple, and they can send word when the king decides to receive visitors."

Tristan blew out a breath, and Karina sensed his frustration. Without telling him what she was doing, she slid off Dom's back and landed with a thump. Praise the Creator, she had not fallen over. She smoothed her tunic and then smiled sweetly at the guard. "Pardon me, good sir."

The guard squinted down at her, a frown pulling at the sides of his mouth.

"I am Queen Karina of Aletheia. It is I who seeks an audience with the king."

The guard's eyes widened, then he quickly bowed his head. "Queen Karina, I ask your forgiveness." He looked up with furrowed brows. "Why have you come unannounced and without a proper escort?"

"My reasons are my own. The matter I must discuss with King Rufus is of an urgent nature."

"We will have you escorted to the palace immediately and inform the king of your arrival." He signaled to a guard up on the wall, and a series of shouts followed. The gate began to swing open, and the portcullis behind it rose with minimal creaking.

Once through the gate, a squad of four guards on horseback met them. The one with a white plume sticking out of the top nodded and offered a pleasant smile. "Please follow me," he said shortly. The four guards surrounded them as the head guard led them up the cobblestone path to their destination.

The palace itself was a marvel to behold. Towers stretched to the sky, each one higher than the next, no two the same height. Each tower had a gold-tipped roof and crystal windows. White stone shone in the late afternoon sun. Elegance at its best.

A part of Karina bristled beneath the surface, breaking the trance the city had over her. So much opulence. What of the people in the first section of the city? What of the orphans like her carted around in caravans, begging for homes? What point did it serve to have such extreme extravagance when your own people were hurting?

Karina leaned over to look around at Tristan. His grim expression hinted he might be having similar thoughts. He did not seem impressed by the white and gold everywhere. Rashka flew overhead, racing ahead and circling back, over and over.

After skirting a white marble fountain—edged in gold—they reached the palace entrance. The massive doors echoed the gold leafing on the last gate. Four more guards stood on the sides. When they dismounted, all four guards worked to open the overbearing doors.

A blond-haired stable boy, no more than twelve, scurried up to them. "I'll take your horse for you, m'lady. The stable is over yonder." He pointed off to the right. "When you have need of your horse, inform one of the servants, and I will ensure your steed is readied."

"Thank you, good sir." Karina offered him a small smile as he took Dom's reins from Tristan.

Dom nickered. "Be careful in there, Prophetess. Something is in the air."

She nodded, not wanting to sound crazy for talking to a horse. "Please see he has an extra measure of oats and a good bath. We have been on the road for many weeks."

The stable boy grinned and hurried off with Dom trailing behind him.

Karina turned her attention to the open doors before her. What had Dom meant by his warning? Was something amiss behind these gilded doors? She pursed her lips, mentally preparing herself for whatever lay ahead. Only the Creator knew, and so far he was not telling her.

"Ready?" Tristan whispered in her ear.

"No."

He was silent for a moment. "How about now?"

She shot him a twisted smile as her mind flashed back to the morning they stood before the cave with an opening as massive as the one before them. They'd had the same conversation.

With renewed confidence, she smoothed her tunic, lifted her chin, and took a step forward. Then again, maybe they should have stopped at one of the shops and purchased a dress, something more appropriate in which to greet royalty. She blew out a breath as she glanced down at her tattered tunic and dirty pants. Nothing she could do about her clothing now.

A light flashed behind them, sending the guards into a frenzy as they pulled out swords. As she stretched her arms, Rashka glanced at the stunned guards. "Have you never seen a guardian before?"

The guards eyes were wide. One shook his head, while another mumbled a quiet no.

Karina suppressed a smile. "She is with me. Please let her by."

The guards stepped back, keeping wary eyes on the elven shapeshifter.

The three of them entered the palace, stepping into a cavernous front hall. The inside of the palace mimicked the outside, white and gold everywhere. Crystal windows let in the sunlight, which made the room sparkle.

An older man, with shoulder-length brown hair peppered with gray, hurried to greet them. He wore a green tunic, intricately woven with gold threads, atop green pants. Holding his monocle, he offered a deep bow, to which Karina nodded. There was something familiar about him. "Greetings, Queen Karina. How nice to see you again. You are welcome indeed. I am sure you have forgotten by now, but I am Bormain, steward of the roy—by the Creator, Tristan Lemur, is that you?"

Karina fought to maintain her composure as she turned to Tristan, who stiffened before holding out his hand in greeting. "Bormain, my good man, it is good to see you again."

Bormain looked a bit flustered. "I did not realize we had two royal guests." He quirked a brow. "Much less that you were traveling together."

Several memories resurfaced concerning this strict steward—especially getting into trouble for childhood antics with the princess. Karina stepped forward, brandishing a warm smile. "I have an urgent quest that requires the king's assistance. Tristan and Rashka, Guardian of Shadowed Forest, are providing escort."

Bormain frowned. "I apologize, Your Majesty. The king is not seeing anyone today. Perhaps if you shared your need with me, I can be of assistance."

"I thank you for your offer, sir. However, the quest is of a sensitive nature. I must insist on seeing the king himself."

His frown deepened, making the wrinkles around his mouth even more apparent. "Really, Your Majesty, I must insist."

"If I cannot see the king today, I will have to wait to see him tomorrow."

"But he may not be seeing anyone—"

"He will have to see me at some point. The fate of the Three Kingdoms depends on it!" Karina narrowed her eyes at the steward, and the man practically shrank under her glare.

"Very well, Your Majesty. Of course, the king would insist you stay here in the palace. Let me show you to your rooms." He turned to Tristan. "Would you like your usual rooms as well?"

Tristan shook his head. "No, I need to stay with Queen Karina."

"Of course. We will put you in one of the larger suites granted the royalty of Aletheia then. It is wise to keep everyone together."

Was that an observation or a warning? This place seemed odder and odder the more she saw of it. Why would everyone be so adamant about not seeing the king? What kind of king would not receive royalty upon arrival? The King Rufus she remembered from her childhood would not have stood for such rudeness.

CHAPTER FIFTEEN

Yosef paced across the marble steps to the public temple, wringing his hands. His breathing was too shallow, making his head light and dizzy. He tried to shake the anxiousness from his hands.

He had seen Queen Karina and Prince Tristan arrive at the palace gates. While he had recognized Prince Tristan—for it had not been long since he had last visited Gundow, and he looked much the same—he had not realized who the woman Prince Tristan traveled with was until she swung down from the horse and introduced herself to the guard on duty.

Why had another monarch arrived in such a manner? Normally, the king informed the priests of such an arrival so they could ensure a proper reception.

The moment Queen Karina had ridden up to the gate, Yosef had sensed a change in the air. The chill cloaking the city of late had been sliced through by a ray of light. He could think of no other way to explain the change. Whatever was infecting Gundow was afraid of her.

So why had a knot of anxiousness settled in his stomach?

Elder Thomas, with his white robes hanging oddly over his round belly, waddled out onto the steps. "What are you doing out here?"

"I am not sure. Pacing."

"Why?"

"Something is about to happen."

Elder Thomas eased down on the top step and looked up at him. "What do you mean?"

Yosef stopped and turned to the palace towering over the public temple. "I am not sure."

"You are full of answers, huh?" His mentor chuckled and patted the marble step next to him. Yosef sat down, hanging his arms over his knees. "Tell me what's on your mind."

"Have you noticed a difference in Gundow of late?"

"A difference how?"

"I sense a presence. An evil, if you will. I do not know when it arrived or how it has affected the people … but it is here."

Elder Thomas regarded him with concern etched in the folds of his face. "I am not sure I would go around spouting that kind of nonsense, son."

Yosef closed his eyes and let out a long sigh. "I have kept it to myself. I just needed to tell someone. Do you not sense it?"

He shook his head, dashing Yosef's confidence.

"Excuse me?" The female voice startled him.

Yosef held back a groan, then immediately stood to greet a middle-aged woman with two young children in tow. "The Creator's blessing on you, madam. How can we assist you today?"

By her tattered appearance, she had traveled through the middle gate, meaning she had bypassed the other two temples in the city. What brought her to the main chapel so far from her home?

"Good day, honored priest." The woman's bright smile belied her disheveled hair and dirt-smudged face. "We have been searching for food these last two days. The other temples appear to be out."

Yosef glanced at Elder Thomas, who frowned and wiped his hand across his sweaty forehead. When he did not reply, Yosef took her hand. "I believe we have fresh bread and water."

In the past, the king had kept the temple pantries stocked for those in need. Of late, again, things had changed. The king barely saw to any of his charities, even when Elder Thomas, as Head Priest, petitioned him in person. After a nasty threat from the king to close down the pantries completely, Elder Thomas had quit trying. Was the kingdom in such dire straits?

He led the woman inside the temple. Elder Thomas followed them in but continued on into the sanctuary, probably to go hide in his office again. Yosef angled toward a small room off the side of the entrance where they kept the food for the poor. The stone room had no windows, so it stayed dark and cool, perfect for storing dry food and any special treats like milk or cheese. Though those special treats did not happen much anymore.

He pulled two loaves of bread from a table in the middle of the room. "Ah, and we have some dried meat left as well!" He tried to sound cheery, but his heart was not in his words. Too many dark thoughts.

"Thank you so much," the woman said as she tried to comfort the whimpering child in her arms. "It's been so hard since my Aaron got killed before the last full moon. I can't work with these two, and we got no family here."

Yosef bagged the dried meat and the bread before handing them to the lady. "Do you have family elsewhere?"

"My sister's in River Branch in Aletheia."

"Is there a way for you to join her?"

The woman shrugged. "She don't got the room. Her husband wouldn't like it anyway."

Yosef said a quick prayer. The woman was in need, but they no longer had the resources to help her—or families like hers. He could help her find a job, though she would still have the children to worry about.

"Do you have any skills? Cooking or sewing? Something people might pay you for?"

She shook her head, then paused. "I suppose I keep house well."

"I know most of the nobles around here. Check back with me in a couple of days, and I will see if any of them are hiring house servants."

The woman looked at the child in her arms and then at the one hiding behind her skirts. "What about them?"

Right. "I will see if I can find anyone to watch them. You should check around too."

Her doubt was evident, but she smiled anyway. "Thank you, honored one."

"No, it is my honor to help you."

When she had left, Yosef stayed in the cool, dark room, soaking in the quiet. While his anxiousness had disappeared for now, the now-familiar sense of evil overwhelmed him once again.

Karina gaped at the room she had just stepped into. The suite of rooms was indeed large enough for all of them. And then some. On the third floor of the north wing, Bormain had led them into a sitting room with two fireplaces—one at each end—with two separate sitting areas and a long table surrounded by eight chairs in the middle. Unlike the rest of the palace, this stone was a slate gray, the floor covered in burgundy and gold rugs. Rich hues decorated the couches and chairs, even the curtains hanging around the windows—though colorful—were not as light and airy as seen around the palace.

Bormain pointed to the doors on either side of both fireplaces. "Each one leads to a separate bedroom with its own washroom. You may have your pick."

A knock sounded at the main door.

Bormain opened it and ushered in an older woman with dark hair and sharp eyes, along with two younger women close to Karina's age. "May I introduce Lady Moriah, your lady in waiting, and Mary and Hallie, your handmaidens while you are here."

All three women bowed, and Karina nodded to each of them.

"Lady Moriah will see to your needs. She will inform me if there is something she cannot provide, and I will see what I can do."

"Thank you, Bormain. Your kindness is much appreciated." As the steward opened the door, Karina cleared her throat. "Please remind the king that my business is urgent. I need to take my leave as soon as possible."

"I will, Your Majesty. Enjoy your stay at the palace." And then he was gone.

Karina turned back to the room. Tristan stood in the corner, not bothering to hide his smirk. Rashka paced by the windows, looking out over the courtyard below and the sea beyond. Lady Moriah and the two handmaidens stood off to the side, watching them expectantly. What now?

Sensing Karina's hesitation, Lady Moriah stepped forward. "Greetings, Your Majesty. Welcome to Gundow."

"Thank you, Lady Moriah. It is a pleasure to make your acquaintance."

The older woman smiled, smoothing her dark green skirt, then she quickly dropped her hands to her side. "I see you have no luggage. Do you not have any other clothing with you?"

Karina winced. She would have to deal with that poor planning at some point—might as well be now. From the sound of things, she might be here longer than she planned. Perhaps a couple of days? "Indeed, I do not. Our quest is urgent and required swift travel. I am afraid this is all I have."

Lady Moriah's hands rose from her side. "Girls, let us get to work." She grinned at Karina. "We will have you a proper wardrobe by dawn. At least one dress before the dinner bell."

"Lady Moriah, really, one dress is all that is necessary."

"Nonsense. You need to be prepared. We do not mind at all." She clapped her hands sharply.

The girls flew into a frenzy, measuring and writing and a myriad of other tasks. Despite rather loud protests, they did the same with Tristan and Rashka as well. By the time they disappeared out the door, promising to return to draw hot baths for everyone, even Karina was ready for them to go.

Karina plopped on one of the overstuffed couches, leaned back, and closed her eyes. All she wanted to do right now was bathe and sleep. She had no strength left. She sensed someone had sat beside her, but she still did not bother to open her eyes.

"What do you think?" Tristan's deep voice came from her left.

"I do not know. Something is off." Rashka said.

"I agree," Karina mumbled as she opened her eyes. "Why would King Rufus not receive royalty?"

"Maybe he is not able to? Maybe he is ill." Tristan groaned as he sat further back on the couch.

"Why would they not say so?"

He shrugged.

"At least we are all together in a suite," she said with a sigh as she closed her eyes again.

"What will we do for dinner? Will we dine with the king? Will they bring food here?"

"Surely the king would receive us at his table," Rashka said. "It would be rude not to do so."

"Something tells me social tradition may not be the most important priority to him right now." Karina struggled not to let frustration get the better of her. "If he only knew ..."

If he were aware of the urgency behind their quest, he would give them directions to the Soteran temple immediately. And then, they could be on their way.

Weary from traveling and lack of sleep, the three of them let the conversation taper off, and Karina became lost in her own darkening thoughts. She had almost managed to fall asleep when a loud knock at the door startled her. Tristan shot her a look. When she nodded, he opened the door.

Lady Moriah rushed in, pink-cheeked and out of breath. "Are you ready to prepare for dinner?"

"Indeed. It has been a great many days since we had a good meal." Karina offered the woman a wide smile, hoping to hide the exhaustion pulling at her eyelids.

The older woman huffed. "A hot bath, a good meal, and a good night's rest in a comfortable bed will do wonders, I assure you."

Karina was unsure if her lady-in-waiting had just insulted her or meant to agree with her, so she kept her mouth shut as Lady Moriah ushered in a host of servants behind her. They brought large pails of steaming water, which required two to carry. Once directed, they hurried into the three bedrooms to fill tubs that were assuredly already in the washrooms.

When done, Lady Moriah clapped her hands. "Now off with all of you. Get cleaned up." She bowed to Karina. "The girls and I will await you in your chambers after your bath, so we may help you dress."

Karina bowed her head. "Thank you."

Tristan merely shrugged and sauntered off toward his chosen room, while Rashka surveyed the courtyard below the windows once again and then wandered into her room on the opposite side of Karina's.

Karina offered a tight smile to Lady Moriah and made her way to the bedchamber.

Karina was not sure what she had expected. Her chamber was a sharp contrast to the rest of the palace as well. Edged in dark stone, elaborate and colorful tapestries hung on the wall. A deep purple quilt lay on the bed, surrounded by the same color drapes. If Karina had not known better, she would think she had entered a room in Aletheia's royal house—her home.

Her legs weakened, and she eased into a cushioned chaise made from purple and gold cloth set in front of the warm fireplace. While day-time temperatures were warming up, the air still tended to chill with the sunset. Soon there would be no need for an evening fire. Still, the crackling flames added to the ambiance, making her long for home—for Jace and Mauri.

A quiet knock sounded on the door she had forgotten to close. "Is something wrong, Your Majesty?"

Karina raised her head to find Mary—or was it Hallie?—standing in the door. Her flaxen hair was tucked under a white cap, and she wore a simple green dress that hung about mid-calf.

Karina sighed. "No, nothing is wrong. I miss my home. Forgive me, what was your name again?"

"Mary, Your Majesty." She clasped her hands together and took a step into the room, a big smile on her face. "I am glad to hear this reminds you of home. This is where your parents stayed when you first left Aletheia as a child. King Rufus had it decorated just for them."

"Oh really?" Karina looked around again, a deeper pang hitting her heart. "I do not remember."

"We were only children, Your Majesty. The only reason I know is because my mother was assigned to your family's service while you were in the palace." Her cheeks pinkened. "We played together a few times, or so my mother says."

A whole lifetime ago, and one Karina barely remembered. She refused to dwell on the past, especially the time between when she had left Calliope and when she had returned with Jace years later.

"I am sorry I do not remember, Mary. I promise my poor memory has nothing to do with you."

"We were children, Your Majesty." She wandered over to the large wardrobe in the corner and opened the doors. "You had best get to bathing. Lady Moriah will be up shortly with your dress. I hear the king will be seeing you briefly tonight."

Briefly? Karina rose from the chaise and hurried into the washroom. If she would only have a short visit with the king, she needed to ensure it counted.

CHAPTER SIXTEEN

Sam's eyelids fluttered open, letting in a small shaft of brilliant light. Every part of his body ached as if he had been trampled by a horse. He moaned as he rolled over and opened his eyes. Dirt. More dirt. It piled up around him, closed in on him. The ogre's trap. His memory came back in a rush of images. How was he going to get out of here?

"Welcome back to the land of the living—again." Sabreen's voice floated in from behind him, and, with effort, he rolled to face her.

"Are you sure I'm alive?"

She grinned as she popped a piece of dried meat in her mouth. "You are. Unfortunately, I did not have enough herbs for all your wounds. At least, I managed to heal the life-threatening and more serious ones. You will be sore until either I find more herbs or you heal naturally."

There were more limits to her kind of magic. Figured. Sam took a deep breath and forced himself into a sitting position. "Water?"

Sabreen handed him a water skin, and he greedily drank in half the silky, cool liquid. His body longed for more, but he could not afford to make himself sicker by drinking too much too fast.

After handing back the water skin, Sam tested his body. Although there were a good number of scratches—some deeper than others—and his muscles ached more than they ever had before, none of his bones seemed to be broken—nothing twisted or sprained. Gingerly, he tried to stand. Nausea washed over him, and he stumbled back against the dirt.

Sabreen laughed. "It would not be wise to move too much yet, my friend."

He looked up at the top of the pit. "How do we get out of here? Do you have a plan?"

She ate the last bit of her meat and pushed herself off the ground. "See here." She pointed to deep grooves in the dirt on one of the walls. "Hand and foot holds. They go all the way up."

"Who made those?"

"I did, silly. I needed something to keep me busy while you were passed out." He glared at her, and she giggled. "Excuse me, recovering," she added with a smirk.

"Looks like the sun is pretty high. How long did I sleep?" Sam pushed off the wall.

"All night and all morning. I was starting to wonder if the herbs had done you in."

Indeed. He wondered if *she* would be the one to do him in with all that had happened since he'd met her. He rubbed his cheeks, then accepted the bit of dry meat and bread Sabreen passed to him and ate quickly.

Sabreen did not say anything as she watched him. Her eyes were kind and curious, but he still suspected some ulterior motive to her assistance in helping him to Gundow. He watched her watching him—all she did was smile in return.

Finally, she stood, shading her eyes with her hand as she surveyed the opening. "The sun is beginning its descent. We should try to get out of the pit now."

He nodded. "It would be better not to spend another night down here."

"Once we are out, we can set up camp by the river. You can bathe and then rest for the night. I will brew you a tea to help with your recovery, and—after a good night's sleep—hopefully we will be able to continue our journey tomorrow."

"May it be so," Sam said with a grin.

Sabreen held out her hand. With her help, he managed to push himself to a standing position, though he still leaned against the dirt wall for support once he was up.

"I am going to climb first. Can't have you falling on top of me." Sabreen giggled, and Sam rolled his eyes.

"Go on, then."

She reached for a high foothold and began to climb rather quickly, up and out in only a couple of minutes.

Sam gazed up at the mouth of the pit. Rationally, he knew the top was not very far. But being so sore and his energy level so low, he might as well be climbing a mountain. With a deep breath, he reached for a foothold and pulled himself up, arms and legs working together to push him upward. Each measure of progress felt like fire in his muscles, and his body begged for relief. He gritted his teeth. He could do this. He *would* do this. His arms trembled, and his legs strained to move.

"You are doing well, Sam. You're almost there!" Sabreen's words did little to encourage him.

Sweat streaked down his face and his back. His hand knocked a clump of dirt lose. Before he could turn his head to the side, the dirt fell into his mouth. Ugh. He ducked and spit the nastiness out, gagging on the grit still left. When he got out of here, he would dive into the river headfirst and stay under for a good long time. Let the water wash away all this dirt, this agony, this frustration.

His hand reached the top of the pit. *Praise the Creator*. He resisted the urge to sigh and pulled his left leg up to the next foothold. Unable to find a hold, his leg slid down the packed dirt, and he lost his balance. Oh no. He couldn't fall back in. He'd never get out.

"Whoa. I got you." A strong hand snaked around his arm.

He glanced up at Sabreen, whose smile lit her face. With the sun behind her, her hair looked like flame surrounding gorgeous green eyes. He shook his head and found his footing. With her added help, he hauled himself out of the pit.

Splayed out on the ground, Sam stared at the sky, gasping in massive amounts of air. He wasn't sure he could move now with all the pain and other misery. Perhaps he should camp here for the night.

"Get a move on, you big oaf."

He strained his neck to glare at Sabreen. "Excuse me?"

"The water is over there." With one hand on her hip, she pointed the other to the left. "You need to bathe while I grab a few herbs and start a fire."

He moaned as he rolled to his belly, then pushed himself up. He stuck his tongue out at Sabreen as he shuffled past her. To his surprise, she stuck her tongue out right back at him.

A smirk tugged at his lips as he headed toward the river. It called his name. He stood on the bank in awe of the water before him. In fact, his eyes moistened as he contemplated how much relief would be found in the river's watery depths. He stripped off his tattered shirt and, after glancing behind him to ensure Sabreen was not watching, his trousers. Easing into the water, he reveled in the cool glory and submerged himself in the river's darkness.

The water surrounded him, shutting off the rest of the world. There was no Sabreen. No ancient evil. No quest. No Karina. Here, he was at peace.

Well, until he ran out of air.

He shoved off the bottom of the river and surfaced a moment later. Inhaling deeply, he ran his hands over his face and his hair. Sabreen had not packed any soap, so he did his best to wash himself. Water was a marvelous healer. His energy returned bit by bit, and his muscles relaxed.

"Hey, are you going to stay in there all evening?"

He shot a grin at Sabreen. "I might if you join me."

Her cheeks reddened as she laughed. "Oh, I don't believe you could handle me."

"That sounds like a challenge." He froze. Was he flirting with Sabreen? A forest witch? What about his feelings for Karina? Suddenly, his insides knotted again. Had he somehow betrayed his best friend?

When a realization hit him, he furrowed his brows. Karina had made her choice. She had gone and fallen for a blasted bounty hunter—one who had kidnapped her and tried to lead her to her death, no less. Sam glanced toward Sabreen. Before him stood a spirited woman with hair like fire. She made him smile. Why not flirt a bit?

"I have tea waiting for you when you—uh—get dressed." Sabreen ducked her head, a blush coloring her cheeks, and hurried back to a fire pit down and away from the river.

Reluctantly, Sam climbed out and did his best to dry off before putting his clothes back on. He made his way over to the fire where Sabreen now sat, pouring hot tea into two bowls. The tea didn't smell familiar … spicy and tangy all at once.

"What kind of tea is this?" he asked as he accepted one bowl and sat on the ground next to the fire. His body soaked in the heat, reveling in the delicious warmth.

"A few herbs and spices native to the Heart of Soter. Their healing qualities make them highly sought after—and very expensive if you try to buy them anywhere else."

He contemplated the contents of the dark brew, before shrugging and holding the bowl to his lips. A conflicting taste—bitter, yet edged with a sweet tangy flavor. He wouldn't say this brew was his favorite tea ever, but it beat the Scorch flower concoction Jace made him drink whenever he got injured sparring with the royal guards.

"You hungry?" Sabreen asked, rifling through her pack.

He was. In spite of the meat and bread from earlier, he was ravenous.

She handed him another hunk of bread and dried meat. "Sorry I don't have anything more appetizing. We haven't had any opportunities to hunt or gather fruit."

He shook his head. "Don't worry. This is fine." True enough. He gobbled down every morsel in record time and then finished the tea.

"So, tell me more about this woman we are meeting up with." Sabreen poked at the fire.

"Karina? I do not know what else you want me to tell you."

"Well, you know her pretty well, right?"

He nodded slowly, memory flooding his mind. "Yes, though she is royalty, Karina has been my closest friend for years. She's compassionate—always thinking of others. Probably why the people adore her. She's always quick to laugh and is generally up for an adventure." His heart ached a bit as he talked about her. He wished she were here.

"You love her, don't you?"

"No. Well, yes. That is—I did." Sabreen's puzzled look mirrored exactly how he felt trying to answer her question. He sucked in a deep breath. "I never really thought of Karina in that way for many years. She was the king's ward, out of my reach anyway. But when all this"—he waved his hands around—"happened, I realized how much she really meant to me. Even when Queen Anaya insisted Karina was dead, I didn't believe the report. I searched for her myself."

Sabreen clasped her hands together and held them near her heart. "And you found her." The words sounded sarcastic, yet there was a hint of some other emotion—something Sam could not determine.

He chuckled. "Yeah, I found her with a bounty hunter."

She gasped. "How did you all get away?"

"We didn't. Turns out the bounty hunter was helping her. At least he was by then. After he kidnapped her. After he took her to Faramos."

"Faramos? The king of Tzedek?"

"Karina is some kind of Chosen One and was threatening all his plans."

"So, what happened next?"

"Well, we met up with an elf guardian and continued on Karina's quest."

"A quest to what?"

Sam paused, twiddling his thumbs a bit. Should he tell her the rest? He eyed her closely before sucking in a deep breath. "Retrieve the sacred armor of the temples in order to defeat an ancient evil infecting our world."

Sabreen mouth hung slightly ajar, her eyes wide. "The sacred armor?"

He nodded. "In the midst of all of this, I realized how much I love her. How much I want to protect her. But …"

Sabreen seemed to recover from her surprise as she leaned forward and placed her hand on his knee. "But what?"

He let out a deep sigh. "But she was already falling for another."

"Another? Who?" Sabreen's eyes widened. "Don't tell me she was falling for the bounty hunter!"

He nodded.

"What? Why? He kidnapped her!"

He got up and poured himself more tea, his angry thoughts knotting his muscles once again, constricting his chest as he struggled to breathe. How many times had he had those exact same thoughts himself? Why would she choose a flawed man like Tristan? Sure, he was nice enough now. But all those things he had done in his past—the people he'd killed, the lives he'd ruined—and all for an evil warlock.

Yet Sam had been by her side ever since she'd returned to Aletheia. He'd helped Jace nurse her back to health after he'd brought her to the royal house. They had played together in the courtyards and the stables. He'd taught her to ride a horse properly and had tried to teach her to wield a sword, though Queen Anaya had put an end to sparring rather quickly. He'd been a listening ear, a shoulder to cry on, a friend.

And she still chose the bounty hunter. The assassin.

He stared at Sabreen, who was searching for something in her pack again. Maybe he should forget about Karina and move on.

CHAPTER SEVENTEEN

Refreshed and in clean clothes, Tristan paced around the sitting room of the Aletheian suite. Patience was not one of his virtues, and he was anxious to talk with the king about their quest. If only Karina would hurry …

Rashka sat on a cushioned seat built into the windows overlooking the courtyard and the ocean. She wore a white satin dress with gold inlays and embroidery, which stood out against her black hair. Her guise was quite different from the elf he'd only seen in leather pants and fitted jerkins. She glared at him. "Quit pacing, Tristan. You are making me nervous. And there is nothing to worry about for the moment."

"What's taking Karina so long? For that matter, what's taking the king so long? The dinner hour has come and gone."

"Maybe he knew we would need the extra time to prepare, given our travels and late appearance."

He held in a growl, huffing instead. Why did she have to be so rational?

The door on the other side of the room opened. Karina entered in the most elaborate gown he'd ever seen her wear. Her coronation gown might have been more elaborate, but he had not been present for the event. This gown had a dark-blue satin bodice that showed off her feminine curves, and he could not imagine the weight of the voluminous layers of skirts. Lady Moriah had braided Karina's hair, pinning the locks up beneath a silver circlet. This dress, though, magnified her blue eyes.

He sucked in a breath. "My, Your Majesty, you are a breathtaking sight."

Lady Moriah clapped her hands. "She is, isn't she? The miracle of a bath and new clothes."

Karina blushed and ducked her head, then returned her gaze with a small curtsy. "Thank you, good sir."

Rashka moved between them, interrupting their moment. "Now all we need is for the king to send for us."

A knock sounded at the door.

"See how I command the dinner bell?" Karina laughed as Lady Moriah moved to answer the door.

Bormain entered and gave them a quick bow. "The king would appreciate your presence for dinner in his private dining room."

Tristan resisted the urge to snort. They had a list of many things they would have *appreciated* upon their arrival. He straightened his tunic, the same color as Karina's dress. No use getting off on the wrong foot now. They needed information from the king.

Karina eyed him warily, nodding to the steward. "Thank you, Bormain. We are ready." Tristan offered her his arm, which she accepted.

Bormain led the way out of the suite and down the hall. They spent several minutes following him down a flight of stairs and then through a maze of hallways to another wing. At last he stopped in front of an elaborate, open double-door.

"If you will wait in here, I will alert the king of your arrival." Bormain bowed again before hurrying off in the opposite direction.

Tristan ushered Karina into the white marble and gold-accented dining room. Guards stood on either side of the double doors, as still as statues. Much like the rest of the palace, the dining room was sparsely decorated, splashes of color added with murals inlaid in the wall itself. The middle of the room held a wooden table shining with flecks of gold somehow integrated into the sheen.

"These rooms are awe-inspiring, are they not, Tristan?" Karina wandered around the room, observing each mural before moving on to the next.

"Indeed. Though I think I prefer more color and a darker room. Makes things more—homey?"

She grinned. "I know what you mean. All this light and beauty—it does not give me the same joy as curling up with a good book in a dark room, next to the fireplace."

"Indeed."

Rashka, ever the guardian, manned one of the windows flanking the small fireplace. "These windows face the gardens below. Quite an extensive array of floral plants."

"Really?" Karina hurried over to Rashka's side. "Look at how many there are! I do not think I have ever seen so many in one place before." Karina pulled back. "Calliope is too cold to grow most plants. However, we do have some hearty ones that have beautiful blooms in the summer." Her eyes misted.

Tristan frowned. "Is something wrong, Karina?"

She blinked and looked up at him, forcing a smile. "I suppose I am still a bit homesick."

"Aren't we all. This quest has taken us away from our homes, our families."

Her shoulders drooped. "I have no family anymore."

His heart broke for her. Truth was he really did not have any family either. Faramos might be his brother, but he was not family. Not like his mother. His father. Tristan reached for Karina's cheek, longing to comfort those ghosts living behind her eyes these days.

Someone cleared his throat, and Tristan dropped his hand. They all turned. Bormain bowed his head. "King Rufus has arrived."

King Rufus, a tall, lanky man, entered the room with his head held high. His dark hair fell below his shoulders, and he wore a white outfit— complete with a long cloak. More surprising than his regal appearance, the king was shrouded with a strange glow. As he approached, light reflected off the flecks of gold adhered to his skin. Paint?

Tristan glanced sideways at the others, who seemed as astonished as he felt. They all bowed, giving the king the courtesy his station demanded, and waited for the king to return the gesture. He merely nodded.

"Good evening, Queen Karina, Prince Tristan." He took Karina's hand in his golden palm. "I pray you will forgive my inability to greet you properly today. I have been ... busy with matters of state."

Tristan honed in on his words. The king's voice, while strong, held a hint of uneasiness.

Karina smiled. "We cannot help what duties arise in our day, can we? And we have come with no warning. You have been gracious enough to host us."

"You are as beautiful and kind as you were when you visited my palace so many years ago, Queen Karina. I am pleased to have you here again." He acknowledged Tristan, a smirk on his face. "And what brings you all the way from Tzedek?"

Tristan raised an eyebrow. "I am here with Queen Karina. We are on a quest to—"

"Would you all like to be seated?" The king gestured toward the table, where servants had brought in goblets of wine. He moved to the head of the table and waited for them to follow suit.

Servants pulled out the chairs for Tristan and Karina on either side of the king, and one for Rashka beside Karina. When they were all seated, the king finally acknowledged Rashka. "And we have a Guardian with us today. It has been a long while since we have had the honor."

Rashka bowed her head. "I am honored to be here, Your Majesty. I have not been to Gundow in many moons."

"I trust the city is as beautiful as you all may remember. Maybe more so?"

Tristan shot a critical look at Karina, who also worked to mask her confusion. She offered the king a small smile. "Indeed, Your Majesty. More beautiful than I remember."

He nodded and took a sip of wine.

Tristan leaned forward. "Before we enjoy a meal together, Your Majesty, we have urgent business to discuss with you."

The king patted his hand as if Tristan were a lad. "There, there, Tristan. There will be time enough for such deliberations."

Karina cleared her throat. "Actually, Your Majesty, there really is *not* much time. We need to be on our way as quickly as possible. Before we leave, we need information from you."

The king shook his head. "I can appreciate your situation, but I really must insist on postponing this discussion. I have other matters that need attention."

Tristan clenched his fists. Why did the king behave in such an odd manner? King Rufus had always been a rational and quick-witted leader. "Since we are having dinner now, could you not hear us out?"

The king's eyes darkened. "I am not accustomed to being argued with in my own home. Did your brother not teach you some respect?"

Karina gasped.

Tristan clenched his jaw to keep from retorting in an impolite manner.

Bormain appeared at the door. When the king acknowledged him, he nodded.

King Rufus pushed back his chair and stood. "Now, if you will excuse me, I must attend to those matters I referred to earlier. As my guests, I invite you to stay and enjoy the meal." He emphasized the word guests in a manner Tristan took as a warning.

Karina stood as well and stepped away from the table. "When might we be able to speak to you about our quest?"

The king did not bother to answer as he strode out of the room.

"Your Majesty?" Karina took another step, but the guards moved to intercept her. Tristan rounded the table quickly, grasping Karina's elbow. She looked up at him, confusion haunting her beautiful blue eyes. He shook his head.

Bormain stepped in, hands clasped in front of him. "Please forgive the king's hasty departure." He held out his hands as several servants entered with trays. "Here, the food has arrived. Please, be seated."

At long last, Tristan made his way to the Aletheian suite with Karina and Rashka. Bormain bid them good night, and Karina sent Lady Moriah away for the evening. Although, the lady insisted Mary wait for her in her room to help Karina ready for bed. With the complicated dress Karina wore to dinner tonight, she would need the help.

He paced in front of the grand fireplace. Karina sat quietly on the couch, while Rashka stretched her legs out on the window seat.

Several times, Tristan opened his mouth to voice his concerns—each time, he could not quite form the words. So many thoughts clashed in his mind.

Rashka finally faced him. "Yes, Tristan. Something is going on."

He grunted. "If I were the kind of royalty who stood on tradition, I would be insulted by this behavior."

"What is he hiding?" Karina asked.

Tristan stopped pacing. "Hiding?"

"Well …. by his behavior at dinner, I assume we have come at an awkward time. Something is going on—something he refuses to share with us. What could be so bad?"

"And if our timing is poor, why would he not give us the information we came for, so he could be rid of us?" Rashka added.

So many questions. He was an answers man. He had to restrain himself from marching to the king's quarters and demanding those very answers.

Karina's eyes widened. "Do you think the evil's influence could have reached this far already?"

No, he had not thought of that. "Why would the ancient evil make him skittish? Would he not have become hardened, like Faramos?"

Karina shrugged.

Rashka stood. "Perhaps the evil is here but has not affected King Rufus. Perhaps he is afraid and cannot defend against it."

Tristan did not like this kink in their mission. If Faramos's evil had reached this far, they were all in danger. The sooner they were gone from this place, the better. "I will request an audience with the king in the morning and demand answers so we can leave. In the meantime"—he glanced at Rashka—"we treat this like a night on the road. Rashka and I will do four-hour shifts."

"I can set up for a shift as well," Karina interjected.

Rashka gently grasped Karina's shoulder. "It is better for you to get some rest, Karina. You are the Prophetess and already carry a heavy burden."

"Rashka is right. Besides, you told Bormain that Rashka and I are the protection, right?" His lips twitched. Karina did not seem amused. Oh well. He cleared his throat. "I'll take first shift."

CHAPTER EIGHTEEN

"I am fine. Ladies, please, let me be." Karina shooed the well-meaning handmaidens from her room. She had been dressed and primped for the day, and now all she wanted was to be left alone. Mary and Hallie shuffled off, no doubt to tell Lady Moriah how uncooperative their charge was being. No matter, Karina found very few moments of peace.

She had not slept well last night. She tossed and turned with dark dreams of monsters and Faramos's haunting laugh. King Rufus, with his ridiculous golden skin, kept popping into her dream, asking, "Did your mother not teach you respect?" She shivered. Even prayers had not settled her nerves. The quicker they were away from this place, the better off she would be. Maybe she would sleep better on the road tonight.

A knock sounded on the door before Rashka poked her head in. "Lady Moriah has ordered quite the spread for breakfast this morning. I do believe I see some citrus puffs. I thought they were more of a dessert. Apparently, they eat them for breakfast too."

"Indeed." Karina's first memory of citrus puffs was here in the royal palace, eating breakfast with the queen and the princess after they had first arrived. Such a warm memory. "I will be only a moment."

Rashka nodded and closed the door.

Karina looked in the mirror, spreading out the folds in the dark blue satin sheath. Not as elaborate as last night's ensemble, still respectable, nonetheless. Her hair hung in ringlets down her back. She grabbed the Belt of Truth from where it lay on her bed. Not a good match with her attire. Was there a way to hide it beneath the bodice? She aimed to get answers today.

She lifted the bodice as much as she could and locked the belt around her waist. The bodice fit a little too snugly over the belt, but it would have to do for now. She straightened, tossed one last glimpse in the mirror, and hurried out the door. The smells of the citrus puffs and breakfast meats teased her stomach.

Tristan and Rashka were already seated at the table in the middle of the room. An array of bone-white serving platters held pastries, meats, and fruits. Lady Moriah offered her a cold glass of fresh milk.

"Oh, please, Lady Moriah. I do not need to be waited on hand and foot."

"Nonsense!" Lady Moriah laughed. "It is my pleasure. I so enjoyed serving your family when you were here before."

Karina smiled and held her plate up as a cue for Tristan to help load her plate. Lady Moriah prattled on and on about the excitement in the palace. How Karina and Tristan had never been here at the same time, and how delightful to have them both now. Karina tuned out the chatter as her thoughts were still set on the quest. She needed to talk to Tristan before he requested an audience with the king.

"And the king mentioned something about a ball in your honor. How exciting!" Lady Moriah clapped her hands together. "I have the perfect idea for a dress for you."

A ball? No! They were leaving. Tonight. "Lady Moriah," Karina said, a little harsher than she meant and right in the middle of Lady Moriah's description of the dress. "I beg your pardon. You have been so kind. I need to speak with Tristan and Rashka about personal business. Would you mind leaving us alone for a bit?"

Lady Moriah looked mortified. Before she could speak, Tristan interjected, "Actually, I need to find Bormain as soon as possible. Lady Moriah, could you assist me with that mission?"

The noble woman paled a bit. "B-but you need to s-stay—"

Karina crossed her arms. "I am sure Lady Moriah would be more than happy to fetch Bormain for you, so we have an opportunity to talk."

"Perhaps. I would prefer to find him myself." Tristan's sharp gaze implied Karina should know where he was going with this. She had not a clue. She needed him to stay here so she could tell him about the belt, about her plan.

Lady Moriah gestured toward the table. "Really, Prince Tristan, I do not mind. Please, have a seat, and I will find Bormain."

Tristan strolled to the door and opened it. "Lady Moriah, I appreciate your kindness. However, I must insist you lead the way, or I will find him on my own."

Her eyes widened. "Well, if you insist, sir." She bowed to Karina. "I will be back shortly, Your Majesty."

Karina inhaled deeply, trying to calm her mind as Tristan winked before shutting the door behind them.

Rashka leaned over and whispered, "He is trying to find out what is going on."

Karina startled, then turned to Rashka. "I already had a plan."

"If we had sent Lady Moriah after Bormain, she could have come back with any kind of story as to why she could not find Bormain or why we could not see the king. This way, Tristan is the one to confront Bormain."

"I can see how that is wise, but I have the belt to determine who is lying."

"Only if you can speak to them."

Karina sat back down at the table with a sigh. Rashka did have a point.

The conversation had barely lulled when there came another knock at the door.

"Have they found Bormain already?" Karina raised an eyebrow as she glanced toward Rashka. "But then why would Tristan knock?" She crossed the room and opened the door.

An elegant woman, who was as tall as her father, entered the room in a crisp gold sateen gown which matched the golden curls atop her head. Karina would have recognized the woman anywhere, despite the fact she had not seen her since they were children. Or the fact her skin was painted gold. Karina pushed off her chair. "Princess Reina!"

Reina laughed, then paused, sobering before offering a formal curtsy. "Your Majesty."

Karina waved a hand. "Stop with that nonsense and come here." She embraced her friend and held her tight. The years had been long since she had last seen Reina, her childhood companion in most of her foibles. When at last they pulled away from each other, Karina grinned. "I wondered where you were when you were not at dinner last night."

Rashka cleared her throat and gestured toward the window seat. Karina nodded, and the Guardian moved politely away to let them get reacquainted.

Reina grabbed Karina's hand and led her over to the couch. "I apologize. I only arrived at the palace late last night."

"Oh? You were away?"

Reina's eyes glittered with excitement. "Father has been after me to agree to a marriage proposal, so I was visiting a suitor."

"Oh, really?" Karina giggled. "And who would want to marry a girl who climbs trees in dresses and can beat them in a foot race?"

"Ha!" Reina flipped her curls over her shoulder. "Come now, Karina, I have outgrown those childish mannerisms."

Karina gave her a knowing look.

"Well, when it comes to proper society anyway."

"So, who were you visiting?"

"Well, I have just returned from—"

Shouting sounded from the hallway. Karina recognized the voice. She closed her eyes and sucked in a breath. Either Tristan did not find Bormain, or Bormain had said they could not see the king. Either way …

The door opened.

"You tell the king that we may be in his home, but we are still accorded royal treatment according to tradition. And that means he has to talk to us at some point."

Karina massaged her forehead. This would not end well.

Tristan slammed the door behind him. "Karina, you might have to stop me …" He froze, eyes wide.

Beside her, Reina stood, her face paling. "Karina, what is *he* doing here?"

"He? He who? Tristan?"

Reina straightened and held her chin high. "What are you doing here?" Her tone was harsh and as cold as the North Sea.

Tristan's ears reddened as he stared at the ground. Karina had not seen him act this way before. Obviously, Reina and Tristan knew one another. But where did Reina's animosity come from?

Tristan rubbed his face before he brought his gaze back up to face the princess. "Reina, I can explain."

Uh-oh. Karina shrank back. Were they—

"You can explain? You can explain broken promises? You can explain disappearing in the middle of the night? Sneaking out … on me?" Her voice broke at the last sentence.

Karina's chest squeezed so tightly she could barely breathe. What was Reina saying?

"Reina, please." Tristan's eyes shifted from Reina to Karina and back. "I know I hurt you. Please believe me, that was never my intention. My brother—"

"I do not want to hear your excuses." Reina was livid—Karina had only seen her so unraveled when one of the stable boys had told her girls could not race horses.

Karina still struggled to breathe, to put two thoughts together. Why did she feel like this? What did it matter if Tristan and Reina were former lovers? It wasn't like … She swallowed, desperate for a drink of water.

Reina continued to whale on Tristan until Karina could bear no more. She stumbled around the couch, refusing Rashka's offer of help. "I need to get some air."

She rushed past a stunned Tristan and a now red-faced Reina.

"Wait, Karina."

She ignored Tristan's plea as she threw open the door and hurried into the hall. Which way to the gardens?

CHAPTER NINETEEN

Tristan did not know what to do as he watched Rashka take off after Karina. He longed to go after her himself. Instead, he had another situation to take care of … another hole he had dug with his past disgraceful behavior. He regarded Reina, memories of their summer together gradually resurfacing. Why hadn't he anticipated seeing her again? He had been so focused on Karina and the quest and his brother …

If Reina didn't kill him, Karina would. This was a very, very bad situation. Had he ruined everything with Karina? *Was* there anything with Karina? They had shared a kiss once, and just the thought of her made his heart race. He sucked in a breath before his mind could completely topple into petrified oblivion.

Reina stood across the room, arms crossed, her once-warm brown eyes now piercing him with a death glare. He remembered their last night together. The way she jumped into his arms when he arrived, holding him tight as he swung her around. Her laughter as they chased each other through the gardens. The way her soft skin warmed beneath his hands …

He shook his head. The rogue bounty hunter was long gone. While he had cared for Reina, he had not loved her. Not the way she deserved. When his brother had sent for him, demanded he leave her behind, he had obliged.

"Reina, I could never apologize enough for what I did to you. You are an amazing woman. You deserve someone who will love you with all his heart. That person was not me."

Although her body remained rigid, her expression softened a bit.

"I wish I had not left you the way I did. That was a cowardly act on my part. I did not want to see how my leaving would hurt you as I knew it would."

She sniffed and faced the windows.

"Please, forgive me."

"What are you doing here? Why did you come back?" A raw huskiness coated her words.

He closed the space between them, wanting her to hear the regret in his voice. "That is a long story. Suffice to say, I am escorting Queen Karina on a quest of the utmost urgency."

"And is she the one who has your heart now?" She turned back to him. All evidence of anger had disappeared from her face, replaced with open curiosity.

He sighed. "I do not know how to answer that. I joined her quest because I thought it was the best way to defeat my brother. Along the way, our relationship has somehow become something more."

"I warn you, Tristan"—Reina pointed an elegant finger at his chest—"do not break her heart. She is my friend, and I will end you if you hurt her as you did me."

"I promise you, Princess Reina, that is not my intention at all."

She looked down her nose at him. "Very well. You best hurry."

"Pardon me?"

She gestured toward the door. "After Karina. You have a sore amount of explaining to do, and I fear she did not take the news of our tryst lightly."

"Right." He hurried toward the door, then paused. "Thank you, Reina."

She waved him off.

Tristan rushed toward the stairway, taking them three at a time as he made his way to the first floor. Even though Karina had not said where she was going, he knew she would make her way to the garden. He dodged servants, ignoring their annoyed screeches.

"Tristan! Where are you going?" Bormain shouted from behind him, but Tristan kept moving.

At last he arrived at the massive doors leading out to the courtyard where three paths led into the gardens. The courtyard was empty, a bit unusual for late morning. Where were the gardeners? The noble women who enjoyed lounging by the ornate fountain in the middle?

He stood at the edge of the courtyard, searching from one gilded archway to the next, all leading to different parts of the gardens. Which way should he go?

A shout came from his left. Karina.

He ducked under the archway and made his way around the path, passing bushes with white and blue flowers and cascading trees with small pink buds. He didn't know the names of such plants, they had never interested him beyond a tool to woo women.

More angry shouts came from farther down the path. Karina would hate him after this. He would not be surprised if she sent him away, back to Tzedek. His chest seized at the thought. He could not bear to leave her to this quest without his protection. Not because he wanted to best Faramos. He cared for Karina. Maybe more than he should.

He made his way into a wooded area where fruit trees were beginning to bloom. Not ten paces away, Rashka leaned against a tree, while Karina paced around a small fountain in the middle of a manicured clearing.

Rashka heard his approach and reached for her bow, which she did not have with her. When she saw him, she glared, her lips pressed in a thin line.

"I know, I know," he whispered. "I got this. You can go back to the palace."

She glanced at Karina, who was still ranting and had not yet noticed him. "You had better work this out with her. She has more important things to worry about than your past dalliances."

He nodded, suddenly not sure he wanted Rashka to leave. If he could put this off a little longer …

Rashka regarded him with wary eyes and then wandered down the path back toward the palace.

Tristan took a deep breath. At least Karina had stopped shouting. In fact, she was not moving a muscle as he approached her. The tears in her eyes ripped at his heart. He clenched his jaw, working to swallow the knot in his throat. Her eyes pleaded with him, as if he had broken some unknown trust. Unknown? He'd known exactly how she felt for he had felt the same. If only …

They stared at each other for a long time. He had no idea what to say. What defense did he have? He had to say something. "Karina, I—"

"No, Tristan, I do not think I want to hear what you have to say." She shuddered, then wrapped her arms around her middle. Her gaze dropped to the flowers at her feet. "That story is about a different Tristan, a man who was angry and hurt, so he hurt others."

His breath caught.

Her gaze rose to meet his. "I know you have changed … you are a better person. I just—I do not understand why you did not warn me."

Fair question. "Honestly, I was so focused on our quest Reina did not cross my mind. If she had, I would likely have told you about her." Or not. Who knows what he would have done. "I am truly sorry for hurting you."

"I am fine." Facing away from him, she stretched out her arms. "I do not know why this is affecting me so. It is not as if we are betrothed. You have a right to your personal life."

Even though she was right, he did not like how she could brush the incident off like an annoying gnat. "Still, given our—er—history, I can see why this situation would upset you." He eased up behind her, close enough to smell the lavender in her hair, and grasped her arm. She did not turn around, but she did not pull away either. "You have to know I—"

"Well, look at this. A lover's spat smoothed over?"

Karina's heart stopped at the familiar voice. She closed her eyes. How was this possible? She turned around slowly—but Tristan's broad chest filled her vision. She beheld his intense green eyes filled with apparent confusion. Blowing out a breath, she stole a glimpse past Tristan.

Lady Anaya stood at the wooded entrance to the clearing. Clad in a form-fitting white dress with elaborate gold netting across the bodice, the former queen hardly looked like a woman who had been pierced by a blade only three weeks ago.

Karina's mind practically exploded from the impossibility of the woman standing there. "By all that is created!"

Tristan glanced back at Anaya. "What's wrong? Who is she?"

"That," Karina retorted as Anaya ambled into the clearing, "is Lady Anaya, former Queen of Aletheia."

Tristan's eyes widened as he wheeled around and drew his sword. "Do not come any closer," he warned. Cocking his head to the side, he whispered, "I thought you said she was dead?"

Karina leaned into Tristan's back. "I said she disappeared after Captain DeMarco pierced her with his blade."

Lady Anaya held her hands out. "I mean you no harm, Tristan Lemur. In fact, I have been told specifically not to harm a hair on your head. Now, how sweet is that? Your big brother is protecting you despite everything you have done."

Tristan scowled. Likely his brother wanted to end him himself.

Karina struggled to breathe as a storm of thoughts whirled in her head. "W-what are you doing here?"

"Do you mean here?" With a grin, Anaya pointed at the ground, then waved her hands around her head. "Or here in the general sense … alive. I have a feeling you might be wondering about both."

Karina could not respond.

After a moment, Anaya clasped her hands together, her eyes twinkling. "A funny story, actually. You might enjoy this. See, after my dreadful excuse for an ex-husband—DeMarco, not our beloved Pistis—tried to kill me, Faramos whisked me away to his fortress in Tzedek. He healed my wound in no time, then sent me here to befriend the king, to help him see Faramos's vision for a brighter future. To possibly secure a treaty through marriage. King Rufus does have a beautiful daughter."

Karina was going to be ill.

"I have been here about ten days now, and the king has been very kind to me. He has taken everything I have said under consideration. Of course, his daughter is not quite sold on marrying Faramos. We shall see what happens there."

"You need to leave," Tristan growled. His muscles rippled beneath her hand. He was ready to spring at Anaya.

Her mouth formed a surprised oh. "Me? Leave? Now why would I do that? The king has lavished such wonderful gifts on me." She leaned in a little closer and lowered her voice, as if anyone else would hear them out here in the garden. "If you ask me, I think he has been a little lonely since his wife died so many years ago. He seems to enjoy spending time with a noblewoman such as myself."

The very thought filled Karina's mouth with bile. The way this infuriating woman went on and on.

"So, you are the one who has the king's ear." Tristan took a step forward. "You are the reason he will not see us or answer our questions."

"Your questions?" Anaya smirked. "You mean your query about the location of the temple? Yes, I do think I advised him against revealing such information at this time. I mean, we do not know what you want with the temple. You could aim to destroy it—as you did the Temple in Aletheia."

"What?" Karina rushed forward, but Tristan grabbed her and held her in place. "Brusho and Faramos's forces destroyed the temple."

Anaya's fake attempt at horror only sent more fury rushing through Karina's veins. "Faramos? That is not what I heard. Now, dear Karina, you should not entertain such lies."

She pressed her lips together. She would not let Anaya bait her again.

"Perhaps I should let the king know how you two intend to ravage the palace, along with that shapeshifter elf. How you intend to take the kingdom for yourselves."

Tristan let out another growl. "Maybe I should kill you where you stand."

Anaya's loud laugh echoed through the clearing. "Oh, dear man, you don't have the ability to do so. Trust me."

Tristan lunged forward, startling Anaya. She danced out of the way of his blade, shoving him hard enough to knock him off balance.

"Do not think because I was a queen I do not know how to fight."

"I would never assume such a thing," Tristan said as he stood. "But I will not underestimate you again."

He attacked again, then feinted to the right. As Anaya moved to avoid the blade, she caught his shoulder in the chest. She stumbled backward and fell.

"I will give your regards to Faramos before I end him as well." Tristan raised his sword.

Anaya held up her arm. "Guards!"

What? Karina turned in a quick circle. Who was she calling for?

A swarm of steel-clad guards rushed into the clearing. As they circled around Tristan, he let out an angry shout and threw his sword to the ground.

One of the guards helped a now-tearful Anaya up from the ground. "That man, he tried to kill me. Said he was sending a message to the king."

"Arrest him." the guard shouted. Two other guards grabbed Tristan's arms. "What about Queen Karina?"

"I … I do not think she meant me any harm. We were having a lovely conversation."

The guard nodded, then gestured to the others. "Take him to the dungeon until the king is ready to deal with him. Come, Lady Anaya, let me escort you back to your room. I am sure you have had quite the fright. Queen Karina, would you like assistance as well?"

Too stunned to form words, Karina shook her head.

The guard nodded—and everyone paraded out of the clearing, leaving Karina behind. She stood there, open-mouthed, for some time, trying to wrap her head around the realization Anaya was alive and here in Soter.

Rashka appeared after a bit, casting quick glances over her shoulder. "What happened?"

CHAPTER TWENTY

Sam hoisted the pack higher on his shoulders. He had been following Sabreen along the base of the mountain range—the one she had told him yesterday they would follow all the way to Gundow. No further than another day now.

One more night on the road. One more night, then he would have a bed, a good meal, and a proper bath.

"Hey handsome. What are you thinking about?" Sabreen nudged him with her arm.

"A hot meal. A warm bath. A comfortable bed."

"You know, I do not sleep with a man so soon. Or bathe with him for that matter."

He rolled his eyes. "What are you looking forward to when we arrive in Gundow?"

She shrugged. "I am doing this for you. But I suppose I can't wait to meet your friends. They sound like wonderful people, even Karina."

Indeed, they were. He'd already noticed how much he missed them these last couple of days. Sure, he enjoyed Sabreen's company—more than he had thought possible. Yet he still longed for the familiar companionship of his traveling crew. Including Tristan. His thoughts darkened at the memory of Tristan leaving him in the woods. Maybe a lupen killed him.

"So, did you grow up in the Heart of Soter?" he asked Sabreen. Better not to think about his friends right now. He would see them soon enough.

"Yes. My mother raised me in the Heart, taught me all the healing arts and then some. I left the Heart briefly to get proper education in Gundow. That only lasted a season." Sabreen studied the ground. "The haughty people did not take well to people like me."

"People like you?"

She looked up, tears in her eyes. "People who commune with nature. People who think we should live in harmony with the wildlife and creatures around us. People who understand the use of the plants and animals. People like me."

Those people didn't sound so bad. Certainly nothing like the pictures painted in the stories of witches told around the guardhouse fires. Sabreen did not seem capable of hurting a tiny kitten, much less a human being. Even the ogres were wise enough to listen to her.

He leaned over to snatch a wildflower as they passed, then grabbed Sabreen's arm. When she stopped, he tucked the yellow flowers over her ear. "Sometimes the wildest flowers make the most beautiful pictures."

Sabreen blushed. Sam liked the way her sweet smile warmed his insides, made his heart beat a little faster. She slipped her hand in his and drug him down the unseen path.

Later in the evening, they tried to find a suitable place to make camp. Most of the area was barren, with little shelter from the elements and not much kindling or brush to make a fire. Sabreen looked weary from their journey, her shoulders slumped and eyes droopy. Sam took her pack on his shoulder, and she smiled at him as she forged ahead.

"Look, there's a little alcove in the rocks ahead." She pointed with a quivering finger.

"Good. You are about ready to pitch over from exhaustion."

"I am not."

"Are too." He smirked. "Why don't you head over with the packs and sit down for a bit. I'll gather firewood from those trees over there and build you a nice fire."

"You are too sweet." She ruffled his hair and then took both packs from him. She sauntered to the dip in the rocks that created a natural shelter. She tossed a smile over her shoulder, her red curls bouncing with each movement.

He shook his head and grinned—he might be in some trouble now. As he ambled over to the copse of trees, he couldn't help but wonder at what had transpired these last few days. Sabreen made him smile as he had not in a long time. He appreciated her sense of humor and wit—not to mention she was the most beautiful woman he had ever seen.

He gathered the firewood quickly, not wanting to be away from Sabreen longer than he needed to be. Once he had an armful, enough to keep them through the night, he made his way back to the alcove. Sabreen had already skinned the rabbit he had caught earlier and was chopping the meat into pieces, along with potatoes and carrots.

"Is there enough water for a stew?" he asked as he dropped the wood to one side.

She gestured with her head. "On the other side of the alcove, there's a small waterfall from the runoff of the snow on the mountain tops. Once we boil it, the water will be fine. I have the pot already catching water, could you grab it for me, please?"

He nodded as she went back to cutting the potato. Rounding the alcove wall, he spotted what Sabreen had called a waterfall. No more than a rivulet, yet it had filled the pot to overflowing. He dumped some of the water out of the pot, then moved toward the alcove.

"Sam!" Sabreen's sharp whisper startled him.

"Is something wrong? Miss me already?" He rounded the wall and froze.

On the other side of Sabreen, a lupen readied to pounce. Smaller than ones he had faced in the past, this one appeared to be near starvation. Its jowls and sides were gaunt, its eyes wild. A menacing growl came from its chest.

Sam edged toward Sabreen, careful to take slow steps. He beckoned Sabreen toward him, but she trembled and shook her head. Sabreen was afraid? Why? She had faced down ogres and climbed out of pits. She'd lived in the Heart of Soter her whole life.

Maybe she had never seen a lupen before. "Sabreen, look at me."

Her watery eyes found his.

"We will be fine. Do you trust me?"

She nodded.

"Then get behind me." They quickly switched places so he was closer to the ravenous lupen. It stalked closer to them, growling continuously.

Sam grabbed the knife from where Sabreen had been chopping the meat. "I think it wants the rabbit," he whispered. "Back up slowly." He wielded the knife, ready to fight if need be. His blood thundered in his ears. Even if he could only give Sabreen moments to escape, he would ensure she got out alive.

With one hand on her arm, he slowly pushed her backward, careful not to take his eyes off the lupen. For every step they took, the lupen advanced the same. When they were out of the alcove, the lupen lunged at the pile of meat and vegetables.

"Go. Now!" Sam spun and shoved Sabreen ahead of him. If they could get far enough away while the lupen scarfed down its dinner, maybe they would survive the night.

They raced across the base of the mountains, not slowing down. Even at this rate, the lupen could easily track them. They needed to do something. Anything.

Sabreen stumbled, then pitched forward to her knees. Her faint cry exacerbated her heavy breathing.

Sam knelt beside her. "We can't keep running."

"I twisted my ankle. I don't think I could run if I needed to." She grasped her ankle and rubbed the area around it, wincing.

What could they do? To his left, the steep mountain rose before them with nothing but trees. To his right, the forest loomed across a large field. Not much hope in either direction. No, they couldn't die now. They had come so far. He had to at least make sure Sabreen would be safe.

He grabbed the knife. "I will go back. I can distract the lupen, give you time to find a good hiding spot. Get up in the trees if you must. This way at least one of us will survive."

"No!" Sabreen grabbed his arm and rose until her face was inches from his. "I will not let you sacrifice yourself for me. We will get out of this together." She laid back on her elbows.

"Well, then what should we do? We can't go up the mountain, and the trees are too far for us to get to quickly with your injured ankle."

She shot him a rueful look. "Thank you, good sir."

"Sorry," he mumbled.

She bit her lip. "I think I can save us."

"Now who's spinning tales?"

"I can …" Her red face paled, and she pointed behind him.

The lupen stalked toward them—only this time, it brought a couple of friends, all lean and starving.

Sam cursed under his breath. "Time to go." He tried to pull Sabreen to her feet, but she resisted.

"Wait. I can save us." She pulled a pouch from her belt, then chanted words in a language he had never heard before. The wind picked up. Her words grew louder. She tossed the contents of the bag into the air.

The wind howled, gathering together dark clouds above them. Lightning flashed.

Sam wasn't sure how he felt about this. He pulled Sabreen close to him, and she continued to chant, her hair whipping across his face as he held on to her.

A great flash of lightning blinded him.

And then the wind calmed.

The clouds cleared.

As quickly as the storm had swarmed, so did it dissipate. And the three lupens were little more than burnt corpses.

Sam stared, dumbfounded. "What did you just do?"

Sabreen grinned. "That, my dear boy, was magic."

Between the pink blush of her cheeks and her breathy pants from exerting too much energy, Sam was in complete awe of this amazing woman. He could resist her no longer. Licking his lips, he leaned over … a breath between them … he captured her lips with his own.

He expected her to push him away, to slap him or something. Instead, she gasped slightly before her body relaxed and she wove her fingers through his hair. He reveled in the sensation of her soft body in his arms.

When he finally pulled away, her eyes sparkled as she smiled at him.

CHAPTER TWENTY-ONE

Karina stood before two sets of double doors inlaid with gold. She swallowed the growing knot in her throat and willed herself to breathe. Two nights had passed since the guards hauled Tristan to the dungeon. She had not been allowed to see him, nor had she been permitted an audience with the king. Princess Reina had come by to offer her condolences, but the affection from their initial meeting had all but disappeared. Karina's emotions were a mess, her nerves on edge.

After lunch, she had insisted, once again, on seeing the king. Though Bormain had sent the king's regrets—again—she had refused to take no for an answer. She was tired of being pushed around, tired of the runaround, tired of Faramos and his followers.

Now she gave the king no choice. She was quaffed up in a costume befitting Soteran nobility, an elaborate white dress embroidered in a checkered pattern of gold. Her hair had been braided and looped around her head.

"Stop fidgeting with your dress," Rashka whispered from beside her. Though her dress was not quite as fancy as Karina's, it still spoke of wealth and fashion.

"Sorry. I am nervous, I suppose. I am not sure what to expect when we go in there. This is not the benevolent King Rufus I knew in my childhood."

"Nor is it the wise and fearless leader I met just a few years ago."

"That does not dissuade my worries, Rashka."

Her grim expression echoed the sinking feeling in the pit of Karina's stomach.

Karina pushed her shoulders back. "I am going to go in there and plead Tristan's case based on Anaya's deceit. Then I will demand the location of the temple so we may be on our way with haste."

Rashka nodded.

Both sets of doors opened at the same time, and the herald ushered them in before calling out, "Her Majesty, Queen Karina of Aletheia and Guardian Rashka of Shadowed Forest."

Lords and ladies of the court lined the sides of the massive hall. They were dressed in white and gold, much like Karina and Rashka. Though the walls were whitewashed stone, the floor was marble flecked with gold. A gold carpet led the way from the doors to the marble dais, on which sat a gilded throne.

So much gold. How did such wealth fill their hearts? Karina shook her head. Perhaps that is how the evil found its way into this court.

Karina and Rashka made their way up the open aisle. No one said a word, but all eyes were on them. She kept her head high and eyes forward, knowing Rashka did the same.

King Rufus sat on his throne, his golden head propped up by one hand, boredom evident in his drooping eyes. Boredom? Karina pressed her lips together against the scathing comments that came to mind at the thought.

He straightened, clearing his throat as his eyes narrowed. "For what reason do you call me to my own court?" His hollow voice echoed throughout the cavernous room. Whispers followed in the aftermath.

"Your Majesty, I have come to plead for the life of my protector."

"Tristan Lemur is an assassin who attempted to murder a woman under *my* protection."

Karina huffed. "Tristan was trying to save you from the deception of a woman in league with the warlock king of Tzedek."

The king's countenance did not change—nor did he appear ruffled by her words. "I know very well who she works for. She has been negotiating a peace treaty to unite our kingdoms."

"So she says. Faramos wants to rule the Three Kingdoms—and he knows how to manipulate people to get what he wants. Already his influence has started infecting your borders a—"

A door slammed shut to Karina's left. Anaya sidled up to the king, hands outstretched, a brilliant smile revealing her perfect teeth. "I apologize, my lord, for my tardiness. My lady had much difficulty in getting my hair exactly right."

The king rose, grasped her hands in his, and kissed her cheek. "And you look beautiful, my dear."

Karina resisted the urge to roll her eyes, which would not be a very becoming action for a queen.

Anaya turned and finally noticed Karina. For all the woman's graceful acting, Karina was not fooled. Anaya smirked. "Well, what have we here?"

"Lady Anaya, Queen Karina has informed me Faramos wishes to rule the Three Kingdoms himself."

A peal of laughter rippled through the room, coming straight from Anaya's perfectly painted mouth. Karina wanted to stuff a rag in it. "Oh, dear child, that is just ridiculous. What would Faramos want with the other two kingdoms?"

"Pardon me, Your Majesty"—Karina stepped forward, ignoring Anaya's question—"but he offered a marriage proposal to me just a month ago. He told me uniting the kingdoms under his banner was his goal. Now, he is trying to make the same proposal to Reina."

Off to the right, a little squeak drew Karina's attention. In a soft golden gown that blended with her painted skin, Reina sat in a smaller version of the throne, covering her mouth with her hand.

The king cocked his head to the side. "Yes, Faramos offered a similar proposal. We declined as Princess Reina did not wish to marry outside of our kingdom. We saw no great advantage to forcing her into the contract."

Karina bit her lip. This was not going as planned. She sent a prayer up to the Creator, asking for help, for direction. The scene around her faded, and a vision filled her senses:

King Rufus, after his wife had passed on to the Lighted Realm, kneeling at his bedside, begging for answers. Years of loneliness and isolation as he watched his only daughter grow into a beautiful young lady, young men seeking her hand in marriage. Maritime trades failing with a streak of water twisters. Crop failures. The kingdom falling into debt.

Hopelessness. Fear. Anger.

Then Lady Anaya's arrival at a most desperate hour. Her friendship chased away the loneliness. Her wit endeared the nobles to him once again. Best of all, she had a plan to restore Soter's wealth.

The vision faded, and Karina sighed. Bargaining with King Rufus would be pointless. He was too far under Anaya's spell. They could worry about political relations after the Three Kingdoms were safe.

"Forgive me, Your Majesty. We are getting off subject. I only wish for you to release Tristan. If you do and tell us where the Temple of Soter is, we will be on our way immediately. I promise Tristan will not return to Gundow."

The king sat back and laughed. "You expect me to let a prisoner go, especially one who attempted to commit murder?"

"He was trying to protect me."

"Protect you? From whom?"

Karina stared at Anaya, who had a hand on her hip, eyebrow raised.

"Me?" She scoffed. "Why in the world would I want to hurt you?"

Scores of memories paraded through Karina's mind, the last of which was the standoff inside the royal house, when Anaya had demanded Karina's death. "You have tried on more than one occasion, Lady Anaya."

"I have done nothing but love you. I took you into my home, gave you food and clothes, made you a princess. And yet, *you* killed the king."

Karina's emotions were about to get the better of her as she took a step forward, but Rashka placed a hand on her arm. "Do not let her bait you, Your Majesty."

Rashka was right, of course. Karina inhaled slowly. "If I killed the king, why then did they make me queen? I have already been proven innocent. You were the one who killed the king of Aletheia."

Anaya's nostrils flared, but then she wagged her finger and stepped down from the dais. "Listen here, you brat. I am tired of you slandering my good name. I have had about enough—"

"I have had enough of both of you," King Rufus roared. "Lady Anaya, you would do well not to let Queen Karina goad you in such a manner. Remember your station."

Anaya pursed her lips and simply nodded in response.

"As for you, Queen Karina, I will hear no more. Anaya has been nothing but attentive and compassionate in her time here with us. She seeks peace throughout the Three Kingdoms. If you do not wish the same—"

"But I do, sire." Karina stepped forward again. "I may have inherited the throne of Aletheia unexpectedly, but do not think me a fool. The Creator himself has called me to a quest in which I must retrieve the sacred armor from the temples. If you would give me my protector and directions to the temple, I would see the Three Kingdoms at peace as well."

"Under your rule, I suppose?" The king shoved off his chair and was in front of her in an instant.

"Pardon me?" She blinked several times, then glanced at Anaya. What had she told him? "Why would you assume such a thing?"

"If you have all the pieces of the sacred armor, what assurance do I have you will not try to overthrow me and Faramos as well?"

"Because I have no desire to do so. The only reason I am retrieving the armor is because the Creator has commanded me to do so. I did not want to be queen in Aletheia, why would I wish to be queen of the Three Kingdoms?"

"I find a monarch who does not desire power hard to believe." The king stomped up the steps to his throne. "Guards, see Queen Karina to her suite."

Within seconds, a squad of guards assembled at her side. While they did not lay a hand on her, their presence was intimidating. Karina fought to keep her chin high.

The king grunted. "You would do well to mind your manners, Karina. You are hereby banished from my presence until you formally apologize and are willing to negotiate an agreeable peace treaty."

Karina's jaw dropped. He could not be serious. "But—"

"Take her away."

CHAPTER TWENTY-TWO

Later that evening, Rashka sat on the window seat, watching the ocean waves roll in through the rain drops pelting the crystal pane. This activity had been calming in the time they had been in the royal palace. So much anger and frustration had built up inside of her, eating at her sanity, until she wanted nothing more than to strike out at anyone within reach. She breathed deeply and leaned her head against the wall.

A door creaked, startling her out of her peace. Queen Karina wandered into the sitting room from her bed chambers. Dark circles lined her eyes, evidence she had not slept well since Tristan had been taken to the dungeon. The budding relationship between them might be an issue soon—she should have known better than to let it happen. Another mistake.

Karina offered her a wan smile. "I think I shall seek my dreams now. Exhaustion is making anything else impossible."

Rashka nodded. "Indeed, Your Majesty. You need your rest."

"Tomorrow, though, we shall devise a way to free Tristan?"

"Yes, Your Majesty."

"Dream well, Rashka." Karina slowly walked back to her room.

Rashka turned back to the sea. To the vastness so much greater than her. *Creator, be my guide tonight. Be my eyes and ears as well.*

She waited long enough to ensure Karina was asleep before rising from the window seat. She grabbed her bow from her room and slipped a dagger into the scaffold on her belt. Now was the time for answers. She needed to talk to Tristan.

She crossed the main room, opened and closed the door without a sound, and slipped down the hall with elven grace. Silence filled the corridors. Everyone had gone to seek their dreams, except for the guards on duty. She would have to keep an eye out for them, for she was unaware of where they would be stationed.

At the end of each hall, she paused to peek around the corner. When no guards appeared, she slipped by and found the stairs, which descended three levels, past the main floor down into the depths below the palace. While she had learned her way around the main areas of the palace rather well, she had yet to explore the dungeon.

The dank smell of mildew and stale air rose up to greet her, while shadows danced in time with the light from torches on the wall. Hopefully, the hallways were not too much of a maze.

She kept her ears sharp for any sound. Something that would lead her in the direction of the dungeon. Granted, as she continued on, few passages led away from the main one, and those that did were mostly dead ends with storage areas and cold pantries.

Up ahead, chains wrestled and echoes filled the air. Where had the sounds come from?

Rashka feared for Karina's safety. They could not stay in the palace any longer than necessary. Each day was more time for Lady Anaya to build a case against them, to poison the king's mind with Faramos's evil. An evil not limited to Lady Anaya's lies, pouring in from Tzedek. And that evil was growing stronger.

She came to a *T* in the passageway. More torches hung on the walls in both directions, lighting cell doors every few feet. Which way was Tristan?

She moved to the left. "Tristan?" she said in a loud whisper when she reached several of the doors. No response. She moved further down. "Tristan?"

"Go away."

"Let us sleep."

A couple of grunts.

She moved even further down the hall. About halfway down, she whispered Tristan's name again.

"Who goes there?" came a familiar voice.

She moved to a door on her right where she could make out Tristan's face through the bars. Bloodied and swollen, he was almost unrecognizable. "Tristan, it is Rashka. What have they done to you?"

"Oh, this?" He attempted a smirk. "This is nothing. You should have seen me the time a farmer caught me with his daughter."

Stupid human. Rashka shook her head. "Are you well then?"

"I can barely see, but I don't think anything is broken."

Something creaked back the way Rashka had come. She crouched down, honing in on whatever had made the noise. Nothing. Probably someone moving around in their cell.

Tristan coughed. "How is Karina?"

"She is well. Too worried about you if you ask me. I tried to convince her to leave the palace. She will not hear of doing so until we free you."

"I do not think King Rufus will be so kind."

"Not with so many people as witness to your attempt on Anaya's life." Rashka took a deep breath. "What do you want us to do? We can attempt a rescue, but it will take time."

He shook his head. "Get Karina out. Her quest is more important than my life."

"I do not think she sees it that way."

He grimaced. "No, she would not. Your job is to convince her."

Voices filtered down the hall.

"Someone is coming," she whispered, looking to the left and right. The sounds were coming from the main hallway. "Get back. I will see what I can do."

"Be safe." Tristan moved into the shadows of the dungeon cell.

Clinging to the stone wall, Rashka slid down the hall. Her sure, calculated movements belied her frantic heartbeat. She could not be caught down here. King Rufus would have her head for such disobedience.

The clank of armor echoed through the hall. Three men rounded the corner. Deep in conversation, they apparently had not seen her. She reached a small alcove and hid within a dark indent.

The footsteps drew closer. "King Rufus wants a ball prepared for three nights from now," a deep voice said.

"So quickly?"

"He wants all the nobility in the kingdom present."

"Why?" The second voice was not quite as deep—younger.

"I am not sure. All I know is he plans to execute the fellow who tried to kill his lady friend. What was his name?"

"Prince Tristan?"

"Yes, him. He plans to execute Prince Tristan and Queen Karina at the end of the ball."

Rashka's eyes bulged. A royal would never risk such a move. Executing another monarch would ensure all-out war with that kingdom. Granted,

Faramos would not care about the demise of his brother, but Jace would see the Lighted Realm moved to avenge Karina's death.

And so would she.

She wanted to put an arrow through every one of the men in the hallway. Instead, she used all of her willpower not to move. Best not to raise suspicion. No one could know she had overheard the guards talking. She continued to eavesdrop on the conversation.

"Why would the king want to kill Queen Karina? She was one of his favorite visitors when she was younger. I thought he would welcome her back with open arms."

"Seems to be the only way he can seal a treaty with Faramos and ensure the embargoes are fair for his trade fleets—since the princess refuses to marry Faramos."

"Well, he is quite a bit older than her." They all chuckled.

Rashka's stomach soured. She could not believe what she was hearing. Would King Rufus really go so far?

"How'd you find out all of this?"

"Broderick was ill the other night. Puking his guts out in the guard house. I filled in for him and stood post outside the war room."

"I'm glad I'm not the king," the younger one muttered.

Their voices carried from around the corner. Rashka tucked her body against the wall as tightly as she could, dagger in hand if needed. She did not doubt her ability to dispatch these three men but prayed the deed would not be necessary.

They were mere steps away. She held her breath.

The three men—two of them tall and clad in armor, one shorter with a cloak denoting his noble status—strolled by. Caught up in their conversation, they did not glance toward her alcove. They continued down the hall, plotting their shenanigans for the night of the ball. After a moment, they turned down another hall and then a door slammed.

Rashka let out her breath and sagged against the wall. They were in more danger than she had guessed. She gathered up her wits and hurried back to Tristan's cell.

"Tristan?"

"Rashka." He stumbled to the door. "Get her out of here. Get her out of here now!"

"I do not know how. I need help. I do not have you or Sam, and I fear I will need you both. When we leave, the king will have his army searching for us."

Tristan blew out a breath. "I do not know how I can help you from in here."

"I will come up with a plan. I will try to let you know if I can. In any case, be ready to fight."

He nodded. "Be safe."

"I will try."

Sam and Sabreen slogged into Gundow about mid-morning. Torrential rains had slowed their journey, but they had pushed forward rather than hiding out in some makeshift shelter. Now they looked like drowned meadow rats as they passed beneath the gates of the capital city.

"I'm starving." Sam grasped at his growling stomach.

"Well, would you rather find something to eat now or go straight to the palace?"

If his stomach had any say, he'd be grabbing the fresh bread from the cart near the gate. The fancy palace food would probably be too rich for his taste anyway. "Wait here." He purchased a loaf of bread with coins Sabreen had given him, split it in two, and handed one of the halves to Sabreen.

She smiled. "Thank you. I was hoping you would choose to eat something now. My body was beginning to shake from lack of food."

He slung an arm around her shoulder. "I'm glad I could help."

She didn't shrug away from him, and he kind of liked the feel of her tucked beneath his arm. Sure, they got a few disapproving frowns from passers-by. He'd never cared what others thought before nor did he now, especially since life was looking good for him.

Sam nibbled on his half of the bread as they strolled through the town. Gundow really was quite the sight to behold, all white marble and gold trim. Even Calliope in the cold beauty of winter did not compare to this. He wrinkled his nose. Of course, imagine all the people Soter could help if they paid heed to the people rather than the trim. He snorted. "Nobles."

"Is something the matter?" Sabreen peered up at him from beneath her long eyelashes.

His heart skittered. "No. I'm contemplating the vast errors in creating a city like this."

Something akin to a snarl marred her pretty face. "The nobles care more about outward appearance than feeding the people around here. They would rather lock themselves away, counting their gold, while regular peasants starve on the streets. They could pay farmers and feed the likes of the entire kingdom for ten years with what they have put into building this city. Instead, they increase taxes, raise prices—more crap."

He cringed. He hadn't realized how she felt about the leaders of her kingdom. Had it been wise to bring her on a journey that might require more … tact?

She laughed. "Don't look so worried, Sam. I have been around enough royalty in my life to know how to act. I will not disappoint you, I promise."

This time, he smirked. "Are you sure? Your last statement sounded quite passionate."

Her lips tightened. "Yes, I do have strong opinions when it comes to the rulers of this kingdom. I do not agree with the way they have handled many things of late. However, I do not intend to disrespect anyone. Then I would be as bad as they are."

She had a good point. He nodded, and they continued on, snacking on their bread in silence. They passed through another arch and finally came to a golden gate intricately carved with vines. Quite stunning. Even Sabreen's eyes bulged a little.

As they approached the gate, four guards stepped forward, moving together, their pikes tilted to block him and Sabreen.

"Who are you and what business do you have in the palace?" the guard to Sam's left asked.

"My name is Sam, and this is Sabreen. We are to meet our friend Queen Karina in the palace. She is expecting us."

"Hold please." The guard nodded to the one next to him, who then ran to the guard house.

Sam stood there, rather awkwardly. What was going on? Sabreen seemed somewhat impatient herself, tapping her shoes on the cobblestone, hand on her hip. Every couple of minutes, she huffed and rolled her eyes at him. If he weren't so anxious about seeing Karina, he would have found Sabreen's antics amusing.

After a while, the guard returned. He murmured something to the first guard—apparently the squad leader—before hurrying to his post.

The first guard removed his helmet. "I apologize, good sir. You are not on the list today. You will have to move along for now. If you would like to send a message to Queen Karina, alerting her of your presence, you may do so at the public temple."

Though he clenched his fists, Sam forced himself to appear relaxed. "I understand your protocol. However, our business is of the utmost importance. If you could spare a guard, I am sure Queen Karina would appreciate being informed of our arrival immediately."

The guard sneered. "I do not think you understood me. If you would like to get in touch with the queen, you will have to send a priest from the temple. Good day." He shoved his helmet back on, then nodded to the other guards. They took up their posts on either side of the gate.

Sam growled and spun away. He would have stormed off … if he had any inkling of where to go or what to do next. A soft hand on his shoulder reminded him to exhale his frustration. He turned to Sabreen.

"I think we should find a place to stay and then we can go to the temple as the guard suggested. So, we have to wait another day." She shrugged and pointed at his hair. "We get a nice warm bath, some hot food, and a day to rest before Karina calls for us."

Another good point. Sam grinned. He was beginning to appreciate having this witty woman around. "Lead the way, m'lady."

CHAPTER TWENTY-THREE

Sabreen led him back down the cobblestone road toward the second gate. Right after they passed through, she angled to the left and strolled down a dark alley. For someone who had not spent much time in Gundow, she seemed to know her way around. Sam had to hurry to keep up with her.

At the end of an alley, a sign hung above a rickety door—no words, just a circle with three dots inside. Sabreen stopped on the stoop and tugged at her bedraggled clothing. She heaved a long sigh and knocked on the wooden door.

A rustle, followed by stomping, came from inside. The door creaked open an inch. "What do you want?" an older voice snapped.

"Madam Claire, it is Sabreen of the Heart." She brought her face into the thin ray of light shining from inside the building.

"Sabreen of the Heart?" The door flung open, and an old woman with few teeth and a disheveled gray bun, stepped out and swept Sabreen into a hug. "Land's sakes, child, what brings you back to the city?"

Sabreen glanced at Sam. "We need shelter for a couple of nights. This is Sam."

The older woman eyed him, a frown pulling at her lips. "A boy, huh? You let a boy start dragging you around?"

"No, Aunt Claire. I'm helping him out."

"Hmm …"

Sabreen crossed her arms. "May we come in? Please?"

Madam Claire gave a dismissive wave. "Fine. Fine. Don't pay me no mind. Consider me an old hag who don't know no good."

Sabreen huffed. "That's not what I meant, Auntie."

Madam Claire shot a grin over her shoulder. "Don't just stand there. Get in here."

Once they were in and had shut the door, Madam Claire pointed to the top of the stairs. "There's an open room on the right and another on the left. Feel like some stew?"

"I feel like a bath," Sabreen muttered.

"Well, I figured you would. There's a full bath in both rooms. Take your time. I'll get the table set."

Dumbfounded by the whole conversation, Sam's mouth hung ajar until Sabreen grabbed his hands and dragged him up the stairs.

"What is your problem?" she hissed. "Aunt Claire is going to think you're dumb or mute the way you are behaving."

"How did she know to have the baths ready?"

Sabreen chuckled. "Auntie can tell the future at times."

"Then how come she didn't know we were coming?"

"Obviously she knew someone was coming." Sabreen pointed to the door on the left. "You take that room. The window faces the alley. When you're ready, come downstairs. I will probably already be down there."

Sam walked into the tiny room. The tub took up half the space. A narrow bed lay beyond it, beneath the window. A short table and a chair to his right were the only other items in the room.

He bathed and dressed quickly, not entirely comfortable in this—what? Was this place an inn? A home? He would be more comfortable when he was next to Sabreen again.

Downstairs, Sabreen was indeed already seated at the table, sipping something from a mug and laughing with Madam Claire. They glanced at him simultaneously.

Madam Claire cackled. "Come, Sam. I have delicious stew for you to try."

Sam sauntered over and sat next to Sabreen. She pushed a bowl toward him and raised an eyebrow. Did he dare? Were they testing him? He took a small bite ... then choked. By all that was created! The stew was spicier than the stories the guards told in the barracks. "Water," he croaked.

"Naw, water won't do you any good." Madam Claire snorted between deep gasps of laughter as she passed him a chunk of bread. "This is the only thing that will help."

He bit into the bread, letting it absorb all the spiciness as he chewed and swallowed again and again until the fire in his mouth gradually subsided.

Sabreen patted him on the back. "Is something the matter, handsome?"

He glared at her. "What was that?"

Sabreen grinned. "Oh, just Aunt Claire's five-spice special. It is the only reason the respectable people have not run her out of town yet."

"Run her out of town?" He looked at the old hag and back at Sabreen. "Why would they do that?"

"Oh, you hush, child." Madam Claire swatted her with the dishcloth in her hand. "Mind your manners."

Sabreen stood, smoothing out the skirt of the new dark green dress she wore. "It is time we get busy."

"Yes, of course." Sam stood, finishing off the last of the bread. He thanked Madam Claire for the meal, though he had not eaten much, then followed Sabreen outside to the main road.

"The public temple is located down from the palace. Do you think you could find it?"

He nodded.

"We are going to split up so we can accomplish more then."

"What? Split up?"

Sabreen gave him a quick kiss on the cheek. His heart soared. "You will be fine," she whispered. "You go get your message to Karina. I need to run a few errands for Aunt Claire."

"Are you sure?"

"Yes, yes. We will meet back here in time for dinner."

Sam watched her wander toward the main gate to the city. What kind of errands did she have in that direction? At one point, she spun around and blew him a quick kiss before ducking inside a shop on the other side of the cobblestone street. He couldn't tell from this distance what kind of shop it was, but he was not sure he liked the disheveled people congregating around the door.

He blew out a breath and turned to head in the opposite direction. While he did not mind finding his way around this big city, he didn't want anything to happen to Sabreen. She had been so kind to him over the last days—weeks—how long had it been?

He watched the other people meandering along the street as he made his way to the temple. The closer he got to the inner gate, the fancier the clothes and demeanor. By Madam Claire's place, many people were dressed in rags, their shoulders hunched, and their eyes darted back and forth. As he drew closer to the temple, people's clothing seemed nicer—richer colors, pricier material, more adornments. The people smiled, but seemingly only at others with whom they were acquainted. Not like the streets of Calliope, where everyone always had a kind word and often a warm embrace. Why were things so different here?

The temple was a large building with many of the same gold trimmings as the palace. Even the marbled steps leading up to the temple had gold flecks that sparkled in the afternoon sun. Sam ambled up the steps and into the wide-open space of the main temple area. Although the walls were no less fancy than the steps, the room was sparse. No furniture except for what was on the alter dais. People must have to stand for services.

Sam barely had time to scan the room when a red-faced, older priest with a round belly hurried over to him. "Good evening, sir. We were ready to close up for the day. How may I help you?"

Close up? Public temples in Calliope stayed open until sundown, and still a priest remained in the temple for emergencies. "Uh—I needed to get a message to Queen Karina."

The priest's eyes became mere slits. "I do not believe the king is allowing messages into the palace at this time."

Sam gritted his teeth. "It is of the utmost importance that Queen Karina know of my arrival … immediately."

"Even if I could get a message to her, it would not be until tomorrow." The priest shook his head as he turned away. "Like I said, we were about to close for the night."

By the Creator! What was wrong with these people? Sam blew out a breath and hurried after the priest. "Excuse me, sir. Please. Queen Karina is on a quest for the Creator to retrieve the sacred armor … to waylay the destruction of our world. I am part of her group, and I must see her as soon as possible."

The priest stared at him for a moment, then broke into a fit of laughter. He held his belly as it jiggled. "You are a riot, my boy. Such an imagination. Still, you will have to come back tomorrow to see if the king has decided to allow messages into the palace again."

"But, sir—"

"Do I need to call the guards?"

Sam held up his hands. "No, of course not."

"Then I suppose I shall see you in the morning." The priest stuck his nose in the air before he disappeared through a side door.

Sam growled as he stormed out of the temple. What in all creation was going on around here? What kind of king didn't give his people a way to contact him? He grumbled to himself as he skulked down the steps and across the square. He shot the guards a steely glare.

Yosef startled as Elder Thomas stormed into the Scribe's Room and slammed the door. At the sight of the smudged marks on his paper, Yosef clenched his fists and tried to breathe. "What ails you, sir?"

Elder Thomas plopped into a chair so hard the legs creaked. He blew out a breath. "Ungrateful ingrates who cannot take no for an answer."

Oh no. Not another one. Why did Elder Thomas become a priest if he did not understand the plight of his brethren? "Sir?"

"Some loon wanted to get a message to Queen Karina even though I told him the palace is not taking messages today." He paused, shook his head, then laughed. "He concocted a tale about our world on the brink of destruction and needing to retrieve the sacred armor. Have you ever heard such a tale?"

Yosef stiffened. The sacred armor? Destruction? "Did he give you any details?"

Elder Thomas waved him off. "I did not allow him to speak further. I do not have time for such ridiculousness."

"But, sir …" Had the elder not sensed the pervasive evil cloaking Gundow? People were uneasy and did not know why. More unrest. More fear. More of people looking out for themselves and not each other. Crime was at an all-time high. And something was going on inside the palace. Despite being the head messenger, he had been reluctant to go these last few weeks. "Do you not think there might be some truth in what he said?"

"Of course not." His face darkened. "And don't you go believing his foolishness either. The boy looks like he's nothing but trouble, and that is the last thing the king needs right now."

Yosef looked down, noting again the smudges on his paper. He would have to start over later. "Yes, sir."

Elder Thomas pushed off the chair. "I will be in my quarters for the rest of the evening. See I am not disturbed."

He nodded. As soon as the head priest disappeared through the door, Yosef scrambled out of the room and into the sanctuary, his footsteps echoing through the emptiness. The temple had been too quiet of late. He feared what the dwindling need for the Creator meant for Gundow, for Soter.

When he made it to the court square, he stopped and surveyed the few people strolling through. Most were lofty nobles in their regal dress, noses in the air. A few food merchants still remained in the aftermath of the midday meal.

One man with messy brown hair stared at the guards who stood by the gilded gates to the palace. With a vigorous shake of his head, the man stalked back toward the other gate. That had to be him. His clothing was not typical of Gundow residents, definitely not of the upper class. Yosef scurried after the man.

When he caught up to him, he cleared his throat. "Excuse me, sir."

The man continued on as if he had not heard Yosef.

He tapped him on the shoulder. "Excuse me, sir."

The man turned and surprise highlighted his young features. "Yes?"

"Are you trying to get in touch with Queen Karina?"

The man nodded slowly. His mission was probably secret, which may make him nervous to trust anyone.

Yosef scanned the area to ensure they were not being watched before he leaned in ever so slightly. "I think I may be able to help you."

"The Head Priest said the king was not allowing communication."

Yosef shrugged. "I have my ways."

This time, the young man crossed his arms. "And why would you want to help me?"

Why indeed? Yosef would be risking his place at the temple by disobeying Elder Thomas. Still, his heart had a peace about this. He breathed deep. "Something is not right in the palace … in this city. I have been saying as much for weeks, but no one will listen. I met Queen Karina, briefly. She is a good woman, no matter what her protector might have done."

"Her protector?" The man's eyes bulged. "What happened to Tristan?"

"Apparently, he tried to kill a friend of the king. Landed himself in the dungeon. Queen Karina has been unsuccessful in getting him released."

The man closed his eyes and sucked in a breath. "You are willing to get a message to her for me?"

"My name is Yosef, and I am a palace messenger. My quarters are in the main palace, so I can be summoned without notice."

The man smiled. "It is a pleasure to meet you, Yosef. I am Sam. Now, here's what I need you to tell Queen Karina …"

Karina paced in front of the sitting-room fireplace while Rashka stood in the doorway, conversing with Bormain. Neither Lady Moriah nor the handmaids had appeared today to help Karina prepare for the day. No breakfast had been delivered. Karina was at her wits end with the way the king had been treating her. Even if King Rufus refused to release Tristan, Karina had not done anything wrong. Why was she being punished?

Rashka bowed her head to Bormain, who glanced over her shoulder, pity in his gaze, before dashing off down the hall. She shut the door and turned, letting out a long sigh. "He did not bring good news, Your Majesty."

Karina blew out a quick breath, pressing against her stomach. "Let me sit down." She sat on the couch but could not get comfortable and quickly moved to a chair at the dining table. But that too felt stiff. She stood again, tears in her eyes. Of all the confounded reasons to cry …

With a good measure of patience, Rashka grabbed her hands and led Karina to the window seat. Beyond the glass, wave upon wave rolled in from the sea. Karina watched them, longing for them to whisk her troubles away to the open waters. Finally, she looked back at Rashka. "I am ready."

"The king has restricted us to this suite. We are not to leave the suite unless we have requested permission and are escorted by his guards."

"I am not a prisoner!" Karina shrieked.

Rashka patted her hand. "Of course not. King Rufus would not want to bring war to his doorstep so quickly. I think he is trying to control the situation—and your influence on his people—the only way he knows how."

With a loud growl, Karina pulled her hand away and crossed her arms. "I am not surprised at the decisions he has made with Anaya around."

The elf nodded, gazing out at the waters. Karina also soaked in the peaceful, rolling waves. They made her somewhat sleepy, and what she would not give for fluffy pillows and a big blanket right now. Burrowing under the covers sounded absolutely delightful compared to the frigid chill she had received from the king.

She hung her head. "What do we do now?"

"I am not sure." Rashka inhaled and let her breath out slowly. "The other night, I—"

"What about Princess Reina?" Karina straightened.

"What about her?"

"Maybe she can help." She rose and opened the door.

Two burly guards in silver and gold stood outside the door. The one on the left sneered at her. "What do you want?"

"I would like to request an audience with Princess Reina, either in her chambers or, if she would prefer, here would work as well."

"We'll pass along the message." The guard resumed his stance, but neither of them moved.

She glared at the two of them. "I thought you were going to pass along the message."

"We can't leave our station. We have to wait until someone else happens by," he replied without looking at her.

Before she lost her temper, Karina closed the door and marched to the window seat. Rashka had not moved. Nor did she say anything as Karina plopped down on the soft cushions. "I have not been treated with such disrespect since my days on the orphan caravan."

Rashka shook her head. "I am not sure Princess Reina could help us anyway. As princess, her hands are probably tied."

"But without her, how can we get Tristan out of the dungeons? Especially since we cannot leave the suite without permission and an armed escort?"

"It does present quite a quandary. I do not believe Tristan would want us to attempt a rescue under these conditions."

"Tristan? What do you mean? And how do you—" She let out a gasp. "You know something. What do you know?"

Rashka held up her hands. "Karina, I—"

"No." She stood and towered over her elven friend. "I want to know … right now."

"I went to visit Tristan last night."

"What? When?"

"After you had gone to bed." Rashka shuffled over to the fireplace. She related the whole sordid tale, much to Karina's growing horror.

Karina sank onto the couch, wishing the furniture would swallow her whole. "King Rufus is going to have us killed? Does he not realize Aletheia would be forced to retaliate?"

"Like you said before, something is off about him. I am not sure he cares at this point. Or maybe Aletheia's retaliation is part of his plan. Maybe he wants Aletheia to attack?"

What was going on here? Had Faramos's evil so pervaded this kingdom—had so possessed the king himself—that someone would see war as preferable? She could not even fathom an acceptable response. How could she be expected to? She was only seventeen.

Tears filled her eyes. "I am not ready to die, Rashka." She looked up as the guardian pulled her close.

"I do not think that will happen, Karina," she cooed. "The Creator has great plans for you. He will not let you fall to the likes of King Rufus."

They sat in silence for a long time. On the couch, Karina dozed off and on as her mind wondered about the insanity of the last weeks. She might have fallen asleep if there had not been a knock at the door.

Rashka rose to answer and then ushered Bormain inside. He bowed quickly. "I took your message to Princess Reina." He paused, an uneasy expression on his face. "Unfortunately, she declined to meet with you today. And King Rufus still refuses to let you leave the suite."

"Could we at least get some food?" Rashka retorted, arms crossed.

"Indeed, Guardian Rashka. Lunch is being prepared as we speak. I deeply apologize for the missed breakfast. The servants were supposed to bring something up. There must have been some sort of miscommunication."

"Like death by starvation," Karina muttered before letting out a long sigh.

"Excuse me, Your Majesty?" Bormain looked genuinely surprised.

"I beg your pardon, Bormain. An empty stomach has left me quite cross this morning."

"Quite understandable, Your Majesty. I will see lunch is brought up immediately. If there is anything else you need, let the guards know. They will get a message to me." He bowed again and skittered from the room quicker than a mouse from a mountain cat.

Karina shot Rashka a dumbfounded frown. Of all the nerve. Bormain had acted like nothing was amiss, as if the imprisonment of a queen—

treating her like a common criminal—was perfectly normal. She shook her head. "We need a plan. Now."

CHAPTER TWENTY-FOUR

Tristan kicked at the dank straw strewn across the impacted dirt floor. He tilted his head as far left as it would go and then to the right, stretching his neck. Every muscle in his body ached, every joint shouted with agony. The guards had ceased torturing him. But with no way of getting proper rest, he could not recover as he should. What he would not give for Rashka's healing powers right about now.

With nothing better to do to pass the time, he sought his dreams for most of the day. Even when the guards brought the measly excuse for food, he barely managed to down the dry bread and crusty meat before dozing off again. How many more days would he endure this dungeon?

He remembered what the men had said the night before. In another two days, the king would have both him and Karina put to death. His breath caught. While he cared little if he lived or died on this quest, Karina's life meant everything to him. Surely, the Creator would not allow this to come to pass. Surely, he would intervene somehow.

He let out a growl. And he probably wouldn't be around to witness any kind of said miracle.

Unfamiliar sounds filtered in through the bars on the door. Curiosity wanted to see what was going on, but the wiser part of him did not desire another beating if the guards were to discover his eavesdropping. Coarse words signaled an argument between two guards, and a swishing sound indicated they were perhaps dragging something.

Tristan decided to chance a glimpse and hauled himself off the floor, swallowing the groan rising in his throat as his body screamed at the quick movements. He shuffled to the door and peered through the bars, careful to stay in the shadows the best he could.

"I'm telling you, George, the king ain't going to care if he is dead or not."

George was a tall, lanky guard, who seemed kind of familiar. His face was an angry crimson. "But we were told to keep him alive. What were you doing?"

"I was questioning him like the captain told us to." The other guard was shorter and stockier, yet his face was just as red. But perhaps more from the body he was dragging around by the feet rather than from anger.

"Questioning does not always mean torturing the prisoners, Marcus."

"It does if you want the real answers."

"How do you know they don't give you a random answer, so you'll quit torturing them?"

"I don't. Which is why I push them a little more to see if they really are telling the truth."

George shook his head, his fists clenched at his side. "You sadistic"—he swallowed his words—"I ain't backing you up when the captain demands to know what happened. I keep telling you not to go too far. And this time you went and done it."

And this time you went and done it. The words rolled around in Tristan's mind. So familiar until a memory slapped him upside the head. He did know George … a friend from long ago. Both sons of noblemen, they had spent time sparring together on several of Tristan's visits. Like when he had been courting Reina. Did George know his friend was here in the dungeon?

Marcus huffed, drawing Tristan's attention back to the conversation. "I do not need you defending me, no how. Now help me get this body to the dumping ground."

"Not a chance." George crossed his arms. "You there," he said, flagging someone down the hall. "Help Marcus get this body away before it starts stinking up the place."

Quickly, the new guard and Marcus lifted the body and shuffled off down the hall. George blew out a breath and sagged against the wall opposite Tristan's cell.

Tristan sucked in a breath. No better time than now. "Some people never learn."

The young guard straightened, glancing up and down the hall. "Who goes there?"

"It's me, fool."

George squinted in his direction before his eyes bulged in their sockets. "Tristan?"

"Yep."

"What are you doing in there?" George crossed the hall in three steps, looking both ways again before peeking into the cell.

"Wrongly accused, as always."

George chuckled. "I don't know that *wrongly* is the right word. At least in some cases."

"Maybe not." Tristan leaned his forehead against the bars, peering out at his old friend. "But this time it is. I was merely defending a friend from someone who has tried to kill her in the past. That someone happened to be close to the king."

"Tough situation. You sure know how to get on the wrong side of important people."

Tristan bared his teeth. "George." His voice held a sharper warning than he intended, but he was tired and sore and ready to be done with this place.

George held up his hands. "It was only in jest. But you really must watch who you try to kill around here. From what I hear, you're not Faramos's bounty hunter anymore."

"Thank you."

"But those bounty hunter charges could bring the noose if the king ever found out."

Tristan let his body sag against the door. Although he was well-known in the underworld for his bounty hunter and assassin jobs over the years, the only nobility who really knew the extent of his missions was his brother. Now that Tristan was no longer in Faramos's good graces, would his brother betray him to King Rufus? Would he be able to spin a tale without implicating Tzedek in the process?

Tristan let out a sigh. "I do not think I have to worry about my past. Faramos would be unable to reveal my secrets without revealing his own."

George merely nodded. "Well, I will see you are properly taken care of until the king decides what to do with you. For what it's worth, regardless of what you did, I hope he releases you in the end."

Tristan nodded and watched George amble down the hall and out of sight. George had too much loyalty to Soter to go against the king—even if Tristan had some sort of solid proof, which he didn't. He growled as he pushed off the door and then crossed the small cell. His body groaned as he sank back to the cold ground.

"A blanket would be nice!" he shouted, though George was probably too far down the hall to hear him.

The late afternoon sun cast long shadows across Karina's sitting room. She had been locked in here all day. Even her request to walk around the gardens had been denied. Anger burned in her stomach and had turned her lunch sour, so the absent dinner was probably for the best anyway. She had perused the bookshelf along the wall next to the main door to the suite and found a suitable book on the history of Soter to lose herself in for most of the afternoon.

Rashka sat on the window seat, also engrossed in a book. She had been quiet for most of the day, only speaking when spoken to. Karina knew, though, she was working on a plan to free them and Tristan. They were running out of time, and they did not have a lot of options.

A knock on the door interrupted their silence. Rashka started to rise, but Karina jumped up. "Please, let me get it." She opened the door to find Bormain in the hall, looking as uneasy as he had every time she had spoken to him the last couple of days. "Yes?"

He cleared his throat and adjusted the monocle covering his right eye. "I came to let you know dinner will be served shortly."

Finally. Karina kept her expression neutral.

"And also, you have a visitor."

"A visitor?"

Bormain stepped back as Princess Reina moved in from his right.

"Your Highness," Karina gasped and bowed her head. "To what do I owe this privilege?"

Princess Reina offered her a small smile and grasped her hands in both of hers. "My dear friend, we have much to discuss. May I please come in?"

Karina furrowed her brow. Had the princess refused her request for an audience just yesterday? In her confusion, she seemed unable to form an appropriate response.

Princess Reina's eyes bulged a bit, and her head jerked slightly toward Bormain before she pasted on a pleasant smile once again.

"Oh, of course, Your Highness. You are always welcome. Please, come in."

Princess Reina turned to Bormain and nodded.

"I will have all of your dinners delivered here," he said gruffly before bowing and hurrying away.

Karina ushered Princess Reina in, shut the door, and then offered her a place to sit on the couch. Rashka had not moved from her spot at the window but cocked an eyebrow in their direction. Karina could only shrug.

Princess Reina sat and then patted the cushion next to her. "Please, join me. I meant what I said. We have a lot to talk about."

With what she was sure was a wary countenance, Karina eased onto the couch beside Reina. "I must admit I am confused. You denied our request to speak to you yesterday."

Reina chewed on her lip for a moment before readjusting her dress. "I apologize for that. I was otherwise engaged and could not get away, especially to speak with you—though I assure you I wanted to." The princess wrung her hands, her face falling from the peaceful candor of royalty to that of a crestfallen youth. "Oh, Karina, I am afraid things have gone terribly wrong." She burst into tears.

Karina was too stunned to move, but then her instincts took over. She wrapped an arm around Princess Reina. "There, there," she cooed. "I am sure everything will be fine."

Rashka flung a handkerchief in their direction, and Karina scooped it off the couch.

"Whatever is the matter, Princess Reina?" She handed her the square of cloth.

"Oh, please." She sniffed. "While we're in here, call me Reina. And I shall call you Karina. Like we did as children. Do you agree?"

Karina nodded.

"I am afraid something has befallen my father. Something no one can determine. He is not himself."

Karina shot a knowing look at Rashka, who pretended to be absorbed in her book. However, Reina glanced Rashka's way, then pivoted in her seat. "Rashka, please come join us. I think you should hear this as well."

"As you wish, Your Highness." Rashka closed the book and joined them by sitting in the chair next to the couch.

Reina sighed, wringing the kerchief in her hands. "I do not even know where to begin. I guess I shall start with the worst news." She paused and stared at both of them with wide eyes. "My father intends to have Karina and Tristan put to death tomorrow night at the end of the ball."

Karina did not move, neither did Rashka.

Reina's face twisted, her brow furrowed. "Why do you not look surprised?"

"We already knew that," Rashka growled.

"How?"

Karina patted her hand. "Rashka overheard some guards talking about the king's plan before we were officially relegated to the suite."

Reina gasped in surprise, then she clasped her hands together. "I do not know what has come over him! He adores you, Karina. He used to speak so highly of you and your family."

No doubt Anaya's encouragement had something to do with his change of heart. That or Faramos's influence. Karina offered Reina a small smile. "Indeed. He was always so kind to us when we were staying here. I have found his current actions shocking as well."

"His behavioral changes began before you all arrived." Reina stood and began pacing in front of the fireplace, now cold from lack of attention. "He's more withdrawn. He does not listen to his advisers nor to me anymore—only Anaya. And she is a manipulative vixen! She seemed so nice at first—still does most of the time—but she gets this look every now and then where I can tell she is planning something sinister. And now she's been pushing harder for me to marry Faramos, even though we have been working out other plans in the treaty.

"But I digress, I was referring to my father's changes. He's quicker to anger. And when it comes to the kingdom, he has no desire to hear about the people—their struggles, their frustrations, nothing. He used to allow them at the palace to log complaints, but no more. Instead, they must file their grievances with the priests at the public temple. Then he hardly ever reviews the people's concerns. All he cares about is building his fleet and his roads for commerce. It is infuriating!"

Rashka grabbed Reina's hand, and the princess stopped pacing. "Have you tried to talk to him?"

"Yes! Over and over. All he does is brush off my counsel. He tells me I am too idealistic, and I do not understand what it takes to rule a kingdom. He warned that I had better find a man who would be stronger than I am to help me rule this kingdom when he's gone."

Karina covered her mouth. How could King Rufus say such a thing to his own daughter?

Rashka crossed her arms.. "I am afraid the evil has too strong a hold on this kingdom, or at least on the king. I do not think there will be any change until you have completed your quest."

Karina could only agree with the guardian. She looked into Reina's heartbroken eyes and immediately felt her misery. She prayed the woman would feel the Creator's comfort until this was over. And hopefully King Rufus would come out of this with his legacy still intact.

"Reina, we need your help."

The princess straightened, wiping away her tears. "Yes, of course. Anything."

"We need—"

Another knock sounded on the door.

Rashka stood. "That must be dinner. I will get it."

Karna squeezed Reina's hand. "Remember your father as he was before. Hopefully, if everything goes as planned, he will revert back to his benevolent self soon. In the meantime …"

Movement by the door distracted Karina from what she was saying. Rashka allowed a young man in priestly white robes to enter. His tan skin highlighted his dark hair and hazel eyes.

Both Karina and Reina stood. "Rashka, who is this?"

Quickly, the man bowed. "Forgive the intrusion, Queen Karina. My name is Yosef, and I am the palace messenger—I have news for you."

Immediately, she grabbed Reina's arm. What kind of news would find her here? Had something happened in Aletheia? Were Jace and Mauri well? She fought against the urge to tremble, willing her body to still, though horrible thoughts rolled through her mind.

Inhaling, she pursed her lips into a tight smile. "Please, go on."

The messenger grinned. "Your friend, Sam, has arrived in the city. He wishes to see you."

CHAPTER TWENTY-FIVE

Sam stoked the fire yet again, as Madam Claire berated him in the background.

"Don't let the fire die down, boy. Otherwise the potion won't ferment properly." She smacked him upside the head as she crossed the room to grab more supplies.

"Excuse me, I don't know who you think—"

"Is everything all right?"

With all the yelling, Sam had not heard the door open. Sabreen slipped in and pulled off the hood covering her delightful red hair. In spite of his anger toward the abusive hag, Sam grinned. "Where have you been?"

"Getting ingredients for dinner. I thought we would have chicken and fresh vegetables tonight." She plopped a full bag on the table.

"How'd you go affording all that?" Madam Claire asked, rubbing her scraggly hair.

"I did a favor for the butcher," she replied, shooting a look at her aunt, who nodded and went on about her own business.

Sam was not sure what the exchange meant. "A favor?"

"Never you mind, handsome." She started pulling food out of the bag, including a whole chicken, already plucked and prepared.

"Wow. You must have really impressed him with whatever it was you did."

She grinned. "I always do. Now what has Aunt Claire been having you do?"

Sam turned to the fire where the pot boiled over. "Oh no." He grabbed it, but the handle was so hot he dropped it. The pot fell to the floor, spilling its contents onto his pants. He howled.

"What in the world is going on?" the old hag crooned, then gasped. "What have you done?"

"What?" Sam gripped his hands and bent over, then hobbled to the chair. He spat at Madam Claire, "You. This is your fault."

"Goodness, Sam." Sabreen rushed over. "Let me see."

His first instinct was to pull away, until he recalled how helpful she had been in his other scrapes. And he had been in several since meeting her. Good thing she was around. And he was rather enjoying the fact she was around—and not just because her magic was convenient.

He held out his hand, which she took it gingerly in hers, inspecting the swollen, red skin. "I've got salve for this." She quickly cleaned and dressed the burn and then moved to check his shins, already blistering as well.

Sabreen's aunt stood in the background, mumbling about thoughtless brutes who were no good in the kitchen. Hey, he was not going to deny his lack of culinary skills. He was better with horses and swords—as he had tried to explain to Madam Claire before she browbeat him into helping her.

Sabreen swiped something across Sam's foot … then came a pain like he'd never known. He swore and jumped out of the chair. She laughed. "Careful, Sam! You might—"

Someone knocked on the door.

All three of them froze. Sabreen looked at Madam Claire, and they both shrugged. Madam Claire nodded to Sabreen, and she grabbed a pouch off a side table as Madam Claire shuffled across the room. What were they doing? Were they worried? Scared? When Sabreen was behind the door, Madam Claire opened it. "What do you want?"

The person gasped—a woman. She cleared her throat. "I am not sure I have the right place. I am looking for Sam Bennett of Aletheia."

Sam would know that voice anywhere. His insides did a flip, and relief swam through his veins. He fairly pushed the old hag aside to get through the door. "Karina!"

The beautiful brunette squealed at the sight of him. He swept her up in his arms, pulling her into the room and spinning her around in circles. When he finally placed her on her feet, she was breathless but smiling ear-to-ear. "Sam, I was so worried. I thought for sure you were dead."

"Me?" He was suddenly sheepish, rubbing the back of his neck. "It takes more than a couple of lupens—or ogres—to get the best of me."

"Is that a fact?" Sabreen coughed.

Her obviously sarcastic question pulled him from their reunion and allowed him to take in the rest of the guests, as well as the somewhat-annoyed

Sabreen and the overly irritated old hag, who crossed her arms as she tapped her feet.

"Rashka!" Sam rushed over to envelope the elven guardian, who stiffened, probably as uncomfortable as he felt. He quickly pulled back and shook her hand instead. "Good to see you."

Two other people were with them. He recognized the priest he had sent with a message for Karina and nodded to him. But he did not know the other woman. Given her dress, Sam took her for nobility … perhaps not royalty.

Karina stepped between them. "Sam, this is Princess Reina. Princess, this is my most loyal friend, Sam."

So, she was royalty. Maybe she was dressing down to wander the streets so late in the evening? Sam kissed the back of her delicate hand. "It is a pleasure, Your Highness." In the background, Sabreen rolled her eyes. Sam stifled a chuckle.

"Quite the same, Sam. Karina has told me so much about you, I feel I already know you." Her big smile lit up her face, though a sadness lay in her eyes. What had transpired to make a princess appear so miserable?

Sabreen cleared her throat.

"Oh, right." Sam backed away, again sheepishly, and gestured toward Sabreen. "Everyone this is Sabreen and her aunt, Madam Claire. Sabreen has been my guide"—she coughed sharply, and he changed his words—"and, more so, my friend these past couple of weeks. She led me out of the Heart and brought me here."

Karina stepped forward and clasped Sabreen's hand. "Oh, then I am most pleased to meet you, Sabreen. Thank you for bringing my Sam back to us."

Instead of replying in kind, Sabreen stiffened, as if offended. She opened her mouth to speak, but Yosef stuck his head into their circle. "I really should not be here. If it is all right, I will take my leave now."

Sam nodded. "Of course, if you must, Yosef, but you are more than welcome to stay."

"No, Sam." Yosef eyed the old hag and then shook his head more vehemently. "I cannot. If you have need of my services again, you know where to find me."

"Yosef, would you be so kind as to let my guards know we found the right place and may be here awhile." Princess Reina offered him a rewarding smile.

He nodded quickly, then, without a backward glance, scurried out of the house.

"Well, he is an odd one." Karina shot Sam a curious look, but he could only shrug. With Yosef's spooked behavior—did he know Sabreen was a witch? Being a priest, he would likely be uncomfortable.

Madam Claire waved her hand. "Men like him never like having anything to do with back alleys like this. Pay him no mind." She grinned and bowed. "Welcome to my home, ladies."

Rashka eyed the woman, suspicion evident in her expression. But Karina and the princess nodded. "Thank you for your hospitality, Madam Claire," Princess Reina said.

"We were just preparin' dinner. You all are more than welcome to join us."

Karina leaned on Sam, and he held her close. "That would be wonderful. Thank you," she murmured with a contented sigh he recognized.

Over the next hour, while Madam Claire and Sabreen prepared dinner, Karina relayed her adventures in the time they had been parted. Princess Reina kept quiet most of the time, listening as well. Karina's trust in her must be strong, or she would not have been so candid in front of her.

Every once in a while, even though he was enthralled by Karina's tales, he found his gaze drifting toward Sabreen. For the most part, she ignored his several attempts at eye contact. Had he done something wrong? Was she angry with him for spilling the potion? Was it—Karina? Surely not. Sabreen was aware of how close he and Karina were, how much she meant to him. Still, he couldn't shake the feeling Sabreen was annoyed at him.

When dinner was finally on the table, everyone gathered around. Sam sat with Karina on one side, Sabreen on the other. Princess Reina, Rashka, and Madam Claire sat across from them.

Karina grabbed his hand and grinned. "Thank the Creator for reuniting us, for new friends, and for this wonderful food."

"Indeed." Sam couldn't help but return the smile. At the mention of the Creator, however, Sabreen and Madam Claire exchanged terse glances. Maybe they would come around.

Karina took a small bite and then leaned forward, her attention on Sabreen. "I have been hogging the conversation this whole time with my stories. How did the two of you meet?"

"It is actually quite interesting. I was about to be ..." Sabreen nudged him hard, and he quit talking.

She pasted on the most fake smile he had ever seen on her. "I ran across him wandering in the woods. Took him in, fed him, brought him here."

"That was very nice of you. It must have been quite a trip to bring him all the way to Gundow."

Sabreen glared at him very pointedly, as if to say Karina didn't need to know their stories. "Indeed. We traveled for many days on foot." She flashed her smile back at Karina. "But I am glad to see him reunited with his friends. And, of course, if I can be of any help on your quest, please let me know." She stuck a piece of chicken in her mouth.

The blood drained from Karina's face as she tore her gaze from Sabreen and glared at Sam. Suddenly, the room got rather stuffy. Karina would never speak to him again.

"I appreciate the offer, Sabreen. You are very kind. I do not know that there is anything for you to do. Mostly, we need protectors."

"I can do that. Can't I, Sam?"

Sam did not like where this was headed. He sucked in a breath. "I am sure—"

Karina put her fork down. "Thank you for the offer, but I have everyone I need."

"Well, maybe Sam wants me to come along anyway. Don't you, Sam?"

"Sabreen ..." he warned.

"Why would he want you to come along?" Karina laughed, until she wasn't laughing anymore. She looked at Rashka, who shook her head. Her eyes widened. "Oh."

Sam's cheeks burned. This was not how he had imagined this conversation going. He did not know if he wanted Sabreen to go along on the quest. Did he enjoy her company? Did he possibly see her as more than a friend? Yes and yes. Still, a romantic relationship could wait until after Karina put the evil back in its place.

He ran his hand over his face, avoiding eye contact with everyone. Silence stretched on. No one was even eating. Sabreen had crossed her arms and turned one way, while Karina continued to stare at a spot past his head.

Madam Claire and Rashka both tried to hide smiles, though Rashka did a better job than Sabreen's aunt. Probably because she was an elf.

He had to say something … anything.

Princess Reina cleared her throat and stood. "I am afraid I must return to the palace, and Queen Karina and Guardian Rashka must come with me. Sam, I would like to invite you to the palace in the morning, as my guest. Your name will be left at the guardhouse, so they should see you in directly this time." She nodded to the old hag. "Thank you, Madam Claire, for your hospitality. The food was delicious."

Karina remained silent as she gathered her skirts and stood. She shot Sam a pointed glare. "I will see *you* in the morning."

What was he supposed to say? What did he want to say? He sucked in a breath. "I'll be there."

Rashka silently passed, shaking her head as she followed Karina. If they hadn't been in polite company, he might have pried Rashka to speak. She usually had the best advice.

After the final stilted farewells, Karina disappeared into the night with Princess Reina and Rashka. Sam closed the door behind them. With a long sigh, he turned around. The old hag had disappeared, but Sabreen stood in the middle of the room, arms crossed, toe tapping.

Sam swallowed. A part of him had dreaded this moment since he'd noticed her silent treatment earlier in the evening. "Have I angered you in some way, Sabreen?"

Her eyes bulged. She threw up her hands with a screech. "Of all the incompetent men!" Spinning on her heel, she marched over to the table and began clearing the dishes.

"Sabreen." He really did not know what to say. If only she would give him a clue. She continued to pile dishes, each one banging into the next. He sauntered up behind her, then placed his hands on both her upper arms.

She paused and lifted her head. Gently, he wheeled her to face him. He waited until she looked him in the eye. "I am not sure what I have done … how I have offended you. But I am sorry I did so. Your friendship is important to me."

Her brow furrowed. "Is that what we are? Friends?"

He huffed, taking a beat to analyze that question. Earlier, he had mulled over such thoughts. While he would certainly enjoy getting to know this feisty woman better, his mission right now was to help Karina defeat Faramos and the evil. As he tried to figure out how to explain his purpose, Sabreen's countenance shifted from curiosity to confusion to anger.

"Very well, then. I understand." She spun back around, grabbed the dishes, and rammed him in the shoulder as she shoved past. "Tomorrow morning, we will go our separate ways."

"No, that is not what I want at all!" He closed the distance between them as she dropped the dishes by a large washing bucket. When she moved away, he snatched her wrist and drug her close. She struggled to push him away, hurt evident on her pretty face, but he refused to let her go and pulled her closer. At last she stilled, glaring at him, her lips pursed. "Are you ready to listen?"

She did not move.

He breathed deeply. "We are friends. And, yes, I would very much like to be more. I simply did not want to engage in a relationship I could not fully devote myself to until after the scourge on our world is gone."

Sabreen's breath warmed his cheek, making his heart beat a little faster. "Why does it have to be one or the other?"

"What do you mean?"

"Why not let me come with you? I understand what you are up against, and I am willing to fight. If we are together, we can still find time to … get to know each other better."

"You would want to join our battle?"

"For you? Of course."

Sam's blood rushed to his core. His ears reddened. "To get to know me better?"

She nodded, eyes wide.

"Like this?" He leaned in, then brought his lips to hers, closing their argument with a soft kiss. Sabreen's body shuddered and then melted into his embrace. Maybe having her along would be a good thing.

CHAPTER TWENTY-SIX

The final day had come. Tristan laid his head back against the cold stone of his last room. All he had been through … all he had done, and he would be killed for a crime he did not even commit.

"Tristan? You awake?" George's voice drifted between the bars.

"Unfortunately."

"Rumors are the king plans to see you run through tonight."

"So it would seem."

"What are you going to do?"

He shrugged, though unlikely George could see him in the darkness of his cell. "What can I do? I'm stuck in here. And with how friendly the guards are, I'm in no condition to stage an escape at any point. Thank you for the blanket, by the way. Made sleeping a lot easier."

"You are welcome, friend." George's voice sounded thick, sad.

"No worries. I will be fine."

George didn't say anything for so long Tristan wondered if the man had walked away … then he coughed.

Tristan pushed off the ground and limped over to the door. "George, can I ask a favor?"

"Sure. I may not be able to get you out of here, but I will do whatever else I can to help."

This is a good man—wish there were more like them in the world. "I don't mind dying for whatever perceived slight I have caused the king. Karina has done nothing wrong, however, and does not deserve to die. Find a way to sneak her out of the palace. Get her out of here so she can complete her quest."

George leaned in closer. "Her quest?"

Oh, right. He didn't know about the mission. Tristan sucked in a breath. "Well, I cannot tell you why we are here. But trust me, the fate of the world depends on Karina."

Through the bars, confusion masked George's face, as if he wondered if he should laugh or cry or be angry. "Are you serious?"

"I know it sounds like I'm spinning tales. I assure you, I am not. As I said, I am willing to die for this so-called crime. Karina must not. Promise me you will do your best to rescue her."

George shook his head. "I cannot."

"Yes, you can. You must. Bad things are about to happen."

George licked his lips and looked away. *Let him be for a moment. Let him wrestle with his inner thoughts.* Useless to push him further at this point.

Finally, he steeled his gaze. "I cannot, in good conscience, go against my king. I have sworn an oath."

Tristan punched the door. His hand blossomed with pain, and he cursed again.

"But," George added, leaning in close to the bars, "I will go to Princess Reina. Things have not been right around here for a while. I think she will want to know about … all of this."

"We do not have a lot of time, George," Tristan bit out between clenched teeth. "Remember, Karina and I are both supposed to die. Tonight."

George bowed his head and then rushed off down the hall.

One way or another, their fates would be decided tonight.

The morning light did little to lift Karina's spirits. By the time Bormain knocked on the door, she was more than ready. She had hardly slept a wink the night before, too worried about Sam. She was not sure what she had done to offend Sabreen. Karina had tried to keep conversation friendly without sharing their desperate situation.

Sometime this morning, Sam would be here on his own, and they could talk more candidly then. Since Rashka was in the wash room, Karina opened the door for Bormain to usher in servants with food to break their fast.

"Bormain, I am fam—"

Not Bormain, rather the young priest from the night before. Yosef bowed. "My apologies, Your Majesty. Obviously, you were expecting your breakfast. I am sure it will be here shortly. I am meant to bring you a quick message."

"Yes?"

"Your friend Sam was a bit delayed, but he will be here shortly."

"Oh. Very well." Karina hid her disappointment, though something pushed against her mind, bubbling in a most unsettling way—something she could not define. When Yosef turned to leave, she suddenly felt the need to talk to him. "Yosef? Would you have time for a chat?"

He quirked an eyebrow but nodded. "Indeed, Your Majesty. I am at your service."

"Please, come in." She welcomed him inside the suite and guided him to the dining table. "Rashka will be out shortly, in case you are wondering."

Yosef nodded as he sat. "What do you need to discuss?"

Karina did not sit down. Anxious energy hummed through her body. Why would she talk to a priest? Something prodded her heart. She needed to share her story with him. "Do you know who I am, Yosef?"

"Of course. You are Queen Karina of Aletheia."

She nodded. "But do you know who else?" His blank expression told her he did not understand what she was trying to say. She sighed. "I am also Prophetess for the Creator."

Yosef's eyes widened and his face paled.

"An evil is infecting the Three Kingdoms. Already, villages and people are starting to see the effects of the evil. Even here in Soter."

Yosef straightened, then leaned forward. "Indeed. I have noticed certain changes and have wondered how we had wronged the Creator."

She would have to question him on those changes later. For now, she needed to continue. "The Creator has tasked me and my friends with retrieving the sacred armor from the temples."

"What?" He sat back in his chair, his jaw wide.

Karina inhaled deeply. "We have already retrieved the armor from the Temple of Aletheia. We received this"—she placed her hand on the Belt of Truth around her waist— "and the Shield of Faith. We came to Gundow to inquire about the location of the Soteran temple, but the king will not hear us out."

Just relating the story to Yosef made her blood boil. She plopped in a dining chair in a most ungraceful way. "And now he has also imprisoned my protector for protecting me. Our quest is looking more and more hopeless." She sighed. "Even so, I do not want to abandon my quest. I trust in the Creator, and I know he will see me through. I just cannot see that end right now. Does that make sense?"

"Indeed, Your Majesty. And I can certainly understand your frustration. Perhaps I can offer you a bit of hope."

Karina stared. Was it possible?

"I know where the Temple of Soter is."

"What?"

"Every priest does. We train there before we are stationed anywhere."

"You know where it is?"

He nodded.

Karina did not know whether to jump for joy, squeeze the man, or run in the other room to tell Rashka. Unfortunately, someone knocked on the door, so she did none of those things.

"That should be breakfast now." Karina grinned. "I hope you will join us."

"It would be my pleasure."

Rashka appeared from the washroom. "What is going on?"

"Yosef knows where the temple is, and breakfast is here." Karina waved her hand as she pulled opened the door. "It's about time …" She sighed.

Once again, breakfast was not at the door. No, it was Princess Reina—with Sam. And Sabreen.

Karina pursed her lips, trying not to scream. The princess had the graciousness to look guilty and shrugged. "Please, come in. The servants should be bringing in breakfast any minute."

Sabreen sauntered in, surveying the room. "I'm fine. Thanks."

Princess Reina mouthed an apology as she passed by. Karina grabbed Sam's arm. "The invitation was for you alone."

He glowered at her. "So we found out when we arrived this morning. Good thing Princess Reina was already out for a morning stroll and heard the commotion or we would not have been allowed in at all."

"Why would you think the invitation was for the both of you when Princess Reina specifically said you only?"

"Because I thought it only polite, seeing as Sabreen saved me."

Karina stepped back, but she did not let go of his arm. "Saved you? I thought she just happened upon you."

Sam pressed his lips into a thin line. She knew that look. He would not say anything more on the matter. She shook her head. He was being impossible. What kind of spell had Sabreen cast over him?

"Well, since we are all here …" She shut the door and turned to her friends—and Sabreen. "I hope you all are ready for breakfast, which should be on its way very soon. In the meantime, there are some important matters to—Yosef, where are you going?"

Everyone stared at the young man, who had risen from the table and was crossing the room. He stumbled over his words. "I apologize Queen Ka—that is, Your Majesty. I must be going."

"But I thought you were staying for breakfast? We need to talk more about the temple."

"Maybe some other time. I cannot now." He cast a furtive glance in Sabreen's direction. Was she why he had left so abruptly last night as well?

She crossed her arms. "Yosef, is there something you are not telling me?"

He turned his gaze to her, his eyes pleading. "Please, I will come back. But I must go now."

Princess Reina strolled over and put her hand on Yosef's shoulder. "Yosef, you are with friends. Please, tell us what ails you."

He wrung his hands as if he were not used to fretting in such a way and the very act bothered him as much as whatever caused his worry. He glanced at Sabreen again. "I do not know if I should."

This time, Sam must have caught the look because he moved in front of Sabreen and grasped her hand. His eyes narrowed at the priest.

"You are under my protection, Yosef. I very much want to hear what you have to say. Especially if it concerns the well-being of anyone in this room, including yourself." Princess Reina offered him a reassuring smile.

Yosef seemed distant for a minute, then cleared his throat. "I apologize for my behavior last night and just now. I have not been in such a situation before and am not quite sure how to handle this dilemma. For the protection of you all, I feel you must know. That woman"—he pointed at Sabreen—"is a witch and so is her aunt. They are members of the Tri-Goddess coven. A coven which we have been trying to rid the city of for some years." He glared at Sabreen. "A coven that has caused much heartache for this kingdom."

Sabreen's face contorted with hatred. "You do not know what you are talking about," she roared. "How dare you disparage my name or the name of my aunt."

Yosef ignored her and faced Karina and Reina. "The sign above their door was a circle with three dots. That is the crest of the coven and is hung above their safe houses around town, usually in back alleys like the home we were in last night."

What he said made sense. And from the look on Sam's face—shock, not surprise—told Karina the words were true as well.

"Thank you, Yosef, for your honesty." Reina heaved a sigh. "He is right about the Tri-Goddess coven. They have been making trouble around here since before my father was king. When he took the throne, he organized a witch-hunt and had almost eradicated the coven. More recently, we discovered they are working underground."

All eyes pivoted back to Sabreen, whose face had flushed red. She trembled where she stood. Before she could speak, Sam raised his hand to stop her. Karina could not remember seeing Sam so angry … at least not since the time one of the guards made inappropriate comments to her after the Winter Ball a couple of years ago.

Sam clenched his jaw. "I do not care who or what you think she is. Sabreen has been nothing but kind and respectful in the time I have known her. She saved my life more than once. She may not believe the same things we do, but she can still be trusted."

Karina could get angry too. In fact, she kind of was. "But—"

"No, Karina. No buts. Do you remember how I accepted Tristan because of what you said, even though he was the bounty hunter who kidnapped you?"

Reina gasped, covering her mouth with her hand.

Karina blew a long full breath. Sam had a point. Other than a few grumblings, he had followed her lead when it came to Tristan, although he had every right not to trust him. She inhaled slowly, casting a sidelong glance at Reina, who looked as uneasy as Yosef. But Sam had been a lifelong friend. He deserved her trust. "You are right. Of course. My apologies, Sabreen, for our behavior." She turned to Reina.

Reina's lips twisted to the side before she cleared her throat. "Of course. You are most welcome here. Any friend of Sam's …"

Yosef shook his head. "I do not know that I can go along with this. The Head Priest would not be happy if he found we were associating with a witch."

"A witch that has done nothing but good since I met her. She even—"

"Let him think what he wants." Sabreen sneered. "I've spent years trying to change the opinions of these close-minded men. They still refuse to see the good I have done. What I have sacrificed for the good of …" Sabreen's sobs strangled the rest of her words.

Sam put his arm around her shoulder and pulled her close. Karina was not buying the act, but she could not say so in front of Sam right now. She did not know what kind of game this girl was playing, but if she hurt Sam in the process, Karina would not hesitate to end her. She paused. Where had that outburst come from?

"We have more important things at hand right now." Rashka pushed her way into the crowd. "Tonight, King Rufus plans to have Tristan and Karina executed."

"What?" Sam let go of Sabreen and crossed the room to Karina's side. "And you waited until now to tell me? Why didn't you tell me last night?"

Karina paused. Last night, she had been happy Sam was alive. How could she mar that happiness to share their personal struggles with total strangers?

Reina clapped her hands. "Tonight is the ball. Afterward, the king plans to murder the queen and her protector. But we are going to save them before that happens."

Sam grabbed her hand and brought it to his chest. "How?"

CHAPTER TWENTY-SEVEN

Yosef raced to the palace kitchens. He only had so much time before Queen Karina and her friends attempted to escape the palace tonight. He needed to gather food and supplies—and plenty of it. The trip to the Temple of Soter would be at least two days, if not more.

He skidded to a stop at the large set of doors to the main kitchen, and his jaw dropped. A flurry of activity gave the room a chaotic spin. Of course. With the ball tonight, every cook and apprentice was probably working today. He blew out a breath. He would find no help or provisions here. He would have to take the coin Princess Reina had given him and purchase food and supplies in town—if there was anything left out there.

He returned to his own bed chambers in the servant's wing. Grabbing a bag from his wardrobe, he filled it with clothes and other items, including some healing supplies he kept on hand. Although he was a priest scribe and a messenger, he had still taken time to train in the healing arts. With one last check to ensure he had everything, he stepped out and closed the door behind him.

"Yosef, I am glad I found you." Elder Thomas strode down the hall with all the confidence of the king, a wide smile on his face.

"I am sorry, sir, but I am in a hurry."

"You have not been at the temple the last couple of days."

He studied the ground, unwilling to meet his mentor's eyes. Their once-easy relationship had suffered in the last couple of weeks since Queen Karina had arrived in Gundow. Perhaps even before then. Several months ago, he would have confessed everything to Elder Thomas, no prodding needed. Not true now. "Queen Karina and Princess Reina have kept me busy with personal tasks."

"Do I need to speak with Princess Reina about your proper duties?"

His eyes bulged a little. "No, sir."

"So, will I see you at the temple tomorrow?"

He did not want to answer. Part of him knew the outcome of this conversation without letting it run its course. He scuffed a toe over the smooth stone floor. "With respect, sir, I need to take my leave for a while."

Elder Thomas's face flushed a deep purple as he leaned forward "What?"

"I need to …" What excuse could he use? He could not reveal his plans to lead Queen Karina and her friends to the Temple of Soter. The head priest would have him thrown in the dungeons—especially after their previous conversations. "I am seeking to commune with the Creator in the Heart. So much is happening here in Gundow, and I fear there is more horror to come."

Elder Thomas crossed his arms. "I do not give you permission to leave, Yosef."

"I am sorry, sir. I am not asking for permission."

"If you leave, you are banished from the temple. You will no longer be a priest."

Yosef bit back a sharp retort and instead breathed deep through his nose. "With respect again, sir, you do not have the authority to strip me of my priest title. However, I acknowledge I will be giving up my position here in Gundow."

In truth, the thought of not having a home when he accomplished his task terrified Yosef. For his entire life, he had always been secure in the knowledge he had a plan for what was coming next. He strived his best to educate himself growing up, knew from an early age he would be a priest in Gundow. What would he do upon his return?

Perhaps he would not come back. Perhaps he would find a position at the Temple of Soter. Maybe the Creator had a different plan altogether. His stomach knotted at his unknown future.

Elder Thomas grunted. "I am disappointed, Yosef. I always thought you would succeed me as Head Priest."

"I am not the one who will not let me return." He looked Elder Thomas straight in the eye. "But I do not bear you ill will. I pray when this is all over the temples of Gundow will rise to glorify the Creator as they have always done."

His mentor sputtered, but, before he could respond, Yosef pushed past him and hurried down the hall. He still had supplies to purchase before he could make his way out of the city.

Karina emerged from her bedchamber in a most uncomfortable ball gown made up of layers of white and gold lace that shimmered when she moved. Of course, the gown was made more uncomfortable by the leather pants she wore under her petticoats. Once they rescued Tristan and were beyond the palace walls, she would shed the confining dress.

A whistle greeted her as she entered the sitting room. Sam rose to escort her. "You look beautiful, Karina."

"Thank you. I have not had an occasion to dress so formally since the coronation. I feel rather awkward."

He leaned his head in toward her. "Well, you do not come off that way."

She giggled as the blush spread from her cheeks to her neck, but she caught Sabreen's glare and sobered. "Reina will be along shortly to escort me to the ball."

"What did the king say about Rashka being too ill to attend?"

"Reina said he seemed all too ready to accept her excuse. She figures he did not mind because there would still be guards outside the doors."

Sam ran his hand through his messy hair in his true stressed-out manner.

"Are you sure you are up for this?" She eyed Sabreen. "Both of you?"

"Indeed, we are." Sam smiled. "Don't let my nerves deceive you, Your Majesty. We are at your service."

Sabreen rolled her eyes but nodded to Karina.

When a knock sounded at the door, Karina shot Sam a bright smile. "I guess it is time."

Sam moved his lips as if he wanted to speak. Karina hesitated, ready to listen. Instead, he only nodded. Her shoulders fell, but she crossed the room to answer the door.

Princess Reina looked resplendent in a gold, off-the-shoulder gown with white pearls sewn across the top. The bodice fit her form well, and the skirt was sufficiently poufy. Even with her gold-painted skin, her smile made her shine the most.

Karina greeted her with the Blessing of Three Kisses. "On the forehead for wisdom, and on each cheek for joy and love," she added with a smile.

Tears shown in Reina's eyes. "If I do not get a chance to tell you after tonight, I am so glad I got to see you again. Even more so, I am glad Tristan found you. It seems you two bring out the best in each other."

Karina blushed again. Not much had changed between her and Tristan when it came to romance—not enough time to let her feelings blossom. And then they were separated. Maybe when this was all over ... "I am blessed to call you friend once again. Thank you for everything."

Reina squeezed her hands. "We had better get going." She nodded to Rashka, Sam, and Sabreen. "May the Creator's strength go with you all. Be brave."

They all bowed to her and offered their farewells.

Out in the hall, Princess Reina instructed the guards to stay at the door as Rashka was still in the room. "I will ensure the queen gets to the ballroom."

"But, Your Majesty—"

Reina pierced the protesting guard with her authoritative glare.

Karina stifled a giggle as they made their way down the hall and toward the stairs. "It must irritate them not to argue sometimes, don't you think?"

Reina grinned. "I would imagine so. Then again, watching them simmer is one of the things that makes being a princess so fun."

They lapsed into silence, both of them nervous. Reina led her in the general direction of the ballroom, though that was not their destination.

"Do you remember what you do once you reach the tunnel?"

Karina nodded. "I will follow the tunnel until I come to the third intersection. From there, I go right to the first intersection, and then go left. That will lead me to a ladder that will bring me up outside of the city walls. At the bottom will be a bag with a shirt, boots, and some provisions. I am to change and then make my way to the cottage we discussed and wait for Rashka and Sam to arrive with Tristan."

"Very good." Reina frowned. "I wish I could go with you. It would be so grand to go on such an adventure."

"Trust me. It is not as glorious as it sounds."

Reina squeezed her shoulder. "You will make it through this. And you will save the world."

Or watch it fall into chaos when the ancient evil infects every last person. She shook away the useless thoughts. Reina took her to a different staircase which led into the bowels of the palace. "This is where I leave you." She handed her a torch and a key. "At the bottom of the staircase, turn right. You will find the barred gate to the tunnel at the end of the hall."

Karina nodded, her heart racing. The time had come. She swallowed, not knowing what to say.

"May the Creator's might go with you, Queen Karina."

Karina hugged her friend. "And with you, dear Reina."

With a deep breath and a last look at the princess, Karina held the torch high and began her descent. A distinct chill reached up to wrap around her as the staircase spiraled downward. She shivered despite herself. When she stepped off the last stair, the hall was dark. No lights. No sounds. Karina could hear the unevenness of her breathing. *Creator, guide my steps.*

She swerved right and used the torchlight to guide her through the surprisingly wide hallway. Her footsteps echoed in the darkness, louder in her own ears. At last, she reached the tunnel with the locked iron gate. She hung the torch on a nearby sconce and then held up the key.

"Well, well, well. What have we here? A mouse trying to escape the cat?" That all-too-familiar voice had chastised her for years.

She spun around to face Anaya. "What are you doing down here?"

Anaya was by herself. Somehow a crimson glow radiated around her, like she was producing her own light. An odd sight. Karina stepped back until her foot bumped the gate.

The former queen held her hands out. "No one is supposed to be down here. I saw a light in the staircase and came down to inspect."

"You did not send the guards?"

She wrinkled her nose. "Well, I figured I knew who the pesky sneak might be. No need to pester the worthless guards."

"What do you want, Anaya?"

"Do not get sassy with me, little miss. You are getting too full of yourself if you ask me. Do not forget who raised you."

Karina pushed away from the gate. "Excuse me? I believe you mean I should not forget who tried to kill me. Who killed my uncle. Who drove my kingdom into the ground not long after his death. Because, trust me, I have not forgotten. I only thought you were dead."

"Pity things do not always work out as we hope." Anaya sneered, twirling something in her hands. A silver-handled dagger with a large ruby in the center of the hilt. Karina gasped and Anaya chuckled. "And you thought you could defeat me. You should have aligned yourself with Faramos. At least then you would have your life."

Karina stuck out her chin. "I would never align myself with such filth. And the Creator will see his legacy brought to ruin. Mark my words."

Anaya threw her head back and cackled. "My child, you are so naïve. Faramos has won, and you cannot seem to fathom his victory. He already has a hold on this kingdom. Yours is in disarray, and he will soon see Aletheia fall under his flag."

"Over my dead body."

"Well, that *is* the plan." Her upheld dagger glinted in the light of the torch. "Time to end this."

Anaya lunged at Karina, but she ducked out of the way. Anaya swung the dagger, but Karina twisted Anaya's arm and kicked her knee. She let out a howl. Still clasping her dagger, she brought herself to her full height.

With a screech, she lunged again. This time when Karina sidestepped Anaya's movements, she changed her trajectory and shoved the dagger toward Karina's stomach.

Karina caught the blade between her hands. Despite the bite in her palms, they were all that kept the dagger from plunging into her body. She prayed for the Creator's help. When the visions of Anaya's past revisited, Karina quickly reflected them into Anaya's mind.

The woman froze, her face contorting in horror. She let go of the blade, placing her hands on either side of her head. "What is this?"

Karina held the dagger in her hand and looked down at Anaya. This battle needed to end, as the former queen had said. Could she take a life? Like this? Anaya squirmed and ranted at the memories flooding her mind.

Heavy footsteps echoed down the staircase. Soldiers. Had they heard the struggle or had Anaya somehow signaled them to come?

Karina dropped the dagger. She had to get out of here. She fished around for the key. There … near the edge of the wall. Hurry! She snatched it up, her breath coming in ragged gasps. Fear raced along her spine, grating her nerves.

She fumbled with the lock as the footsteps grew louder, closer, heavier. "Oh, come on." Forcing the key inside, she twisted hard, and the door swung open.

Violent hands grabbed her by the shoulders and yanked her backward. Karina stumbled several steps before falling on her rear. She heard the dress rip as she skidded to a stop. Anaya stood over her, a victorious grin on her face.

In the next moment, guards crashed into the hall behind them.

"Arrest her," Anaya screamed. "She tried to kill me! Revenge for her lover, I would guess." She straightened her dress, smoothing the skirts.

Karina glowered at her aunt as the guards picked her up. "You will not get away with this, Anaya."

She leaned in close to Karina's ear. "I already have. And you better believe, I will be sitting on Aletheia's throne before the next full moon. And anyone who has ever helped you had better beg for my mercy. And even then …"

Karina's stomach roiled. The woman was pure evil.

Anaya waved her away. "Take her to the ballroom. I am sure the king would much like to hear of tonight's events."

Rashka waited until the guards had passed before waving Sam and Sabreen forward. She had already disabled her own guards and tied them up in the sitting room, so they were making their way to the staircase leading to the dungeon. She figured the best place to intercept and extract Tristan was at the bottom of that stairs. Then they could make their way out the front under the guise of guards leading a peasant off palace grounds.

Sam slipped past Rashka, his hand in Sabreen's, pulling her along behind him. She stayed close to his back. Wary, but not afraid. The little witch was quite the curious conundrum. On one hand, the Creator warned against the motivations of a witch as they did not align with the Creator. For now, though, she appeared to be on their side. And Sam seemed to truly care for her. Their relationship would never work, but at least Sabreen took his mind off Karina—someone unattainable for Sam.

Rashka crept along behind them, keeping her eyes and ears alert for the slightest sounds. Most of the people had already gathered for the ball. Reina had been tasked with ensuring the king was distracted enough for the evening and not searching for Karina during the festivities. Hopefully, she had enough excuses stored up to last a couple of hours.

Once they made it to the staircase, Rashka motioned for them to stay behind her and for Sam to be the rear lookout. They descended the stairs quickly and without incident. When they stepped into the open landing at the bottom of the stairs, two soldiers stood on the walls to the left and right. Not in the plan.

"Hey!" one of them shouted, pulling his sword.

The other, though startled, jumped to the ready.

Rashka's bow would do little good down here. Too cramped. She slipped a dagger from her belt. "You do not want to—" She stopped when Sabreen rushed past her. "Wait!" The woman was going to get herself killed.

She stopped out of reach of any blade and lifted her hand. With a giggle, she blew something from her hand into the face of the two guards. They coughed and sputtered, then slumped to the ground, snoring softly. Sabreen spun around and clapped her hands together, dispelling whatever was left. "Sleeping dust!"

Rashka shook her head. Not what she would have chosen, but it worked. "Thank you, Sabreen."

"You're welcome," she chimed. A little too cheery for a secret mission.

"What do we do now?" Sam asked as he relieved the guards of their weapons.

"If we work quickly, we can remove their armor and put it on before the guards bring Tristan out. We can move more stealthily that way."

"What about Sabreen?"

Rashka acknowledged the woman with a nod. "There is nowhere for her to hide right now. She will have to stand behind you once we are ready."

"Fine. Let's do this."

CHAPTER TWENTY-EIGHT

Karina tried not to tremble as the guards led her into the grand ballroom, a display of radiance and splendor. Candlelight glittered off the gold and marble everywhere. In contrast, her dress was torn and dirty from being thrown around on the ground. She did not even want to think about the mess her hair must be. She was anything but a queen in this moment. Tears of shame and fear crowded her eyes, blurring the crowd.

The gaiety of the night seemed to mock her, streams of music and melodious laughter like a burr. One by one, the nobles stopped when they saw her shuffling through the crowd. Small gasps and whispers began to float through the room. At some point the music stilled, and the room fell silent.

She refused to be crushed by this turn of events. The Creator had not left her before, he would not leave her now. She pulled her shoulders back and jutted out her chin. She would not let these people see her shrink away from what was to come. She was the Prophetess and a queen.

Off to her right, Reina pushed her way through the crowd, her face contorted with horror. Karina avoided her stare. Reina had tried so hard to help her, and Karina would not let her friend take the fall for this. Shaking her head, Karina hoped Reina discerned the meaning.

King Rufus sat atop his throne, a golden goblet in his right hand, his free arm snaked around Anaya's thin waist. Despite their fight not too long ago, the evil enchantress looked as severe and perfect as always. Instead of her normal black attire, she had changed into a gold gown that shimmered and shone however she moved. The whole thing made Karina sick.

When the king spotted her, his face darkened. He looked up at Anaya, who raised an eyebrow, and then glowered. "What is the meaning of this?"

One of the guards stepped forward and bowed. "Excuse me, Your Majesty. We were instructed by Lady Anaya to bring the prisoner, Queen Karina, before you immediately."

The king rose from his throne and stepped down from the dais. "Was it not good enough that I welcomed you into my home? You and your lover had to attack my guests?"

Karina also arched an eyebrow. "Welcomed?" She laughed. "I have been anything but welcomed since I arrived. Your court has lost the charm I remember from my youth, Your Majesty."

"Does your opinion of my court excuse your behavior? Why in the name of the Creator would you attack Lady Anaya?"

"I would choose words to defend myself if they would not fall on deaf ears, sire."

"Watch your words, Queen Karina. What do you mean?" he growled as he moved uncomfortably close.

"It means no matter what I say, you will not hear me. Lady Anaya obviously has your ear and your friendship. What I say does not matter."

For some odd reason, the king actually paused as if stunned. He regained his composure quickly. "What is it you want, Queen Karina?"

"I have told you. The only thing I want is my protector and directions to the Temple of Soter. With those, I can be on my way and out of your hair."

"Or I could have you executed and be done with you."

A collective gasp rose from the crowd.

"Father!" Princess Reina stepped forward. "What right do you have to treat a fellow monarch so? She has done nothing to deserve this."

"Both she and her lover have attempted to kill Lady Anaya!" the king roared.

Reina stepped a little closer. "Does that sound like the Karina you remember?"

"People change as they grow older, my child."

"Indeed, they do. And you most of all." Reina's eyes welled with tears. "You are not the man who raised me."

The king marched over to Reina, his arms quivering with anger, but she refused to back down. He glared down at her. "You would do well to remember your place, daughter. Or you could very well spend a few nights in the dungeon yourself."

"That is not necessary." Karina squared her shoulders. When Reina's face flushed crimson, Karina shook her head again. "Let us go. We will leave, and we will not return. Lady Anaya will have your protection for whatever perceived slight we have done."

"I will not let you go." The king waved his hands. "Take her away. Tell the captain there is a change of plans and to leave both of them in the dungeons tonight. They can be in the same cell for all I care. Let them enjoy their last few days together."

The guard nodded.

Karina swallowed what little pride she had. "Please, sire, you cannot do this. The Creator tasked me with defeating the ancient evil before it destroys our world. Do not let our kingdoms fall into chaos and ruin on the words of an enchantress." She glanced pointedly at Anaya.

The king chuckled. "My, you really will say anything to get your way. Lady Anaya is right. You manipulated your way into King Pistis's good graces. Why else would he have allowed the daughter of the traitor back into the royal house?" He looked down his nose at her. "Take her from my sight. I do not want to see her again until the day she dies."

Gasps rose from the crowd. Out of the corner of her eyes, Karina was sure she spied a few tears. These people knew their king had taken a turn for the worst, but they had no idea how to right the wrong. Just like Reina, whose tears streamed down her cheeks like rain on a glass pane. With one glance back, Karina caught Lady Anya's sardonic grin.

Sam stood as still as he possibly could. But with Sabreen tucked so close to him, his body tingled with feelings he had only experienced a couple of times when he was near Karina. The sensations were fascinating. He wanted to kiss her. No. That would earn a stern glare from Rashka, who had not moved a muscle since they had taken up their positions.

Instead, he surveyed the small landing again. While it resembled a square room with stairs leading in on one side and a hallway leading out the other, there was no furniture or adornments. Nothing of note.

"I'm glad we're still here together," Sabreen whispered in his ear. "This is exciting. I wouldn't want to share this adventure with anyone but you."

He couldn't help the grin tugging at his lips. "I feel the same way."

"When we get out of here …" she went on to whisper all the things she wanted to do with him. He groaned. She was going to be the end of him.

"*Psst.* Pay attention." Ah, he'd earned the stern glare.

Footsteps and the clank of armor resounded down the hall as the guards brought Tristan up from the dungeon. Rashka nodded to him, and they readied their swords.

"Let me use my sleeping dust first," Sabreen whispered. "You may not need your swords at all. Put them away."

Sam looked at Rashka. She regarded Sabreen with a wary expression but then agreed. They sheathed their swords and stood still as guards came through the hallway entrance.

One man led a squad of six guards, two in front, two behind, and one on either side of Tristan. From the bruises and cuts on his face and arms, Tristan had been beaten—and recently. Sam fought the urge to swing at the nearest guard.

"What is going on here?" the guard in front barked. Must be the captain.

"Nothing, sir," Sam said. They had agreed he should speak because they were not aware if King Rufus allowed any females in his guard.

"Who are those two men off to the side?" The captain regarded them, his features hardening. "And who is this woman?"

Sabreen stepped out from behind Sam, a sweet smile on our face. "I am a witch of the Tri-Goddess Coven."

The man's face turned ashen.

Sabreen blew sleeping dust in his face with enough force the particles reached the two guards behind him. The captain hit the floor immediately, while the other two bent over in a fit of coughs. Sabreen moved in closer to blow more dust.

Before Sam could move, Rashka had incapacitated the rear guards. Sam pulled his sword and lunged for the middle guard on his side. The guard stepped back, but Tristan shoved a shoulder into him, pushing the man forward. The guard cried out as he fell into Sam's blade. Sam pulled the sword as the man sunk to the ground.

Sabreen had put the front guards and the last middle guard to sleep with her magic dust. She placed the pouch back on her belt and shot a victorious grin his way.

"Sam! Rashka! I have never been so glad to see two people in my entire life." Tristan sagged against the wall, blowing out quick breaths.

Sam chuckled. "I'll be sure to tell Karina you said that."

"Karina!" Tristan's eyes widened. "Have you seen her? Is she safe?"

Rashka nodded. "If everything has gone according to plan, she is outside the city walls by now, waiting for us."

"Then we need to get going."

Sam held out his hand. "First, you need to change."

With help, Tristan quickly changed into one of the guard uniforms while they filled him in on the plan to pose as guards escorting the witch out of the palace. Sam noticed the curl of Tristan's lip when they mentioned Sabreen was a witch. At least he had the decency to keep his comments to himself.

Once Tristan was ready, they arranged themselves with Rashka in the front and Sam and Tristan on either side of Sabreen. They made their way up the stairs and down the hall with no issues—most of the nobles and attendants in the palace were still attending the festivities.

As they neared the grand hall, voices floated into the corridor. From somewhere beyond, a group of people approached. A loud group. Well, with one loud—familiar—voice. Karina!

"You cannot do this to a queen!"

Sam's muscles tightened. As he reached for his sword, Tristan held out his arm, shaking his head as a warning. Sam gritted his teeth, knowing his friend was right. No use giving up their disguises until necessary. They exited the corridor into the grand hall in silence.

Crossing the large room, guards surrounded Karina as she struggled against the grip of two of the men, her face red with anger and her gown in disarray.

"Please. The Creator has sent me on a quest. It's life or death," she pleaded. In the next moment, her gaze fell on their crew. Her eyes widened when she saw Sabreen, but she did not say anything. Likely she did not want to draw attention to the connection between them, not wanting to put Sabreen in any more danger.

Rashka stepped forward. "Halt."

The guards stopped, the ones in front eying her. "Who are you?" he asked.

"Where do you think you are taking Queen Karina?"

The large guard sniffed. "Not that it's any of your business, but the king wants her thrown in the cell with her lover until he decides how she's going to die."

How had she been discovered? Sam clenched his jaw, resisting the urge to give away his ruse. This wasn't good. They had to get her out of danger.

The guard jerked his head toward Sabreen. "What are you doing with this one?"

Rashka squared her shoulders. "Found her wandering the palace. She must have sneaked in with the crowds. We're escorting her beyond the palace walls."

"Indeed." He sniffed again, then turned to his guards. "Let's go."

"Wait." Although Rashka radiated a sense of authority, Sam could tell she was unsure how to keep them from taking Karina to the dungeons. There were four guards and four of them, plus Karina. Surely, they could take them out. Might even avoid killing anyone if Sabreen used her dust.

A faint growl strained from Tristan's throat. Rashka nodded ever so slightly. "I cannot let you do that."

The guard's eyes narrowed. "Can't let me do what?"

"Take the queen to the dungeon."

"Why not?" He crossed his arms instead of going for his sword. Big mistake.

"Because, as Prophetess of the Creator, she is my charge." Rashka drew the bow from her back. Before anyone knew what was happening, she had sent an arrow flying right into the big guard's shoulder.

A flurry of movement broke forth. Guards drew their swords, as did Sam and Tristan. The clank of metal against metal echoed through the massive hall. Sabreen pulled Karina to the side, then used her sleeping dust on one of the guards.

Sam engaged with his target—a man equal to him in size and strength. He was good, but Sam was quicker. In a few swift moves, Sam swept the man's legs out from under him and then plunged his sword into the man's side.

With all the guards down, Karina and Tristan had a tearful reunion. Well, tears on Karina's part anyway. Then she rushed over, and Sam swept her up in a bear hug. Praise the Creator, she was safe.

"We must go." Rashka looped her bow back over her shoulder. "More guards will be here any moment."

Sam grabbed Sabreen's hand as they followed Rashka out the front doors.

CHAPTER TWENTY-NINE

Tristan rushed out of the palace gates, left open this evening because of the ball. While they had hurried their pace down the palace paths, they slowed outside the walls as they wandered through the streets of Gundow. No sense drawing more attention to themselves by running than they already were by being out tonight.

"We should go to my Aunt Claire's and regroup," Sabreen whispered loudly.

Rashka shook her head. "No, we need to get out of Gundow now."

"But we need resources."

Tristan ran a hand over his face. "Rashka is right. At this point, the most important priority is getting out of the city. The king will likely stop at nothing to get us back."

With her hand snuggly tucked inside his, Karina smiled up at him and then nodded to Sabreen. "Besides, Yosef will have plenty of provisions for the trip at the cottage where we are supposed to meet."

"We will not reach the main gate for a while, even at this time of night. How do you expect to get out now that our covers are blown?" Sam asked.

"I think I can help you."

They all spun to the approaching stranger. Tristan huffed a sigh of relief. Princess Reina sat atop Dom, leading servants with horses up the cobblestone road. He had not been this happy to see the princess since they were young teenagers.

He shook his head. "Well, well, well ..."

With his help, Reina slid down from Dom. "A thank you would suffice."

"How did you get away?" Karina asked.

Reina shrugged. "After my father sent you away, I retired to my room. Or that is what I told him after I said I would never speak to him again. Once in my room, I had my handmaid send for the stable boys to gather horses and provisions. I had hoped to meet you at the cottage."

"Our plans didn't quite go as planned," Sam said.

"Apparently. For now, here are horses so we may get out of Gundow quickly."

Tristan froze. "We?"

"I am coming with you."

"No. You cannot." Karina pushed to Reina's side.

"You need my help to get out of Gundow."

Of all the times for her to decide to be a hero. The last thing Tristan needed was two royals to protect. He shook his head. "We need you here. Your people need you here. With the king falling to darkness—"

"Exactly!" Reina grabbed his arm. "I am no longer safe here. And if my father finds out I aided your escape, he will have my head."

She was probably right. Tristan wanted to say yes—but when he looked at Karina, he knew that was not the plan.

Karina pulled Reina's hand from his arm. "Reina, in the short time we have been your guests, you have once again become a dear friend. I do not want to see anything happen to you. This quest is more dangerous than staying here, especially for you. The king may not be long for this world. And if that is the case, your people will need you here to lead them. I should know." She gave Reina a pointed look. Reina's face showed her disappointment, but she nodded. Karina continued, "In all likelihood, we will need your help for the final battle. We may need reinforcements even sooner. You need to be here to orchestrate these things."

With a deep breath and teary eyes, Reina nodded again. "I know in my heart you are speaking truth. But I do not want to send you off alone."

Karina's eyes shone with tears as well. Tristan swallowed the lump growing in his throat. He would not turn sentimental. This is why he avoided emotional farewells.

Karina smiled. "I am not alone. I have these amazing friends here who have protected me from the beginning." She shot a sly look in Tristan's direction, and his lips twitched. "Well, mostly. More importantly, I have the blessing of the Creator. He will not let his Chosen One be waylaid. He will see my quest to completion. Of that I am sure."

Rashka swept in. "We need to go. Something is happening within the palace walls."

Tristan helped Karina swing up on Dom—why she got his horse, he still did not understand. So what if they could talk to each other. To his surprise, though, an even larger white stallion stood behind Dom. He quirked a brow at Reina.

She grinned. "Roan was to be a gift for Father at his birthday celebration next week. However, I think you have need of this magnificent beast more than he."

With a nod to his old friend, he mounted the beautiful stallion. "Roan," he murmured, patting the horse's neck.

Once everyone was ready, they set forth toward the gate at a brisk pace. He and Karina led the way atop their stallions. What a pair they made. Was this an image of how they might be after they returned to Aletheia?

He startled. Why was he thinking of these things? He had not been the type to be tied down to any one place since his mother died. And here he was thinking of the future—and a future with a queen no less. What was happening to him?

"If you do not watch where you are going, I fear you will kill that horse before we make it to the temple."

"What?" Tristan shook himself from his thoughts and turned to a grinning Karina. Her eyes twinkled in the moonlight. "I suppose I should pay attention."

"What thoughts are rolling around in that head of yours?"

What to tell her without scaring her away? She cared for him, but would she be willing to share a life with him? "Just wondering what will happen once we complete the quest and you save the world."

She forced a laugh. "I am not sure I will survive this quest to have a future."

He gazed at her. "I do not think death will be your fate. You are destined to rule Aletheia as a strong queen worthy of King Pistis's legacy."

Tears reformed at the corners of her eyes as she meekly nodded. They fell back into a comfortable silence and easily made their way out of the main gate.

Once beyond the outer walls, Rashka took the lead. Apparently, they were headed for a cottage not far off the main road where they would meet up with someone who would take them to the temple.

A quick dash through the woods, and they indeed came to a small white cottage with a thatch roof. The woods around them were dark and quiet, a contrast to the warm light shining through the windows. Still,

Tristan's senses were on alert as they dismounted and tied their horses to nearby trees.

"Wait here." Rashka took her bow in hand. "Let me make sure it is safe."

Tristan hung back, scanning the woods for any sign of trouble. But all was quiet. They had not been followed.

Karina appeared at his side. "You should let Rashka heal your wounds before we set off on the next journey."

"I am fine."

"Travel would be easier if you would let her."

"I can help." Sabreen sauntered up with Sam, holding a pouch. "I am a healer too."

"Indeed." Sam rubbed the back of his neck. "She had to save my skin a couple of times."

"Does she heal like Rashka?" Karina's eyes were wide.

He shook his head. "No, her magic doesn't work exactly the same."

Tristan crossed his arms and sized up Sabreen. She looked harmless enough, although Sam had called her a witch at one point. Tristan did not know much about witches except sage advice warned to avoid them. "How exactly does this magic work?"

"My healing magic comes more from the earth than from the Creator."

"So, you are a practiced healer like I am?" Karina asked.

"No." Sabreen sighed. "I mean, I can use herbs and plants and such like trained healers, but I also use the magic of the earth … the power of life and water and air."

Karina stared hard at the girl. Tristan could not be certain what she was thinking, and he was more puzzled by Sabreen's reply. "I think I will let Rashka assess the injury, but thank you for your offer."

Sabreen shrugged. "Suit yourself. I only wanted to help." She tugged on Sam's hand, and they wandered off together.

Rashka reappeared from inside the house with a young priest at her side. "It is safe. And Yosef has prepared dinner."

So this was the priest who would lead them to the temple. Tristan sized him up. He did not look like much of a warrior, but a priest would not. Hopefully, they would avoid resistance on their journey.

Everyone crammed into the small cottage—too small for them all to fit comfortably—where the aroma of meats rubbed with herbs and roasting vegetables filled the air along with the tang of sweet berries. They piled their plates with food from the table in the middle of the room, sitting wherever they could find a chair or spot on the floor.

"Yosef, this is delicious!" Karina crooned, and others echoed the sentiment.

He blushed and bowed his head. "It is my honor. We have a long journey ahead of us. Who knows when the next full meal will come?" He waved his hands. "So, eat up!"

The group ate and chatted, the sense of relief to be out of the palace palpable in the conversation and smiles. When the group atmosphere became too much for him, Tristan excused himself to check on the horses and secure the perimeter.

He stepped out of the cottage and breathed in the night air. The hour was late, and they all needed to seek their dreams so they could get on the road at dawn. Unfortunately, the cottage would not hold them all. Karina should stay inside to get some real rest. He did not mind sleeping out here, as he imagined Rashka and Sam would not either. Better to keep an eye on the surrounding woods. He checked on the horses and did a quick sweep around the house. Everything was quiet.

"Good evening, brother."

Tristan startled at Faramos's voice. He surveyed the clearing, the cottage … where had the voice come from?

"Check the tree line."

He scanned the trees and found his brother standing beneath a tall oak. Unsheathing his sword, he raced to the edge of the clearing, only to discover the image was another mirage. He would not have the satisfaction of killing Faramos tonight.

"What do you want, Faramos?"

"Just checking in." He grinned. His dark hair swished around as he moved, the vision incorporeal on Tristan's end. "I hear you escaped King Rufus's palace. You must be headed to the Temple of Soter."

Tristan crossed his arms. "What do you want?" He emphasized every word.

"Want?" His brother threw his hands out to his side. "To end the fighting, of course. I want nothing but peace in the Three Kingdoms."

"Your idea of peace comes at too steep of a price. You unleashed evil on this world."

"Sometimes it takes extreme measures to make people see what is good for them."

Tristan shook his head. "No, Faramos. People like you bully others into following them, causing strife and hatred in this world."

Faramos chuckled as he paced back and forth. "Your narrow view of the way things are in the Three Kingdoms shocks me, Tristan. You, the shining star of the underworld, cannot understand the measures needed to bring peace."

"Indeed. My time in your service taught me your way does not breed honest loyalty. Rather, your methods create fear—a fear that keeps the heart longing for something more."

Faramos considered this before the smirk returned to his face. "Unless you beat that fear into submission, and they lose all hope. Then you build them up with hearts for no one but you."

Tristan suddenly felt a deep sadness for his brother. Evil had twisted his mind to such an extent he no longer understood love or happiness. Hope? What did a man without hope have to strive for? To hang on to? In his own darkest hours, hope is what Tristan clung to—he would one day see his family avenged.

Shouts reached his ears—fighting inside. Had someone sneaked in while he was talking to Faramos? He turned.

"Beware, brother. I have already sent my people after you."

Tristan stopped and looked back over his shoulder. "Let them come. You will not stop us." Refusing to waste another moment with his sorry excuse for family, he rushed to the front of the cottage and threw open the door.

Karina stood in the middle of the room, hands on her hips, her face a scary shade of crimson. Only inches from her, Sabreen clenched her fists. "I do not have to explain myself to you, Your *Majesty.*"

Tristan cringed at Sabreen's blatant disrespect.

Karina's sigh seemed hinged with determination. "If you intend to stay on this quest, you will. As Prophetess, it is—"

"Oh, get off your high horse, Karina. You may well be the Creator's chosen or whatever, but you are not in charge of me. Nor does your so-called position give you the right to dive into my personal life … to pass judgment on stuff you know nothing about."

Everyone else watched from the sides, mouths open, eyes wide. Even Rashka. Tristan glared at her. When she finally noticed, he shook his head. He stepped between the two women. "What is going on here?"

Karina crossed her arms. "I asked her about the Tri-Goddess coven and her involvement with them."

"The what?"

Yosef stepped forward. "The Tri-Goddess coven is a group of witches who set about to overthrow the kingdom some years ago. When they failed, they began to cause other problems within Gundow. The king had most of them executed. Only a few survived."

Sabreen glared at him. "Soter's government is corrupted. The king no longer cares for his people. They are starving, they are weak, and he keeps filling his coffers."

Yosef clenched his jaw. "His choices do not excuse the likes of the plagues and massacres that have been instigated by the Tri-Goddesses."

"I was not born when those happened," Sabreen screamed. "And I have lived in the Heart most of my life."

"She means well. She even got the ogres on her side—got them to stop killing people."

A gasp rippled through the group as everyone's eyes turned to Sam. Though he had boldly stepped forward, he now shrunk back from the light of the tiny fireplace.

Tristan glared—first at Sam, then Sabreen, and back at Sam. No one controlled the ogres. Even Faramos had tried and proclaimed them mostly useless. "Better to leave them alone and let them clobber our enemies than to deal with them and risk being killed ourselves," he had said.

"Ogres?" Karina's eyes widened.

Sam growled. "When we met, two ogres were trying to make me their dinner. She sent them away and took me to her tent in the ogre camp to heal my wounds." His eyes found hers, and his face softened. "If it weren't for her, I would not be here now."

Tristan could not be certain if Sabreen's red cheeks were a result of a blush or if she was still angry. Her fists balled, she glowered at Karina. "Yes, I may be a witch. Yet obviously I do some good in this world."

"Depends on your definition of good." Yosef frowned. "Ogres are not the kind of creatures to be messed with. How did you befriend them? Why? For what purpose?"

She stuck her chin out. "To keep them from killing the other people in the Heart."

"To control the Heart, more likely."

She screeched. "I do not have to take this from the likes of you all." She flipped her red hair over her shoulder, pushed past Tristan, and stormed out the door.

"Wait. Sabreen!" Sam called, hurrying after her.

"Sam!" Karina grabbed his arm.

He glared at her, yanking his arm from her grasp. "Why are you acting like this?" He hastened out the door without another word.

Karina stared after him, her mouth ajar.

Tristan shook his head. This was not good. He looked to Rashka for help, but she shrugged her shoulders. Her thoughts entered his mind. *It is better if she does not go with us. The Creator warns against using magic that does not come from him—it corrupts the soul.*

He nodded, still worried infighting could very well tear their group apart.

The morning dawned too early after a night of tense silence. From atop Roan, Tristan watched the sun rise as the group readied their steeds. Except for Rashka. She soared into the sky to scout the area ahead of them.

"I see they did not leave." Karina pulled up beside Tristan. Dom nickered and she patted his neck.

"What did he say?"

"We do not always see what is going on beneath the surface."

"What does that mean?"

"Your guess is as good as mine."

Though Sam and Sabreen had stayed the night at the edge of the clearing outside the cottage, they had indeed not deserted them. Now, Sam approached with a rather solemn expression. He stopped next to the horses and gazed up at them. "I can't abandon the quest, and I will not send Sabreen off to make her way back home alone."

Karina pursed her lips but said nothing.

"Let us come with you. Sabreen promises not to use any of her magic unless asked."

Luckily for them, Rashka had already taken to the sky and could not argue the case against them coming along. The struggle to make a decision cast an uneasiness across Karina's features. She sucked in a breath. "Fine. She will have no say in what happens. And no magic."

Sam grimaced as if ready to argue, then sighed. "Agreed."

"Then mount up. We need to leave."

Within minutes, the party was ready to depart. Both Rashka and Yosef were not too keen on letting Sabreen come along. However, Karina had made her choice. At least for now.

From atop his horse, Yosef turned to the group. "We are heading south and west. The temple is on an island off the southern coast … about a two-day ride from here, more if there is turbulent weather."

"Do you expect bad weather?" Tristan asked.

He shook his head. "We are between rainy seasons. However, spring is famous for its sudden intense storms."

Tristan remembered the last storm he had encountered. Karina had almost gone over a cliff. While her wits had saved her, the horse still plunged to its death. Afterward, Karina had been plagued with nightmares for days—not to mention a broken arm.

"Well, let us pray the Creator's blessing is with us." Karina grinned. "Lead on!"

CHAPTER THIRTY

Rashka eased into the clearing. With a shake of her feathers, she shifted from her hawk form to her normal self and then stretched her aching muscles. While she loved to fly, taking to the sky all day would make her sore tonight.

She took a moment to enjoy the quiet before the rest of the group arrived. The thing she loved most about flying was how quiet it was up there. No voices. No arguing. No nothing. Although, from what she could tell, the group had not been much for conversation today.

At lunch, Yosef, dear man that he was, had tried to get people talking more than once. Mostly they grunted or kept their response as brief as possible. Eventually, he quit trying.

The tension seeping into the group worried Rashka. Tension could prove to be costly. They needed to stick together if they were to get through the trials ahead. If Sam had not been so insistent on bringing that witch along … Rashka inhaled deeply. Just the thought of something as vile as a witch made her blood boil. Did Sam not realize the dangers a witch could bring on them? Never in all her years had Rashka met a good witch. If they were not blatantly evil, they had always had selfish intentions. Never for the good of anyone outside themselves or their coven.

She shook the mounting anxiety from her hands and arms and legs. She felt like a trainee preparing to spar as she hopped from one leg to the other, bouncing with frustrated energy.

Voices carried through the trees, followed by the clomp of horse hooves. With a cacophony of noise, the group appeared. First Yosef and then Karina and Tristan. Sam and Sabreen brought up the rear.

"Rashka!" Karina grinned. "Are we stopping again so soon?"

"We should make camp here tonight."

Tristan dismounted and glanced around. "There are still a few hours of daylight left. Should we not continue on?"

"I scouted ahead. The terrain gets rougher from here for quite a while. We would be wise to pass when we are sure of the daylight."

He nodded. "We make camp then."

Everyone set about getting the clearing ready for the evening. Everyone except Sabreen, who sat off to the side by herself. She had some sort of book in her lap and seemed to ignore the bustle around her.

Karina noticed too. She sneered and then stomped over. "We would appreciate your help with the camp."

Sabreen did not even look up. "I am sure you would. I would like an apology for last night." She slammed the book shut and stood. "It seems neither of us is going to get what we want." Pivoting on her heels, she hurried over to Sam, who had started a fire in the pit he had finished clearing.

Karina, in turn, wandered over to Tristan. They put their heads together in intense discussion.

Oh, if they could be rid of the witch, everything would be fine.

Rashka walked over to Sam. "I am going to find more firewood, so we have enough for the night."

"Do you want me to go with you? Or Sabreen?"

Rashka eyed the woman but offered a small smile. "I will go alone. It should not take long."

He nodded and went back to stoking the small fire.

Rashka had only been with the group for a short time now, but already she needed a break. She prayed the Creator knew what he was doing by bringing all these vastly different people together. The woods were a nice reprieve from the tension in the clearing. Bird calls and insect hums were much more pleasant than arguments. She picked up a few downed branches.

So much had happened over the last few months. She had lost her brother, her former husband, and her childhood friend in a matter of weeks. Yet the overwhelming grief hardly touched her heart. She had closed the pain off, squashed the emotions. This was not a time for weakness. The quest was more important than any one loss.

She blew out a breath and continued to collect branches and twigs. The woods teemed with life, stretching and growing and pushing on. How she missed the calming time she spent in Shadowed Forest. She inhaled the earthy scents of trees and dirt. Animals scurried about in the undergrowth. Still, inside she had changed.

"Well, who would have thought to find the Guardian of Shadowed Forest in the woods beyond the Southern Plains? Are you lost?"

Anaya. Immediately, Rashka dropped the wood and pulled the bow from her shoulder as she turned.

Anaya sat atop a brown mare with at least ten soldiers behind her. The woman's skin-tight leather riding apparel did not seem appropriate for pursuing an enemy, but she had perfected the evil scowl marring her face.

With a nod from the former queen of Aletheia, the soldiers rode out to surround Rashka. But these soldiers did not wear the colors of Soter. Instead of the white and gold, their tabards were black and silver with the crest of a dragon. Soldiers from Tzedek. What were they doing out here already? Tristan had warned Faramos was sending his people after them, but a pursuit should have taken more time.

Rashka forced herself to keep breathing. This was not good. She could not let Anaya take her hostage. "What do you want, Anaya?" She pulled back the string of the bow, and a black arrow appeared. Small, precise. She should end the tricky vixen now.

"I assured King Rufus I knew where you were headed, and I would be sure to bring back Karina." She leaned forward on the horse. "In fact, if you were to hand over my niece, I would gladly let the rest of you go free. So long as you agree to leave Soter, of course."

"No."

"Are you sure?" She looked around. "You are outnumbered. And if we get rid of you, how likely are the others to escape these men? Or the power of Faramos?"

Tristan had filled Rashka in on the confrontation with his brother the night at the cottage. No, Faramos's power would not reach them here. His influence, on the other hand …

"You have ten seconds to take your men and leave, Anaya. Or I will put this arrow through your heart."

Anaya threw her head back, cackling. "Do you remember what happened the last time someone tried to kill me?" She held her hands out. "As you can see, death did not suit me well."

Rashka held the bow steady, unsure of what to do next. Would an arrow through the heart kill her? "How did you escape?"

"Oh, Faramos saw to it I would not die at the hands of that pitiful excuse for a king. He snatched me out of the royal house just in time. Saved me. Gave me a new purpose."

"What purpose is that?"

Anaya regarded her with narrowed eyes, but then she smirked. "I suppose it would not hurt to tell you, since you will be dead in a matter of minutes." She giggled before continuing. "I am making way for Faramos to take over the Three Kingdoms."

Information Rashka was already aware of. She squinted at the ruined queen.

"What?"

"Your declaration is not news, Anaya."

"Yes, well, let's just say Faramos has given me the tools to sway whoever might need some extra persuasion, to ensure the ancient evil continues to sweep across the kingdoms. But that will be my secret for now." Anaya pulled on the reins of her horse as she shouted at the guards. "Kill her."

Rashka blinked, and her body shimmered with light. She was a hawk again, soaring up into the sky. Arrows flew past her as she angled away to avoid their pointed heads. She had to warn Karina.

CHAPTER THIRTY-ONE

While Tristan and Sam argued rather intensely about something, Karina groaned and dropped her pack and blanket. She turned to Dom. "What are we supposed to do?"

He shook his mane and stomped at the ground. "I know you are frustrated, child. It is not easy to lead people who disagree with each other. What has the Creator told you?"

The Creator? She had not even thought to stop and ask him what to do in this situation. She had prayed in passing, tossing up prayers to the Lighted Realm in the heat of the moment. But had she stopped to listen?

Dom nudged her shoulder. "You will know what to do."

She would rather lay out beneath the velvety black sky and count the stars, lose herself in the vastness of everything the Creator had done.

Instead, she eyed Tristan and Sam again. Sam was angry. She could tell by his clenched fists and the way he leaned in slightly. If he did not back up, he might end up with a bloody lip. Tristan would only tolerate so much.

Tristan's face darkened as well but was less volatile than normal. He seemed to be entertaining whatever argument Sam was exploding at him. Then his eyes narrowed. Karina cringed, waiting for the punch.

Before a fight could break out, Sam marched over to the fire where Sabreen sat by herself again. The sight of the woman bristled the hair on Karina's arms. She could not describe the impression that came over her when Sabreen was around—like a crisp winter breeze in Aletheia. Only, there was no wind. And the cold came from within. She took a deep breath, afraid to exhale.

Karina sensed Sabreen was not the good person Sam claimed she was, despite what she had done for him. If only she could make Sam understand this. Karina's hand fell to the purple braided belt around her waist. Maybe if she used the Belt of Truth …

Before she had a chance to pray, a familiar hawk landed in front of her, followed by the usual burst of bright light. Then Rashka stood before her. "Come."

Rashka led her over to the fire. "I have news," she said loud enough for the group to hear.

Everyone gathered around. Tristan and Yosef sat on a fallen log with Karina in between them, while Sam and Sabreen sat on the ground on the opposite side of the flames. Karina stared at the huddled pair. She wanted Sam to be happy. Really, she did. But this was not the woman for him. Who was? Was she jealous of Sabreen? Karina glanced up at Tristan. No, her heart belonged to the handsome ex-bounty-hunter, whether he was aware of her feelings or not. Right? She bit her lip. Did she worry because Sam was her best friend or because she secretly loved him?

Rashka interrupted her thoughts. "Anaya is in the woods." She began kicking dirt over the fire.

"Hey, what are you doing?" Sam jumped up.

"Anaya has a dozen soldiers with her." She looked at Karina. "And not guards from Soter."

Tristan grabbed her hand. "Faramos."

Rashka nodded.

Karina sucked in a breath. This was not what she had expected. She knew King Rufus would send soldiers after them, but they could avoid leaving a trail. Depending on Faramos's power, his men could prove to be a whole different challenge.

Rashka finished dousing the fire. "Anaya and the soldiers have most likely seen the smoke. We should move now."

"I thought you said the terrain was too uncertain to travel without light," Tristan said.

In the west, the sun had already settled beneath the horizon. While not completely dark, the woods would not have enough light to see adequately. Karina squeezed Tristan's hand tighter.

"Indeed." Rashka's frustration was evident in her tense muscles as her gaze traveled over the tired group. "But I do not think we can fight either."

Sam and Sabreen whispered to each other on the other side of the fire. At last, Sam nodded and then looked over at Karina. "Perhaps, Tristan, Rashka, and I should stay behind, fend off whoever is pursuing us. Yosef can take Karina and Sabreen on ahead. Sabreen can protect them if any get past us."

Karina shook her head. Everything inside of her screamed against the idea. One side-long glance revealed Yosef's dark scowl. He was not keen on the idea either. "No. Splitting up is not a good plan." She stood and wiped her hands on her pants. "We need to stick together."

"But where should we go?"

Yosef shrugged. "I have not been out this way in a few years."

Rashka sighed. "If we go north, we will end up in the Southern Plains. No rough terrain but no shelter either. If we go straight south, the terrain is not so bad now. But we will end up on the rocky cliffs."

"Great. Three choices, none of which are ideal." Tristan growled.

"I'm telling you, we should split up." Sam said again.

"No!" came an almost unanimous shout.

Sam scowled and turned away. Sabreen whispered something to him, then he stopped, his back to the group.

"What do you think, Karina?" Yosef asked.

"Could you give me a minute? Start packing up the camp and load the horses."

Everyone nodded and went about breaking down camp. Karina stood in the middle, inhaling the remnant of smoke and the freshness of night air. *Creator, hear me tonight. Our journey is in peril, and I need your guidance. I have learned I cannot do this without you.*

Nothing happened. Karina bit her lip. She had expected an answer. Something. When she had prayed for direction under the mountain, lights had guided her steps. Scanning the trees, she did not see any light. In fact, the only thing she could see beyond the tree line was a wide swath of ground where there no trees grew. Her stomach warmed as their way was revealed.

Tristan led Dom over to her. "Do we have a direction?"

She nodded. "We take the path for now."

"South it is." He handed her the reins and leaned close to her ear as he whispered, "You are doing well, Your Majesty."

She closed her eyes against the tears that welled at those words. How did he know what she needed to hear?

Rashka cleared her throat. "I will travel in hawk form again. I am going to swing back and see where Anaya is. Then I will fly south and find you again."

Tristan grasped her forearm. "Be safe."

She nodded. Light flashed, and she rose above the trees, disappearing into the growing darkness.

Tristan gave the order to leave. The group mounted their horses, and he led them into the woods along the path.

Since the trail was not wide enough to travel side-by-side, they rode in a line. Considering the dangers, they kept quiet, the sounds of the night drifting over their silence. Night owls called from the trees, bugs hummed, and the moon shone onto their path, illuminating their way.

By the time they stopped again, the early wisps of dawn reached over the horizon. The path had gone from grass to hard-packed dirt to stone and then to dirt again. Karina's back ached, her muscles were sore, and she had trouble staying awake atop Dom. Every now and then, he would say something and startle her back to consciousness.

When Tristan called for them to halt, she let out a sigh and slid from Dom's back, sinking further as if her body had melted into a puddle. Yes, she felt like a puddle.

"You plan to sleep right there?"

She opened one eye to find Yosef grinning ear-to-ear as he stood over her. "I may never move again."

"I am not sure that is the best way to save the world, but I am not the Prophetess." He winked and then held out a hand to her. She let him help her up as the others went about unloading packs and spreading out blankets.

"No fire. We will only sleep a couple of hours, until the sun is high." Tristan dropped his own pack. "Then we must continue on the journey."

Karina yawned. "Have you seen Rashka yet?" He shook his head, and Karina prayed she was safe.

Tristan had chosen a small clearing on the edge of the woods. Somewhere in the distance, too dark to see but close enough to hear, waves crashed against rocks. Though Karina settled near Tristan and Yosef, Sam and Sabreen were once again off by themselves. In fact, their blankets were next to each other, Sam's arm around Sabreen as they talked. They were getting a little too close, bordering inappropriate.

"Lay down before Sam catches you spying."

Tristan's words were meant to be a gentle chastisement, but they still stung. Sam was heading down a very dangerous path—and not because he was possibly having an inappropriate relationship—but because that relationship could get him hurt. Or worse.

Still, she lay her head back against her not-so-soft pack and stared up between tree branches at the cloudy sky. No stars now. No moon either. Just dark clouds to add to her darker thoughts.

Karina and her friends picked their way along the rocky cliff edge where a narrow swath of land stretched between the cliffs and the woods. Because of the rocky terrain, Karina walked with Dom by her side. While they had not talked much this afternoon, the time had passed in companionable silence.

"Maybe you should talk to him."

Karina sighed. "I do not feel it is my place."

Dom nickered. "Are you his friend?"

"Well, yes. Still, it is none of my business who he chooses to have a relationship with."

"Why not? If he could not see and was about to walk into a fire, would you not save him?"

She rolled her eyes. "Of course I would."

"How is this any different?"

"Because he loves her."

"A man who loves fire can still be burned."

Karina groaned. "I do not know whether your words are profound or ridiculous." She glanced over her shoulder.

Sam and Sabreen leaned toward each other as they walked, heads together, whispering as always. Why was this woman's presence so bothersome? Yes, she was a witch, but she was hiding something as well.

Dom was right, of course. A friend would warn a person if they were headed into danger. She felt like a petulant child being forced to perform daily chores. Still … she squared her shoulders and raised her chin. Dom nudged her on. "Fine."

She fell back to where Sam and Sabreen were. They both looked up, surprise on their faces. She smiled as sweetly as she could muster. "May I please talk with Sam?"

Sabreen glanced at him, then seemed about to agree when Sam cut her off. "Whatever you want to discuss, you can talk about in front of Sabreen."

Karina chewed on her lip. She could see how that conversation would go. She would need to choose her words wisely. "Sam, I appreciate your openness with Sabreen. That speaks well of your relationship. However, I would like to talk to you alone for my benefit."

Sam studied her face intently. He turned to Sabreen, whose expression quickly morphed from shock to anger. She pasted on a tight smile. "I think I will go see if the horses would like to graze. Or something." She stalked off without a backward glance.

"What do you want, Karina?"

"Walk with me a bit." Up ahead, Tristan paused, a quick glance over his shoulder, but she gave him a reassuring nod and moved to follow after the others. Now that she had Sam alone, how did she broach the subject? "Did I tell you how happy I was when Yosef told me you were in Gundow?"

He nodded.

"I thought I would never see you again. After all our years together, I was devastated at the thought of not having you in my life."

"Good grief, Karina. Get on with it."

Karina stopped again, stunned. Sam had never spoken to her in such a manner, even when she was annoying him. She stumbled over the words while Sam's gaze darted everywhere but at her. She fidgeted with her fingers.

When he did finally look at her, he seemed bored and distant. He raised an eyebrow. "Well?"

His obstinate attitude hit the wrong nerve. Her frustration and hurt transformed into fury, and she had to ball her fists to rein in her anger. Cross words would do nothing to help the situation. "I am worried about you."

Sam let out a half-hearted chuckle and resumed walking "Oh, no."

"Hey!" Karina hurried to catch up. At her shout, Sabreen stiffened. But, when Karina glared at Sabreen, she swung back toward the horses. "Sam, please hear me out."

"If you have come to disparage Sabreen, I have no desire to hear what you have to say."

"Even if I have legitimate concerns?"

Sam stopped and crossed his arms. "Like what?"

Karina huffed. "Like she is a witch. Someone in direct opposition to the Creator."

Sam rolled his eyes and started walking again.

"You know it is true." She fell in step with him, but he would not look at her. "And … I do not know how to explain this … but I get a bad feeling whenever she is around."

He shook his head.

"I know it sounds odd. I mean, I thought about using the belt—"

"You what?" Sam stopped so fast, she staggered and reeled at the same time. "How dare you—"

"No!" She held up her hands. "I wanted to, but I didn't. Not yet anyway." She glanced toward Sabreen who stood near the horses. They were docile around her, except for Dom, who kept a wide berth. "I wish I could make you understand the impressions I get."

"Have you had a vision from the Creator?" His tone was laced with sarcasm.

She shook her head. "Sam, you are my best friend. I do not want to see you get hurt, I hope you know that."

He did not respond.

"And because I am your best friend, I cannot ignore these impressions without saying, at least once, I do not trust Sabreen … and I think she is trouble." There. She had said what she had to say.

Sam's face reddened. His jaw twitched.

Karina waited for the explosion she knew was coming. She had never been the object of this kind of outburst but had seen him lash out at people before, particularly in her defense. His strong feelings for Sabreen made her feel that much worse. But saying what needed to be said was the right action.

"Who are you to judge?"

"Pardon me?"

Sam stopped again, his scowl darker than any Karina had seen. "Who are you to judge my relationships?"

"I … I …"

"You"—he jabbed a finger in her direction—"who flirts with the ruthless bounty hunter who kidnapped you. You, who lived under the comforts and care of the man who banished your parents. You, who relies on the whims of an all-powerful being to show her how to make her life meaningful."

Karina stepped back as if she had been slapped. Her breath caught.

"Do not dare to cast disparagements on my relationship choices." He stormed off.

"Sam, I …" she squeaked.

He stalked back, shoulders hunched over. Inches from her face, he was all hard lines and crimson with anger. "You had your chance. All those years I loved you, and you did not even see me. Now that I have found my happiness, all you want to do is ruin it." He gave her a once over and stalked away.

Tears trickled down Karina's cheeks. She did not know how to respond to Sam's outlandish response. Of all the things she had expected, this had not even been in the realm of possibilities. She did not think Sam could possibly be so … cruel.

CHAPTER THIRTY-TWO

Sam's anger had been growing for hours now, burning in his belly like a late-night Scorch-flower ale. He blew out a breath, hoping to expel some of his tension, but his muscles only tightened again.

He had lashed out at Karina unfairly. He had not meant any of the things he'd said. Tristan may have started off a bounty hunter, but he had turned into the closest friend Sam had next to Karina. And King Pistis was a saint! Oh, the hurt reflected in Karina's eyes after his outburst! How he wished he could take it all back. He let out a groan.

Or maybe he didn't. After all, she had called into question his judgment concerning Sabreen—Sabreen, the woman who had saved him on more than one occasion, the woman who made him laugh, the woman who was nothing but open about her life with him. About everything, including the witchcraft.

He had to admit he had been surprised by her candidness when she explained witches only embraced natural magic. Apparently, anyone could do the things she did—even him. Not that he wanted to.

"Why the long face?"

Sam startled as Sabreen sidled up next to him. Her fiery red hair danced in the breeze sweeping in off the ocean. "Karina does not trust you."

Sabreen pushed ringlets of hair away from her face. "We knew that already."

"Yes." He sighed. "But then I threw it back in her face, accused her of being jealous."

"Really?" Sabreen raised an eyebrow. "You believe that?"

"Yes. No. I don't know!"

"Hey, calm down." Sabreen rubbed his shoulders. "She's your best friend. It has to be hard for her to see you with someone new, regardless whether she had romantic feelings for you or not."

He nodded. "I wish I could see what was going on in her head."

Sabreen offered him a small smile. They walked on in comfortable silence for a long while and had fallen behind the group. Karina strode alongside Tristan, also quiet from what he could tell. Occasionally, she would look back at him. Then, when she noticed him watching her, she would quickly turn away. What kind of games was she playing?

"I've got it!" Sabreen jumped a little, snatching his hand in hers.

"Got what? What are you talking about?"

"How you can know what is going on in her head."

He put both his hands on her shoulders to hold her still. "What are you talking about? Whose head?"

"Karina's! Earlier you said you wished you knew what was going on in her head. Well, you can."

Oh boy. This should be interesting. He quirked an eyebrow and waited.

She leaned in. "You need to get your hands on her belt."

"What? The Belt of Truth?" Well, it could help him decipher her actions. "She would never let me use it."

Leaning forward, she cocked her head to the side. "Who said anything about her letting you?"

"You want me to steal it?" he responded in a harsh whisper.

"Steal. Borrow. Whatever." She shrugged. "The point is with the belt you would be able to figure out what is going on. Maybe settle whatever issues stand between the two of you."

True. And he could give it right back. "How do I go about retrieving the belt?"

"I noticed she removed the belt this morning when we laid down to sleep. Maybe she'll take it off again tonight?"

At that moment, Karina glanced back. Even from this distance, he could tell her cheeks were wet with tears, her eyes red. Maybe the time had come to find out the specifics behind her aversion to Sabreen.

Sam pretended to be asleep. Everyone in camp had wound down for the night inside the tree line beyond the cliffs. The only sounds were soft snores, the crackling fire, and a distant lapping of waves. Yosef had said they would reach the temple by tomorrow evening, so tonight was his only opportunity to retrieve the Belt of Truth.

Karina had indeed taken off the belt in order to remove the riding tunic and replace it with a nightshirt. She'd put the belt in her pack.

"Hey, Sam," Tristan whispered.

He rolled over, rubbing his eyes. "What?"

"Your turn for watch."

Perfect. "Fine." He reached for his water skin and took a long drink, but it did not help his dry mouth. If anyone saw what he was about to do next, they would think he was betraying Karina … sabotaging the quest. He only wanted to know what was really going on.

Tristan plopped down on his bedroll and closed his eyes. Sam rose and threw another branch on the fire. Though she made no move to get up, Sabreen rolled over to watch him from her makeshift bed. This was all up to him.

He did a quick search of the perimeter as Tristan had shown him so many weeks ago. By the time Sam returned to the fire, Tristan snored as softly as Yosef. Sam waited a bit longer, stoking the fire, searching the tree line again.

Finally, he made his way across the camp to Karina's bedroll. Tonight, she had her cloak rolled up for a pillow as she curled up under the thin blanket. Her pack lay next to her feet. That made things a lot easier for him as he bent over and opened the pack. The purple braided belt nestled between her tunic and her extra pants. He snatched the belt and hustled back to the safety of the fire.

"What are you going to do now?" Sabreen sat down next to him.

"Figure out how it works?"

"How are you going to do that?"

He shrugged, rolling the belt over in his hands. Such a simple piece.

"What are you two doing with the Belt of Truth?"

Sam jumped and Sabreen let out a squeak.

Beyond the flames, Rashka's golden eyes flashed. "I asked you a question, Sam."

"N-nothing," he said, his heart beating so rapidly, he could not catch his breath. Around them, the others began to stir.

"Sam?" Rashka prodded him once more.

Tristan leapt from his place on the ground with his sword at the ready, then scratched his head in confusion. "What's going on?"

"Nothing. Nothing is going on." Sam's hand, the one holding the belt, fell to his side. "Sabreen and I were just talking."

"Oh." Tristan rubbed his face and then went to sheath his sword.

"Wait." Rashka raised her hand. "Sam has the Belt of Truth."

"What?" Karina appeared from the darkness behind Rashka. "The belt was in my pack."

Sam's heart stopped. This would not end well. No one would listen. He could feel their judgment already. He inhaled deeply. "Karina, I can explain."

Tristan stepped forward with his sword upright, his normally nonchalant expression replaced with suspicion. "Explain what."

Yosef appeared by Rashka, yawning and stretching. "What is with the noise? Is it time to leave? Why is it still dark?"

"It seems we have a traitor in our midst." Rashka glowered at Sam.

He crossed his arms. "Now, wait a minute. I am not a traitor."

"Then why did you take the belt from my pack?" Karina asked, hurt already evident in her voice.

"Because. Sabreen and I—"

"Sabreen?" Rashka's hardened gaze cut over to the love of his life.

Sam saw the error in his words. "No, that's not what I meant. I was worried about the fight I had with Karina."

"So, you decided to steal from her?" Yosef pointed a finger at him. "Were you going to magically find the belt later?"

"No, nothing like that. I wanted to use—"

"Use!" Karina's eyebrows shot up. "Why would you—"

"Karina, you will gain little discussing this with them." Rashka's eyes were cold, despite the reflection of the fire.

Sam shivered. The whole situation was getting out of hand. "Look, I'm sorry. Here, take the belt and then let me explain fully."

"No!" Sabreen lunged forward and snatched the belt from his hand.

He cringed. "What are you doing?"

"We are not giving in. Especially not because they say so." With a dagger in her other hand, she jabbed in the direction of the others. "You are your own person. Stop letting them take advantage of you."

"Sabreen, give me the belt." Tristan's voice held a warning that demanded obedience.

Sabreen aimed her dagger in his direction. "Sam spoke so highly of all of you after we met. He could not wait to be reunited with his friends. After being here with you all, I am hard pressed to understand why. You all are ruthless. Heartless. You have treated me with nothing but disdain no matter how kind I have been toward you. And the way you treat Sam?" She scoffed.

"Hand over the belt, Sabreen." Rashka loosed the bow from her shoulder and pulled back the string. A small black arrow appeared, almost invisible in the darkness. "Now."

Sam had to stop this insanity. They were behaving like he and Sabreen were working for Faramos. Sam stepped in between Rashka and Sabreen. "Wait, please. I promise this is a misunderstanding." He turned to the feisty redhead he had come to adore. "Sabreen, give them the belt. Obviously, they will never trust us. At first light, we can make our way back to the Heart."

She glared at him. "No. I have worked too hard and too long to get my hands on one of the pieces of armor. I am not giving it up now."

Tristan could have punched him right now, and he would not have been more surprised than hearing Sabreen's words. "W-what?" The only word he could manage.

Sabreen's normally complacent face contorted in a sneer. "Yes, Sam, you are nice enough. I even enjoyed our time together. How unfortunate we could not have met under better circumstances."

Karina stepped up next to him, but he took a larger step away from her. This could not be happening. "Was this your plan from the beginning?"

She shook her head, curls bouncing over her shoulders. "You were a cute puppy that needed a friend. Like I said, I do like you. Your stories about the quest for the armor convinced me to tag along. To put up with"—she waved her hands around the group—"all this."

Could a heart crack without being pierced by a blade? This pain impaled him as if he'd been skewered. Unable to breathe.

Karina sighed. "We cannot let you leave with the belt, Sabreen. And as much as you may believe to the contrary, we do not want to hurt you either."

Sabreen faced Karina and took another step toward her. "And you are worst of all, looking down from your haughty horse. You are worse than Soter's nobility. The way you treat your friends as if they were your servants." She laughed. "I'm surprised they have stayed by your side this long."

Sam clenched his fists. "Now, wait just a minute ..."

Karina reached for the belt, but Sabreen recoiled and sliced forward with her dagger. The blade slid across Karina's forearm. Crying out, she gripped her arm.

Tristan ran toward them, but he was not close enough. Sabreen struck out with the knife again.

Before he knew what he was doing, Sam jumped in front of the blade. With a sickening sound, the dagger rammed into his chest, below his ribs. His breath caught. And then pain rippled through his body. Karina gasped.

His gaze fell to the protruding dagger ... and he admired the silvery beauty, the red jewels adhered to the hilt. He turned his eyes to Sabreen, his love. Though her jaws were clenched, a storm raged in her eyes. She shook her head as she slid away from him.

His energy waned ... life drained out of him, bit by bloody bit. He stared at Karina. She covered her mouth with one hand, reaching out to him with the other. Tristan held her back.

What could he say? In this moment, what would matter?

All those years. This one mistake.

"I'm sorry."

And he slumped to the ground.

CHAPTER THIRTY-THREE

"No!" Karina dove toward Sam, trying to break his fall. He hit the ground too hard.

Kneeling beside her best friend, she covered the wound with her hands, tried to stop the bleeding. She did not dare remove the blade yet. Tears blurred her vision.

"No, Creator. Please, no!" Mounting panic threatened to stop her own heart. She bent her ear to his mouth. No breath. "No!" she shouted as she beat her hands on his chest.

"Karina." Tristan knelt beside her. He guided her gaze to look at Sam's eyes.

They were open but unseeing. Vacant.

Sam was gone.

Her best friend was dead.

A mournful wail escaped as she sank the rest of the way to the ground. Tristan circled his arms around her and pulled her close. The wails deteriorated into sobs, an unyielding pressure as the pain and grief strived to explode from her chest.

Sam was gone.

"What have you done?" Yosef's voice sounded distant, as if sifting through a waterfall.

"I did not mean for him to die." Sabreen pointed at Karina. "Silly fool. Still defending *her* at the end of it all."

Karina pushed through her agony enough to dry her tears, to steel her resolve. She looked up. Rashka still had her bow at the ready, arrow aimed at Sabreen's heart. "Give us the belt, Sabreen. You will not make it out of here alive any other way."

With a malicious laugh, she pulled the belt around her waist. Rashka loosed the arrow, but the witch dodged to the right. Sabreen locked the belt in place. "With this armor, I will bring the Tri-Goddesses to a new level. We will rid this kingdom of its corruption."

A most disconcerted feeling hardened like a rock in Karina's stomach. The impression was not grief for Sam but something else. Something was going to happen.

Sabreen continued to rant. "Even better that the armor I have is the Belt of Truth. What better piece to reveal the truth of the corruption for my people?"

Rashka had another arrow ready to launch.

"If only you all could see past your narrow-minded view of the world. Past all the stuff holding you back from—wait. What?" Sabreen stopped. She held up one arm and then the other. "What's happening?"

Karina leaned forward but did not see anything unusual.

A shriek ripped from Sabreen as she stumbled around. She grabbed her head, still screaming.

Instinctively, Karina used her body to cover Sam. Tristan leaned over her. But they did not take their eyes off Sabreen.

"What is wrong?" Karina croaked.

"I don't know," Tristan breathed in her ear.

Sabreen fell to her knees, her cries fading. Without warning, she burst into flames … bright and intense. Her final scream echoed through the trees and then everything went dark.

And silent.

Karina gawked at the spot where Sabreen had just stood. What had happened?

Rashka hurried over. "Ashes." She shoved her bow around a dark pile.

Tristan stood, keeping one hand on Karina's back. "What was that?"

"Holy fire," Yosef replied. "Only the armor bearer can wield the armor."

Rashka leaned over and picked up something. The Belt of Truth dangled from her hand. She walked over, then kneeled as she held the belt out to Karina.

Karina reached for the armor and noticed her hands were drenched in blood. Sam's blood. She pulled back her hand and let her head fall forward. A stream of tears fell again.

Whispers went back and forth, but she ignored them. She did not want to be here anymore. In this moment. On this quest. Anywhere that was somewhere without Sam. Sobs wracked her chest again.

"Someone is coming!" Yosef's voice turned frantic.

Horse hooves pounded through the trees.

"Anaya. They must have seen the flames," Rashka hissed. "Yosef, help me grab the horses. Tristan …"

Silence fell as they went for the horses.

Tristan knelt by her again. "Karina, we need to go."

She shook her head.

"It is not safe here. You know what will happen if Anaya finds you."

She did not care.

Tristan grabbed her under the arms and pulled her away from Sam.

"No!" She lunged for Sam, burying her face in the crook of his neck. She could not leave him here. They had to give him a proper burial.

Tristan grabbed her again, holding more tightly, the pain in his grip barely penetrating her already-broken spirit. She fought against him as he pulled her upright. She pounded him with fists when he scooped her up and held her close to his chest.

"I'm sorry," he whispered in her ear.

And with those words, all the energy left her body. She went limp. She did not care to move, to think, to live. She barely felt Tristan throw her up on Dom's back. He tried to hand her the reins, but she could not grab them. Even if she had wanted to, her body would not have obeyed. He slid into the saddle behind her.

"Don't worry. I've got you."

CHAPTER THIRTY-FOUR

Tristan followed Yosef as they plunged into the forest on horseback. Leading Roan, the white stallion, Rashka brought up the rear. Karina slumped against Tristan's chest. Not the casual comfort of a lover but the heavy weight of a dead body. She seemed unable to move or think.

He cursed himself for not seeing Sabreen's deception sooner … for assuming Karina's suspicions were nothing more than spikes of jealousy. She would never forgive him for allowing Sam to die.

"Faster," Rashka hissed.

Yosef glanced back before leaning forward and urging his horse onward. Dom dipped his head and pushed harder without a cue from Tristan. In the dark, they could only go so fast.

Panic threatened to override Tristan's thoughts. Deep breaths. He would be of no help if he allowed his mind to succumb to the direness of their situation. He glanced down at Karina again. She stared off into the trees, eyes open yet unseeing. If it were not for the sensation of her chest rising and falling, she would appear as deathly still as Sam had been back at the camp.

Ahead, Yosef stopped so quickly Dom skidded to a stop, almost throwing Tristan and Karina from his back. "What's going on?"

Rashka trotted up beside them. "We need to keep going. Though I believe we are outrunning them in the dark, they are still not far behind."

"There are not many places to go, and the road is too dangerous from here at night." Yosef gestured off toward the right where the tree line thinned. "There are empty caves in this direction as you reach the edge of the land. Tristan should take Karina there and hide. Get some rest. Rashka and I could continue on through the woods, leaving a trail for them to follow."

Rashka nodded. "That is actually a decent plan. Are the caves easy to find?"

"In the moonlight, Tristan will have to look carefully. They should not be too difficult to locate."

"Very well." The elf raised an eyebrow at Tristan.

Though he understood Yosef's plan, splitting up right now did not seem like a good idea. "How long do I stay in the caves? I do not know the way to the temple."

"We should return to you by midday," Yosef replied. "If we do not, you should follow the sea, always keeping it to your left. Eventually, someone from the temple will find you."

Tristan gave a curt nod.

Rashka took up her reins again. "May the Creator's might go with you, Tristan."

He urged Dom toward the right. The path was stonier, and the trees thinned even more as they rode onward. The sounds of the night pressed in on him without the comfort of companions.

Comfort? Had he really changed so much he considered the presence of others to be comfort? Before Karina, he had preferred to work alone. He cared not for companionship, except to fulfill physical needs rather than a need for a relationship. Of course, he realized he had been so wrong in that area. What he hoped to develop with Karina was so much bigger, purer.

Karina shifted slightly beneath him, but then nothing. He needed to get her off the horse, so he could talk to her.

With only the moonlight to guide them, Dom wandered down the path aimlessly as Tristan attempted to seek out a cave through the shadows. In the distance, the sound of waves hitting the shore welcomed him like an old friend. The castle in Tzedek had been on the edge of a cliff, as had Faramos's fortress. Even when the nights stretched endless and despairing, he found comfort in the sounds of the ocean.

Dom nickered and tossed his head. What he wouldn't give for Karina's ability to hear the stallion's thoughts. To his right, a rock face rose and stretched a short way before descending into the ground again.

He allowed Dom to lead them over to the large hill. On the north side, a notch in the rock indicated a cave entrance, hidden by shadows unless a person was right next to the entrance.

Tristan dismounted and pulled Karina down after him. He expected she would find her feet, but she toppled over as soon as he let her go. Immediately, Dom knelt on the ground. Tristan smirked. They may not be able to communicate with words, but they still understood each other. He hoisted Karina over to the horse and laid her against his side like he had after she almost drowned a few weeks ago.

"I'm going to ensure the cave is safe. Watch her. Let me know if anyone approaches."

Dom dipped his head a couple of times. Tristan assumed the horse understood and quickly gathered a stick and dry grass to make a torch. Once he lit the torch, he entered the cave.

The opening was not large, but it was tall. He could easily fit Karina and Dom in here with him, maybe a small fire to add light and warmth. The cave was dry, which was good. More comfortable that way.

He set about getting everyone into the cave and started a fire. Finally, he eased down by Karina. Flames crackled underneath a pot of water waiting to boil. He hoped hot tea would sooth whatever ailed her. "Karina?"

She did not respond. Did not even blink.

Tristan took her hand. "Karina, look at me."

Nothing. What was going on in that head of hers? He studied her face. Her beautiful, smooth, perfect face with those endless blue eyes. Once so full of life and hope, they were empty now. As if Karina's soul had left her body. What was he supposed to do? How was he supposed to reach her?

"Karina," he said, louder this time. He grabbed her shoulders and shook her. "Karina, wake up. Snap out of it. What is wrong with you?"

Dom let out a sharp whinny.

Tristan glanced over at him. "Yeah, I know. I don't know what else to do."

Yosef plodded along, leading two horses, while he slumped wearily atop his own. Rashka soared through the sky, her golden feathers highlighted by the coming dawn. He had heard of the shapeshifting powers of the Guardians appointed by the Creator but had never seen one for himself. Now, staring in awe at the hawk gliding on the wind while he rode a horse below, he counted himself lucky to be able to witness such amazing ability.

The sight almost quelled the guilt of betraying his mentor, though he had made the right decision … what the Creator would have wanted him to do. Still, the decision cost him much. He would never be welcomed back at the temple in Gundow. If word made it to the sacred Temple of Soter, chances were he would not find a permanent place there either.

Still, he had to ensure Karina and her friends were able to continue their mission. He had already seen the affects the ancient evil was having on the people of Soter, and it all weighed heavy on his heart. Dark times were ahead if Karina failed. Why Elder Thomas could not see the truth, Yosef did not understand. Maybe his mentor had been affected by the evil as well. He shook off that particular thought.

The hawk swooped down, and, with a flash of light, Rashka appeared in her elven form once more. His eyes widened as he shook his head. Inspiring.

Rashka stretched her arms to the sky and then down to the ground before facing him. "I believe we lost Anaya and her soldiers farther back. They have stopped to rest. For how long, I do not know. She sent scouts out in different directions. If we double back the way we sent Tristan, I believe they will not be able to follow us."

Yosef nodded. "Very well. Let us leave then." He held out the reins to her horse.

Tristan awoke to Dom's restless stomping on the stone floor of the cave, then rolled over to the dying embers of last night's fire. Dom snorted and stamped a hoof. With a groan, Tristan stretched and then pushed himself up on his elbows. "What's with you?"

His question was met with a blank stare.

Tristan shook his head and glanced behind him to where Karina lay on her blanket. She didn't move. Her eyes were closed, so maybe she was actually sleeping. Though she was in the same position she had been earlier when he laid her there—on her back, hands folded over her stomach. That could not be a comfortable way to sleep for any amount of time.

He stood, brushed off his pants, and glanced toward the opening of the cave. The boulder in front of the entrance blocked most of the light, but the golden rays of daylight seeped in through the crack. He walked outside and looked around.

The clearing between the cave and the forest was large but relatively quiet. Bugs buzzed in the patches of long grasses while birds called from the trees, the rest of the silence only broken by the constant crashing of waves behind the cave.

He glanced up at the sky. Midday was only a couple of hours away. If Rashka and the priest did not return, he would have to continue without them. According to the priest, they would follow the shoreline for a ways to find the temple.

Irritation besieged his thoughts. Nothing was going as planned. This whole journey through Soter had been a disaster. Even if they got to the temple, what were they to do? Sam was no longer with them. Did his death mean Yosef was supposed to take his place? How would they know? The mind of the Prophetess had disappeared. What was the next step?

Instinct told him to abandon the quest and go after Faramos himself. He knew his brother. He had the best chance of getting to him, of killing him. Granted, years of opportunities proved he would never follow through. Tristan sighed. Maybe he was a coward.

No. That was his old self talking. He had followed his instincts all his life, and where had those gotten him? He was an assassin, a bounty hunter who had no loyalties, nothing holding him back. And yet he had never been satisfied with his life. He had joined Karina on her journey because he had been searching for one thing. Hope.

With a countenance only slightly lighter than before, he sauntered back into the cave. Dom tossed his mane and snorted in greeting. Karina had still not moved, except her eyes were open. He knelt beside her and brushed a stray hair away from her face. "Let me help you sit up."

She stared at the cave ceiling. Had she even heard him?

He lifted her up and leaned her against the cave wall, careful to make sure the spot was clean and dry. "How about some breakfast?"

Karina did not respond. Tristan watched her for a moment. Of course, he understood she had lost her best friend. And in some strange way that was completely Karina, she probably blamed herself. However, he could not comprehend how she could simply go limp, physically and emotionally. Why did she persist mourning to this degree?

He pulled a bag of bread from his pack. If she were not responding, he probably did not have a chance of feeding her something like porridge. He sat on his haunches and held the bread out to her. "Do you want some?" When she didn't move, he broke off a bite-size piece and held it up to her lips. She did not open her mouth. He used his other hand and forced a piece on her tongue, but she didn't move.

Dom nickered and pranced.

Tristan glowered at him. "I don't know what you're saying. The Creator did not grant me ears to hear you." He rolled back to sit on the ground, blowing out a long breath. "And I'm out of ideas." He bit off a part of the loaf and chewed hard.

From outside, the call of the Barren bird made its way into the cave, an annoying caw that sounded nothing like a song. Tristan closed his eyes, trying to block out the noise.

His eyes snapped open.

What was a Barren bird doing this far south? And in a forest? He had hardly encountered them anywhere but in the Barrens, except when the occasional one found its way over the river into the northern parts of Tzedek.

He pulled his sword from its sheath on the ground and tiptoed to the entrance. At first glance, the field was empty. He crouched by the boulder to listen. Through the whistling of the wind, the Barren bird called again, the sound coming from his right, near the cave. Keeping to the rocks, he edged toward the sound. The call came again. On closer inspection, the voice was human. And they were right around the bend in the hill.

He pulled his sword to the ready. Took a step …

An elf with dark hair appeared from around the hill, and Tristan lunged forward. Rashka! He pulled his sword before it could reach her stomach.

"By all that is created!" she cried, leaping away from the blade. "Tristan, what are you doing?"

He let the blade dip toward the ground. "What are *you* doing sneaking around like a grave robber?"

She let out a shrill whistle before turning back to him. "We have been searching for you for hours. I figured you would hear the Barren bird call and realize it was us."

Of course, he should have. If he had not been distracted by Karina's odd behavior. Understandable that she would be grief stricken, perhaps cry uncontrollably … but not become this motionless block. And it all had him so flustered he couldn't think straight.

Yosef appeared, leading three horses by the reins. His stringy, dark hair hung down to his chin. He grinned and tossed a wave at them.

Rashka leaned in. "How is Karina? Has there been any change?"

Tristan shook his head.

Minutes later, they were all tucked into the cave, a cozy fit with four people and a horse. Rashka led Dom outside with the other horses while Yosef knelt by Karina to look her over.

"Is there anything you can do?" Tristan hovered by the wall, afraid to get any closer now. The ball in his stomach clenched tighter.

Yosef sighed. "There is nothing physically wrong with her. This is her mind's way of dealing with losing Sam."

"So, what do we do?"

The priest shook his head as he stood. "It's up to her. She has to work through this."

"What happens if she doesn't?"

His lips pulled into a deep frown. "People in this state cannot eat or drink. If she does not find her way back, she will die in a few days from dehydration."

Tristan's heart plummeted. His world had just been ripped out from under him. "There has to be something we can do." He nearly choked on the words.

Yosef shook his head. "I am sorry. The rest is up to her."

CHAPTER THIRTY-FIVE

Karina stood in the middle of a forest. Flames shot out from the trees around her. She was trapped. No way out. Every time she thought she saw a gap in the inferno, she took a few steps, then the flames would blaze even bolder to cover the spot. *Creator, help me!*

But the fire burned brighter, hotter. Sweat drenched her skin, plastering the plain cotton dress to her body. Voices called out from beyond the flames. Some of them screamed for help. Others taunted her like Faramos had done.

How had she gotten here? Where *was* here? Black smoke blocked the sky from her view.

More voices joined in, growing louder and louder.

She crouched down, hands over her ears. "Make it stop, make it stop," she murmured.

Something poked at her side.

She peeked out of her left eye. The flames were gone. The forest had disappeared. She was surrounded by inky black darkness, save for one blazing light that did not seem to have a source.

A man stood in front of the light, the brightness shadowing his face. Something about him was familiar. She raised her hand to block the light, to try to get a better look. "Hello?" Her voiced echoed around her. Were they in a cave of some sort?

The man did not respond. She took a step forward, and he took one as well. She tried again. "Hello?" Her voice cracked, still raspy from all the smoke.

He still did not say anything. When she took a step, so did he. When she stopped, he stopped. Finally, they were a mere arm's reach away from each other. His face… she gasped. At last, someone she knew. "Sam?"

He did not smile but regarded her as he often did when he did not approve of her latest plan.

"What are you doing here?"

He held out his hands. Hesitant to tear her gaze from his eyes, she glanced down. His hands were covered in a crimson liquid. Blood.

"What happened?"

He met her gaze once again. A red spot blossomed on his chest, soaking through his white shirt too quickly.

"But—but—" What had caused the wound? She did not see any weapon, had not heard anything. Blood seeped from his lips. He opened his mouth, but no sound came out. "Sam? Sam!"

He stumbled toward her.

She reached out to catch him, but there was a dagger in her hand. She froze. Where had that come from? Tipped in red, the silver dagger had bright red rubies in the hilt. Something about it was familiar …

Sam's body crashed into hers. She careened backward, releasing the dagger and crashing to the ground. His body landed on top of her, and she fought to breathe.

Her heart thundered … her pulse raced. What was going on? She shoved him off of her, rolled over, then searched his body. His eyes were vacant.

"Sam, oh my goodness. Sam!" she cried. Tears fell in rivulets down her cheeks. "Don't leave me. Please don't leave me." Her tears became sobs that wracked her chest. She looked again at his vacant blue eyes. No, he could not be gone. He was all she had left. Her only family.

Her chest tightened, strangling her breath. She leaned over Sam's body, trying to suck in air. But there was none to breathe. Nothing in the darkness as it closed in on her like water … the heavy darkness pushing her down.

Sam's body disappeared. But she could not worry about that. Instead, she clutched at her throat, willing her lungs to work properly. She staggered to her feet, glancing around. Nothing. No light. No air. Nothing.

She opened her mouth in a soundless scream. Her eyes closed …

And suddenly she was drawing in air again. Deep, desperate gulps. She coughed, hacked, and then blinked against a disruptive light. She was in a field of wheat at harvest time, and the golden stalks shone in the late afternoon sun. What had happened? Where was she?

Far off, she heard someone call her name. She turned in a slow circle.

"Karina, where are you?" The silky voice sung over the field. Karina opened her mouth to respond, but the voice continued. "You cannot hide from me."

Anaya.

A light flickered out over the tops of the wheat. Karina ducked between the stalks, moving away from the disembodied voice.

"Karina, your time has run out. The Creator cannot help you here."

She shook her head. She would not believe Anaya's lies anymore. The woman brought death to those who followed her.

"She cannot hide for long," The man's voice shouted from the other side of the field—from the side she was headed toward. "Let her try to run." Faramos. His raucous laughter echoed over the field, making Karina's blood run cold.

She angled to the right and ran. Pushing past the stalks of wheat, she dodged through the rows. Her mind sorted through escape plans, discarding them as quickly as they came. How was she going to get out of this? Anaya on one side, Faramos on the other.

Panic clawed her stomach, stealing her breath. She shook her head. She had to focus … had to keep running.

"Karina!" Anaya sang once more, closer now.

She glanced over her shoulder but did not yet see the former queen. *Deep breaths. Keep going.* She turned back to the path in front of her and crashed into a solid body.

Strong hands gripped her arms to keep her from falling backward. "Whoa, Karina. What's going on?"

She looked up into Sam's blue eyes. Her breath caught and then she threw herself into his arms. "By all that is created, Sam, I thought you were dead."

"Dead?" He held her at arm's length again. "Why in the world would you think such a thing?"

Why indeed? Confusion fogged her brain. She could not think straight. "But … I saw … You were on the ground."

He shook his head. "You must have been dreaming."

"It does not matter." She grabbed Sam's hand and tried to pull him along. "We have to get out of here, or you really will be dead."

"What do you mean?"

"Faramos and Anaya are here. They're searching for us … well, me."

Sam stopped. "What is going on?" She tried to pull him after her, but he refused to budge. "Tell me what is happening."

"We need to get out of here first."

He crossed his arms over his chest. Why was he so stubborn?

She huffed. "I am not sure what is going on. I woke up here in the field, and Anaya …"

Sam grunted, staggered, and then groaned.

"Sam, what's wrong?" As he stumbled away, she grabbed his elbow, pulling him back toward her.

He hunched over. Blood seeped through his shirt in the same spot as before.

She gasped. "No, not again." Tears stung her eyes.

Sam stared at her and then grinned.

Stunned, she stopped trying to help him and took a big step backward. His sinister smile sent chills up her spine.

His smile widened, showing his teeth as he laughed. Karina shuffled back all the quicker. As he continued to laugh, his face contorted and began to melt. Like the demons in her challenge for the Belt of Truth.

The belt! She placed a hand on her waist. Gone. What had happened to it?

She glanced back up at Sam. The flesh on his face melted away to bone, and she screamed. Then the flesh began knitting itself back together— muscle and sinew, then skin. Karina's stomach rolled.

And then she was looking at Faramos. Still laughing.

She shrank away and tried to run. But her feet were planted in place. Like a tree, they sunk into the ground with roots spreading out from them. Despite her frantic struggles, she was unable to move.

Faramos stepped forward as Anaya appeared behind him. She did not say anything … her smirk was enough to understand her intent. Faramos stroked Karina's cheek. "To think, you could have lived a life of leisure, never wanting for anything. All you had to do was say yes."

Now everything from her neck down refused to budge. Her arms were stuck to her side as if she were bound. She could not even bend her neck to see what was going on.

Anaya sidled up to Faramos's side and caressed his shoulder. "What should we do with her now?"

Faramos lifted Anaya's chin. "Thank you for helping me."

Her eyes shone with pleasure. Then, her head snapped to the side with a crack, and she slumped to the ground.

Karina's stomach clenched. She could not look away. She breathed in through her nose, willing her body to calm despite the panic crawling through her veins, latching on to every nerve. Anaya was not a good person, but she did not deserve to die in such a horrid manner.

Faramos turned his casual grin back to her. "There now. Where were we?" He took a step toward her, hand outstretched.

"No!" Karina squeezed her eyes shut.

And then the sunlight disappeared, and a crackle replaced Faramos's words. She opened her eyes and found herself in the middle of a ring of fire in the middle of a forest.

Again.

Rashka leaned against the cave wall as she watched Karina. The way she seemed unable to move was uncanny. She hardly blinked. This would not do. Rashka was not used to feeling helpless—but staring at the unmoving prophetess, with nothing to fight, no way to help …

She pushed off the wall and wandered outside. Over by some recently downed trees, Tristan went through practice paces with his sword. Sweat soaked the back of his tunic, and his grunts and shouts reached all the way over to where she stood. She could not imagine what he was going through right now—all the pent-up emotions.

Part of her wanted to go over and commiserate with him. Help him through this. A larger part of her wanted nothing to do with these pesky human emotions. Not after all she had lost.

Tristan lunged with his sword, stumbled, and fell to his knees. He sat there, heaving, staring at the ground. Better to leave him to his own thoughts.

She moved toward the cave as Yosef came over from attending the horses. "Any change?"

She shook her head.

"We need to get going. We cannot properly care for her here. She should be resting somewhere comfortable. If we get to the temple, they will have a place for her."

Rashka looked off to where Tristan was climbing to his feet. "I do not know how we will convince him to move her."

"But we must. Now."

She remained quiet for a long time.

"We do not know how long we will be safe here. Anaya could find us—"

"I know," Rashka snapped. Closing her eyes, she breathed deeply. "Go gather our things in the cave. I will talk to Tristan."

Yosef disappeared into the cave while Rashka tried to prepare herself mentally for the upcoming conversation. Tristan had resumed his paces, but they were not quite as energetic as before. "Your advances are a little sloppy. You need to be sharper."

Tristan stopped. Hands on his hips, he studied the sky.

"Tristan, we need to go."

"Karina is not well enough to travel."

"Karina is fine. Physically, she would survive any trip right now. The sooner we can get her to the temple, the better."

"The better?" He spun around. "How do you know? What can they do that we cannot? That the priest cannot?"

Rashka gently touched his arm. "They can give her a comfortable place to rest. They can watch over her, so we can rest as well."

He shrugged her off.

"And if Anaya should find us out here …"

Tristan straightened. "I would kill her where she stood."

Men! Why were they so stubborn? "Tristan, you know we cannot stay here. Get your emotions under control, because I need your help to protect Yosef and Karina on this journey."

Tristan glared. Well, let him be upset. He was putting his emotions above his duty. He had sworn to protect Karina. This is what was best.

"Fine." Tristan sheathed his sword and stormed past her.

Within minutes, their supplies were packed and loaded onto the horses. Rashka helped Tristan get Karina on Dom's back and held her there while Tristan swung up behind her. When he assured Rashka he was ready, she stepped back.

"I am going to fly over the area to be sure Anaya is not following us. Then I will come back and ride with you." She turned to Yosef. "How much further?"

Yosef scanned the area from atop his horse. "If we hurry, we may reach the temple before the midnight hour. If we take it slower and rest, we should arrive by midday tomorrow."

"Then let us hurry." Rashka raised her arms. A bright light engulfed her as her body transformed. She gave in to the swirling heat and relaxed. With a flap of her wings, she lifted into the sky.

Below her, Tristan and Yosef headed west, keeping the sea to their left. She flew in slow circles, small at first then larger, keeping them at the far side as she flew east and north.

Trees drifted under her, and clearings came and went. No sign of Anaya or her soldiers. Had they abandoned their mission? She surveyed the area for a couple of hours until convinced Anaya had left. Still, she flew farther to the west to be sure they had not gotten ahead of them where they could take them by surprise.

Far off to the horizon, she spied an island. The glint of gold caught her attention. Could that be the temple? Although she had visited the sacred temple of Tzedek in her early years before she became a Guardian—in fact it had been the first place in the Three Kingdoms she had set foot after leaving the island of the elves—she had never been to Soter's temple.

Time to return to Karina's side. She angled away from the late afternoon sun, making a lazy turn back to the east. Her wings were tired, and her head was foggy. She needed rest.

Finally, she found Tristan and Yosef. Even from way up here, she could tell they were hunched over and solemn. Karina's condition must be weighing heavy on both of them. If only she knew how to heal Karina, she could bring some life back to their traveling party. She circled down and landed in front of them. With a flash, she was herself again. She stretched her sore muscles.

"We were wondering what became of you." Yosef tilted his head to the side, looking so much like a curious child.

"I apologize if I was gone too long. Perhaps Anaya has given up her search for now. I saw no one else in the area."

"Good." Tristan nudged Dom forward again.

Rashka took the reins of her horse from Yosef's outstretched hand and climbed up. She took her bow from the saddle holder and swung it over her back. Better to be prepared for the unexpected.

Tristan forged on ahead, though Yosef stayed at her side—quiet as he stared off at the ocean to their left. She peered over at him. His perplexed expression said a lot, though he had plenty of reasons to fret. He had been thrown into all of this somewhat unexpectedly. His future was now as unsure as the rest of theirs.

"Is Soter's sacred temple on an island?" she asked.

He nodded. "The only way to get to the temple is by ferry. Most of the time the area is shrouded in mist."

"Interesting. I wonder why the elders decided to make it so inaccessible."

"I am not sure. I often wondered the same thing." He fell back into silence, not offering more of an explanation, which was odd compared to his normal chatty demeanor.

The rest of the afternoon and evening trudged on in silence. Little changed with the scenery. Trees far off on the right, ocean to the left. As they continued through the hills, the intermittent rocky terrain gave way to grassy knolls. Sometimes the sea was below soaring cliffs, and at other times a mere trek across a thin beach.

The sun slanted to the horizon and began to slip below the sea. They came upon a shallow valley between two large hills. Tristan halted and waited for them. "We should make camp. We will not be making it to the temple tonight."

Rashka glanced at Yosef, who shrugged. She would have preferred to push through until they at least had reached the ferry to the temple. But Tristan had already dismounted, pulling Karina off with him. He laid her on a patch of grass.

"Rashka, find some wood. Yosef, please check over Karina." He did not wait for them to respond but began unpacking the horses.

Rashka nodded to Yosef, and they both set out to accomplish their assigned task. She quickly found an armful of sticks and branches and returned to the camp to make a fire. By that time, Yosef was helping Tristan brush down the horses.

Everyone worked in silence. A tension hung over the camp, which did not tempt Rashka to break the silence. The others were lost in their own thoughts of what was to come just as she was. Who knew what waited for them at the temple or beyond? Would she be tasked with one of the challenges? Of course, it only made sense. The thought made her anxious as she set about creating fire with flint stones.

Finally, they settled around the fire for dinner. Yosef had roasted a rabbit Tristan had caught earlier in the day. Still, nothing but silence.

Rashka stared at her empty bowl. Uncomfortable with the deafening stillness, she was yet unable to bring herself to break it. Why had the Creator tasked her to deal with any of this? She wanted to complete the quest as soon as possible and return to her home in Shadowed Forest.

"Who knows what tomorrow will bring." Yosef cleared his throat as Rashka and Tristan glanced his way. "I fear we may be on the edge of failing this quest."

Tristan glowered, staring into the fire.

"Do not say such things, Yosef." Rashka sat her bowl to the side. "Despite all the setbacks, the Creator has always provided. And I trust he will continue to do so."

Yosef did not even look at her. "You are a fool."

She frowned. Why did he—a priest—say such things? He had not been through many of the struggles the rest of the group had been so far on this journey. "I understand you are discouraged—"

"Discouraged? I am facing the truth, the reality of the situation."

She shook her head. From his perspective, their quest surely appeared on the verge of toppling into failure. "You have to have hope."

"There is no hope out here." He still refused to look at her, studying the fire even more intensely than Tristan, who let his gaze flicker over to Yosef now and then.

No hope? That was a depressing thought. There was always hope. The more she tried to convince herself, the more his melancholy slipped into her soul. She did trust the Creator's plan, though all this was overwhelming, even to her. Every delay. Every mistake. Every mishap. Why did they think they could accomplish any of this when the quest promised only to worsen from here on out? She sighed.

"We are all going to die."

Tristan threw a rock in Yosef's direction. "Stop that."

Yosef did not move, did not blink.

Rashka leaned forward. In fact, he had not blinked at all during this conversation. "Tristan …"

He had already reached for his sword. "I know."

Yosef laughed. "So, you figured it out, did you?"

Rashka furrowed her brow. What did he mean?

"Faramos." Tristan angled his sword toward their new friend.

"Good to see you again, brother."

"That's a new trick," she said as she stood, pulling her bow from her back.

"Good evening, Rashka. You are looking well."

"What have you done to the real Yosef?" Tristan demanded.

"Just a little magic. No harm to him."

"Release him."

Yosef grinned. "I will, soon. I only wanted to peek in to see how your journey was going. Where is my beloved?"

Rashka glanced at Karina, lying on the other side of the fire. She did not seem to be aware of what was going on.

"Ah, something has happened to her, has it? Tristan, could you not care for one woman?"

Tristan growled and took a step toward Yosef.

"Tristan, you cannot harm him."

He narrowed his eyes, dropping his sword to his side.

"And where is Sam, the best friend, the unrealized lover?"

Rashka cast her gaze away, not wanting to remember the horror from a few nights ago. Sam …

"Dead?" Yosef's eyebrows wagged. "Officially this time? No chance of popping up again?"

Tristan clenched his jaw, raked his hair with his fingers, and turned away.

"Well, I guess I shall leave you all to mourn your loss—or losses rather. Pity about Karina. She may never recover from this."

Tristan kicked a clod of dirt into the fire and wandered away from the camp, far enough to not be seen by Faramos but close enough to jump in if he posed any danger.

Yosef grinned again. "Until we meet again." His body convulsed for a moment and then the real Yosef shook his head. "What happened? Where did Tristan go?"

Rashka sighed and dropped her bow to the ground as she sunk down next to it. Her head drooped. She was tired, so very tired.

"Rashka?" Yosef laid a hand on her shoulder. "What happened?"

CHAPTER THIRTY-SIX

Karina could not catch her breath. No matter what she did. The air was too thin, the watery darkness closing in too tightly. She fell to her hands and knees. *Breathe, Karina, breathe. Oh, Sam. Tell me I have not lost you.* No answer. No life next to her. She could not see his body anymore. *May I see you in the Lighted Realm.*

When she opened her eyes, though, she was not in the Lighted Realm. She was in a wheat field. In the middle of the day. "How did I get here?" she whispered.

"Karina!" A sing-song voice floated across the stalks of grain.

This scene was all-too familiar, as if she had been here before. The sting of Sam's death hung heavy in the back of her mind, but she could not deal with her sorrow right now. She had to figure out what these images meant.

"Karina, where are you? You cannot hide from me," the voice sang again. Anaya.

This had happened before. All of this. She ducked, knowing a light would blast across the field.

"Karina, your time has run out. The Creator cannot help you here."

She shook her head. What was going on? She felt like there was something else she should be doing. How did she get out of here?

"She cannot hide for long," another voice shouted. Faramos. He was here too. "Let her try to run." His cackling laugh still chilled her blood.

She should run. No … not this time. She had to do something different. *Creator, help me. What do I do?*

"Karina!" Anaya sang once more, the tones closer now.

She glanced around, more of the scene coming back to her. Sam would appear next.

Sure enough, he stepped through the stalks of golden wheat. "Whoa, Karina. What's going on?"

Sam's blue eyes distracted her. Her breath caught. If only this were real

…

A memory flashed through her mind. Sam, lying on his back while Sabreen backed away slowly. Sabreen. She had killed Sam. She had meant to kill Karina and would have if Sam had not stepped in the way. Sam had given his life to save her. Her best friend was gone.

Tears prickled the corner of her eyes, but she could not afford to let them fall now. "You are not Sam," she whispered.

"Am I not?" Sam tilted his head, peering into her eyes. His lips pulled into that playful boyish smile she loved so much. "Are you sure?"

She nodded, backing away slowly. "Faramos."

"Excuse me?"

"You are not Sam … you are Faramos," she screamed.

He laughed as his face began to change again. This time, she was able to tear her gaze away, to avoid the horror. She remembered everything.

The silver dagger with rubies appeared in her hand again. Confusion swept over her as Faramos's laughter echoed in the background. She looked up in time to see Anaya walk up behind him, her smirk telling a story all its own.

No. This would not happen again.

She plunged the blade into Faramos's gut. "I will not fail."

Karina blinked against the warm midday sun. What was going on? This—this was not part of the loop she had been experiencing. She was riding atop Dom, leaning back against …

She shifted slightly against the hard planes of a toned chest and stomach. Tristan! She immediately tried to arch her back, but it was like her body refused to obey her thoughts. Her movements were too slow.

"Karina?" Tristan whispered into her ear.

She groaned. Her muscles were sore, her head ached, and she struggled to stay upright on the horse. Praise the Creator, Tristan's arm held her safely in place.

"Karina!" Tristan reined in Dom and angled around to look at her face.

"What happened?" she croaked like a frog. Rashka and Yosef appeared in her line of vision. She smiled. "Why do I feel like it's been awhile since last I saw you?"

Yosef laughed, but Rashka's eyes misted before she had a chance to turn away. The three of them dismounted at the same time, and Karina allowed Tristan to pull her off Dom.

"Welcome back, Prophetess," Dom said with a toss of his head.

"Back? Did I go somewhere?"

Tristan bent over until his forehead touched hers. "You were lost."

She let his nearness warm the icy pit in her stomach, even if she did not understand what he meant. They helped her over to a rock mound, and Yosef handed her a water skin. She gulped the water down, the lukewarm liquid respite for her raw throat. When she had handed the water back to Yosef, she regarded all of them. They seemed so happy to see her, but someone was missing.

"Where's Sam?"

Immediately, everyone's face changed. No one would meet her gaze. And in an instant, the memories returned.

"Sam's dead."

Her words were more of a statement than a question, but Rashka nodded. Tristan turned away, his hands interlaced behind his head. Yosef studied something on the ground. Tears trickled down her cheek. Her best friend was really gone. "He—he saved me."

Tristan wrapped her in his arms and kissed the top of her head. "Yes, he did."

A sob escaped her throat, and Tristan held her tighter. She let herself cry for the loss—for all her losses. What would she have at the end of this? Would she even have her own life?

When the well of sorrow had run dry, she pulled away, wiped the tears from her cheeks, and offered her friends a small smile. "We have to move on from this now. Sam would want us to continue on the quest." She nodded—more for her own benefit than theirs—and then surveyed the rocky terrain with patches of grass and trees. Behind her, the sea stretched seemingly forever, sparkling in the sunlight. "Where are we?"

They took turns relating to Karina the events of the past couple of days. Yosef gestured further down the shoreline. "We are not far from the ferry to the temple."

"Then let's go!" She attempted to stand, but her legs were too weak. She slumped against Tristan.

"Whoa there." He looped an arm around her waist.

Yosef took a minute to look her over. "You will be fine. You are dehydrated from lack of water, your weakness exacerbated by lack of food." He handed her the water skin again. "I will grab you something to eat from the packs. You do not want to eat too much too quickly, but a small amount of bread will not hurt."

"Once you have rested a bit, we will move on." Rashka patted Karina's arm. "I am so glad to see you talking and moving again." She glanced toward Tristan. "I am going to take to the sky and scout the area before we come upon the ferry. We do not want to tip any of Anaya's scouts off."

He nodded. What did Rashka mean?

"Where is Anaya?" Karina asked.

Rashka, already in hawk form, flew off. Tristan helped Karina sit again and scooted in close to her. "We don't know. We think she may have given up the search, though that is unlikely. For now, we want to make sure we don't tip her off on the location of the temple."

"Oh." She nestled against Tristan's side, soaking in the continued warmth. She did not feel cold—on the outside at least. Yet, there was an emptiness inside, a hollow where Sam used to be. She sighed.

CHAPTER THIRTY-SEVEN

All the arguments this morning made Rashka want to throw the men in the ocean to cool down.

Tristan glared at Yosef. "You want us to do what?"

Yosef let out an exaggerated sigh. "Get in the boat."

"You called that boat out of nowhere. It's floating on its own … no oars. How is that possible?"

Rashka rolled her eyes. Dumb oaf still did not understand the depth of power the Creator possessed.

Tristan scowled. "It's not magic, is it? You saw what happened with Sam."

Yosef shook his head earnestly. "It is not magic—a gift from the Creator. The boat does not appear for just anyone. Only for priests and other chosen ones." He gestured toward Karina.

"But …"

Rashka stepped between them, holding up her hands. "Tristan, get in the boat. Help Karina."

"Fine." He grumbled but held Karina's hand as they both boarded.

Rashka could not see any land beyond the water, though Yosef had assured her the island was hidden by a mist that covered everything beyond a few feet from the shoreline. While she trusted Yosef, she did not like to be blinded to what was in front of her.

She climbed into the boat behind Yosef, who sat on one of the middle boards and then settled onto a seat at the opposite end from Tristan and Karina.

"What now?" Tristan asked.

Yosef said a short prayer, and the boat began to move.

Rashka stretched, willing her body to relax. Most likely, nothing lurked out here for them to fear. Like in Aletheia, the priests protected the area surrounding the temple. She should be able to breathe more easily. Still, with the disasters that had befallen them so far, she steeled herself to expect the worst.

They were all quiet as the boat drifted on the glassy sea, the only sound was the gentle lapping of water against the side of the boat. Across from her, Karina rested against Tristan's shoulder while he held her close. Inseparable since she had awoken, Tristan had ridden behind her atop Dom the rest of the way. Though she seemed weak, her color had returned, much to Rashka's relief.

The tranquility of the water mixed with the foggy air relaxed Rashka more than she had expected. She inhaled deeply and let her mind drift.

"Come on, Rashka."

She startled and jumped up, almost falling into the water as the boat rocked beneath her shifting weight. "What happened?"

Karina smiled. "You fell asleep."

Sleep? She had never done such a thing before. She got only as much rest as she needed and pushed on. What was wrong with her? She frowned. Perhaps she was more tired than …

Tristan helped Karina onto a shadowed dock. The sun was high in the sky, but mist still clung to the air. Yosef climbed up behind them and then stuck out a hand to help her. Though unaccustomed to such courtesy, she allowed him to help her out of the boat.

A large shadow loomed beyond the fog. The shape was familiar, the same as the Temple of Aletheia. As they came to the end of the dock, an archway came into view—the same shape and build as the Aletheian temple, but the gate was gold instead of silver.

Several priests in long white robes rushed out to the archway, opening the gate for them. A massive bald man stepped forward. "I am Elite Elder Samson. How may we assist you?" He surveyed the ragtag group, his widening eyes settled on Rashka. "Forgive me, Guardian. We were not expecting anyone."

Karina stepped aside to let Rashka to the front.

Rashka bowed her head to the elder priest. "All is well, Elder Samson. We have come on a quest from the Creator." She gestured toward Karina, who offered the priest a small smile even as she was still tucked under Tristan's arm. "This is the Creator's chosen one, his Prophetess."

Whispers broke out among the small group of priests. Elder Samson held up his hand, and silence fell in the courtyard.

"This is big news," he said. "Please, come inside the temple. Once you are refreshed, you can relate your tale to the rest of the Trium."

Rashka nodded and steered Tristan and Karina ahead.

The priests led them to a corridor and settled each of them into private rooms. Rashka was grateful to have some time to herself as she bathed and dressed. With time to think without interruption, she sorted through the last few days. Sam's death still weighed heavily on her. She concentrated on what was most important—the quest. There would be a time to mourn later.

She pinned up her freshly braided hair, then donned the pale green dress already in the wardrobe. She much preferred her leather pants and vest to the prim and proper attire expected in the temple.

When she had dressed, she sought out Karina's room and knocked.

"Come in," Karina called.

Rashka entered and quickly shut the door behind her. "I came to see if—oh."

Karina sat at a vanity while two priestesses fussed over her hair. She glanced at Rashka and offered a forced smile.

"I suppose you do not need my assistance," Rashka said with a smirk.

Karina giggled. "No, I suppose not, but I am glad you are here."

"Indeed. As I am glad you are here."

A distant look clouded Karina's lively eyes. "I cannot believe what happened. It's all so … much. I am overwhelmed by all these emotions."

"*Tsk*," said one of the priestesses. "Hold still, Prophetess."

Rashka sauntered over and shooed the priestesses away, assuring them Karina was well taken care of and they would be out shortly. "Karina, all is well. Yes, we have suffered great losses, but the Creator's light is still on our path." Despite her encouraging tone, her heart did not echo the compassion in those words. Worse, she felt nothing.

Karina sighed. "I know."

"What is it that bothers you so?"

"I do not know." She stood and smoothed the skirt of her dark blue dress. Her balance was still a little off, but she appeared to be able to move on her own now. "The more that happens, the less equipped I feel to complete the quest."

"Maybe that is the way it is supposed to be?"

"What do you mean?"

Rashka headed toward the door, suddenly uncomfortable in this conversation, though she did not know why. "If you were able to rely on your own strength, why would you need the Creator at all?"

"But I trust the Creator. I do not need so many reminders!"

Rashka paused as she opened the door. "Maybe the reminders are not for you."

Once in the hall, they met up with Tristan and Yosef. "We were coming to check on you ladies. The Trium is ready to convene in the sanctuary."

Karina accepted Tristan's arm, and he led them out into the great hall. The layout was almost exactly like the Aletheian temple, except the color scheme was green and gold, giving the whole temple a different ambiance. Warmer in some ways …

They ascended the golden staircase to the sanctuary doors, also plated in gold. The opulence reminded her of Gundow … excess everywhere. Had the temple always been like this?

The doors opened, and Elder Samson escorted them in. The sanctuary was bigger than the one in the Aletheian temple, space enough for the many priests and priestesses lining the seats along the sides. Everyone bowed their heads in reverence as their group moved up the aisle.

This time the other two elders of the Trium were already standing behind their chairs on the dais—a short female elf with dark curls on the right and an older human male in the middle. Elder Samson made his way around the chairs to his seat to the left of the head elder, where he easily dwarfed the other two elders. He addressed everyone in the room. "May I present Prophetess Karina and her friends, including Rashka, Guardian of Shadowed Forest. They have quite the tale to relate."

He nodded to the head elder, a slender man with graying hair, who smiled at Karina. "I am Eliandor, Head Elder of the Temple of Soter. It is a pleasure to have you all in our sanctuary on this day."

"Thank you, Elder Eliandor. I am Karina, Queen of Aletheia and Prophetess of the Creator. What a blessing to find such kindness here in your temple." Her voice, loud and clear, belied the exhaustion she must still be experiencing. She continued, introducing them all in turn.

Rashka found herself restless already. A sense of change resonated within her soul. Something was coming. She peered around the room, yet all seemed well.

"What brings you to us, Prophetess?" Elder Eliandor asked.

"How much have you heard of Faramos, king of Tzedek?"

Eliandor's face darkened. "There has been rumor of this warlock and his most despicable plans."

Karina nodded. "He has unleashed an ancient evil that has become a blight on the people of this land." She shuffled in a circle, addressing the whole room. "Faramos seeks to become supreme ruler of our world, though he does not have the Creator's blessing to do such a thing."

The priests began murmuring amongst themselves until Eliandor silenced them. "We have heard of this evil, though we did not realize it had become so prevalent."

"The Creator has sent me to retrieve the sacred armor,"—a collective gasp went through the room—"and I am here for the next two pieces of armor."

Eliandor narrowed his eyes. "How do we know you are telling the truth? Though we certainly trust Rashka, we need to be careful."

Karina touched the braided belt around her waist. "This is the Belt of Truth." She nodded to Tristan, who held up his right hand. "And he wears the Shield of Faith."

The whispers started up again. Eliandor looked at Samson. They spoke with their eyes, not saying anything, until Eliandor turned back to Karina. He waited while the room quieted. "This is serious, indeed. What do we need to do to help you?"

Karina hesitated, glancing at Rashka. Perhaps she did not know how to respond either. Should the Trium not know about the challenges?

"Pardon me, sir, but do you not have the next two pieces of armor at the other end of challenges like the Temple of Aletheia?"

He frowned. The elf woman leaned over and whispered in his ear. His eyebrows shot up. "Apparently we do have challenges you must face. Who will be embarking on those challenges?"

"Rashka, Guardian of Shadowed Forest, and Yosef, Priest of Gundow."

Rashka's eyes widened. Although she already knew by deduction she and Yosef would be the ones, hearing the declaration aloud secured her fate. From the expression on Yosef's face, he must be feeling much the same way.

"Very well. We will begin at dawn tomorrow. For now, let us retire to an evening meal, and then we will let you get some sleep."

Karina bowed her head and then flashed Rashka a bright smile. As they walked, she wrapped an arm around Rashka's elbow. "Are you ready?"

That was a very good question. Was she?

CHAPTER THIRTY-EIGHT

The morning dawned gray and dismal. The fog was denser today, making it impossible for Rashka to see anything beyond her window. The sound of ocean waves did little to soothe her spirit. She inhaled the salty air, praying for encouragement.

She was not as attached to the ocean as her brother had been when they were children. Asharan spent many of his days on the seashore—whether practicing with his sword or learning his ciphers. Rashka much preferred the forest, to be on solid ground. Still, the waves often soothed the chaotic places in her mind.

Thoughts of her brother, now gone as well, saddened her. So much loss. So much pain. What was the purpose of such things in this life? Perhaps this is why she preferred the solitude of the forest. Except for checking in with the temple from time to time and stopping in River Branch for supplies, she did not have to converse with people very often. Maybe that is why the Creator chose her to serve in Shadowed Forest.

A soft knock on the door brought her out of her memories. She retreated from the window as Karina let herself in. She wore the same long, lace-layered white dress as Rashka, an aspect of this place that differed from the Temple of Aletheia. "Ah, so you are awake."

Rashka raised an eyebrow. "As are you. Is everything well?"

Karina nodded and eased down on the bed. While she acted sprightly, dark circles lined her eyes and her shoulders were not as straight as usual. "I could not sleep. As dawn approached, I thought I would see how you are doing."

"Oh, Your Majesty, do not worry about me."

"Rashka …"

She hid a smile. "Sorry, Karina."

"You were expecting this, right?"

She turned back to the window. "I was. I am prepared." But was she? If her experience were to be anything like Karina's and Tristan's experiences, the Creator would be exposing some weakness. While she could not fathom what that weakness might be, she had no desire to face the reality of imperfection. Had she not served the Creator well until now? She was strong, fast, quick-witted. She had protected Shadowed Forest and the Temple of Aletheia for years. So, why had this quest been so hard for her? Why had she not been able to protect Karina and the rest of the people entrusted to her care?

"I believe there is more you are not saying," Karina said gently. "But I will not press you further. I know the seriousness of what lies before you today."

"Do you have any word from the Creator to share with me? Did you have a vision?"

Karina shook her head. "He has been oddly quiet on this. Other than naming you two."

Rashka breathed out a long sigh.

"Shall we head to the great hall? The priests should be arriving soon."

She stood and followed Karina out the door and down the corridor. "Have Tristan and Yosef already made their way to the great hall?"

Karina shrugged. "I have not seen them this morning. Did you break your fast? The tray in your room was untouched."

Rashka placed a hand on her stomach. "No, I could not eat this morning."

The prophetess nodded but said nothing more.

While a few priests dotted the great hall, with its gilded pillars and marble floors flecked with gold, she and Karina were among the first to arrive. Rashka stood straight, chin high, determined to face this challenge with all the dignity and integrity expected of a Guardian. She would not let the priests see any sign of fear, lest they deem her unworthy.

She remained quiet as the rest of the priests arrived, including the Trium. Finally, Tristan and Yosef made their appearance as the fog outside began to lift.

"Are we going outside?" Karina asked Head Elder Eliandor.

"Indeed. The entrance to the challenge is in the temple gardens."

They followed the head priest out the large double doors and around the side of the temple. Flowers of all colors lined the pathway, but the thick fog hid the world beyond the flowers, like a haunted garden. Sounds of life filtered through the mist, though Rashka could see nothing.

Karina walked beside her. Rashka smiled at how comforting the prophetess's presence had become. No matter what transpired, she knew Karina was on her side, would be there for her. Still, it was *her* job to protect the prophetess, not the other way around.

In the middle of the garden, Eliandor stopped and addressed the crowd of priests and priestesses in a loud voice. "Elite Servant Duma will lead us in prayer."

Duma, the elven woman of the Trium, stepped forward. She asked everyone to bow their heads and said a rather lengthy prayer. Rashka's mind wandered, though she tried to focus on the words. *My apologies for lack of attention, Creator.*

At last, the prayer was over, and Eliandor stepped forward. "Once again, Prophetess, who has the Creator chosen for this challenge?"

"Rashka, Guardian of Shadowed Forest, and Yosef, Priest of Gundow."

"Thank you, Prophetess. Rashka and Yosef, please come forward."

Rashka glanced at Karina, who patted her arm and offered a bright smile. "You will be fine," she whispered.

Whatever Karina thought, fine was not how Rashka felt. Her stomach suddenly bunched into knots. What if she failed? What if she could not face her weakness? What *was* her weakness? Thoughts collided in her mind, muddling her concentration even more. What had gotten into her? She was not so easily ruffled. Why was this challenge taxing her composure?

Eliandor launched into a diatribe on the history of the armor, all stories Rashka had heard before. Which was a good thing, because her focus was not getting any better. Her gaze chased imaginary shadows in the fog. Her mind flitted from one thought to the next. She inhaled a slow, deep breath, but it did little to help.

Had this quest broken her mind? Was this the weakness the challenge would expose? If her mind was broken, would she survive? She clenched her fists. Of course, she would survive. She was a Guardian!

Eliandor concluded his speech with these final words: "So without further delay, we usher Rashka and Yo—"

"Excuse me!" Karina raised her hand. "Do you not have any instructions for Rashka and Yosef? Or supplies maybe?"

Duma's dark curls bounced as she shook her head. "They will have no need of outside supplies for this challenge." Her gaze slipped to Rashka.

"Although, be warned. Your shapeshifting ability will not work in the challenge."

Rashka chewed on her lip. "What about my other abilities? Healing?"

"I believe you should still be able to use them."

She nodded as Karina rejoined Tristan. He whispered something in her ear. She shrugged. Yosef glanced at Rashka, and she smiled at him. They would get through this.

Eliandor stepped aside, revealing a golden gate that opened into a beautiful garden. At the gate, Yosef paused and waved to the crowd as they cheered them on.

"We will be waiting for you when you finish." Karina called after them, her words an encouragement.

Rashka took a deep breath and plunged into the garden. Unlike the cave, there appeared to be only one path. "This is odd. Are we supposed to stay together?"

"What do you mean?"

"Karina and Tristan were separated for their challenges. Karina followed a path labeled Truth, while Tristan followed the one that said Faith."

"But we have only one path here."

Rashka nodded. "Which is why I thought it was odd."

"Maybe the requirements for this challenge are different?"

"Maybe so."

They continued in silence for a while. The path seemed to wind around the garden, no particular direction, no particular destination in sight.

"Do you know anything about the challenges?" she asked Yosef.

He shook his head. "Only the Trium of the temple know the particulars about them. I thought it peculiar when Eliandor did not know."

"Last night, before I retired for the evening, I believe Duma mentioned he was newly appointed. The previous Head Elder passed away unexpectedly."

"Ah, so maybe the information had not been passed down yet."

The mist gave way to a tall wall. Dense bushes arched out from both sides. No way around it.

"What are we supposed to do here?" Yosef turned in a circle.

Rashka could not see any other paths or exits. They had to do something with the wall. A light shone through the mist, highlighting letters etched in gold on the pale stone plaque. She pointed at the lettering. "Look, Yosef."

He traced over the symbols. "On your own strength you cannot depend. Up and over, or you will meet your end." He stepped back and surveyed the wall. "What does that mean?"

"I am not sure. But something tells me we do not have much time to figure it out."

"What?"

Growls sounded in the distance.

"What are those?" Yosef glanced back the way they had come.

"I do not think we want to find out." She studied the top of the wall. She might be able to … She moved backward to get a running start, then jumped as high as she could, her fingertips sweeping the top. She landed in a crouch.

A loud creak and then the sound of stone rubbing against stone. "What was that?"

Yosef cleared his throat. "The wall just got taller."

Rashka rounded on him. "What?"

"After you landed, the walls grew about a hand's width."

"Not possible." She reached up. Sure enough, the wall had grown. Trick of the challenge.

Howls echoed through the mist, sending a shiver up her spine. She did not want to deal with lupens today. If they were lupens.

Taking a deep breath, she tried again. Her fingers did not reach quite as high but still hit the top of the wall. She landed with a huff. The wall creaked and groaned again.

Dusting off her hands, she stared at the growing walls. "How do we get over this?"

Howls again … closer this time.

Yosef let out an unsteady breath. "Well, it says we cannot rely on our own strength."

"Whose strength are we supposed to depend on? It's not like the Creator is going to reach down, pluck us up, and drop us on the other side."

Yosef grinned. "But that would be pretty spectacular."

She glared at him. The sound of pattering paws reached them from beyond the fog. They were running out of time. "Think!" She paced in front of the wall. "Not my own strength, not *my* own strength—"

Yosef hurried to join her at the wall. "That's it!"

Howls echoed just around the corner. They would be dead any minute. She waited impatiently for Yosef to continue. "Well?"

"Not *my* own strength—our strength."

"You are not making any sense, and I do not want to die, Yosef!"

"Our strength. We need to help each other."

"How?"

His eyes flitted around for a moment. Then he clasped his hands together and bent over. "Step into my hands, and I will boost you up. When you are at the top, pull me up with you."

Brilliant. Hastily, she stepped into his palms and between his push and her leap, she grasped the top of the wall and pulled herself onto the smooth stone top. From her vantage point, she could barely see the outline of the lupens as they entered the clearing.

"Yosef, hurry!" She flattened herself on the top of the wall and reached out her hand. "Grab my hand."

But Yosef was frozen in place. He saw the lupens too.

"Yosef, listen to me." He did not seem to hear her. "Yosef!"

He glanced up, wary of taking his eyes off the lupens now stalking him. "Jump."

He faced the wall and reached up. Not tall enough.

"Jump!"

He leaped and his fingers grazed hers … but he fell back to the ground. The soft growl of a lupen reached through the fog.

"Again."

Yosef took a couple of steps back, ran forward, and leapt. Rashka reached down as far as she could. When his hand hit hers, she closed her fingers, vise-like. Throwing out her other arm, she grabbed onto both his hands and then pulled as hard as she could. His legs scraped against the stone wall as he scampered up and over.

They both lay on their backs, panting. They had almost been lupen fodder. Why would her mind not work like usual? Why was she so slow? She groaned. She was not herself.

Yosef let out a long sigh as he sat up. "So, how do we get down from here?"

CHAPTER THIRTY-NINE

Yosef's sore muscles were a testament to how long it had been since he had ventured beyond the public temple to run on the sandy shores below the city. Climbing the wall and then using hand and foot holds to descend the other side tried his strength. By the time he was done, his mouth was parched. What he would not give for a drink.

As if answering his prayer, the sound of rushing water sliced through the fog. They had been at this for a couple of hours, and the fog had not thinned in the least. The rushing river grew louder and eventually revealed itself through the mist. Though wide, its roar was like one of the biggest rivers Yosef had ever seen. Not that he had seen many. He had not traveled much, save one trip to Calliope in Aletheia as a child.

He ran to the bank of the river and drank greedily.

"You sure the water is safe?" Rashka asked as she sat down next to him.

Before the words were out of her mouth, he spit the water out. Saltwater. He had not considered the possibility this might be the next test. He shot her a sheepish grin, wiped the water from his mouth, and sat back. "It was saltwater anyway."

She shook her head, a smile playing at the corners of her lips. His heart warmed at the sight. She had been so serious in the time he had known her. Even before Sam's death. Not that he had seen much reason to smile, even then.

"I suppose we have to cross here." She nodded toward the opposite bank. "The path continues over there."

He looked up and down the river. "Well, I see steppingstones to my left and a rickety old bridge to my right."

"Past experience tells me only one way is the right way."

"How do we know which one?"

She shrugged.

What was the purpose of these challenges anyway? He did not understand why the priests could not just hand over the pieces of armor so

Karina and her friends could be on their way. More than that, he wished he would have known what he was getting into when he left Gundow. He had only meant to show them the way to the temple, not join the quest in such a personal manner.

"I say we take the steppingstones. They look sturdier than the bridge." Rashka stood, wiping dirt off her pants.

"Sounds as good a reason as any."

Yosef followed the guardian over to the stones, where about a dozen were scattered in a zigzag fashion across the width of the river. Some were larger than others, while some were flatter and others more rounded.

"Be careful," he warned as Rashka leapt out on the first one.

She landed with the grace only an elf could possess. After flashing a triumphant grin, she continued to the next one. When he did not follow behind, she paused and put her hands on her hips. "Are you coming, priest?"

"I suppose." He tried to ignore the rushing water. While he enjoyed his runs by the sea back in Gundow, he had never learned to swim. He would do well to keep his balance if he did not want to end up fighting for his life.

He jumped to the first rock, waving his hands wildly when he landed. Rashka reined in an amused smile but then leapt to the next rock. He followed onto the second one.

"See? Nothing to—"

The rock below her began to move.

Rashka's arms flailed. "By all that is created!"

The rock careened sharply, tossing her to the side.

"Rashka!" Yosef knelt on his stone, hand extended.

She landed in the water with a mighty splash, disappearing beneath the surface. Behind her, large eyes and a long snout with a mouth full of sharp teeth appeared. What matter of water beast was this? It opened its massive jaw which then snapped shut with a loud crack.

He did not have time to be properly terrified as Rashka broke the surface with a gasp for air. "Rashka, hurry! The beast!"

She shook her head, slinging water from her face, then glanced behind her. Her eyes bulged as she twisted back to him, reaching for his outstretched hand. He struggled to grasp her slick hand.

Beyond the beast, the other steppingstones began to move, six creatures in all.

"C'mon," Yosef muttered, pulling Rashka onto the stone next to him, water sloshing all over him as well. There was not enough room for the two of them as they fought to maintain balance. With a deep breath, he lunged back to the first stone and then back onto solid ground.

Snapping jaws hastened Rashka's retreat as she leapt across the two stones and onto the riverbank. They stood, side-by-side, heaving deep breaths. Yosef's body began to relax.

Until the first water beast began to waddle out of the water.

He jumped back. "What is that thing?"

In addition to its lengthy snout, the creature had a long body and a sturdy tail. Its four appendages resembled stout fins, made for the sea yet allowing it to move slowly on land as well.

"To the bridge!" Rashka grabbed his arm and pulled him along. They dashed along the bank to the dilapidated bridge.

Glancing over his shoulder, Yosef counted three beasts on land while the other three sashayed down the river, reminiscent of a sea serpent stalking its prey.

Before them, the bridge was a simple rope contraption with boards across the bottom. The rope was frayed in places, and some of the boards had fallen away. Not the sturdiest way to cross. Certainly not the safest. But right now, it seemed their only choice.

"One at a time?" he asked Rashka.

She shook her head. "Together." She took a cautious step onto the first board. When the bridge did not sway, she took another. "Step exactly where I step," she whispered.

Yosef followed along behind her. They moved slowly, Rashka testing each step before she put her full weight on it. The further away from the bank they moved, the more the bridge swayed. Yosef grabbed onto the rope for balance, as did Rashka.

They came to a gap where two boards were missing. The next board beyond that did not appear to be very sturdy either. Yosef said a quick prayer and glanced at Rashka, who seemed to be praying as well.

"We have to be quick but try not to move the rope too much. It is already straining under our weight." She paused and then leapt across the gap, keeping slightly to the right. When she landed, the rope creaked and swung but remained intact. She steadied herself. "Your turn."

He crept to the edge and surveyed the water. All six of the beasts circled below, churning the water as they carefully avoided running into one another, their bumpy eyes watching Yosef. He swallowed past the knot in his throat. Falling was not an option.

With a deep breath, he launched himself across the gap. As he landed squarely in the middle of the board, he threw himself forward, falling across the next three boards as well. A good thing, because the first board cracked, and his feet slipped off the bridge.

So did Rashka's entire body.

She let out a screech and grabbed for the rope. The bridge swayed wildly, the ropes creaking … and then a couple snapped.

Gripping the board in front of him, Yosef glanced back. The rope Rashka had grabbed was fraying more with each swing of the bridge. Should he move to grab her, or would such a move make their dire situation worse?

The rope on his left started to wear under the added tension as the rope on his right weakened. Either way, they were no longer safe. He scooted over ever so slightly. "Grab my legs," he hollered at Rashka.

"No! You cannot hold my weight."

"Yes, I can. Trust me."

The bridge vibrated as she shook her head.

"Rashka, I may only be a priest, but I have put a lot of time into keeping my body strong. And these boards are sturdier than that rope. Now move!"

She did not say anything. Then a moment later, he felt her hands on his legs, her added weight pulling on him. Not too soon, either. The right rope snapped completely, and they tilted to the right.

Rashka gasped and tried to readjust her hold on his legs. Yosef's fingers curled harder around the edge of the board as he prayed for extra strength.

Below, the hungry sea creatures rose out of the water, snapping their jaws. No doubt they knew dinner was on its way. Yosef struggled to breathe. Sweat stung his eyes. He could not give up. He would not.

The left rope groaned and then snapped. They both let out a shout as the bridge fell quickly toward the water while swinging to the other bank. He had not thought he would die this way.

No, he would not fail.

"Start climbing," Yosef shouted.

Rashka's hands moved up to his waist, her nimble movements pulling at his fingers, which clung to the board like a knight to his sword.

The bridge hit the river with a sickening slap. Immediately, water soaked his tunic.

"Hurry!" Rashka was next to him now. Yosef scrambled up the bridge, using the boards first for leverage, then as a ladder … up and out of the water.

On dry land once more, they did not even stop to rest. Those creatures could come after them. Yosef, with Rashka at his side, dashed into the trees and followed the path away from the riverbank.

Their narrow escape made his heart beat faster than the time Elder Thomas had caught him and the other scribes with the sacrament wine. He thought for sure his mentor would throw them all to the streets.

"Wait, wait." Yosef coughed and bent over, hacking, trying to breathe. At least the creatures were far behind them now.

With a grimace, Rashka stalked back over to him, not saying anything.

His side ached, his muscles were sore, and he wanted nothing more than to curl up next to a fire and sleep for a week. What kind of madness was this challenge?

"What do you think we will face next?" He looked up at Rashka.

She shrugged. "No one has seen these challenges in hundreds of years. The elders are the only ones who know anything about them."

He straightened, then arched his back, stretching the muscles.

"Are you well enough to continue on?"

He glared at the elf. "Of course I am well enough to continue on. I just needed to catch my breath."

Rashka led the way again as the path continued to wind through a dense forest. They had obviously left the confines of the garden now. He searched the unfamiliar trees. He did not remember the island being quite this vast when he had trained here. Everything was … different. Unknown. Unsettled, he could not be sure of any thought blazing through his mind.

You don't need to do this.

"What did you say?" Yosef hurried to catch up with Rashka.

She shot him a confused look. "I did not say anything."

"Oh." He fell back a few steps. Maybe he was over-thinking the whole situation. His mind was playing tricks on him.

Why are you here?

He glanced around and then ahead at Rashka. Her gait had not changed as she charged forward along the path.

You got the prophetess to the temple, why are you putting yourself through this?

His gaze darted back and forth, searching the trees. "Rashka …"

She turned to him and waited. "Is something wrong?"

"I think there might be someone—or something—in the trees."

Rashka's muscles tensed, as if her guard went up. "What makes you say that?"

"Someone keeps talking to me."

"I have not heard any voices." She continued to survey the forest herself.

Come to think of it, he could not say he actually *heard* voices. "I think—I think the voices may be in my head."

She leaned in closer, her eyes scanning his face. "What do these voices say?"

He shrunk back from her, suddenly self-conscious. "They keep telling me I do not need to be here, that I do not need to do this."

"This, like the challenge?"

He nodded.

"I suggest you ignore those voices."

He glared at her. "Is that the best advice you have?"

She looked around them one last time. "It is all we can do, given the situation we are in."

Yosef tried not to snarl as she spun around and continued down the path.

She does not understand you, the voice crooned inside his head. *Why listen to her?*

Because listening to her was better than listening to a voice without a body. He hurried after Rashka.

Rashka tried to hide the searing pain. Somehow, she had twisted her ankle in the incident on the bridge and then the fall had wrenched her shoulder. Still, they were not finished with this challenge yet. There had to be at least one more trial after this, if not more.

She glanced over her shoulder at Yosef. Though his face was drenched in sweat, he seemed to be holding up better than she had expected. Except for the voices in his head. Maybe he was not doing well after all. Maybe he was cracking under the pressure. He was a priest from Gundow, not a Guardian or a trained soldier.

His shifty eyes darted to either side of the path and along the tree line. He tensed at each shadow. Ironically, she could not bring herself to worry about anything, her movements sluggish at best. If something jumped out in front of her, she was not entirely sure she could best it in close combat— or any kind of combat, for that matter. She was not even sure she could see clearly enough to shoot an arrow straight.

What was going on with her mind? Her body? She was losing control.

A thought niggled at the back of her mind, like a knock on a door, something she could not let in. Hard as she tried to access it, the thought continued to elude her. With a disgruntled sigh, she pushed forward. She would complete this challenge on her own if need be.

A brilliant white light from the path before them blinded her. She shaded her eyes with her upheld arm. From what she could tell, a dark form stood in the middle of the brilliance.

"Who goes there?" she called.

"I am Garon," he said. The light began to fade until a Servant of the Creator stood before them clad in a white robe, wings tucked behind him.

Behind her, Yosef fell to his knees and bowed his head to the ground, though he said nothing. His body shook.

Rashka regarded the servant. "Garon? You are the one who appeared to Karina."

He nodded.

"Why are you here?"

"You are about to embark on the final part of the challenge. I am here as a warning."

She raised an eyebrow.

"These trials will end in either life or death. As you have put your ability to work together to the test in the first two minor challenges—"

"Minor!" Yosef jumped up from his prone position. "We almost died both times." His eyes lost focus, and his lip curled in a snarl. "No, of course, we cannot give up. The others are counting on us." He shook his head.

Rashka furrowed her brow as Garon continued. "The maze will require you to work together to complete the challenge." He glanced behind her at Yosef. "Alone, you will fail."

"What is the next challenge?" she asked, her hand on her hip.

"I cannot reveal everything." He moved aside and gestured beyond where he stood. "The path will lead you to a maze. You will find the final trials there, along with the armor you seek."

"No!" Yosef shouted, spinning in a quick circle. "He is a servant. We must listen to him!" He clamped his hands over his ears.

Rashka waited for Garon to say something. He merely stared, a serious frown waylaying any possible comfort. "I suggest you hurry." And then he vanished into thin air.

Rashka groaned. The servant was more cryptic than she had ever been. This was not good. What would they find in the next leg of the challenge?

Beyond a bend in the trees, they came to a large archway made of two large trees, its high branches intertwined in an elaborate series of knots.

"Is this the entrance to the maze?" Yosef whispered, then cringed and batted at the air by his ear.

Rashka nodded. "I believe so."

"It would have been nice if the servant had given us a map."

"Indeed. But I have a feeling that would have defeated the purpose of whatever we are supposed to learn in the maze."

Yosef wrinkled his nose. "I do not like this."

She glanced at him and offered a half-smile. "Neither do I. But we will do this anyway. For Karina and for the Three Kingdoms."

He grunted and gestured for her to lead the way.

With a deep breath, she took the first step beneath the archway.

CHAPTER FORTY

Karina stretched out on a chaise in a parlor off the great hall. The shades of green melded with the gold accents all blending into a detailed mural on the ceiling. The artwork and décor created the atmosphere of an opulent forest setting. She watched the empty fireplace.

Sometimes, she missed the year-around cool temperatures in Aletheia. She could curl up next to a fireplace with a mug of spiced cider and one of her uncle's books. What she would not give for those quiet times now.

Instead, her worries gave her a headache and soured her stomach. Rashka and Yosef had been gone for a very long time. Granted, their challenges could take all day, maybe longer. Who knew what kind of trials they were facing, if they were even similar to what Karina and Tristan had faced in Aletheia? Maybe their challenges were completely different. Maybe the challenge would take more than a day to complete. Maybe it …

She groaned as her head drooped. Not knowing what was going on would be the death of her. While the destiny of her friends was not in her hands but in the hands of the Creator, she still could not help but claim responsibility for them. She wanted to *do* something. In the temporary stillness, she again lifted a prayer to the Creator—*Protect my friends*.

Tristan walked in, carrying a tray full of pastries and fruit along with two goblets. "Would you like something to eat?"

She shook her head. "I am not sure I could eat anything. My stomach is all in knots."

"They will be fine." He set the tray down on the low table beside the chaise. "Rashka is quick-witted and strong, and Yosef is, well …" He paused for a long moment, long enough that Karina raised an eyebrow. "Well, I am not sure yet what Yosef's strengths would be in a situation like this. Although, he is a healer like you but maybe not as talented." Tristan winked.

She blushed as his smile warmed her insides, a balm for her worried soul. She pulled her legs off the chaise to allow room for him to sit next to her. Since coming out of her prolonged sleep, they had not had any time alone together. Odd. They were both aware of their feelings for one another, but there had not been much time to nurture their relationship in the past weeks. Still, just being near to him gave her hope, encouragement.

He plopped down on the chaise next to her, his green eyes tracing her lips. She was pretty sure she frowned instead of offering him the smile she had intended. Her stomach fluttered at his attentions.

He reached up and tucked a strand of hair behind her ear and then his thumb skimmed the line of her jaw. Yes, she just wanted to enjoy these times with him. She read the same longing in his eyes. His fingers cupped her chin, lingering there.

Somewhere outside, a door banged open. Shouts echoed through the great hall.

Tristan's hand dropped away, and Karina groaned inwardly. So close to a peaceful, perfect moment. With a tight smile, he took her hand in his, helped her up, and together they hurried into the great hall.

Two men, an elf and a human, stood in the middle of the room, trying to catch their breath as Eliandor and the other two members of the Trium descended the spiral staircase.

"Well, this is ominous," Karina whispered, grasping Tristan's arm with her free hand.

"Not to mention familiar."

She smiled, but his attention had already deviated to the men.

"What is the meaning of this?" Eliandor's big voice boomed through the great hall.

"We are sorry for the noisy intrusion, sir. We come bearing ill news," the elf replied with a quick bow.

"Continue." From inside the tight circle of people, Eliandor shot Karina and Tristan a disapproving look, however, did not make them leave.

"We have come from the western border. Faramos's forces crossed over to our lands last night. If they are headed here, as their path suggests, they will be here by tomorrow afternoon at the earliest."

Eliandor's face reddened. "What does he think he is doing?"

"He knows we are here." Karina's said, barely above a whisper. All eyes turned to her. She reached up to cover her throat, a protective gesture as she contemplated the ramifications of the news. "He is finally bringing the battle here." Her eyes widened as she glanced up at Tristan.

His features hardened to steel as he wheeled back to the scouts. "Was Faramos with them?"

"We do not know." The human male gave Tristan a questioning once over. "What should we …"

The door banged open again, and a man stumbled in. This one was dressed in a temple guard's attire. "Word from the docks. There is a boat approaching."

Eliandor glared at the scouts. "I thought you said the forces were still a distance away."

The men swallowed hard, and the elf stiffened. "We did, sir. There has to be another explanation."

"Do we know who is in the boat?" Eliandor inquired.

The temple guard shook his head, seeming to shrink beneath the intense stares. "Someone said something about a royal and her guards."

"A royal and her guards?" Karina replied in a breathy whisper. Had Anaya returned? Had she somehow found the temple on her own? Or maybe she had followed them at a distance and was now making her move with Faramos's reinforcements behind her. Panic threatened to overwhelm her.

Tristan squeezed her hand. "Don't worry," he whispered. "I will protect you."

"It is not me I am worried about." She looked around at the people in their circle. Once again, a sacred temple was in trouble, and she was to blame. What would they do? She could not send them to Gundow like she had sent the Aletheian priests to her capital city. The king of Soter would not so readily take in the remnant of a battle at the temple. She could send them to Aletheia, but the journey would be long. And if Faramos was determined to destroy them, they would never arrive in time.

Another temple guard raced in the open door. "She's here! She's here!"

Karina put a hand over her stomach. The final confrontation. Her and Anaya. *Breathe through the panic.* She had to keep her wits about her if she wanted to live.

A shadow fell over the entrance where the sun's afternoon rays shone in the doors. Karina squeezed Tristan's hand. She wanted to shut her eyes against what was coming, or perhaps run away.

No. She would be strong. Brave. She was a queen. The Creator's Prophetess. She inhaled sharply through her nose.

And in strolled Princess Reina.

All present gasped, and the rush of air sounded like a gust of wind.

"Ah, Princess." Eliandor swept in and bowed. "We have never been graced with your presence here at the temple. What can we do for you?"

Princess Reina smiled graciously as the head elder kissed the back of her hand. "Thank you for the warm welcome, Eliandor." She looked around the circle, her eyes widening slightly when she spied Karina and Tristan in the background. "But I have not come to visit the temple exactly."

Eliandor cocked his head to the side. "Are you in need of help?"

She sidestepped the head elder. "I am here for Karina." She made her way over and grasped both of her hands. Reina's smile lit her face. "As soon as you left, I realized I should never have let you leave without me. My place is not with my father, not right now. And the way Anaya acted after you were gone?" She let out a sigh. "She called me a traitor and had my father restrict me to my suite."

"What?" Karina's gulped. That a man would betray his own daughter … "I am so sorry, Princess Reina."

"It is not your fault. My father has made his choice. It is up to me to stop him—to stop the evil infecting my kingdom. I want to help you."

Karina nodded. In her heart, she felt the Creator meant for this to happen. This was right. She continued to nod. "I am glad to welcome you on this journey."

Tristan leaned in. "Not to mention she's pretty handy with a sword."

Reina giggled. "Bested you a time or two, did I not?" He harrumphed and backed away again, then she turned to Karina. "I brought fifty soldiers who are loyal to Gundow and to me. They are stationed on the other side of the river. Anaya is maybe a day behind me."

How had she returned to the palace and organized her own reinforcements so quickly? Karina closed her eyes. They were headed for trouble. How much longer would Rashka and Yosef be? They needed Rashka's insights.

Tristan gestured to Eliandor. "We need to gather your temple guards, as well as any priests who are versed in battle."

Eliandor, his face ghost-white, nodded.

Reina surveyed the gathered group as if seeing them for the first time. "Did you already know I was coming, or did I interrupt something?"

CHAPTER FORTY-ONE

Yosef followed Rashka beneath the blended archway and onto a dirt path hedged by bushes so densely intertwined one could not push through them. The leaves were a bright green, new life in the mid-spring season. Even a few florals dotted the towering bushes, filling the air with the scent of sunshine and waterfalls. He stopped to lean in, so he could sniff the nearest one.

"Stop!" Rashka grabbed the back of his now-tattered robe and gave him a swift yank.

He landed in an ungraceful plop on his rear. "What are you doing?"

"The scent of dragon lilies will knock a man out for two days if it's too strong." Rashka glared at him.

Dragon lilies? He had heard of those in his training as a healer. A deadly poison if ingested. But if the healer needed to tend a more sensitive wound, inhaling the lilies worked like a sleeping potion.

But sunshine and waterfalls …

He shook his head against the voices rising in his head, a chorus egging him on.

"We need to keep moving," Rashka said, her chin up as she surveyed the path behind and before them. "We do not know what all awaits us in this maze, and I would prefer to be done before darkness falls."

"How long do we have?" Yosef stood and dusted off his robe.

"It is just past noon. So, we have several hours yet."

"Well, at least that is one good thing."

He followed her down the path. Not a minute later, they came to a fork in the path where they had to turn either left or right. Rashka peeked around the corner, then stepped into the perpendicular path and looked both ways. Probably trying to discern which way to go.

Go left!

No, go right.

Go left! Go left!

Right.

The "go left" voices were like a melody of instruments, blending together into one harmonious sound. The voice urging him to the right was singular but sure, firm.

"Do you have …" Rashka paused, then regarded him. She shut her mouth, let out a burdened sigh, and glanced both ways again. "We go left."

A signal buzzed in his mind. He pushed it away like an annoying fly on a summer day. Rashka tore a piece of cloth from the bottom of her tattered dress and then tied it to the bushes in the direction they were going. It took him a second, but then he said, "Ah. To keep track of our direction."

They walked down the path to the left, which resembled the one they had been on save for the angle of the sun, which now kept shadows to his left. The signal still hummed in Yosef's head, then died suddenly. He glanced around but did not see anything.

Wait.

In front of Rashka, the ground shifted somehow. Slightly. As if something were moving, though he could not see anything, nor was there any wind strong enough to move the dirt like …

"Rashka!"

Too late. Rashka stepped into the quicksand. Immediately, she was sucked in up to her knees. She flailed her arms to keep her balance before leaning forward. She reached out, hands searching for solid ground.

Yosef shouted again and fell to his knees beside the pit. "Grab my hand!"

Rashka slowly angled her body toward him. But as she twisted, she sunk further. By the time she reached for him, she was already waist deep. "Hurry, Yosef!" she rasped.

He grabbed her hand with both of his and pulled with all his might. With her free hand, she pushed against solid ground … but her arm slipped toward the quicksand. The sucking dirt claimed another couple of inches of her body.

"Give me your other hand."

Though Rashka reached, Yosef could not connect. Her arm fell back into the quicksand. Nearly covered, Rashka managed to yank her hand free and lunged toward Yosef. He caught her hand. Her chest had sunk below the sand. He pulled and pulled. His feet started to slip.

Just let her go …

No, he could not lose her. The servant said they had to do this together. *She'll only hold you back.*

That was not true. She was the one who kept him going, who assured him they would survive this. He dug his feet into the ground. "Aaaah!" He yanked with all his might.

With a sickening squelch, the quick sand released Rashka. He fell on his rear again, Rashka tumbling on top of him.

He lay there, trying to catch his breath. He did not remember the last time he had to do anything as vigorous as today's events.

Rashka pushed off and sat back on her knees. "Way to go, priest," she said, her breath almost as weak as his. "I thought perhaps you did not have it in you."

He waved a hand of dismissal. "However I can serve." A twinge of pain pulled her lips downward. "How's your shoulder?"

She stared at him. "How did you know?"

"I'm a healer, remember? I notice these kinds of things. You twisted your ankle, too, but it seems to be doing better."

She chuckled as she stood and then offered him a hand up. "My shoulder is quite sore, but I can still use it if that is what you were wondering. Now what should we do?"

Why did she think he would only be concerned about how she could help on their challenge? He looked both ways. Beyond the quicksand was a dead end. "Was this area closed off before?"

Rashka shook her head. "I do not believe so. I would have spotted it and gone back."

Go right.

"So, I guess we go back and take the path on the right."

They hurried back the way they'd come. Rashka untied the white cloth from the bush and retied it on the other side. Then they continued on, taking corners at random. Yosef tried to follow the singular voice, but the chorus was getting louder, drowning out the singular one. What would happen if he could not hear that voice at all?

On the last turn, the voice had been a whisper within a cacophony. Still, he heard the definite direction to go left and urged Rashka to do so. The path curved to the right and ended at a lava pit too wide to jump across. What was a lava pit doing in the middle of a forest island?

"Brilliant, priest," Rashka muttered, hands on her hips, legs apart in a warrior stance.

"But I am sure this is the way we were supposed to go."

"Sure? You are sure? How are you sure?" She rolled her eyes and turned back the way they had come from.

Follow her. You do not want to die here.

No, you must cross—The single voice was drowned out by a chorus of no's.

Follow her! Follow her! Don't die down here.

Cross here! The voice surged a little louder, like someone who was trying to yell but could still only whisper.

"Rashka!"

She stopped, her expression not as trusting as before.

He cleared his throat, suddenly a little unsure under her scrutinizing glare. "We need to cross the lava."

"Why?"

"Because the way out is on the other side."

"How do you know?"

He considered his response. How could he tell her about the voice? "I just … do."

She crossed her arms, obviously not buying his flimsy reasoning.

Yosef took a deep breath. "Fine. I have been hearing voices this whole time. They've been telling me—"

Rashka let out a growl. Without a word, she spun on her heels and stormed away.

Sure the singular voice was right, Yosef would not be cast aside so easily. "There are two kinds of voices," he shouted as he jogged after her. "One is a chorus of voices telling me to do one thing, slowly getting louder and louder. The other is a single voice, strong and firm. When we have followed the single voice, we have found the path to be true. When we did not— when we went left instead of right at that first intersection, you ended up in the quicksand."

He caught up to her, and she regarded him out of the corner of her eye. "Then why would that voice send us to the lava pit?"

"Perhaps there is a lesson? Something about working together like the servant said. I do not know. I only know if we do not obey the single voice, we are not going to get out of here."

Rashka stopped, closed her eyes for a long moment, then let out another growl. "Fine. I do not know if I believe you. But I will take a closer look."

They returned to the lava pit. Molten fire boiled and hissed. Somehow, the bushes on either side did not disintegrate, though they did hang a little limp, as if begging for water. Rashka surveyed the rest of the surroundings. From what Yosef could see, there was no way across—nothing to grab.

"Do you suppose it is a faith thing?" Yosef asked. "Like if we have enough faith, we can walk across the lava without dying."

Rashka smirked. "I do not believe so. Our challenges have not been about faith. They have been about working together, about trusting each other." Her words were sure, but she slurred them together and spoke slowly. Whatever had been bothering her through this challenge was getting worse.

Walk across the lava. Show the Creator how great your faith is.
Better yet, take a running leap!
There's still time to go back …
Up. The single, small voice. Simple instructions.

Yosef looked up. Above the pit, above their line of vision, a branch stuck out over the molten rock. Though not overly thick, the branch appeared sturdy. "Rashka?" When she turned his direction, he pointed up.

"Yes, I saw it. But it is too high." Scuffing her boot on the ground, she sighed. "Shapeshifting would be nice right about now."

He considered her dismissal. The ability to fly would indeed be useful. Then again … "I have a really bad idea."

Hands on her hip again, she smirked. "Let's hear it."

"At the new year celebration, the king invited a circus to perform in the large courtyard. There were these acrobats who swung on bars that hung from ropes between two of the buildings."

Rashka's features contorted in confusion, so Yosef rushed on. "The man had his legs over the bar, and when he swung up to the platform, the woman grabbed his wrists. They performed a few tricks before he swung her over and deposited her on the other platform."

Rashka's expression had not changed. He let out an exasperated sigh. "If you assist me, I can jump to the branch, curl my legs over it, and then swing you over to the other side. Then, from the top of the branch, I can safely jump over."

A smile spread across her face. "That is a truly horrible idea. What if you miss the branch? You will fall to your death. And why you and not me? I am nimbler than you are."

He was not sure he agreed with her, but that was not the point right now. "Perhaps on most days. Right now, your shoulder is injured. You may not be able to carry your weight … or mine."

She looked back at the branch and then at him, her silence deafening. Of course, she did not trust him, despite the fact he had pulled her up out of the water in the second trial.

"Very well."

He cringed. Now they actually had to execute this idea. Even though he knew his plan would work, part of him had hoped she would veto his idea and demand they go back. No. This was the only way. He wiped his sweaty palms on his dirty robe.

Rashka knelt, holding her hands out with her fingers crisscrossed. "You will need to push off at the same moment I lift you. That is the only way you will get enough power to reach the branch."

He nodded. Placing his foot in her hands, he eyed the angle and height of the branch. He only had one chance. His heart skittered, and he thought he really might faint. *Breathe.*

"Ready?" Rashka asked, her voice steady and strong.

He blew out a breath. Then another. He met her gaze. "Yes. Let's do this."

"On three. One. Two."

He stared back at the branch, calculated the projection, took a deep breath …

"Three."

He shoved off the ground with his left leg as Rashka lifted her hands, giving him an extra boost. At the last moment, he pushed off from her. Reaching out with his right arm, he pushed his shoulder forward. A little farther. Almost there.

His right hand wrapped around the branch, but momentum kept him sailing beneath it. He thrust his left arm up and back, then swung and grabbed the limb. The branch shook violently. He hung there, eyes squeezed tight as he waited. No cracking sounds. No signs the branch would break under his weight. Everything settled.

"Are you well?" Rashka shouted up to him.

"Yes. Fine." He grunted as he worked his feet up and over the branch. "Rashka, I'm going to swing back and forth. You are going to have to time your jump with my rhythm so when I swing your direction you jump out and catch my wrists. Aim for the wrists because they are easier to hold than my hands."

She nodded.

With another deep breath, Yosef rocked back and forth. He kept his movements steady, not trying to go faster or slower, making sure his legs held tightly around the branch. Back and forth with his arms outstretched. "Get ready," he called.

Rashka's head moved with the sway of his body. She was timing him. Her right foot was in front of her left, readying, calculating when to jump.

Back and forth. Back and forth.

Blood pounded at his temple. The voices in his head taunted him.

He swung away, and Rashka took a step back, then stepped forward.

He began his return swing—she took another step. And leaped. As he came to the apex of the swing, her hands slid around his wrists. He grabbed hers as well. Success!

As he swung away, the full weight of her body pulled at him, slowing his motion. He could not let go of her at the other side. She would not make it all the way across. When she let go of his wrists, he did not release her. She looked up, her eyes wide with uncertainty.

"Not enough momentum!" he shouted. "Pump your legs!"

The heat from the lava caused them both to sweat profusely. Salty water dripped down his arm and over his hands. If they did not hurry, she would slip from of his grasp.

She readjusted her grip once again and began to pump her legs, pushing out and then pulling back as they swung back and forth. He inhaled through his nose, blowing each breath out. She seemed heavier, though she could not be. His arms were sore. He was tired.

Just let her go.

"No!" he shouted.

Rashka did not hear him. If she did, she had chosen to ignore his outburst.

It'll be easier.

Ready. One more time. The still, small voice.

"Next time, Rashka!"

She tucked in on the back swing. When they swung forth, she pushed out with all her might. Right before the apex, Yosef released her. Her body arced through the air. She did a front flip and landed in a crouch on solid ground.

Yosef exhaled as his body came to a stop. Energy sapped out of him like a water trough with a hole. He huffed. He still needed to get down himself. With a groan, he reached up and grabbed the branch. Very carefully, without losing grip, he loosed his legs and pulled himself on top of the branch. He took the time to regain his strength, to let his blood flow return to normal. At last, he stood, readied himself, and jumped.

He was not afraid of heights. In fact, he often liked to linger at the top of the temple or the palace to take in the beauty of the city. Falling, however, was a different story. His heart pounded in his ears.

He tucked to absorb the landing with a roll, only not quickly enough. His right foot fell forward as he slammed into the ground. He heard something snap as his body followed in a roll to the right. He lay on his back, dazed, breathless.

"Yosef?" Rashka leaned over him, concern etching her face.

Told you.

Who do you think you are? A hero? The voices taunted him, called him names. Almost louder than Rashka.

"My ankle," he gasped, rolling onto his side. Blinding pain shot up his leg. "I think it is broken."

"Here, let me." Rashka pushed him gently onto his back again. She prodded his ankle. No matter how gentle, each touch seared like lightning. He howled. "I can heal you, priest."

He lifted his head. "What?"

She offered another one of her smirks, and then a warmth invaded his ankle, spreading to his foot and up his leg. There was pressure, heat—the pain lessening until it disappeared.

"Done." She stood and offered him a hand.

He ignored the offering and sat up on his own. His ankle did not hurt at all. In fact, it felt fine, normal even. He tested his injury by pushing his foot into the ground. Nothing. No pain. He breathed a sigh.

"Now may I help you up?" Rashka grinned as she put her hand out again. This time, he grasped her hand and let her pull him up. "Ready to go?"

He nodded and followed her down the path. The voices in his head rose to a deafening scream. He covered his ears, trying to block them out.

When they came to another fork, Rashka turned to him. "Which way?"

He could not tell her. The single voice was silent—or it had been drowned out by the cacophony of other voices. "I do not know." *Creator, help me.*

The voices died. All of them wailing and screaming into silence.

Go right.

Yosef sighed at the soothing assurance of the single voice, strong and firm once again. He nodded to the right and led Rashka down the dirt path, around a curve. Into a dead end.

Yosef groaned. Why would the voice lie to him now? Or had it?

In the middle of the dead end was a stone bowl upon a pedestal of wooden stems woven together. As they approached, he could see something shiny in the bowl … not liquid … solid.

Rashka stopped and gestured toward the bowl. "I think you should go."

He crept forward, his breath shallow. What was that thing? A cross between a crown and a helmet, the headpiece had an odd shape. The metal was burnished gold, circular like a crown, with two long pieces that curved down slightly on the sides. A flap of purple cloth hung from the back. Odd, indeed. He lifted it from the bowl and placed the helmet-like object on his head. The two long pieces came down the side of his face, in front of his ears. He turned to Rashka.

"How very regal," she said before she placed a hand over her mouth.

"Very funny. I feel ridiculous."

"What is it?"

"I am not sure. I did not see any …" He peered back at the bowl and found an inscription on the bottom of the bowl.

A gift to the one who made the journey thus far … the Helmet of Salvation. May your thoughts be clear and your mind always your own. Listen for the Creator's gentle voice—for his clear guidance and his righteous admonishments. In dire situations, may the Helmet offer a blessing as your way out.

He read the words aloud to Rashka. "What do you think the last part means?" he asked as he moved away from the bowl.

She shrugged. "I have not a clue. I suppose we will find out if you are ever in dire need. Where to next?"

The branches to their right peeled back, revealing another path. Yosef's mouth fell open. "Well, how about that."

CHAPTER FORTY-TWO

Rashka walked, more like hobbled, along the hard dirt path. Every muscle in her body ached. Her mind was so muddled she could not grasp one thought … not even for a moment. Her body felt cold in spite of the late afternoon heat. She was losing motivation, perspective. Something was very wrong.

Beside her, Yosef looked a bit ridiculous in his new helmet. But ridiculous was fine if his mind was clearer than hers. She needed to push through.

A howl echoed over their heads.

She jumped. "What was that?"

Yosef grasped her arm to steady her. "Are you well?"

She jerked away. "Of course. I am fine."

His brows drooped with concern as he squinted toward the sky. "I believe that was a lupen, which should mean …" A chorus of howls replied to the first. "Yes, there they are."

With her mind addled, lupens were the last thing they needed. "They are in the maze."

"What do we do?"

She glanced at him, then back to the path in front of them. "Hurry."

They followed the voice of the Creator as he gave them directions through the maze. They avoided any further traps until they came to an open arena. On the other side, a golden gate shimmered in the sunlight filtering through the towering trees. The gate was closed.

And between them and the exit were three lupens. Their massive snouts rose and pointed to the sky, sniffing, honing in on their scent. Slowly, the glowing red eyes swung in their direction.

Had they not been through enough already? Rashka clenched her hands into fists. "Have you ever fought a lupen before?"

Yosef shook his head.

"I will try to keep their attention. You slip around the side and see if you can open the gate. It is our way out."

"Are you sure you can take on all three?"

No, she was not sure. In her current state, she was not even sure she could take on one. She reached for her quiver, which should have been slung over her back. Only they had not been allowed weapons in this challenge. She bit back a curse. If the Creator saw fit for her to fight without her bow …

But how *could* she fight without her bow? How does one walk without legs? Her bow had become like an extension of her. Maybe that was the problem.

No, the problem was the three lupens now stalking toward them. How could she garner their attention away from Yosef? "Go," she whispered.

She walked straight toward the mighty beasts as the leader yawned, revealing its belief she was not a threat. The lupen on the left growled, then changed direction toward Yosef. Rashka leapt to the left, pulling its attention to her. She was only a three-man's breadth from them. She had to do something.

She jumped up and down, shouting at the top of her lungs. The lupens stopped. Breathless, she inhaled … the lupen on the left turned away again, bent its head further, and stalked toward Yosef.

"No!" she shouted and ran toward the beast.

The leader of the pack snarled ferociously. And while she knew she should have stopped, she could not. She would not let the lupen near Yosef. Out of the corner of her eye, she saw Yosef cowering against the wall. While he seemed determined to keep moving, he hugged the wall like she would at a royal ball.

Something hard bowled over her, and she toppled to the ground. The leader landed on top of her, squashing her beneath its massive weight.

The lupen rolled off. She could hardly move. Everything hurt. She gasped for breath. The leader circled her, snorting, daring her to get up. Now both other lupens headed toward Yosef. She had to move. Had to get up.

Still, her battered, broken body refused to listen. Useless. She was useless. She could do nothing. A thought niggled in the back of her mind. She fought to grab hold of the memory. Something familiar about this scene. She knew something. Someone.

Tristan. How he faced a dragon on his challenge.

How he almost died before he called out to the Creator. *Oh, Creator, how could I have been so stupid. You are trying to teach me that I do not do this on my own strength but on yours. You are the one who called me. You are the one in control. Not me.*

Strength returned to her body. Pain still invaded each joint, each muscle, but she could move. She sat up as the lupen continued to circle her, closing in. On the other side of the beast, she spied a short sword she had not noticed before.

The fuzziness cleared, and she was finally able to concentrate, to plan. *Creator, help me.*

She pushed past the pain in her body and rolled beneath the lupen. It snapped at her as she rolled again, picked up the sword, and swept up to her feet.

The lupen lunged, but she leapt to the side. As it passed, she shoved the sword into the side of its neck. Blood spurted from the wound, and the beast whined as it crumpled to the ground. Its breathing ceased, and its body stilled.

With a cleansing breath, Rashka snatched the sword from its body. What a relief to have her senses back, to feel strong again, to feel … powerful.

Facing the other two lupens, she let out a battle cry and ran toward them. They scattered. She chased the one that ran toward the gate, zigzagging around the arena.

As she passed the gate in pursuit of the lupen, she noticed it was open. Their challenge was complete. "Get out!" she shouted to Yosef.

He pivoted to the gate and ran. She kept the lupens on the other side of the arena, daring them to cross over the invisible center line she guarded with her sword.

Call on my name.

The lupens looked at each other, as if communicating with their minds. Then they turned to her, approaching quickly, readying to lunge. She could not fight off both without risking injury to herself.

Call on my name.

Creator, whatever your plan, let me stop them.

Call on my name.

"In the name of the Creator!"

The sword began to hum, then to vibrate, then to shine.

A brilliant light shot from the sword as it divided in two and struck the lupens as they launched. Simultaneous yelps echoed through the arena, then silence. Two blackened bodies thumped to the ground.

Rashka let out the breath she had been holding. Her shoulders slumped forward. *Thank you, Creator.* A warmth spread through her body—not of healing, rather a peace and acknowledgment. She savored the moment and remembered. This was the feeling from when she was first called, when she first stepped into Shadowed Forest. Back when she laid everything at the feet of the Creator.

She held up the sword. A weapon like she had never seen before. Perfectly balanced, perfectly sharp on both sides. Simple steel with a simple gilded hilt. Simple—but strong.

"Rashka?"

She blinked, taking in the surroundings again … the large arena hedged by tall bushes, smoking lupen bodies, golden gate. And then Yosef. She waved.

"Are you well?"

She sauntered over, sword in hand. "Yes, Yosef. Finally, I am well."

CHAPTER FORTY-THREE

Tristan stabbed at the salted meat on his plate and shoved it in his mouth. Tasteless. Dry. It could hardly be called meat in this state. He glanced at the overcooked potato and slimy carrots. What kind of meal was this? At least the rolls were good. He snatched another one from the platter in front of him.

Beside him, Karina sat with her hands in her lap. She had not touched her food. Not that he could blame her. At least she was unaware of how bad the meal was. On the other side of Karina, Reina engaged in conversation with Duma, though Tristan was unable to overhear.

He leaned in close to Karina. "What's wrong?"

She shook her head, still staring at her plate.

"Worried about Rashka and Yosef?"

She looked up at him, then to the door and back at him. "Why haven't they returned? Do you think something could have happened to them? What if they did not survive?" Her voice rose with each question. "How would we know?"

He stroked her hand. What words could he say to comfort her? "Rashka is strong, Yosef is smart. They will complete the challenges." Karina sighed, and Tristan wished he could do more to ease her mind. Truth was he did not know if their friends were fine or not. For all he knew, they were both dead. Would someone or something alert the elders if they had failed? He chewed on the roll as if Rashka's life depended on it.

He intended to approach Eliandor and ask for word concerning Yosef and Rashka when the door to the dining hall slammed against the stone wall. His hand immediately went for his sword, but Rashka and Yosef strolled in, clothes now tattered rags, scratches covering both of them. Overall, they seemed to have faired the challenge well.

Yosef had a strange crown on his head, and Rashka carried a sword—one which she had not taken into the challenge. Where had she found the weapon? Was it a piece of the armor?

He glanced at Karina, already out of her seat and running to their side. She threw her arms around Rashka with a squeal of delight. When at last Karina let go, she embraced a surprised Yosef as well.

Tristan sauntered up to them. "It's about time."

Rashka smirked. "Well, I would like to see you put down three lupens by yourself."

"Or scale a tree so you can get over a lava pit," echoed Yosef. "Or survive a collapsing bridge …"

Rashka glared at him, and he clamped his mouth shut.

Eliandor appeared at the edge of their reunion. "Ah, I am pleased to see you have acquired the Sword of the Spirit and the Helmet of Salvation."

Tristan glanced at his ring and at Karina's belt. Four pieces. Four pieces toward defeating the ancient evil tearing their kingdoms apart. Only two more pieces remained. And they would have to sneak into Tzedek to retrieve them.

"What do they do?" Karina ran a finger down the shaft of metal on the side of Yosef's face.

"If I understood the inscription correctly, the Helmet protects my mind from being controlled by others, like warlocks." He looked pointedly at Tristan. "But it does something else as well. Though the inscription was not clear, only saying it would bless me in dire situations."

"Odd." Karina grinned. "But I am sure you will have an opportunity to use the helmet on this quest."

She turned to Rashka … but before Karina could speak, Rashka raised the sword. "It's a double-edged sword that shoots lightning."

Tristan's jaw dropped Why could he not have a weapon like that? He held up his hand with the ring. Though incinerating creatures was nice too. Still …

"Wow!" Karina giggled. "Can you show me how it works?"

Rashka scowled. "Of course not. The gifts are only to be used when necessary."

"Of course." Karina dropped her chin and stepped back.

Rashka looked torn, and Tristan could understand her hesitation. They were all feeling their way through this situation. The elf sighed. "I apologize for being short with you. I suppose I am overly tired."

"Ah!" Eliandor clapped his hands. "Then eat quickly so you may retire to your bed chambers. You must get your rest as you will be leaving first thing in the morning."

Tristan started. So soon?

"What about the battle?" Karina cried. "We cannot leave you here to face a two-front battle—Faramos's army as well as Anaya's."

"We are not alone," Eliandor said as he ushered them all to their chairs. "We have our own temple guard, which is bigger and more experienced than the guard you had in Aletheia—as we have already discussed. Plus, we have Princess Reina's soldiers fortifying the seashore."

"But—"

"I will hear no arguments. Your quest is far more important than the fate of this one temple." He clasped his hands in front of him and bowed his head. "We have the Creator on our side, so I do not fear what is to come." He gave Karina a knowing look. "Even if standing our ground means my final trip to the Lighted Realm."

Karina pursed her lips but did not say anything. Tristan rubbed her shoulder, trying to relieve some of the tension. He would be glad to be done with this place, to move on. He would be even more ecstatic when this whole quest was completed. When he could finally move forward with a certain prophetess, who also happened to be a queen.

The next morning dawned too early. Or rather, the servant entered Tristan's bed chambers before dawn, awakening him from precious slumber. He groaned and buried his face in his pillow as the servant shuffled around the room, dropping a tray on the table, opening the wardrobe, and whatever else he was doing.

"Time to rise, sir," the cheerful servant quipped. "Your party will be leaving soon. I have already prepared your possessions for travel. You need only break your fast and dress."

"I need to sleep until the sun is up."

"I am sorry, sir, but the Head Elder says you must rise now."

Tristan groaned again and rolled into a sitting position, feet hanging off the bed. "There, I'm up."

"Do you require any help dressing, my lord?"

"No," he snapped, a little harsher than he intended.

"Very well." The servant bowed. "I bid you good day and may the Creator's light go with you on your journey."

"Thank you," he muttered as the servant scurried out of the room.

Tristan dressed quickly and ate a hearty breakfast of bacon, eggs, and pastries. How long before the next full, home-cooked meal now that they were venturing into Tzedek? At least he knew where the next temple was. No reason to hunt down someone for directions. Unfortunately, the temple was on the other side of Tzedek—granted in the southern part, a good journey from Faramos's fortress. An advantage … if Faramos had not already sent soldiers there.

He gathered what little remained in his room and ventured over to Karina's door. After his third knock, she finally answered, her face scrunched in a scowl. "Now is that anyway to greet your protector?"

"It is when he is impatient." She retreated from the door and finished latching the Belt of Truth around her waist. Clad in a light red tunic and brown leather pants, her hair hanging in a fat braid down her back, she looked as stunning as ever. He inhaled a contented breath as he watched her move about the room. Finally, she smiled and met him at the door. "What are you looking at?"

He shook his head. "You get more beautiful every day."

She giggled. "Yes, I can just imagine what the weeks in the forests have done to my hair, my skin, and my hands." She rolled her eyes and pushed past him.

"Think what you will, Your Majesty, but I still say you are the most beautiful woman I have ever seen."

She stopped in the middle of the hallway, hands on her hips. "Tristan Lemur, what are you up to?"

He raised his hands, feigning innocence.

She cocked her head ever so slightly to the left. With a smirk, he leaned over and kissed her on the cheek. Before she could object, he sauntered down the hall, leaving her sputtering behind him. Maybe they would find some romance on this journey yet.

They met up with Reina, Rashka, and Yosef out by the boat. Their belongings were already loaded in the front. While Karina talked with Rashka, Tristan strolled over to Reina. "You're really going with us, huh?"

She quirked an eyebrow. "Did you think I was not?"

He chuckled. "I thought you did not like the bugs. Nor the hard ground."

She sniffed indignantly.

He smiled. "Seriously, I am glad Karina will have the company. With Sam gone …"

Over on the dock, Karina was talking excitedly with Rashka, using her hands to express whatever it was she was trying to say. Despite her enthusiasm, her shoulders drooped as if weighted down by boulders.

Reina followed his gaze. "She will grieve for a while, Tristan. But she will pull through. She has you."

He turned back to her. "And now she has you too. A blessing."

Eliandor sashayed down the stone path. "Time for you all to be on your way. We need you far from here before soldiers arrive. Do you know how to make your way to Tzedek?"

Rashka nodded. "Tristan has a good enough idea. And if we need more detail, I can always fly overhead and get the hawk-eye view—now that my shapeshifting ability has returned."

"Very good." Eliandor bowed to Karina and then to Reina. "Thank you both for your presence here. I was honored to meet you, Prophetess. May the Creator's light go with you."

Karina inclined her head. "And with you."

They filed onto the boat and within an hour unloaded on the other side. The fog had not been as heavy on this trip as on the first day. In fact, on this side, the air was practically clear. As Reina had said, her soldiers were camped at the edge. They all rejoiced when they saw the princess.

"We are glad to have you back with us, Princess Reina," a tall soldier said.

Another soldier, wearing captain's colors, sauntered over. "What are the plans now?"

Reina glanced over at Tristan and Karina. She licked her lips and then straightened her shoulders. "You all will remain here," she said, loud enough for all to hear. "The temple will need your protection as Anaya's and Faramos's forces converge on the temple. Captain Franks, I am leaving you in charge. You are well-versed in battle strategy and will know best how to handle the situation. Also, the temple does have a sizable guard at your disposal. You would do well to coordinate with them."

Captain Franks, an older man with thinning hair and a squat frame, glanced nervously in their direction. "That is all well, Your Highness. But should I not send a squad of our best soldiers with you? Your protection is of the utmost importance as well."

Tristan stepped forward. "We will move faster and with more stealth as a smaller party. I assure you, the rest of us are well-trained and can protect the princess. Although"—he winked at Reina—"she can hold her own pretty well in a sword fight."

Reina rolled her eyes, and the captain coughed. "Are you well, Captain Franks?" she asked with the most serious look on her face.

Beside him, Karina grabbed her stomach as if to thwart a laugh.

"Very well, then. Should we send word to your father?"

"No!" Reina leaned in toward Captain Franks. "You are not to breathe a word of this to my father. For now, you are to remain here at the temple unless you have lost the battle. Then you should head for …" She glanced at Karina.

"Head for Aletheia. On the other side of the border is a small town called River Branch. If you tell them Tristan and Queen Karina sent you, they will find refuge for you until Princess Reina sends new orders."

Reina smiled and nodded. "As Queen Karina has said, Captain Franks."

He nodded brusquely. "May the Creator's might go with you, Princess."

"And with you, good captain."

"Well done," Karina said as Reina came up to them and linked arms with her.

"You think?"

Tristan nodded. "You will make a fine queen one day."

"Maybe."

Yosef and Rashka strolled over, leading four strong horses and one familiar black stallion.

"Dom!" Karina rushed toward his horse and threw her arms around his neck. He nickered, saying something only she could understand.

Tristan followed behind her and snickered. "Are you ever going to give me back my horse?"

She shrugged. "I had not planned to." She looked up at him with shining eyes. Her words only slightly bothered him. Confounded horse. At least he still had Roan. He patted the white steed's flank.

"Let's ride, my friends," Reina said. With one smooth motion, she swung up on one of the other horses. Everyone else mounted and waved goodbye to the soldiers.

"Lead the way, Rashka," Karina sang above the din.

Rashka steered her horse west and led them away from the sea.

Karina was tired of riding horses. Even Dom. She could sit and chat with him all day. But riding him—or any horse—grated on her last nerve. And they had only been riding for a little more than half an hour.

"Do you know what challenges Rashka and the priest faced?" Dom asked as he plodded along through the clumpy grass and dirt.

"A bit. Rashka gave me a quick recap last night. Their experiences were quite a bit different from Tristan's and mine."

"Different how?"

"Well, for one thing, they got to go through the challenge together."

"That is different."

"Indeed. I would have liked to have Tristan by my side—"

"Everyone be quiet." Rashka raised up off her horse slightly, ears perked.

Yosef scowled. "I do not hear—"

"Ssh." They all quieted as she listened. "Horses. Three of them. Following us."

"Three?" Tristan scoffed. "Scouts, most likely. If they knew where we were, they would send more than three."

Karina rolled her eyes. He was getting a little too arrogant.

"What do we do?" Yosef asked.

"There's not time to—"

"Well, hello, there." Anaya's grating voice sang out as her chestnut horse trotted through a grove of trees. "Going somewhere?"

Two men rode up behind her. Not soldiers. At least they were not dressed like soldiers or guards. Who were they? She glanced at Tristan, who clenched his jaw but said nothing. Rashka's eyes widened slightly, then her face seemed numb as if she'd blanked.

"What do you want, Anaya?" Tristan growled.

"I was told to apprehend you and the brat of a queen you cannot get enough of." Her smiled widened, showing her bright white teeth.

"And you only brought two men with you? Not even soldiers from the looks of it." Tristan's voice took on an incredulous tone.

"Careful, Tristan," Rashka warned. "Those men are more than they seem."

"Meaning?" he asked without taking his eyes off the trio.

"Warlocks."

Karina's stomach dropped. The ground swayed below her. She inhaled deeply several times to keep from fainting or falling off Dom.

"Indeed?" Tristan smirked. "Well, isn't that something?"

"Stop it, Tristan," Karina hissed. "What is wrong with you?"

He dismounted, closed his eyes with his arms held out, and wiggled his fingers. A fluctuating light began as a bubble around him and extended to the entire group. He opened his eyes. "They are not getting past the Creator."

The rest of the group dismounted, as did Anaya and her cronies.

"Well, aren't you all high and mighty," Anaya crooned. "A far showing from the man who was in the dungeon only a few days ago."

Tristan grit his teeth. Karina placed her hand on the Belt of Truth. The armor piece was not as much a weapon for offense, though it had disoriented Brusho in the last battle and then again with Anaya at Soter's palace.

Rashka stepped forward, brandishing her sword instead of her bow. "Tristan and Karina are not the only ones with pieces of the sacred armor."

"As I can see." Anaya tapped her chin. "And the priest has an odd headpiece on his head. Tell me, what is that?"

Yosef opened his mouth as if to speak, but Karina shot him a warning glare. No use giving the enemy more information than was necessary.

"Very well," Anaya said as she raised her hands. "Enough small talk."

The sky darkened as roiling clouds collided overhead. With her hands raised, Anaya lifted her face toward the sky and then brought her gaze back to Karina and the others. Her eyes were black, and her features somehow sharper, more disturbing. Karina could not quite comprehend the change. What had happened?

Anaya laughed. "Let's see what your fancy new powers can do against something else that is not alive and has no form."

Surely she did not mean … Had her aunt allowed the ancient evil inside her? Karina laid a hand at the base of her throat.

Lightning flashed above their heads, not quite reaching down. Once. Twice.

The third bolt of lightning arced down from the sky, crashing toward them so quickly Karina did not have time to duck. Before the lightning could strike, it was dissipated by another flash that blinded her momentarily.

When she turned in her saddle, Karina saw Rashka had stretched her sword upward, and streaks of brilliant light had shot from the blade. Now, she narrowed her eyes, murmuring words Karina could not hear, then lowered the blade to point at the trio of warlocks. A bolt of lightning shot out, split in two, and struck at the two men behind Anaya before they could raise their hands.

Their bodies fell to the ground, smoke rising from their smoldering flesh.

Anaya's smile vanished. She growled. "You will not get away with that." A stream of fire shot from her hand. However, when the blaze hit Tristan's barrier, it sizzled as if doused in water and then disappeared.

Anaya screeched. She was breathing hard, her shoulders rising and falling with each breath. She lifted her arms above her head. "I call from the depths an enemy of enemies, a power beyond power." A black ball formed between her hands, writhing and billowing.

Karina could sense the evil from where she stood, like dark slime slithering over her body. She shivered as the hairs on her arms stood on end. She did not dare to even breathe.

The ball grew and shifted, pulsed, as with life.

Suddenly, Anaya squeaked. Her concentration failed, and the ball dissipated. She looked down at her chest where a blade now protruded. Blood soaked her dress around the blade, spreading down the cloth.

"What have you done?" she groaned.

The blade disappeared and, in the next moment, severed Anaya's head. Her body crumpled to the ground in a messy heap.

Karina gaped. Time seemed to slip by in slow motion.

Behind where Anaya had stood was Reina. She held a sword at the ready, a sly grin on her face. "You did say Lady Anaya did not die the last time someone stabbed her, right?"

Karina did not know what to say, how to react, what to think. She willed her muscles to relax. The immediate danger was gone.

Tristan laughed out loud as his forcefield shimmered and then faded. "I knew you had it in you."

"What?" Karina spun on him. "You knew what she was doing?"

His eyes rounded, but he nodded slowly. "She edged around to the left while Anaya was distracted with the lightning. When she saw me watching, she held up her sword. I figured out the rest."

"And you did say I was handy with a sword," Reina quipped as she cleaned her blade on Anaya's dress. She looked at Karina and frowned. "Though I do apologize if it was you who wanted to kill her yourself. You had more reason than anyone of us."

Karina shook her head. That was not what she had meant … not at all. She did not know why she was flabbergasted by this turn of events. It was just—unexpected. "No, Reina, it is fine. I am glad she is dead. Really dead. Really, really …"

Still, a twinge in her soul told her the last of her family was dead. She was alone in the world. Not alone, but she no longer had any family. Even someone who hated her.

Tristan swung his arm around her, distracting her from her sorrowful thoughts.

Reina laughed and sheathed her sword. "I have not had so much fun in a long time."

"Fun?" Karina shook her head. "You call that fun?"

"More fun than the time I beat Tristan in a foot race." Reina ambled back over to her horse. "I am glad I could be of service."

"You know"—Karina glanced toward Tristan—"that was some seriously good teamwork though. I may not have seen what happened nor was this my plan, but you three pulled that off seamlessly." She looked over at Rashka, who merely nodded.

"You and I got stuck with the useless armor," Yosef muttered, tapping his helmet.

"Not useless, Yosef. Trust me. You will find good use for that helmet. I have had to use the Belt of Truth a few times, twice in self-defense."

"Really?"

"I will tell you the whole story when we are on our way again."

CHAPTER FORTY-FOUR

They had ridden at a leisurely pace for three days, keeping to the southern edge of Soter. Far enough from the sea they could not see it but close enough to hear the din, especially at night when all else was quiet. Now, they stood in a low area between two cliffs. Water rushed from the river dividing Soter from Tzedek beneath a surprisingly massive bridge and on out to the sea.

Karina took in the soaring cliffs, so reminiscent of the cliffs on the northern side of Tzedek. They stopped on Soter's side of the bridge to camp for the night. A dry cave offered cover from the wind as well as prying eyes. Although, she hoped there were none of those as she surveyed their surroundings again.

Reina and Rashka had wandered off to find wood for a fire. Tristan tended to the horses while Yosef started a stew with the last of the salted meat and fixings provided by the temple.

She sat down next to him. "Is there anything I may do to help?"

Yosef smiled. "You do enough already. It is an honor to cook for you."

She regarded him, sure the horror must be written plainly on her face. He should not think such a thing. Yosef had given up everything in his life to help her. Still, he dumped everything into their one pot, already filled with water, unaware of her discomfort.

Within a couple of hours, dinner was served. The camp had been readied, and no one had really allowed Karina to help at all. She sighed. Why did they treat her as if she were helpless? She shoved a bite of stew in her mouth and chewed as she dwelled on the frustrating thoughts. Finally, she cleared her throat. "I have something to say."

Everyone quieted.

Suddenly, her palms began to sweat. But she must give voice to her concerns before they ate at her sanity. She sucked in a breath. "I know I am the Prophetess, the Chosen One."

Everyone nodded in agreement. Silly.

She stood. "Still, as you should know, I do not expect to be treated any differently." Tristan started to speak, but she held up her hand. "The last three days, none of you has let me do very much at all to help. I do not know if this servitude is because I am the Prophetess—or a queen—or because of my coma before we arrived at the temple." She turned in a slow circle. "But as you can see, I am perfectly fine. I should help. I *need* to help."

Rashka cleared her throat. "May I speak?"

Karina nodded, her pulse pounding quicker than Dom at a full run.

"I know I speak for your friends when I say this. While we welcome your assistance, it is not always necessary. One, because there are many of us already. Two, because, in spite of what you may believe, you do a lot already. Maybe not the labor, like gathering firewood or tending to the horses. But you are the heart of this team. You are what brings us together. If the Creator had chosen another person to be his prophet, I do not think they could have brought as strong and loyal a group together as you have."

Yosef cut in. "I agree. I have not been with you long, but I already know this. You are the first to jump in when there's trouble. You are the last to fall asleep at night, worried about protecting us. You are constantly thinking, constantly planning, constantly praying. I say this—and I'm a priest!"

Everyone laughed. Everyone except Karina. Tears of happiness and confusion welled in her eyes. "I do not understand," she said. "I should still do my part."

Tristan cradled her hands in his. "That is what they are saying, Karina. You are doing your part. More than your part. Everything you are, everything you do—those characteristics are what make you incredible. It's what made me fall in love with you."

Everything else fell away. The crackle of the fire. The sound of the waves. The titters of laughter among the group. Tristan had just declared his love for her. A bounty hunter in love with a princess—no, a queen. Who would have thought?

She leaned in close to him, so close she could feel his breath on her cheeks, her lips. "I love you too."

He closed the distance between them, sealing his lips over hers. Warmth spread over her face and into her chest, to her core. She had found her perfect match. Her love. Her forever. She breathed in his scent as he bent over her, taking the kiss deeper.

"Oh, please," Rashka muttered. Reina giggled.

At last, Karina pulled away, a smile pulling at her lips as she stared up at him. "What was that?"

His beautiful emerald eyes sparkled back at her. "A promise."

"Indeed? Well, wasn't this a most wonderful moment … deserving of applause, really." Everyone gasped as Faramos's image appeared on the log beside Yosef.

Karina clung to Tristan, eyes wide. How was Faramos here like this— no fiery illusion or possession? Was his power getting stronger the closer to Tzedek they were? Oh, but he had appeared to Tristan in the same way when they left Gundow. Perhaps he was just toying with them however fit his fancy at the moment.

Faramos gave a slow clap. "My brother has secured the love of my former betrothed."

"We were never betrothed, Faramos," Karina hissed.

He wagged a finger at her. "*Tsk tsk*. Manners, darling."

"What do you want?" Tristan growled.

Faramos crossed one leg over the other and layered his hands on his lap. "Well, I come bearing good news and bad news."

"What do you mean?" Karina straightened.

"Well, my dear. The good news is there is no reason for you to make your way to the sacred Temple of Tzedek. Why? Well, that's the bad news. I am afraid I sent my soldiers to burn it to the ground."

His tone was so flippant, Karina froze. Her stomach congealed into a rock-hard stone. He could not be serious. She chanced a glimpse at Tristan, whose clenched jaw could have broken through steel. She inhaled as deeply as she could.

Rashka stood. "There is no way the Creator would allow something like that to happen."

Faramos shrugged, the smirk never leaving his face. "I do not know what to tell you, Rashka. Maybe he was busy with other tasks. The fact remains, as of this evening, the temple is in ruins."

"Wh-what of the people? The priests?" Karina's voice quivered uncontrollably.

"Do you think me an animal?" Faramos waved off the question. "Of course, my soldiers had orders to let the people flee. However, many of them chose to stay and fight." His eyes narrowed in on her. "I was not about to let *my* men die. They fought back."

Karina cried out. Her lungs must have deflated … she could not breathe. All those people. Why? *Oh, Creator, please say it is not true.* But she knew in her heart the report was indeed true, and she mourned the horrific loss of life.

"I see our group has increased again. The beautiful Princess Reina has joined us all the way from Gundow. How is your dear father, gorgeous?"

Reina crossed her arms and scowled.

"Feisty one, is she not?" Faramos stood. "Well, I wanted you to know you can all go home. The sacred temple is destroyed. There will be no final pieces of armor. Your quest has failed." He looked from Karina to Reina and back. "And if either of you should change your mind—in order to save your kingdom from my destruction—let me know." He bowed and then his mirage disappeared into the night.

They all stared at the spot where he had stood for several long seconds. Tears streamed down Karina's cheeks. Her heart hurt for the people who had sacrificed their lives to this quest. Surely, they had not died in vain. *Creator, do not let it be so.*

Rashka crossed her arms. "I still do not believe him."

"I do," Tristan growled as he stood. "This is just like him. He doesn't get his way, so he goes on a rampage, destroying things. The same way he did when he killed our father."

Karina reached out to comfort Tristan, but he shrugged her off. Her senses went on high alert. No, the team could not fall apart like this.

Reina pounded her fisted right hand into her other palm. "He's a snake. Someone needs to put him in his place."

"Someone like you?" Yosef asked from his spot on the log. He continued to stare at the place where Faramos had stood, as if he expected him to reappear any moment.

"If necessary."

"You would not get near him on your own," Rashka muttered.

"You would not fare much better," Tristan countered.

Reina leaned over, elbows on her knees. "What are we to do now?"

Yosef shrugged. "Go home, I guess."

"We're not going home," Tristan growled.

"Enough!" Karina moved between her friends, circling around the fire until they were all quiet. "That is enough. This is exactly what Faramos wants—for us to fall apart, to give up."

Yosef stiffened. "But he said—"

"I know what he said. Contrary to popular belief, he does not know everything. And given that he does not serve the Creator, I am betting there is a lot he does not know about the sacred temple."

Tristan crossed his arms. "Like what?"

She stood toe-to-toe with him, hands on her hips. "Like the fact that, so far, the challenges have not happened in the temples themselves. That the challenges have in fact been outside and away from the temples."

"Right." A smile spread across Rashka's lips. "Faramos burned down the temple, but he does not know where the armor is hidden."

"Exactly." She pivoted back toward Tristan, whose eyes were wide as he returned her glare. "What's more, to get to the armor required completing tough challenges. My guess is Faramos would not stand a chance at any of them."

"Indeed," Tristan murmured as he quirked the corner of his mouth into a smirk—his cute, kissable mouth.

She shook her head. "Our quest is not over. We will not let Faramos tear us apart. We are united under the Creator, and that is what makes us strong. We will prevail. We will—"

"Yes, yes, we understand. Can we get some sleep before we go getting all noble and quest-worthy again?" Yosef yawned and stretched.

Karina let out an exasperated sigh. Then, as she readied to speak again, Tristan wrapped an arm around her waist and pulled her close. "I know what I will be dreaming about tonight," he whispered in her ear. He kissed her lightly on the temple and left her dumbfounded as he gathered everyone's bowls and headed toward the water.

<<<<THE END>>>>

ACKNOWLEDGMENTS

Hello, readers!

No two people experience an event the same way, and the same goes for enjoying a book. No two readers read the same book. I hope the story has spoken to your heart so far! I hope you saw a bit of yourself in the actions and thoughts of Karina and Tristan, maybe even their friends. And I pray a bit of their journey inspired you to step boldly forward in YOUR calling, in YOUR adventure, in YOUR life.

I hope you'll leave a review on Amazon or Goodreads. Be honest! Reviews help the next reader find the right book for them. And no one book is right for everyone.

And if you enjoyed the story, I hope you'll join my newsletter as we start preparing for Temple of Tzedek, the final book in the Sacred Armor Trilogy!

As with any major plan like this, there are so many people involved in bringing this project to life. So many wonderful people to thank. First, though, I would like to thank my Lord and Savior, Jesus Christ. Without the inspiration he gives me, the motivation to #SHINEBeyond the circumstances in my life, I would not be able to write the way I do.

I'd also like to thank Julie Gwinn, my agent, and Deb Haggerty, my publisher at Elk Lake Publishing Inc., for taking a chance on me, for putting up with all my craziness the last couple of years and still trusting that I would see this through.

My husband is an amazing man. Even with all his own health struggles, he still ensures that I have time to write, time to grow, time to daydream. He fills my life with hope and encouragement, with inspiration and love. He never lets me believe I can't do what God has called me to do.

My children are why I write these kinds of stories. I struggled for so long against who I really was. But when I embraced my calling fully, such joy entered my heart! And I hope that my children can skip much of that heartache by believing in themselves early on and not ignoring their call!

To my Ladies of Spec, I owe you all the world! Desiree, Morgan, Jennette, Becky, and Janalyn have been my backbone, my rocks, my refuge over the last couple of years. We've weathered storms together and come out on the other side stronger than before. They've stood by me on this writing journey, and I am not sure Karina's story would have been told without them.

To my Realm Makers tribe, especially Becky and Scott, thank you for your encouragement and support along the way. As a writer and a marketer, I have found so much inspiration and knowledge from the friendships I've made within the Realm Makers community over the years.

To all those who have been with me on this journey through social media and my newsletter. Thank you for all your prayers, your encouragement, and your willingness to share your lives with me! If not for you, this story may not have found its way into the hands of the right readers.

Blessings upon blessings,
Ralene

ABOUT THE AUTHOR

Whether she's wielding a fantasy writer's pen, a social media wand, or a freelance editor's sword, Ralene Burke always has her head in some dreamer's world. And her goal is to help people #SHINEBeyond! She has worked for a variety of groups, including Realm Makers, the Christian PEN, Kentucky Christian Writers Conference, and for several freelance clients. Her fantasy novels are available on Amazon.

When her head's not in the publishing world, she is wife to a veteran and a homeschooling mama to their three kids. Her Pinterest board would have you believe she is a master chef, excellent seamstress, and all-around crafty diva. If she only had the time ...

You can also find her on Facebook, Instagram, Twitter, or at her website.

www.ingramcontent.com/pod-product-compliance
Lightning Source LLC
Chambersburg PA
CBHW052002020726
47501CB00004B/961